Dance, Drama, and Theatre in Thailand

Dance, Drama, and Theatre in Thailand

The Process of Development and Modernization

Mattani Mojdara Rutnin

SILKWORM BOOKS
Chiang Mai

ISBN 974-390-006-3

First published in Thailand in 1996 by
Silkworm Books
54/1 Sridonchai Road, Chiang Mai 50100, Thailand.

Silkworm Books is a registered trade mark of
Trasvin Publications Limited Partnership.

Printed in Thailand by O.S. Printing House, Bangkok.

To my late mother

in gratitude of her love and encouragement

Contents

Illustrations

Illustration acknowledgements and/or source citation appear in parentheses following each description. Illustrations without acknowledgements are photographs taken by the author.

Preface

Dance, dance-drama, and theatre arts in Thailand, from their simple folk and religious origins to the most refined, sophisticated, and ritualistic presentations at the royal court, have been a vital part in the life stream of the Thai people. Their original ceremonial functions relating mainly to agriculture—rice planting, harvest, rain-making, etc.—are still active and alive in both rural and urban areas. The Thai king still plays annually the important role of Father Rice Planter who distributes the best grain to his people and performs the rice planting ceremony. The king also presides over the prediction of the climatic weather and environment by means of the sacred Brahmin's oxen. What the oxen choose to eat in the offering tray will predict the future climatic conditions for agriculture. In all these royal and folk ceremonies, dances and dance-dramas are performed to please the patron gods and the spirits of natural phenomena and agriculture. Buddhism, Brahmanism, and Hinduism interweave comfortably with animistic beliefs, superstition, and magic from primitive folk culture.

In the past, and to a certain extent in the present, the three important centres of Thai culture and arts have been the *ban* (home, village), *wat* (temple), and *wang* (palace). They are interrelated and have influenced one another in the development of the arts, particularly the performing arts. After the Revolution of 1932, the role of the *wang* was diminished by the Revolutionary Party in order to curb the political and social influence of the monarchy and aristocracy. The "Democratic Government of the People" has taken over every aspect of court art and controls them under the central administration and its political policies. Since 1932 national performing arts have become instruments of government propaganda and political campaigns. The most notable are the nationalistic movement during World War II under Premier Phibunsongkhram and the anti-communist campaign of Premier Sarit Thanarat in the late 1950s and 1960s. Premier Sarit restored and promoted the role of the monarchy to the fullest extent for political reasons, as royalistic plays with patriotic themes graced the stage during the 1960s and 1970s to raise funds for royal charities.

The use of theatre for political and social purposes has been introduced as early as in the 1910s and 1920s by King Vajiravudh, Rama VI. However, King Vajiravudh's plays did not catch on with the general public, as they were performed as an experimental theatre among the courtiers and elite society close to the king. It was not until the late 1930s, 1940s, and 1950s that nationalistic plays became popular through the talent of Luang Wichitwathakan, Minister of Culture and Director of the Fine Arts Department during Premier Phibunsongkhram's two regimes (1938–44, 1948–57). Using simple melodramatic plots and popular songs, Luang Wichit (between 1936 and 1957) was able to create successfully "popular theatre" for the masses, with the traditional format of princely heroes and virtuous heroines, who sacrificed their lives for the country. Though intellectual motifs are lacking in these plays, their political and social ideas successfully come through to motivate the general public much more effectively than the sophisticated drama produced by intellectual circles.

It is interesting to note how the Thai monarchy has played a very important political, social, economic, and cultural role in the development of performing arts from early history to the present day. In the past, once regional folk dances and dramas were adopted by the royal court, they became royal prerogatives and taboos for the general public. The Lakhon Phuying Khong Luang (female dance-drama of the royal court) was the exclusive possession of the king and was guarded jealously by that institution. There are many incidents in history in which political disputes were generated from this issue, as in the reign of King Rama I. It was not until the reign of King Mongkut, Rama IV, in the Bangkok period during the nineteenth century that this taboo was lifted and private troupes were able to train their own female dance-drama performers in the style of the royal court.

Despite the efforts of King Chulalongkorn, Rama V, and King Vajiravudh, Rama VI, to democratize the theatre and lift the rules and regulations that divided the royal court theatre from popular theatre, the separation of the two continued to the Revolution of 1932. This issue was taken up and publicized in a negative way by the left-wing intellectual leaders in the 1970s as a political and social attack against the aristocracy and the rising capitalist middle-class, who attach themselves to the royal court. The constant fights and conflicts between the two camps continue even today at the intellectual podium, on university stages, in the National Theatre, at cultural centres, and on public grounds. All of these reactions and counter-reactions make the whole scenario of Thai theatre vibrant and very much alive.

It is my intention to show in this book the life force of Thai performing arts: dance, dance-drama, dramatic literature, and theatre of all forms and styles, which are still living creatively within the bloodstream of the

Thai people. They are interwoven with the political, economic, and social fibres to create a fantastic, multicoloured tapestry of Thai cultural heritage.

I began writing and compiling this book after receiving an offer from The Centre for East Asian Cultural Studies for Unesco in December 1984 to produce a work on the history of Thai drama covering the premodern as well as the modern and contemporary periods. The main emphasis is on the process of development and modernization of Thai dance, drama, and theatre focusing on the nineteenth and twentieth centuries to show how traditional Thai drama and performing arts survived through political, economic, and social changes by way of modernization of forms, styles, and content, as well as how new forms emerged with the new society in each important period under the leadership of the elite groups headed by the king and the court in pre-revolution times and by the rising middle class in the post-revolution period. Meanwhile, the common people either continued with their folk ways and natural expressions or followed the models set by the court and urban elite.

Chapters II, III, IV, V, and VII are based on my doctoral dissertation, "The Modernization of Thai Dance-drama with Specific Reference on the Reign of King Chulalongkorn" (1978) for the School of Oriental and African Studies, University of London, while the section on "Children's Theatre" in Chapter VI was compiled from the research of Ms. Wandee Limpiwattana (1985) to whom the writer is grateful.

I would like to take this opportunity to express my gratitude and appreciation for advice and assistance to the following persons who have made this book possible: Professor Mom Ratchawong Kukrit Pramoj and the late Professor Mom Luang Boonlua (Kunjara) Thephayasuwan for their invaluable information on Thai dance, drama, and theatre, Professor E. H. S. Simmonds, my Ph.D. thesis supervisor for his advice and encouragement, Professor Khun Neon Snidvongs and Thanphuying Warunyupha Snidvongs for consultation on Thai history, the late Peter Bee for reading the original thesis, and Richard E. Hughes for reading a part of this manuscript, colleagues and friends in Bangkok, London, and Tokyo for their assistance in various areas, and above all my family for their continual support throughout my career.

Mattani Mojdara Rutnin
Drama Department
Thammasat University

March 1993

Introduction

Dance (*natasin*) and dance-drama (*lakhon*) have been vital parts of Thai life from the beginning of its history to the present day. This is due largely to their close relationship with Buddhism, the national religion, and with Brahmanistic Hinduism and animistic popular cults in those ceremonies, traditions, and customs so important to the lives of the people. The Thai monarchy has also from as far back as the fourteenth century played a very significant role in the development, enrichment, and patronization of dramatic literature and productions, both within the royal court and outside for the enjoyment and education of the general public. The unfailing efforts of Thai kings, poets, and dramatists to preserve traditional forms and texts and also modernize certain aspects and features of the texts and performances for the enjoyment of contemporary audiences have been major factors in the uninterrupted continuation of *natasin* and *lakhon* in Thailand.

Throughout many centuries of political, economic, and social change, folk and classical dances as well as dance-drama have always been subjected to an unceasing process of modernization which, in most cases, was led by the Thai monarchs. The serious concern with appealing to the tastes and serving the needs of a new generation of audiences in each period has stimulated the leaders in dramatic circles to experiment with new ideas and concepts, in order to present their dramatic works in more effective and attractive ways, and make them more pleasing to the eye and ear in a simpler, more direct manner, thus giving audiences the fullest possible dramatic entertainment.

As political and social problems became major issues in modern times, dance-drama began to change in its role and function from mere public entertainment, or a quasi-religious attribute of the royal court, to an agent for political and social change. This functional change started at the end of the reign of King Chulalongkorn, Rama V (1868–1910), in the Ratanakosin period and increased in significance during the reigns of King Vajiravudh, Rama VI (1910–25), King Anandha Mahidol, Rama VIII (1935–46), and the present king, Bhumibol Adulyadej, Rama IX (1946–present).

The reign of King Chulalongkorn marked the most important turning point in the development and modernization of classical dance-drama. Westernization, which was first introduced during the reign of King Mongkut, Rama IV (1851–68), did not have the most direct and the most fruitful effects on modern adaptations of *khon* (masked dance-drama) and *lakhon* until the reign of King Chulalongkorn. The creative innovations and experimentation that was begun during that reign has continued to influence the works of dramatists until the present day, not only in the modernization of the dramatic texts, but also in the choreography, methods, and techniques of stage presentation, set design, costume, and make-up.

This book attempts to show that *natasin*, *khon*, and *lakhon* are living arts, having been kept alive precisely by this very process of modernization and by a continuous line of succession of dancers and dance teachers, who have passed on from one generation to another the art of this cultural heritage under royal patronage during the times of absolute monarchy and under the sponsorship of the new constitutional government after the Revolution of 1932.

DANCE AND DANCE THEATRE OF THAILAND

Thai dance may be divided into two major groups: folk dance (*rabam phun muang*) and classical dance (*natasin*). Each of the four regions of Thailand has its own indigenous folk dances usually associated with agricultural and social activities, such as rice planting, harvesting, festivals, and religious celebrations (pl. 1). The styles of these regional dances are unique to the localities and temperament of the local peoples.

The northern dance, called *fon*, is slow and graceful with simple hand, arm, and leg movements. It is accompanied by an ensemble of the gong (*khong*), drum (*klong*), oboe (*pi*) , and cymbals (*chap*), resembling Burmese, Tibetan, and southern Chinese music.

The northeastern dances, called *soeng*, are somewhat faster in step and tempo. Hand and leg movements remain simple with the addition of hip-shaking and swaying in a rather sensual manner. The major instruments accompanying these dances are the pipe flute (*khaen*), drum, and gong. Sometimes a kind of wooden xylophone, called the *ponglang*, is used.

The folk dances of central Thailand are more refined, such as *ram srinuan*, *ram prop kai*, and later on during World War II, *ram wong*, an innovation of Premier Phibunsongkhram's government to counteract Western ball-room dancing which was sweeping the nation at the time.

Southern dances are closer in origin to Indian and Ceylonese *Kandyan* dance both in their fast rhythm and swift hand and leg movements. The southern style of dancing is called *ram sat* such as *ram sat chatri*, accompanied by the oboe (*pi*), a pair of drums (*klong tuk*), gong (*mong*), small cymbals (*ching*), a pair of single-faced drums (*thap* or *thon*), and bamboo stick castanets (*krap*). The movements of the body, arms, hands, and legs are sensual, almost erotic, imitating the natural movements of mating birds and animals. Dancers of the north and south usually attach long, curved bronze fingernails.

Thai classical dance (*natasin*) developed from the basic movements in these folk dances and later incorporated the elaborate hand gestures, arm and leg movements of the Indian *Bharata Natayasastra*, either directly or through the ancient Mons and Khmers. However, *natasin* differs markedly from Indian classical dance and maintains its own national characteristics.

Thai dancers, in both the folk and classical styles, hold their bodies straight from the neck to the hips in the vertical axis and move their bodies up and down with knees bent, stretching to the rhythm of the music. Indian dancers, on the other hand, move their bodies often in an s-curve. The arms and hands in Thai dancing are kept in curves, or *wong*, at different levels, high, medium, or low, and the legs are bent with the knees opening outward to make an angle with the legs called *liem* (lit., angles) (pl. 2). The grace and beauty of the dancer depends on how well these curves and angles are maintained in relationship and proportion to the whole body. The curves and angles of male dancers and characters are wide and open, while those of the female parts are narrow and closed. The symbolic hand gesture (*mudras*) of Indian dance are simplified to a few basic hand gestures such as the *chip* (closed fingers [thumb and index] and opened fingers) (pl. 3). Foot movement is also slower in Thai dancing with the toes mostly curved upward or kept flat at an angle with the legs, but never pointed as in Indian dance or Western ballet. The head and neck movements are slight, while the shoulders remain straight as a result of their being at different angles to the body. The body moves in diagonal lines to the left and right and is rarely twisted in curves except in the southern dance-dramas (*nora chatri*). These rules can be more or less applied to most of the Thai dance styles.

The development of *natasin* can be traced as far back as the thirteenth and fourteenth centuries in the Sukhothai period. The terms *rabam* (choreographed dances for specific functions and occasions), *ram* (dancing with emphasis on the hand movements), and *ten* (dancing with emphasis on the foot movements) are mentioned in the first stone inscription of the reign of King Ramkhamhaeng the Great (1279–1300). According to scholars, *ten* probably refers to masked dance-drama (*khon*) and shadow puppet dance-drama (*nang*), because these two sister-arts both use feet movements in a martial style (pls. 4, 5).

However, it was probably not until the Ayudhaya period in the sixteenth and seventeenth centuries that classical dance and dance-drama fully developed into the forms and styles we see today. The long reign of King Boromakot of Ayudhaya (1732–58), a period of peace and prosperity, was also a golden age for Thai classical dancing and the dance-drama of the royal court. The dance teachers and members of the royal family, who were responsible for the training of Ayudhaya court dancers, carried the tradition on to the Thonburi period (1767–82) and then to the Ratanakosin period (1782–present) after the fall of the ancient capital in 1767 in the Burmese war. Incidentally, a large number of Thai court dancers were taken to the Burmese royal court at that time. They settled down in Yodia (i.e., Ayudhaya) village and taught *natasin* to the Burmese. Thus the origin of the term *yodia* dance and music.

King Taksin, the sole monarch of the Thonburi period, as well as every king of the Chakri dynasty, has contributed in one way or another to classical dance, dance-drama, music, and dramatic literature. While trying to preserve the long traditions, many talented artists and dramatists have introduced new dimensions and directions in terms of content, material, style, form, expression, stage presentation, and theatre production. This has involved other fields of arts as well, namely, literature, music, architecture, painting, and design.

The royal court maintained its role as the centre of Thai classical dance and dance-drama and set the royal style as the national model for public troupes and theatres. King Rama II (1809–24) was responsible for most of the royal choreographies and dramatic texts for *khon* and *lakhon* dance-dramas, which are carried on by the royal and national dance troupe even today. Teachers at the Witthayalai Natasin (College of Dance and Music) and the National Theatre come from a long line of artists to the royal court of Ayudhaya, Thonburi, and Ratanakosin uninterrupted by wars or political crises.

After the Revolution of 1932, the Krom Silapakon (Department of Fine Arts) under the Ministry of Education took over the function of training for and production of dance and dance-drama. *Natasin, khon, lakhon*, music, and art are now taught by modern methods from the elementary school level to the college level. The natural, life-long method of teaching has been changed to set courses and curriculum for each academic year. Students attend courses in normal education in the morning, while dance, music, and art are learned in the afternoon. Both teachers and students participate in National Theatre productions for the public. A graduate of the Witthayalai Natasin receives either a certificate of dance or a bachelor's degree in education or *natasin*.

The Witthayalai Natasin has branches in the four major regions of the country (in the north, northeast, central, and south) to teach or give advice to local schools. They also have travelling dance troupes, which perform in the provinces and throughout Asia, Europe, and the United States. Many universities and colleges, both public and private, have elective courses in Thai classical dance, dance-drama, or extra-curricular dramatic activities. The Ministry of Education now requires Thai classical dance and music as compulsory courses in elementary and secondary education.

Students of Thai classical dance start their training usually from the age of between eight and ten with foundation series of dance movements called *phleng cha* (slow movements) and *phleng reo* (fast movements). They vocally repeat the sounds of the *taphon*, single-face drum used in giving rhythm, while exercising in their daily routine: "cha-chong-cha, thing-chong-thing" for the *phleng cha* slow movements and "tup-thing-thing" for the *phleng reo* fast movements. Then they proceed to learn the basic patterns of dance for each character.

Traditionally, there were 108 basic movements (*mae tha*) in *natasin* for the characters of refined male heros (*phra*) (pl. 2) and refined female heroines (*nang*) (pl. 3). They have now been reduced to 68 movements in the major chapter (*mae bot yai*) and 18–20 movements in the minor chapter (*mae bot lek*). The demon (*yak*) and monkey (*ling*) characters in *khon* dance-drama have separate chapters consisting of six patterns of dance movements. The monkey chapter has now only five patterns, however (pl. 5).

The next requirements in the training of classical dance-drama are dances for specific actions and occasions in the play or ceremony (*ram na phat*). The most basic dance tunes and patterns for these actions, *na phat*, are walking and going from one place to another in a slow or moderate tempo (*smoe*) and fast entrance/exit or other fast actions such as fighting (*choet*). There are more elaborate *na phat* for special actions such as supernatural actions (*tra nimit*), very violent and forceful actions (*kuk phat*), and magical or supernatural actions about to happen (*rua*).

Each type of *na phat* is again divided into sub-types for detailed purposes, occasions, and characters. They are all revered as sacred and have to be performed with great respect, concentration, and care as if the dancer is in a magical or religious trance. Certain *na phat* are considered very powerful, to the extent that they could cause fatal accidents or even death to dancers who misbehave, such as the dance of Phra Phirap performed in the Invocation and Initiation Ceremony of Dancers. Phra Phirap is actually Bhairava, a god of dance, a destructive, monstrous form of the god Siva, the creator and destroyer, whose dance gives both life and death to the universe. Phra Phirap is also the name of the demon guardian of Siva's garden in the *Ramakien*, the Thai version of the *Ramayana* epic. The reasons for this confusion is still debated by scholars.

In order to perform well in the dance-drama, dancers have to learn the language of gestures, or *phasa tha*. The narratives and dialogues in classical dance and dance-drama of all forms are interpreted with gestures by the dancer, either word by word or phrase by phrase. The expression of feelings and emotions is also mimed with elaborate hand movements. These gestures are fixed in the classical forms, but more improvised in the folk and modern forms. They have also a certain influence on the language and expression of the people in their daily lives.

Each dancer has to practise how to best interpret the scripts and the character in the play (*ti bot*). Dancers and actors who succeed in interpreting well are said to "have smashed the script and character to pieces" (to *ti bot taek*). Though there are strict patterns of movements and gestures to follow as an artistic skill, dancers can still explore their individual talents and ingenuity as creative artists.

Dance threatre developed in the Ayudhaya period in the forms of both *lakhon* and *khon*. One of the oldest forms of *lakhon* is the *nora chatri* of the south which incorporated movements of Thai *natasin*, Indian *Bharata Natayasastra*, and the indigenous naturalistic style of southern dance (pl. 6). An off-shoot from this ancient art is *lakhon chatri* in eighteenth-century central Thailand. Other forms of dance theatre are *lakhon nok* (folk dance-drama, traditionally performed by male dancers, later by a mixed cast) and *lakhon nai* (female dance-drama of the royal court) (pl. 7). During the nineteenth century, there were many new and modernized forms developed from these traditional ones, namely, *lakhon dukdamban* (from *lakhon nai* and *lakhon nok*) (pls. 8, 9), *lakhon phan thang* (from *lakhon nok*) (pl. 10), *lakhon rong* (Thai operetta) (pl. 11), and *liké* (*likay*, folk dance-drama) (pl. 12). *Liké*, because of its popular themes, wit, and humour, is the form which best survives as a people's art, while the others are performed by the National Theatre as classical dance-drama.

Khon (Masked Dance-drama)

The term *khon* may have derived from the Khmer *lakhol* or *lakhon khol*, meaning dance-drama and royal dance-drama respectively. Scholars have debated the origin of *khon*. In stone inscription No. 8 of the Sukhothai period, the *Charuk Khao Sumanakut* (Inscription of Mount Sumanakut), written under the royal commission of King Lithai, son of King Thammaracha I (ca. A.D. 1370), there is a mention of the word *ten*, literally meaning to jump or to move with legs and feet, which is a technical term for *khon* movements. This is probably the earliest evidence of a proto-type of *khon* developed from the martial arts, in which soldiers stamped their feet in unison to the rhythm of drum beats (pl. 13).

In the chronicles of the Ayudhaya period, there is a description of a martial ritual called *Chak Nak Dukdamban* (lit., pulling a giant serpent), performed at the coronation of a new king by the god Indra (*Indraphisek*), in which military officers and civil officials dressed and masked as demons (*yak*), monkeys (*ling*), and gods (*thewada*) in Hindu mythology, pulled opposite sides of a serpent rope in a tug-of-war, re-creating the myth of churning the Milk Ocean with the great serpent king, Ananta Nakharat, and winding around Mount Sumen (Meru) placed vertically on the back of a giant tortoise (Vishnu Incarnate) to obtain ambrosia of eternal life for these heavenly beings. This ritual possibly originated in India and was then transmitted to the Thai through the Khmers.

At Angkor Wat and Angkor Thom, constructed in the twelfth-century Khmer kingdom of Suryavarman II (A.D. 1113–50), there are stone-sculptured bas-reliefs depicting this ancient rite. The *Indraphisek* and *Chak Nak Dukdamban* rituals may have developed into a complete masked dance-drama form of *khon* or may have co-existed with it.

Another sister art of *khon* is *nang*, i.e., shadow puppet drama. It is known to have been performed as early as the fourteenth and fifteenth centuries in the late Sukhothai and early Ayudhaya periods and perfected in the late Ayudhaya period, parallel to the *khon*. In the *Tamrap Thao Si Chulalak*, the memoirs of Nang Nophamat, a legendary consort of a Sukhothai king, there is a mention of *nang ram* (dancing leather puppets) as a form of *mahorasop* (royal entertainment) in a royal ceremony in the fifth lunar month.

Khon and *nang* were usually performed together, with the *nang* either preceding the *khon* or running simultaneously with it in the *khon na cho* (*khon* in front of a screen). This type of performance is also called *nang tit tua khon* (lit., shadow play with *khon* dancers). Some scholars have argued that *khon* developed from *nang* because of its being performed by dancers in more elaborate patterns. Others have contended that they are off-shoots from the same tree, i.e., the pictorial illustration of dramatic narratives of the *Ramakien*. In both forms the recited and sung narratives, called the *kham phak*, are written in the same poetic forms of *kavya* (*kap*) and *chandra* (*chan*) with dialogues called *cheracha* improvised in *rai* poetic form.

Performers of both theatre forms adopted the aesthetic qualities from each other to perfect their arts. For example, *khon* dancers imitate fighting poses depicted in the exquisitely carved shadow puppets, while *nang* puppeteers manipulate their puppets and use the leg and body movements of *khon* (pls. 4, 5).

There are five major types of *khon:*

1) *khon klang plaeng,* performed in a big field
2) *khon rong nok* or *khon nang rao,* performed on an open stage with a long bamboo rod serving as a bench
3) *khon na cho,* performed in front of a *nang* screen
4) *khon rong nai,* performed in the style of *lakhon nai* (female court dance-drama)
5) *khon chak*, a modernized production style of the nineteenth century performed today in a theatre with painted backdrops

Stories performed in *khon* are taken from the *Ramakien*. Each episode has a Buddhist theme of good defeating evil. The favourite climatic scenes are battle scenes between Phra Ram (Rama), the righteous king of Ayodhaya, and Thosakan (Ravana), the immoral ruler of Longka, a menace to the universe. It is customary that the performance ends with the defeat of Thosakan and his allies who promise a revengeful return, which is the next day's performance.

Though Thosakan is finally killed in the epic, his death is generally not presented on stage, for it is believed to cause misfortune and fatal accidents to the dance company. This is generally respected as a rule in all Thai classical dance-dramas.

Traditionally, *khon* performances begin with a prelude of "Catching the Monkeys in the Early Evening" ("Chap Ling Hua Kham"), a short episode about a hermit and his two monkey disciples, one white, one black, i.e., good and evil (pl. 14). The white obedient monkey receives all the blessing, while the delinquent black monkey is a nuisance. He is finally caught by the white monkey and is punished by the hermit, who later releases him only on probation and after long moral lessons. After this, the show starts with the similar theme of evil caused by the demon king, Thosakan, who is exterminated by Phra Ram or his associates.

All through the play, there are constant comparisons between the two opposing rulers, their politics, social and domestic affairs, systems of government, characters and personalities, as well as their psychological complexities, all of which were originally intended to give political, social, moral, and religious lessons to the audience. However, there are also many comic reliefs by the demon and monkey soldier-comedians, and court jesters, who, being unmasked, exchange witty improvised dialogue.

For other characters, the chorus and narrators, called *khon phak*, recite the narratives and dialogues in poetic rhyme with musical accompaniment. The orchestra called *piphat* consists of one or two wooden xylophones (*ranad*), an oboe (*pi*), a double-face drum (*taphon*), one or two circular sets of gongs (*khong wong*), a pair of small cymbals (*ching*), and two drums (*klong*). There are several dance tunes for special *na phat* actions, such as army processions, fighting, flying, walking, sleeping, and manifesting supernatural power. They are respected by the dancers and musicians as sacred, and therefore are performed as rituals.

Khon masks are worshipped by dancers and artists as sacred objects possessing supernatural power, which could bring both fortune and misfortune to the owners or wearers. There is an annual religious Invocation and Initiation Ceremony for both teachers, students, and artists of *khon*. The new dancers are initiated by the master teacher who wears the masks of Phra Phrot Rusi (Bharata Rishi, great master of dance) and Phra Phirap (Bhairava, the god of dance, one form of Siva), and the head-dress of *nora chatri* southern dance-drama. Only the initiated dancers can perform *khon*. The various masks are placed on altars all through the ceremony.

There are four main differences between classical *khon* and *lakhon*. First, *khon* is a military, political, Hinduistic ritual dance-drama; *lakhon* is romantic and social in its themes and Buddhistic in its messages. Secondly, *khon* dancers use leg and body movements and martial steps, while *lakhon* performers emphasize hand and arm movements more than the legs and body. Thirdly, the style of *khon* is more serious and dignified in contrast to *lakhon*, which is graceful as in *lakhon nai* or worldly and comic as in *lakhon nok*. Fourthly, *khon* dancers wear masks and war costumes; *lakhon* dancers wear make-up and royal costumes. The differences between Japanese *noh* and *kabuki* may be the closest comparison.

Later in the nineteenth century, *khon* adopted romantic scenes from *lakhon nai* and lost many of its original martial characteristics. New songs and sung narratives in the *lakhon* style have been added to the *kham phak* scripts. A major contributor to this new feature was Prince Narisaranuwattiwong (Prince Naris, 1863–1947), younger brother of King Chulalongkorn.

Dancers of *khon* are trained from childhood, usually from the ages of eight, nine, or ten. They are first divided by their teachers into four categories following the types of characters in the *Ramakien*. They are (1) refined male humans or divine beings (*phra*, e.g., gods), (2) goddesses, princesses, or refined females (*nang*), (3) robust or vigorous demons (*yak*, e.g., Thosakan), and (4) monkeys (*ling*, e.g., Hanuman).

Physical appearance and special talent suitable for each specific role are the major criteria in the choice of characters. Each dancer normally undergoes rigorous training for nine to ten years in the character and practises daily the "mother" patterns of dance for each type of character. They also learn acrobatic martial arts for fighting scenes.

Until the 1930s, all *khon* dancers were male (pl. 15). After the Revolution of 1932, female dancers were permitted to play female roles and the *khon* dance style merged with *lakhon* dance-drama. A major contributor to new features in *khon* was Prince Naris, who composed romantic songs and music for his modern production of the *Ramakien* in a new style called *lakhon dukdamban*, which is now used in modern *khon* productions. Present-day *khon* has lost many of its original martial characteristics.

King Vajiravudh (1880–1925) introduced modern politics into his royal *khon* productions and trained his courtiers and close associates in the art as a revival of the ancient military tradition and also as a tool to propagate his political policies in support of the absolute monarchy. A special school under his royal patronage was set up for sons of officials and middle-class families to receive free formal education as well as *khon* training. The school later became an academy for scout cadets and loyal musketeers of the king. The themes of his *khon* productions are loyalty to the throne and patriotic sacrifice for the nation. Thus, *khon* developed in a new political role for modern Thai society.

After the absolute monarchy was replaced by a constitutional monarchy in 1932, the Royal Khon Troupe was transferred to the Krom Silapakon under the administration of the Ministry of Education. Its contemporary trends are more educational than artistic or political. Episodes chosen for productions are geared toward audiences of children. The scripts and dances are now shortened with more comic reliefs to increase its popularity among the younger generation. Modern techniques in set and lighting designs intrigue the new public audience with spectacular effects and glittering costumes.

Despite the threat of Western popular culture, *khon* gradually regained its significance in modern Thai culture during the 1970s through the creative effort of Mom Ratchawong Kukrit Pramoj, former prime minister and an avid *khon* dancer himself, who formed the Thammasat University Khon Troupe with the purpose of training young intellectuals as cultivated future leaders of the country like in the old days. Kukrit's witty dialogues and new political and social interpretations of the stories are major attributes to the success of "Khon Thammasat." Former members of the troupe now hold many important positions in the government and private sector. They form a firm group of *khon* supporters necessary for the continuation of this ancient art as a living tradition in Thai society.

Khon training is now popular in schools, colleges, and universities. The grand national performance, in which two thousand dancers from various schools and the Witthayalai Natasin celebrated the Bicentennial Anniversary of the City of Ratanakosin (Bangkok) in 1982, proves that this cultural heritage, which has been handed down from generation to generation for more than four hundred years, is still a living art in Thailand.

Lakhon/Lakon (Thai Dance-drama)

The term *lakhon* probably derived from the Javanese *lagon* meaning dance-drama, though certain Thai scholars associate it with *nakhon* meaning city, referring to Nakhon Sithammarat in southern Thailand, where old forms of dance-drama, *lakhon nora chatri* and *lakhon chatri*, are most active. The three major genres of *lakhon* are:

1) *lakhon ram*, dance-drama with poetic narratives sung by a chorus and solo singers and poetic prose dialogue spoken by the dancers-actors
2) *lakhon rong*, operetta with narratives sung by a chorus and dialogue sung and spoken by the actors-singers
3) *lakhon phut*, spoken drama in poetry or prose

Up to the nineteenth century, *lakhon* referred only to dance-drama in various styles, both classical and folk. *Lakhon rong* and *lakhon phut* are modern, Western-influenced dramatic forms introduced during the reign of King Chulalongkorn (1868–1910).

Stories performed in traditional *lakhon ram* are taken from *Jataka* tales usually about the adventures and romances of Bodhisattva kings and princes in Buddha's previous lives. One of the oldest forms of *lakhon* is the *nora chatri* of southern Thailand which dramatizes the romantic tale of "Phra Suthon and

Nang Manohra," other *Jataka* stories such as "Phra Rot and Nang Meri," or contemporary stories in the present modernized *nora chatri* (pl. 6). This southern folk dance-drama developed into *lakhon chatri* in the eighteenth century when *nora chatri* dancers were brought to Thonburi and Bangkok during the reigns of King Taksin (1767–82) and King Rama III (1824–51). It incorporated many features of the central folk dance-drama, *lakhon nok*, but maintained most of its indigenous southern characteristics, i.e., the rapid dance with swift hand and foot movements, music, the long, curved bronze fingernails, and *soet* head-dress.

Another old form of *lakhon ram* in the central part of Thailand is *lakhon nok* probably developed in seventeenth-century Ayudhaya or earlier. Some scholars state that it also came from the south, since the term *nok* means "way of the provincial," i.e., southerner, referring to both dance-drama and music. Others explain that the term means "outside," hence, dance-drama *outside* the royal court as opposed to *lakhon nai* (lit., dance-drama of the "inside," i.e., *inside* the royal court). *Lakhon nai* is in fact the shortened term of *lakhon nang nai* (dance-drama of the ladies of the Inner Court), which was a later development in eighteenth-century Ayudhaya during the reign of King Boromakot.

The main differences between *lakhon nok* and *lakhon nai* are in the stories, style of dancing, musical accompaniment, characterization, interpretation and expression, costumes, and dramatic purposes.

Stories in the *lakhon nok* are *Jataka* tales from the Mahayana Buddhist collection of *Panyasa-Chadok* (*Pannasa-Jataka*), meaning the "Fifty Lives of Phothisat," such as "Manohra" from the life of the Bodhisattva Phra Suthon in *Suthon Chadok* and the life of the Bodhisattva Phra Sang in *Sangthong*, with emphasis on comic and melodramatic scenes. The style of dancing is simple, fast, and action-oriented. It is a folk dance-drama for popular audiences.

Lakhon nai, on the other hand, is a court entertainment focusing on elaborate, refined dance movements presented with grace and charm to perfection and purely for romantic and aesthetic effect (pl. 7). Stories are from the *Ramakien, Inao*, and *Unarut* with emphasis on love scenes and domestic affairs of members of the aristocracy and royal family. The expressions of feelings and emotions are therefore very subtle in the sophisticated manner of the courtiers. While characters in *lakhon nok* are usually two-dimensional, those in *lakhon nai* are aristocrats with psychological complexity and depth.

The costumes of both dance-dramas are similar, but *lakhon nai*, being an entertainment for the elite and members of the royal family in the past, could enjoy the richness, luxury, and high fashion of the court, using exquisite costumes and ornaments imitating the royal attire (pl. 16). During the reign of King Mongkut (1851–68), other *lakhon* troupes were prohibited from imitating royal costumes or using gold ornaments, which were prerogatives of the royal family.

Lakhon nok and *lakhon nai* use different styles of *piphat* orchestration and music. The *piphat* orchestra consists of a bamboo xylophone (*ranad*), an oboe (*pi*), a two-face drum (*taphon*), a circle of gongs (*khong wong*), a timpani (*klong*), and small symbals (*ching*). Musical tunes for specific actions, called *na phat*, are shorter, faster, and simpler in *lakhon nok* than in *lakhon nai*, which accompanies elaborate dances for aesthetic beauty. Dance movements and music for both dance-dramas were perfected during the reign of King Rama II (1809–24). The king and his court poets composed many episodes from the *Ramakien* and *Inao* as well as original plays for *lakhon nok* to be performed by the Royal Dance Troupe.

Later the dance styles of both theatre forms merged, and *lakhon nok* developed more refined qualities in dramatic texts, dance patterns, characterization, and even the comic reliefs.

Other dance troupes later imitated the classical style of royal *lakhon nai* and *lakhon nok* and used King Rama II's compositions and choreography. *Lakhon* and *khon* productions of the National Theatre at present depend heavily on his dramatic texts in modern condensed versions, concentrating more on rapid story-telling actions, comic dialogues, dance numbers with modern choreography, spectacular set designs, and colourful costumes, rather than the traditional, complex, and refined movements.

New musical tunes and songs composed by Prince Naris are later additions to traditional *lakhon nok, lakhon nai*, and *khon* made to attract the interest of modern public audiences. These three types of dance-drama are now regularly performed and taught by the National Theatre and the Witthayalai Natasin. Occasionally, private and educational institutions present amateur productions.

During the reign of King Chulalongkorn, due to modernization under Western influence, new forms of *lakhon* emerged from the traditional ones, namely, *lakhon phan thang* from *lakhon nok* with new stories taken from historical legends and chronicles using modernized costumes of the periods; *lakhon dukdamban*, a creation of Prince Naris and Chao Phraya Thewetwongwiwat, which was an off-shoot from the royal *lakhon nai* and *lakhon nok* with new music and songs now sung by the dancers, rapid actions, contemporary dialogues, and modern theatre techniques (pls. 8, 9); and *lakhon rong*, a Thai attempt at imitating Western operetta with Thai music and stories adapted from Western plays set in the contemporary period and fashion (pl. 11).

There was also an introduction of the spoken dialogue play called *lakhon phut*, a completely new dramatic genre from Western tradition. Ever since his childhood and school days in England, King Vajiravudh had been an avid amateur actor and playwright. His translations and adaptations of Western plays into Thai, mainly from French and English including Shakespeare, and his own numerous original plays earned him the title of the "Father of Thai *lakhon phut.*" He also introduced new styles of acting, directing, make-up, and stage production. His political plays served well as an instrument to stir public interest and patriotism necessary in opposing the external threats of Western colonialism and Bolshevism, as well as internal economic and social problems such as the Chinese monopoly of commerce and trade. His political themes are mostly in support of the absolute monarchy led by a democratic, enlightened ruler.

Lakhon phut during his reign became an effective means of fostering a sense of loyalty to the throne as well as educating the public on various subjects. Later playwrights who followed his footsteps were Luang Wichit-wathakan with his patriotic and nationalistic musical plays in the 1940s and 1950s and Somphop Chantharaprapha in the 1970s with his royalistic dance-dramas.

Lakhon phut became more popular during the Second World War and the postwar period, when the import of foreign films was not permitted. Many companies competed and offered high salaries to popular actors. They invested in musical scores, choreography, costumes, and sets. Radio plays also became regular entertainment for the general public and served as a government political and educational tool. The style of acting and manner of speaking are melodramatic and type-cast. These characteristics still prevail in Thai films and television drama. The stories are mostly domestic and romantic, or patriotic when there is a national call for it. Modern music and lyrics are major elements to attract popular audiences. Costumes and make-up in *lakhon phut* still follow much of the traditional style of *lakhon ram* in theatrical qualities rather than being realistic and naturalistic. This phenomenon may also be observed in Thai films and television.

The training of *lakhon ram*, both folk and classical, starts usually from childhood going through the basic patterns of dance handed down from older generations with some modernized choreographies by outstanding artists of the royal court in the past or the National Theatre and the Witthayalai Natasin in present times. In contrast, actors of *lakhon phut* are mostly self-taught.

It was not until the 1970s that Western methods of modern acting in the style of realism began to be taught in the universities. Stanislavsky's method is a major influence and is combined with Thai elements. University plays are mostly adaptations or translations of Western classics and modern plays set in contemporary or historical periods of Thailand or Asia. The most noted productions are those of the Theatre Arts Department of Chulalongkorn University and Drama Department of Thammasat University. Their audiences are limited to the intellectual elite and middle class, as the general public still enjoys melodramatic, domestic, comic, farcical, and musical plays. At present, the contemporary stage plays are produced by groups of amateurs, university graduates, and professionals from film and television at hotels, cocktail lounges, public and private halls. The most successful commercial cocktail lounge theatre is the Monthienthong Theatre at the Montien Hotel. The most recent one is Patravadi Theatre started in 1992 in an open-air style. There are now two or three new theatres being built by commercial groups. Sala Chaloemkrung Theatre is being renovated as a proper theatre for classical *khon* and *lakhon,* to reopen in 1993.

During the 1950s and 1960s, with the influx of Western films, both staged *lakhon ram* and *lakhon phut* lost the majority of their audiences. However, in the present age of television, they are being revived with modern electronic media technology. Tales from traditional *lakhon nok, lakhon nai,* and *khon* are regularly presented with modernized costumes as television dramas. All television channels have their own *lakhon thorathat* (television drama), most of which presents domestic scenes with social or satirical themes. The characters still maintain the major types within *lakhon ram: phra ek,* a handsome hero, *nang ek,* a beautiful heroine, *phu rai,* a villain, *nang itcha,* a jealous female antagonist, rival of *nang ek, phra rong,* confidant of *phra ek* or second important male role, *nang rong,* confidante of *nang ek* or second important female role, and *tua talok,* a clown. Hence the tradition of *lakhon* is still very influential in the Thai entertainment world despite imported Western culture.

Chapter I
Traditional Dance, Dance-drama, and Dramatic Literature

Ancient Times to 1851

The Origin of Thai Dance in the Pre-Sukhothai Period

The history of Thai drama has generally been treated as a part of the study of Thai literature, culture, and customs. Only a few researchers have given careful attention to this art form as a separate phenomenon in itself.[1] Though literature plays a very important part in drama, there are other visual, aural, and oral aspects and forms that co-relate and interweave to make Thai dance-drama and spoken-drama composite arts very distinct from literature.

As a living form of public art, drama involves people in the roles of poet, playwright, dancer, actor, singer, painter, dramatic interpreter and director, producer, critic, and audience. The religious, social, and political functions of Thai drama are essential elements directly related to Thai society, culture, civilization, and way of life. For these reasons, the writer wishes to show in this study of the origin and early development of Thai drama in the Sukhothai period a harmonious balance between dramatic literature and the theatrical arts.

Most research published by both Thai and foreign (mostly Western) scholars have primarily looked to written evidence. Yet it should be noted that dance and drama have long been natural human expressions even from before the documentary and literary evidence came into existence. Therefore, archaeological evidence is crucial for the study of Thai dance and drama during pre-historical periods. Ancient sculpture, paintings, and drawings also help to reveal the pictorial details often omitted, or taken for granted, in the early Thai historical accounts[2] and have been often misinterpreted by Western observers.[3]

Archaeological Evidence

The earliest literary references to Thai performing arts appear in the A.D. 1292 stone inscriptions of Pho Khun Ramkhamhaeng, the third king of the Sukhothai kingdom (A.D. 1257–1377). However, there have been many archaeological discoveries from much earlier periods in various parts of the Indochina peninsula. They show forms of dancers, entertainers, and musicians whose nationalities were uncertain. In the early 1960s a group of archaeologists from the Krom Silapakon (Department of Fine Arts) of Thailand found a large amount of terracotta pottery, many ornaments, and a number of sculptured reliefs in the provinces of Ratchaburi and Nakhon Sawan. Among them are figurines and sculptured reliefs of dancers and musicians.[4] They are believed to have been created in the Dvaravati period between the sixth and twelfth or thirteenth centuries A.D. The Dvaravati kingdom is said to have been a great Mon empire existing long before the Sukhothai kingdom. However, archaeologists and historians are still debating about the exact historical dates and location of that empire.

Dhanit Yupho, an authority on Thai dance and drama, compared the dance poses and positions in these figurines with the dance positions (*karanas*) of the Indian *Bharata Natayasastra*[5] seen in the sculptured reliefs of the Temple of Siva Nataraj (the dancing god) at Gitumbhrum in Madras. There seem to be many similarities between them.

> In the past ten years, we found many Dvaravati terracotta antique figures in the forms of dancers and musicians at Tambon Khu Bua [Khu Bua district], Ratchapuri province. Some dance positions resemble the *catura* positions[6] in the *Bharata Natayasastra*. Another plaster figure found at Ban Khok Mai Den, Amphoe Phayuhakiri, Nakhon Sawan province is in the form of a *kinnari*[7] [a half-bird, half-maiden mythological creature] dancing in a position resembling the *lalita* position[8] in the *Bharata Natayasastra* [pl. 17], and yet another terracotta dancing figurine found in Ban Chan Sen, Amphoe Takli, Nakhon Sawan province in an *ancita*-like position[9] . . . two Dvaravati terracotta dancers figures in the possession of Air Marshal Montri Hanwichai, one of them has a hand gesture like the *lalita* or *krihastaka*[10] while that of the other resembles the *catura*. . . . Before this, that is in 2476 B.E., a bronze figure of a dancer of the Lopburi period was found at the Prasat Hin Phimai, Nakhon Ratchasima province [pl. 18]. Its dance position corresponds with the *vyamsita* position[11] and its hand-gesture is in the *kilakahasta* gesture[12] which expresses love or friendly dialogue.[13] The discovery of these sculptures is an evidence of the long cultural relationship in the *natasin,* the art of dancing, between the people of India and those of the land which is now Thailand, at least from the Dvaravati period [11th–16th centuries B.E.], or even before that, the Lopburi period [16th–17th centuries B.E.] up to the present. Therefore, it may be possible that the native teachers themselves had learned the Indian *natasin*, taught it to their people and had these sculptured

1 Thai folk dances and songs related to rice planting and harvest, in Nakhon Thai Village in Phisanulok, a northern province.

2 (*left*) Thai classical dancer in the *phra* (male) role demonstrating the *wong* (curve of arms) and *liem* (angle of legs) positions, 1950s.
3 (*right*) Thai classical dancer in the *nang* (female) role demonstrating the *chip* finger gesture (closed fingers, thumb and index, and opened fingers) and *lop liem* (non-angular) legs movement, 1950s.

4 *Nang yai* shadow plays: a puppeteer holding up a shadow puppet of a *yak* (ogre) character in an angular leg position similar to *khon*.

5 *Khon* (masked dance-drama). A fighting scene between Thosakan (*left*), a *yak* character, and Hanuman (*right*), the white monkey, a *ling* character. Compare their different physical appearances, costumes, and movements.

6 "Offering Dance to the Gods" (*ram thwai mu*) in *nora chatri* (Southern dance-drama) in the traditional costume, possibly before the 1940s.

7 *Lakhon nai* (female dance-drama of the royal court), possibly performing *Inao* play, in the Fifth Reign.

8 Drawing by Prince Naris, depicting the scene of Rotchana and Chao Ngo in the episode of "Rotchana Choosing a Husband" in *Sangthong*, possibly in the Fifth Reign.

9 "Rotchana Sieng Phuang Malai" (Rotchana throwing a garland to Chao Ngo to choose him as her husband), a scene from *Sangthong*, a revival of *lakhon dukdamban* at Ban Plai Noen Palace in the 1970s.

10 Thai adaptation of Persian costumes for a *lakhon phan thang* production of the *Arabian Nights* by Prince Narathip in the Fifth Reign.

11 Modern *lakhon rong* costume in *Sao Khrua Fa,* a Thai adaptation of *Madame Butterfly.* The heroine (*left*) in a Northern costume; the hero in a contemporary military uniform. A Silapakon production, 1980s.

12 Modern *liké* costumes, possibly in the 1950s. Female (*left*); male (*right*).

13 *Mongkhrum,* a traditional martial dance with drum beating and feet stamping in *khon*-like positions, possibly in the Fifth Reign.

14 *Nang yai:* the opening piece of *Chap Ling Hua Kham* (Catching the monkeys) with the *rishi* (hermit) and two monkeys, black (bad character) and white (good character). The white monkey catches the black one and brings it to the hermit to punish him for his bad behaviour. Photo taken from the backside of the screen.

15 *Khon* dancers without masks for *phra* and *nang* characters, possibly performed by all male dancers, or by a mixed cast, possibly in the Fifth Reign.

16 Elaborate *lakhon* costumes of Prince Narathip's theatre troupe, possibly in the Fifth Reign.

17 Bas-relief of a dancing *kinnari,* a half-bird, half-woman mythological creature, found in Ratchaburi Province, assumed to be of the Dvaravati period.

18 Bronze figure of a dancer showing Khmer and Indian influences. Lopburi period.

reliefs made to depict the dance movements which were seen and performed at that time.[14]

The Dvaravati kingdom was recorded by Hiuan-Tsang, a Chinese Buddhist pilgrim, in A.D. 648 as being one of the notable kingdoms which he was unable to visit during the course of his travels. He referred to it as the "To-lo-po-ti" kingdom. The kingdom was also mentioned by an Arab geographer, Ibn Khordadzebah, in his *Routes and Provinces*, compiled during A.D. 844–48. He referred to Thaton, the state on the eastern side of Dawna mountain range where the Dvaravati kingdom was founded as "Raman'n'adesa."[15] It is generally believed that these people enjoyed a great civilization long before the Khmers conquered them during the reign of the great Khmer warrior, King Suriyawaraman I (A.D. 1002–49). The Khmers consequently fell to the Burmese King Anawahata of Pagan in A.D. 1047. The Mon people of the Dvaravati period had their own script and literature, which are believed to be the first cultural heritage inherited by their conquerers, the Khmers, the Burmese, and later the Thai of the Sukhothai kingdom. Along with their literary culture, Mon Buddhism, art, dance, and music deeply influenced the various tribes living on this Indochina peninsula.

From the study of these Dvaravati sculptured reliefs found in Thailand, it may be assumed that the Thai people may have directly received the art of dancing and music from the Mon, as well as from the Khmer, both of whom were introducing Indian culture into the area. It should be noted, however, that the Mon and Cambodian dances seen today are most probably not direct continuations of their ancient forms. Thai influence in both of them at present is very evident.

The dance positions (*karanas*) and the hand gestures (*mudras*) mentioned above are also reflected in the various poses of Buddha images in India and Southeast Asia. The most notable Thai example is the famous Walking Buddha of the Sukhothai period, with the left hand lifted to the level of the chest and the index and thumb fingers forming a circular hand gesture. Another example is the Standing Buddha in south India with one hip slightly swaying to the left as if in a *contrapposto* position of a Hellenic statue. This position is also a typical Indian dancing pose called the *tripanka*.[16]

Archaeological evidence of the Khmer empire in the Lopburi period found in various parts of Thailand, particularly in the Northeast, also shows a strong influence of the Indian *Bharata Natayasastra*, which the ancient Thais may have indirectly inherited through their more civilized Khmer neighbours, who had been their masters before the declaration of sovereignty by the Sukhothai state. One clear example is a group of sculptured reliefs on the gate lintels of the Khmer Phrasat Hin Phimai in Nakhon Ratchasima province. The temple complex is believed to have been built by King Suriyawaraman I in the same style as Angkor Wat and Angkor Thom in Cambodia. One relief depicts five seated deities, with the largest image in the middle flanked by two identical images on each side. Each deity has three faces and six arms. Each hand holds different objects—a trident, a bell, a noose, a bowl, a drum, and an undefinable object. These attributes are found in most images of the dancing god Siva. The deities are surrounded by dancers, both male and female, arranged in rows on each side. They are bare-chested, with flowing garments covering the lower parts of their bodies. Their hair style is identical to that of the dancing gods (*devas*) and goddesses (*apsaras*) in the sculptured reliefs at Angkor Wat. Each dancer is in a dance position with the right hand lifted to the right knee. In the middle, under the central image, are seated singers and musicians.

Another lintel of the same temple depicts an eight-armed deity dancing on an elephant's head in a similar position to that of the Siva Nataraj of south India. The hide of the elephant hangs upward with its tail falling upside down resembling a cape enveloping the back of the deity. Below the image is a row of dancers in the same dance position as in the lintel described above. According to Prince Subhadradis Diskul, a well-known Thai archaeologist and art historian, the former lintel depicts the images of the "Wacharasatawa Buddha" of the Mahayana tradition, while the latter depicts the "Lokayawichaya Buddha," also of the Mahayana tradition. Both manifest a concept of Mahayana Buddhism which incorporates the Tantric elements of Hinduism into Buddhist form. However, in a close comparative study of these reliefs and the Hinduistic ones in Angkor and south India, this writer is more convinced that these two Buddha images had been modelled after the image of the god Bhairava, who is the destructive form of Siva Nataraj. He is the "terrible destroyer" with three heads and six arms who performs the *tandava* dance with his wife, the goddess Devi. They are surrounded by dancing imps or gods and goddesses.[17] The elephant's head is that of the ogre (*asura*) Gaya, whom Siva destroyed by ripping the skin off his body and throwing it with its head attached over his shoulders like a cloak.[18] The objects in the hands of both images are identical with those of the god Bhairava as represented in a standing sculpture at the Temple of Surya (the sun god) at Konaarka, Orissa, in India, which was built in the thirteenth century A.D.

It could be assumed that the tradition of temple dancing to glorify Siva and the other gods was carried on in this Mahayana-Hindu temple at Phimai by Khmer dancers. This may have been the origin of the sacred ritualistic dance of Phra Phirap, the god or teacher of Thai classical dance and drama, which is still being performed by Thai dancers who have been initiated to do this most sacred dance in the Invocation Ceremony (*Phithi Wai Khru*), which pays homage to the spirits of dance teachers. The Thai name "Phirap" could have been derived from "Bhairava" (as the Sanskrit consonant pronouned "bh" is usually transformed to the "ph" sound in Thai). In Nepal, the same god is worshipped in a more grotesque form. It is more logical that the Thai god of dancing, Phra Phirap, derived from this destructive form of Siva Nataraj rather than from the insignificant demon character in the *Ramakien* who has the same name and who is the guard of the golden mango orchard of the god Isuan (Siva), from which Phra Ram, Sida, and Phra Lak were driven away by the demon. In this episode of the *Ramakien*, Phra Ram later kills Phra Phirap for having tried to abduct Sida. Phra Phirap in the Thai version corresponds with a ferocious demon Viradha in Valmiki's *Ramayana,* who was also killed by Rama.[19] Dhanit Yupho has suggested in an interview with this writer that Viradha was previously a god of music called Tamvaru,[20] who was punished by Siva for having neglected his duty to entertain the gods. He was sentenced to take the form of a demon. After being killed by Rama he resumed his former being. Whichever the case may be, it is evident that the tradition of temple dancing to satisfy and pacify the gods, to ward off evil spirits, or to ask the gods for fertility is of great importance to the people in this agrarian culture. At present, similar dances before the gods which are commonly called *Buang Suang*[21] dance in Khmer, Thai, and Lao. It can still be seen in Cambodia, Thailand, Bali, Java, Laos, south India, and Ceylon.

In Thailand, *nora chatri* dance-drama of the south and the later *lakhon chatri* contain ritualistic dances performed at the beginning of the *Wai Khru* ceremony[22] to pay homage to the gods and teachers and at the *Kae Bon* ceremony to untie a promise made to the gods or a particular god and give offerings as promised for a boon or a fortune received from them. Here the host may hire a dance troupe to perform a dance in worship of the gods as an offering. This type of sacred dance is called *Ram Thwai Mu* (lit., a dance to offer the hands of the dancers to the gods). This dance is also performed by dance teachers and pupils who are initiated in the *Wai Khru* ceremony for each type of dance and dance-drama.

These archaeological discoveries have helped us determine the possible sources from which the ancient Thai people may have been influenced. After a process of synthesizing these influences, the Thais developed their own indigenous performing arts in unique styles quite different from these outside sources.

The first possible geographic direction follows the merchant ship routes from south India and/or northeast India (in the area of Orissa, Banaras), where, as seen from evidence of sculptures and paintings, highly developed dance cultures were centred. From these parts of India the route continues through the Javanese empire of Srivijaya (7th–13th centuries)[23] and the Khmer[24] empire (9th–15th centuries), both of which spread their influence over the whole Indochina peninsula. It finally reached the Thai people who had just founded the first kingdom of Sukhothai in the thirteenth century.

The second route may have been more direct, from south India and/or Sri Lanka (Ceylon) to the south of Thailand, where an Indian settlement was situated in the area now called Nakhon Sithammarat, Takua Pa, and Phang-nga. As Theravada Buddhism was imported from Sri Lanka in the reign of King Ramkhamhaeng (1279–1300), so too dance and art cultures may have been brought in with Buddhism, or even earlier with Hinduism. The *nora chatri* dance-drama of the south, which is believed to be the oldest form of Thai dance-drama, bears a strong resemblance to the still extant *Kandyan* dance in Sri Lanka in the dance movements, naturalistic interpretations imitating birds and animals, hand-gestures, costumes, and musical accompaniment in which the drums have a dominant role and are played in a variety of rapid speeds and rhythms. This close resemblance to the Indian and Ceylonese dances confirms the theory that *nora chatri* of southern Thailand originated in the south around Nakhon Sithammarat. It was possibly directly influenced or even taught by the Indian dance teacher or dancers to the natives and later brought up to the Ayudhaya kingdom (1350–1767), where it developed into a more refined form of dance-drama later known as *lakhon nok*.[25]

The third route may have been a direct one from Java to the south of Thailand during approximately the same period as the introduction of Hinduistic-Javanese civilization to the Khmers. There are many Srivijaya style sculptures found in southern Thailand, notably the famous image of "Avalokitesvara Bodhisattva" in Chaiya. Though the lower part of the image is broken and lost, the s-curve of the upper body shows very clearly a *contrapposto* (*tripanka*) pose of a dancer with hips swaying to the right. Moreover, the Thai word *lakhon*, or dance-drama, is most likely to have come from the Javanese word *lakuan* or *lagon*. In Cambodian, there are also the words *lokkhon* and *lukkhun*. Here again, Prince Damrong hypothesized that *lakhon* may have derived from the word *nakhon*, the name of the city of Nakhon Sithammarat where the dance-drama was originated, as the two words resemble each other in spelling and sound. However, King Chulalongkorn after his trip to Java stated that the Thai *lakhon* probably came directly from Javanese sources.[26] This again is still not finalized. The Royal Academy of Scholars has followed the theory of Prince Damrong. This writer, however, is more convinced by King Chulalongkorn's theory, which seems to have more evidence supporting its argument. It does not seem very logical that dance-drama should be named after the city of Nakhon Sithammarat, since the drama has been performed in cities other than Nakhon Sithammarat. Moreover, the dramatic form of the Javanese *lagon* is quite close to the Thai *lakhon*.

The curious absence of evidence of any forms of dance-drama in the ancient kingdoms of Chiengsaen, Chiengrai, and Chiengmai, in the north of Thailand and Burma prior to the sack of Ayudhaya in 1767[27] (despite the golden periods in which they had manifested great civilization in their Buddhist religion, art, architecture, music, and literature, both oral and written), confirms this writer's opinion that the tradition of dance-drama which was influenced by the Indian *Natayasastra*, and also *Natakam* and other forms, came through the southern route, i.e., from India to the southern end of the peninsula and then up north in later periods. It is therefore most unlikely that the influence should have come through the northern route from India to Burma and northern Thailand. The strong Buddhist influence in Burma and northern Thailand may have been a factor in discouraging the development of any dramatic entertainment. Also, dance-drama forms were more or less a culture of south India in the earlier periods, and therefore influential in the southern parts of Asia and Southeast Asia, which had direct commercial and cultural contacts with it. This dance-drama culture which came up from the southern part of Thailand to the north in the pre-Sukhothai period reached only as far as the Sukhothai area, and did not advance farther north or into Burma. It was only in the Ayudhaya period that the influence of Thai dance-drama came to Burma, when troupes of Thai dancers were taken as captives by the Burmese army after the sack of Ayudhaya. They settled there to perform and teach at the Burmese courts in Ava and Mandalay.

In northern Thailand, there is only evidence of music and dance which continue to the present. The dances, however, did not develop into any dramatic forms until in the nineteenth century, when a Chiengmai princess, Phra Ratchachaya Dararatsami, a consort of King Chulalongkorn, after having seen stage plays in Bangkok, wrote a dramatic plot for a dance-drama in the northern style. She commissioned Thao Suthon Photchanakit to compose the dialogue in verse. The play was called *Phra Lǫ Waen Keo* or *Noi Chaiya* and is still very popular among the northern Thais.[28]

According to the *Phongsawadan Yonok* (Chronicles of the northern kingdom), the ancient culture of the Lanna Thai kingdom had greatly been influenced by the Mon-Burmese culture centred in Pegu, Pagan, Ava, and Mandalay. On the other hand, at the height of the Chiengmai civilization, artists, dancers, and musicians from that court were sent to entertain the Burmese kings.[29] The Burmese court of Ava and Mandalay had Thai dancers come from Ayudhaya to teach their dancers in the *yodaya* or *yodia* (i.e., Ayudhaya) style. The name *yodaya* or *yodia* style remains today as the name of a particular dance and music in Burma. There is also a village called "Yodaya" where these Thai captives settled after having been taken to Burma. Maung Htin Aung, an authority of Burmese dance and drama, in his book, *Burmese Drama*, affirms this fact.

> The play [a Thai *lakhon* performed in Burma] was presented with Siamese . . . dress and costume. . . . The introduction of Burmese elements into the play through the professional actors was prevented by the tradition of rigid faithfulness to the Siamese model. The Siamese courtier-captives of course discouraged any interference with the form of their entertainment, which they took to be a perfect art; probably they thought the Burmese, as far as dramatic representation was concerned, to be barbarians. Moreover, many

of the Burmese scholars themselves were against any substantial changes in the presentation of the play at their court. They were for borrowing from, and imitations of, the Siamese play, but they held that the model must be kept unchanged and intact.... However, changes were introduced in the actual words of the songs and speeches.... The gesture, rather than actual acting and facial expression, was of great importance in the Siamese play, and that the Burmese court rigidly followed.[30]

In the contemporary presentation of the *Ramayana* in Burma, we can clearly see strong Thai influence in the costumes of the male dancers, masks, and to a certain extent, the music. However, the female costumes are genuinely Burmese and the dance movements and gestures more angular and swift, in the style of Burmese dance rather than the Thai classical dance style. This "Burmanization" is only inevitable in the long process of cultural transformation and assimilation from the eighteenth century to the present. The basic tunes of *yodaya* music, however, despite some Burmese touches are still recognizable.[31]

It is interesting to note that the Thai people received most of their cultural influences from India, not only in the political and social aspects, but also in religion, arts, literature, dance, drama, and music. China had long been geographically and historically connected with Thai settlements before their migration into the Indochina peninsula, and has carried on political and economic relations with Siam all throughout history. However, China has not had a strong cultural impact on Thai civilization. Chinese influences are found only in music (tunes and instruments), pottery, ceramics, painting, sculpture, architecture, decorative arts, dressing and eating habits, food, and a few customs and words. These influences are, however, superficial and external. Chinese culture, religious beliefs, political organization, court ceremonies and customs, literature, language, drama, and dance did not penetrate as deeply into the Thai social and cultural structures as did Indian civilization. In dance and drama, there are only a few dance pieces imitating Chinese styles. They include the "flower dance," "lantern dance," and "fan dance." The accompanying music to these dances is basically Thai with Chinese overtones. These dances are, however, later innovations made in the nineteenth century for the sake of exoticism, notably in the dance-drama form called *lakhon phan thang*, which presents tales from foreign lands in modernized Thai classical form. While Vietnam seems to be the only country in Southeast Asia which directly adopted Chinese culture in complete forms, including Chinese opera, other countries on the Indochina peninsula preferred Indian cultrure and remain faithful to it even today.

Mom Ratchawong Kukrit Pramoj, an authority on Thai civilization, remarked in his lecture entitled "The Foundation of Thai Civilization" at Thammasat University in 1971:

If we look at Thai civilization, both in its history and present condition, we could immediately say that Thai civilization is founded more on Indian civilization, the civilization of the "Araya" [of the Aryan tribes of relatively civilized people]. Be it religion, belief, or government, including the Thai way of life in the past or even at present, the inclination has mostly been towards Indian civilization. We can conclude that, on the subject of civilization, Thailand has looked West for a long time. Therefore, if we should follow the West today we should not be criticized, for we have done exactly the same thing for who knows how many thousand years. We have always turned to the West and not to the East. But the real historical reason why the civilization of the people who migrated into Thailand has inclined more towards India is probably because the ancient Chinese civilization did not spread down as far as where we are at present. On the Indochina peninsula, it was known that the Chinese army conquered the area which is now North Vietnam two thousand years ago. The whole area became a centre of Chinese civilization, that is, present-day North Vietnam. But Chinese civilization did not spread south. This was because there were other kingdoms connected to this area [under Chinese rule two thousand years ago]. One in particular was called the Champa kingdom, which had already adopted Indian culture. It was this kingdom that prevented Chinese civilization from spreading southward.[32]

Another reason was that the Mon and Khmer peoples had no racial relationship with the Chinese, and therefore, it was difficult for them to assimilate Chinese culture. When the Thai people migrated into this area, these two tribes of people had already highly developed cultures in the Indian mode. It was only natural for the Thai to adopt them readily and integrate them with the few Chinese cultural elements they had brought with them from southern China, where they were believed to have originally settled before their migration. These elements include musical instruments and tonal spoken language.[33]

Mom Ratchawong Kukrit Pramoj's theory may seem political, diplomatic, and tongue in cheek, but it is quite valid. It helps to explain the Thai inclination towards the West in the modern age.

Lévi in his *L'Inde civilisatrice* seems to support Kukrit Pramoj's theory:

[L'expansion de la civilisation hindoue] vers ces contrées et ces îles de l'Orient où la civilisation chinoise, par une frappante correspondance d'aspiration, semble venir au devant d'elle. . . . Mère de la sagesse, l'Inde donne ses fables à ses voisins qui vont les enseigner au monde entier. Mère de la foi et de la philosophie, elle donne aux trois quarts de l'Asie un dieu, une religion, une doctrine, un art.

Elle porte sa langue sacrée, sa littérature, ses institutions dans l'Insulinde jusqu'aux limites du monde connu.[34]

According to Coedès, the Thai migrants from Yunnan must have had a considerably advanced culture and must also have had some contact with India and Buddhism, via a route that joined India and China through Assam and Yunnan, before they entered the Indochina peninsula in the eleventh century. This may be seen in the Thai Buddhist art in the northernmost region of the "Menam Basin."[35] By the thirteenth century, they managed to dominate those who had formerly been their masters, i.e., the Khmers, Mons, and Burmese. These peoples had also been leaders in adopting Indianized civilization.

However, recent discoveries from the prehistoric civilization in eastern Thailand, at Ban Chieng and Ban Kao in Kanchanaburi province, have considerably upset this theory of the origin of the Thai people and their early civilization. The skeletons, pottery, decorative objects, hand-woven fabrics, terracotta items, stone and bronze instruments and ornamants, and beads reveal that there was a tribe of rice-eating people in the region with a considerably advanced Neolithic and Bronze Culture. From the burial grounds and funeral objects, mainly pottery, it is evident that these pre-historic people believed in the hereafter. Their ritualistic way of life seems to manifest "elements both of fertility and ancestor worship."[36] They had highly developed pottery and tools. Their economy was based on agriculture, with some supplementary animal breeding, hunting, and fishing.

Since ritualistic dances usually connected with the fertility cult are still seen in farming villagers in Thailand and other parts of the world today, it could be assumed that these ancient people may have had this dance tradition as early as Neolithic times, as evidenced by cave paintings in Europe and South America.

A group of Thai-Danish archaeologists concluded from their study of the skeletons found at these sites that this tribe is physiologically related to the present Thai people. However, there were other tribes of Thais who were different from those who migrated from Yunnan into Indochina. The Ban Chieng and Ban Kao people may have migrated from central China and arrived in this area about 1800 B.C. Their culture was probably the foundation of the later Bronze and Iron Ages in the same region. Sørensen has stated,

It is the results of the study of the latter [i.e., burial finds], . . . They show that the culture must have arrived about 1800 B.C. as the result of a migration from the Proto-Lungshan phase in Central China. It has so far been possible only to trace this culture from Western Central Thailand through Peninsular Thailand to North Malaya. A local development of the culture took place in this area, but probably under renewed influences from the Lungshan culture proper in China, arriving not later than about 1500 B.C., perhaps following the Yangtze Kiang and one of the main rivers running South from China. These influences may mark the beginning of a second stage of the culture, chronologically a Neolithic Late subphase, which can be followed regionally down to North Malaya with faint extensions acrose to Borneo. It is probable that this culture is the foundation of the later but so far sparsely known Bronze/Iron Age culture in the same region. . . . Through anthropological studies of the skeletons many good reasons have been found to support a theory of a certain relationship between these Neolithic inhabitants of Thailand and the present Thai population, as distinct from the later immigrated Chinese populations; in other words the recent Thai population—the Thai-speaking peoples—may well have arrived deep in historic times, but at least one branch of their forefathers occupied parts of the kingdom from 1800 B.C.[37]

It is not difficult then to understand why the Thais have received more influence from Indian civilization than from China. Due to this first immigration in 1500 B.C. and finally the third or fourth in the eleventh century, they firmly settled in the area and were developing their own culture, distinct from the Chinese, long before the first wave of Indianization hit the shores of the Indochina peninsula at the end of the fourth century or early third century B.C.[38] Since there is still no archaeological evidence of the culture in the transitional period from the late Neolithic Age to the first Hinduized monuments found in Champa and Cambodia, and since Sanskrit inscriptions were found on stone implements, Coedès has concluded that the people of "farther India" were still in the midst of the late Neolithic civilization when the "Brahmano-Buddhist" culture of India came into contact with them:

> On peut donc, sans grande exagération, dire que les populations de l'Inde extérieure étaient encore en pleine civilisation néolithique tardive lorsque la culture brahmano-bouddhique de l'Inde est arrivée à leur contact.[39]

The more primitive Neolithic dance and music culture of these peninsular people must have been cultivated within this new Brahmano-Buddhist tradition from the third century B.C. onward.

Dance and Performing Arts in the Sukhothai Period

Evidence in the Stone Inscription of King Ramkhamhaeng

The first literary evidence of Thai dance and music is the ca. A.D. 1293 stone inscription attributed to King Ramkhamhaeng, the third king of Sukhothai who also invented the Thai script used to record this inscription.[40] The stele was discovered in Sukhothai by King Mongkut (r. 1851–68) when he visited the ancient city during his monkhood. He brought it back to Bangkok and finally, with great effort and patience, learned to read it.

The style of the Ramkhamhaeng inscription is autobiographic in the first part, using the first-person narrative, referring to himself as "Ku" (meaning "I," an old term used by royal persons to subordinates or by commoners to persons of equal or lower status). It tells about his parents, his valiant deeds during his adolescence, and his ascension to the throne. The second part uses the third-person narrative referring to "Pho Khun Ramkhamhaeng" (King Ramkhamhaeng). It lauds the political and economic stability of his kingdom, the fertility of the land, freedom of trade, and the king's concern for the welfare of his people. It also praises him as a great patron of Buddhism for constructing the Phra Mahathat Temple at Sisatchanalai for the Buddha's relics in M.S. 1207 (A.D. 1285), as a wise king in his audience with the people at the Manangkhasila stone throne in M.S. 1214 (A.D. 1292), and as the inventor of the Thai written language (M.S. 1205). The third part is believed to have been written much later, since the orthography is different from the first two parts. It witnesses mainly to the glory and greatness of King Ramkhamhaeng and his expansion of the Thai territory in all directions.[41]

The form, content, and structure of the Ramkhamhaeng inscription bears a strong resemblance to the Mon-Burmese inscriptions, notably those of King Kyansittha of Pagan. Its propagandistic style, common in most of these inscriptions, confirms the socio-political theory that the new young king, Ramkhamhaeng, had not only wished to glorify his own administration and great deeds, but also to advertise to the neighbouring peoples the political and economic stability of his state, the richness of its natural resources, the freedom of occupation and life style, as well as the equal opportunities offered to all who wished to settle in this land. Manpower, trade, and agriculture were necessary for the development and stability of this newly found kingdom.[42] In the descriptions of state and religious ceremonies in the second part of the Ramkhamhaeng inscription, the author notes the freedom to pursue personal pleasure and entertainment in Sukhothai, of which music and dance were the essential parts.

In the first inscription[43] it is written that the king and the men and women of Sukhothai were devout Buddhists. They all observed the *silas* (Buddhist moral precepts) during *Phansa* (Buddhist Lent). When *Phansa* was over on *Ok Phansa*, they had *Kathin* offerings[44] for a month. In the *Kathin* procession, they carried trays of coins (*bia*), betel nuts, flowers, and pillows for sitting and sleeping as offerings to the monks. They gave two million in unspecified monetary units to the temple. They attended the *Yatti* prayer ceremony for the *Kathin* at the faraway Aranyik mountain. When they returned to the city from the mountain, the procession came to the "Hua Lan" (a large plot of land, possibly similar to the Phra Men Ground in Bangkok where all festivals and state ceremonies take place). There the people enjoyed themselves in playing musical instruments, dancing, jumping, laughing, and singing. All types of entertainment and merry-making were carried out in great freedom. People in great crowds entered the four city gates to watch the candles and fireworks lit by the king. The sounds of the fireworks were so great the city seemed to be exploding.

The fact that in the Sukhothai period there was freedom in seeking pleasure and entertainment is indeed very important. It shows that dancing and music were important to the daily lives of the people. Being propagandistic in purpose, King Ramkhamhaeng might have felt that it was necessary to mention this cultural freedom to impress the neighbouring peoples and to assure his own subjects of the peace and prosperity of his civilized, cultured state and his liberalism. As Mom Ratchawong Kukrit Pramoj comments in his lecture on "The Sukhothai Governmental System,"

> As to the preservation of the rights of the people, there is in many instances in the Sukhothai inscriptions an emphasis on individual rights to all kinds of possessions and the right for children to inherit these possessions from their parents. The king was the protector of these rights. Moreover, there were other rights and freedoms such as "Whoever wishes to play can play, whoever wishes to laugh can laugh, whoever wishes to sing can sing." The right and freedom of the people to laugh is one of the most precious. When people lose this freedom to laugh, other rights and freedoms will also be lost.[45]

This particular emphasis on freedom might have also been intentionally a political strategy to contrast the liberal rule of the Thai king to the dictatorial Khmers, who were known to have demanded sacrifices from the people for their own glory. Khmer dancing and entertainment were also directed to the Hindu gods and the king, who was worshipped as a god-incarnate. They were performed as a form of worship and sacrifice for these divine beings. The Sukhothai people on the other hand expressed joy in celebrating any Buddhist religious occasion. The Thai court had not yet developed its own royal dance troupe. All the entertainment was performed and improvised by the people. The distinction had not yet been established between royal court and public entertainment. The Sukhothai king was the father figure or the patriarch to his subjects, and not a divine monarch like the Khmer ruler. Even later on during the reign of King Lithai (A.D. 1354–76), there is no mentioning of any royal dance troupe or royal orchestra. It was not until the period described by Nang Nophamat that we find the term *chao phanak ngan* (officials responsible for dancing and music at royal ceremonies). However, members of the royal entourage participated also as spectators and performers in public contests for reciting, singing, and dancing on a number of festive occasions. However, according to some modern Thai scholars, the *Memoirs of Nang Nophamat* is a work of a much later period, possibly the Ayudhaya or even the early Bangkok periods, due to the fact that its literary style is far more sophisticated than the Sukhothai literature and the society depicted is far more cultured as well. (This subject will be discussed later on.)

The musical instruments mentioned in King Ramkhamhaeng's inscription are percussion and strings:

1) *dom bangkhom klong*—(v) to repeatedly beat drums in unison,[46] or strike musical instruments together
2) *phat*—(n) percussion and woodwind instruments[47]
3) *phin*—string instruments, possibly *phinpia, phin nam tao,* and *krachup pi,* which are shown on the sculptured reliefs on the north side of the *prang* (pagoda) at Wat Phra Phai Luang depicting the god Indra playing a *phin* or a *krachup pi* in worship to Lord Buddha.

In the inscription there are other terms indicating different kinds of recreation and merry-making by the people. Some of these terms are still unclear.

1) *luan*—assumed to mean "singing," it is yet uncertain (and not in modern usage)
2) *khap*—reciting, singing (a poetic term)
3) *len*—"playing, performing, acting, entertaining, merry-making" as used in the modern language
4) *hua*—"laughing, merry-making, enjoying"; in the modern language it is used with other epithets such as *yim hua* (to smile) and *hua ro* (to laugh).

Phao thien (to burn candles) and *len fai* (to play with fire, i.e., to light fireworks) may have been religious ceremonies influenced by Hinduism. Some scholars have suggested that the king in performing these ceremonies was acting as a god giving light and fire to the world. However, according to this writer's observation of the revival of these ceremonies, *Loi Krathong*[48] day in November 1977, in which hundreds of candles were lit on the temple grounds and fireworks of different types displayed, appeared to be merely festive recreation. Still, the original religious significance may have been lost, or the religious interpretation of the event too farfetched. Nevertheless, it is rather universal to any culture to celebrate with candles and fireworks. In the North and Northeast, there are fireworks called *bong fai,* which are lit in the rain-making ceremony. Scientifically, the explosion of these giant-size fireworks could accumulate clouds and humidity and hence produce rain.

Another literary evidence is Inscription No. 8, the *Charuk Khao Sumanakut* (Inscription of Mount Sumanakut) written under the royal commission of King Lithai,[49] son of King Thammaracha I (ca. A.D. 1370), which was discovered by King Vajiravudh during his visit to Mount Sumanakut in 1908 to worship the replica of the Buddha's footprints (the original is at Mount Sumanakuta in Sri Lanka). The replica was said to have been erected by King Thammaracha I in A.D. 1359.

Side one of the inscription describes the Buddha's footprints on Mount Sumanakutaparvata (Sumanakut), which the Sukhothai people worshipped to obtain prosperity. It mentions the name King Sisuryawongsa Thammarachathirat in the eleventh month of the year M.S. 1281 (A.D. 1359). The second side of the inscription describes the festival and celebration held when the Buddha's footprints were brought to Mount Sumanakut. The road was decorated with *kalapapruk* (decorative, mythological) trees, flower garlands, torches, candles, and lamps. Incense sticks were burned. There were flags and banners everywhere. On both sides of the road people placed trays of betel nuts and *phlu* leaves. They expressed joy in worshipping the sacred footprints. There were all types of entertainment: dancing, jumping, and music. The sounds of *phin* (lutes), *khong* (gongs), and *klong* (drums) were so great that it seemed like the earth was shaking.[50]

The term *rabam* in the inscription means a dance,[51] while meaning of *ten*, literally "jumping," is rather vague. The verb is used in *khon* (masked dance-drama), where dancers representing demons (*yak* or *yaksa*) and monkeys (*ling*) stamp their feet and jump in different positions to the beat of drums and percussion instruments. *Ten* applies only to dancing with foot movement, whereas *ram* implies hand gestures as well as moving the feet.

The term *duriyaphat* means "orchestra," said in the inscription to consist of *khong* (gongs), *klong* (drums), and *phin* (a string instrument resembling a lute). At present, the term includes *ranat* (wooden or brass xylophone), *ching* (small cymbals), *taphon* (two-faced drum), and other string instruments such as *so* (there is a variety of *so—so u, so sam sai, so duang*—each of which has a different tone quality).

The term *len*, which literally means "to play," may also imply performing a dance or a play or some other entertainment or sport. However, there is no mention of the words *lakhon, khon,* or *nang.* This affirms that these more highly refined performing arts were later developments, probably during the Ayudhaya period. Nevertheless, since the *Ramayana* epic was already known to the Sukhothai people, as indicated in various place and personal names such as King Ramkhamhaeng (deriving from the name of the hero, "Ram" of "Rama," meaning "Rama manifesting power") and Tham Phra Ram (Rama's cave), it may be assumed that some of these *len, ten,* and *rabam* may have presented some elementary forms of the *Ramayana* or *Jataka* tales. There is also other archaeological evidence such as the *yak* (demon) guardian figures made of glazed ceramic found in Sukhothai and dated about the fourteenth century, and similar demon figures in the relief showing the Buddha in the temptation scene seated under a *pho* tree surrounded by evil spirits. These demon figures wear costumes and have facial appearances like the *yak* characters in *khon*. It could therefore be concluded that *khon* costumes and masks are most likely to have come from these prototypes in sculpture and painting.

Evidence in Other Sukhothai Inscriptions

The Inscription of Wat Prayun,[52] said to have been composed about A.D. 1371 in the same reign of King Lithai (A.D. 1354–76) and in the same style of language and script as other fourteenth-century Sukhothai inscriptions, relates the great religious event when King Thamikaracha (Dharmaraja), the father of King Lithai, went to Haripunchai[53] to meet the Mahathera Sumana,[54] whom the king had invited to bring the sacred relic of the Buddha to Sukhothai. "The King caused the highway to be decorated with bouquets and banners and had a pavilion built, roofed with pure white cloth. Various offerings were prepared for the lustration of the relic."[55] The descriptions of the procession and musical instruments are very detailed.

> [The day his exalted lordship arrived was in a year of the cock, in the first month, on a Friday. On that day, when his exalted lordship was about to arrive, King Dharmikaraja in person went to receive him, escorted by a numerous throng of officers, subjects, soldiers, princes, noblemen, and ministers, drawn up in formal order.] He had them carry banners and flags, grilled rice and flowers, torches and candles. They struck xylophones and sounded stringed instruments, gongs, drums, clarinets, cattle-horn trumpets, small double-headed drums, curved trumpets, and conches, together with plategongs, hand drums, and tabors, with such excellent and re-echoing sound that the whole people cheered loudly, almost shaking the whole town of Haripunjaya.[56]

It is clear in this text that during the reigns of King Thammaracha and King Lithai there was a great variety of musical instruments similar to those mentioned in the first book on Thai Buddhist cosmology and theology, the *Te Phumikatha*, commonly known as the *Trai Phum Phra Ruang* (The Three Worlds of Phra Ruang, the legendary king of Sukhothai). This literary work was said to have been written under the royal commission of King Lithai in ca. A.D. 1360.

Montri Tramote, an authority on Thai music, has stated that the Sukhothai people had all the musical instruments, except for the *ranat* (wooden xylophone), used today in the classical Thai *piphat* orchestra: consisting of *pi* (oboe), *taphon* (one-face drum), *tabor khong* (gongs), *klong* (drum), and *ching* (symbals). The basic musical instruments used in royal ceremonies in general include a variety of *pi* such as *pi chanai kaeo* or *pi soranai,* and different kinds of drums such as *tat thiat* or *sara thiat* (two-faced drums), *klong chana* or *klong Malayu.*[57] There are also *trae* (trumpets), *sank* (conch-shells), *marathong* (drums), and *kang sadan* (gongs). These are the basic instruments used in royal ceremonies up to the present day.

Evidence in the *Trai Phum Phra Ruang*

In the *Trai Phum Phra Ruang,* more elaborate descriptions are given concerning Sukhothai music, dance, and other forms of entertainment. The book depicts vividly the existence of living beings in the three worlds: Kamma Phum (world of desires), Rupa Phum (world of forms), and Arupa Phum (world of formless existence).

They are similar to Dante's Christian view in his *Divine Comedy* of the underworld, present world, and heavenly world. In the *Trai Phum Phra Ruang,* there are sub-divisions of thirty-one regions, into which living beings are born according to their sins and merits. The purpose of the book is to show that all forms of existence, albeit animal, human, godlike, or devilish, regardless of worldly or heavenly pleasure, wealth, and prosperity, all suffer from the impermanence of existence. They have to continue in an endless chain of different existences according to their past deeds. The only release from this chain is to seek *nirvana* as the Lord Buddha did and be forever released from this suffering cycle of birth and rebirth.

In the Manussaphum (human world), there are four continents: Uttaraguru Thawip, Amarakoyana Thawip, Buppawitheha Thawip, and Chomphu (Jambu) Thawip. In Uttaraguru Thawip, all men and women have perfect beauty. They dance, sing and make merry all day long. They also practise the *panja sila* (five Buddhist moral precepts). In their next lives they will all be reborn as gods and goddesses.[58]

The term *chap rabam* in the *Trai Phum Phra Ruang* means to dance together usually in pairs or in groups. The term *ring ram* is suggested by some authorities to mean *ling ram* (a monkey dance as in the *khon* masked dance-drama).[59] It may also mean *roeng ram,* as in the old Thai spelling where the term means "to dance joyfully."

In the *Trai Phum Phra Ruang,* there is a legend of King Sithammasokarat in which a dance of the birds in the forest is described. The phrase *ma fon ram ti pik chik hang* (to dance and flap the wings and display tails like birds) shows that human dancers usually imitate the actions of animals, especially the mating dance of birds.[60] This type of dance is found in most cultures.

It also mentions that the courtesans in the royal court of King Sitham-masokarat danced the *rabeng* and *rabam. Rabeng* is a dance in which the performers hold peacock feathers to imitate birds.[61] (This dance has been revived at present by the Krom Silapakon and is performed occasionally at the National Theatre.)

In heaven, the gods and goddesses dance gracefully (*fon ram*).[62] In the heaven of the god Indra, there is a mention of a *rabam* (a dance) and a long description of musical instruments. Each instrument has a Sanskritized name.[63] This shows a direct Indian influence in Sukhothai music. However, Thai names for instruments such as the *klong* (drum), *ching* (cymbals), and *pi* (oboe) are also used.

In the *Trai Phum Phra Ruang,* the term *panchangkikduriya* (five-piece orchestra) is mentioned.[64] This may well be the present *piphat kruang ha* (five-piece orchestra).[65] Coedès states,

> Cette Grande Relique fit de grands miracles et de nombreux prodiges et il y avait tout autour d'elle de grandes reliques en quantité. Lorsque le grand sanctuaire en briques fut achevé et inauguré, on alla à la recherche des anciennes statues en pierre du Buddha.[66]

In Inscription No. 4 of Wat Pa Mamuang (the mango orchard), it is related in Khmer that the patriarch, Phra Maha Sami Sangkaracha, who was invited from Ceylon to Sukhothai in A.D. 1362 by King Luthai, gave alms at the *Ok Phansa* (end of Buddhist Lent) and worshipped the life-size bronze image of the Buddha.[67]

The magnificent decoration of the royal avenue and the festive atmosphere on the sacred occasion of the inauguration of the Buddha's image described here must have left a striking impression on all the spectators, in the same manner as the *Kathin* (robes-giving to monks) processions. There was dancing, singing, music, a profusion of sounds and colours, and an assortment of costumes, decorations, offerings, and flowers. They are still impressively carried on in the north and northeast of Thailand today.

Inscription No. 5 of Wat Pa Mamuang relates the same event written in Thai, mentioning the word *chalong* (to celebrate or to inaugurate) twice: "Il fit de grandes donations et inaugura une statue en samrit. . . . A l'occasion de cette inauguration, le roi écouta la Loi quotidiennement pendant cent jours entiers. Les offrandes distribuées. . . ."[68] The celebration of the Buddha's relic was followed by one hundred days of sermons and alms giving.

Inscription No. 11 of Wat Khao Kop (Muang Pak Nam Pho) concerning the inauguration of the Rama Chedi and Rama Wihan at Rama Awat on Mount Sumanakut (Khao Kop) also describes a celebration: "puis il célébra l'inauguration, écouta la Loi."[69]

The celebration also included other princes and officials, as stated in Inscription No. 15 of Wat Sadet. There is a description of the celebration and inauguration of a temple by princes and high-ranking officials of Sukhothai, Than Chao Khun Luang Maha Phian Phraya, Thao Yot Thao, Nai Phan Suriyamat, and Nai Phan Thepharaksa.[70]

It should be noted here that the imaginary world in the *Trai Phum Phra Ruang* reflects all of the aspects of life in the real world, but magnifies them 60,000 times to make a strong impression on the readers by showing them both the horrifying consequences of sin and the heavenly rewards from good deeds. The beauty and magnificence of dance and music in heaven are thus exaggerated to emphasize the happiness and heavenly pleasure of the divine beings who had gained their godly existence through merit earned in their past lives.

It is obvious in most of these inscriptions that Buddhism, under the direct influence of the Singhalese (i.e., the Ceylonese from whom the Thai people received Hinayana Buddhism during the reign of King Ramkhamhaeng in the thirteenth century A.D.), played a major part in all of these festivities. The terms *chalong* (to celebrate) and *chaloem* (to celebrate, to commemorate, or to inaugurate, as upon the completion of a building or the erection of a religious or a national monument, such as a *chedi* [pagoda, stupa, or temple]), frequently appear and are usually followed or preceded by a religious ceremony, such as a *phra thammathesana* (Buddhist sermon) or *tham than* (alms giving), as stated in Inscription No. 2 of Wat Si-Chum.

The influence of the Singhalese immigrants who came to Sukhothai in order to supervise the construction of Buddhist temples and monasteries did not limit themselves to only the areas of art and architecture, but applied their creativeness to all religious ceremonies and festivals. In Inscription No. 2 of Wat Si-Chum, considered one of the most important records of Sukhothai history, archaeology, culture, and religious customs and said to have been written in the reign of King Thammaracha I to glorify the Mahathera Si Sattha,[71] it is stated that the Mahathera followed the example of the Singhalese in meditating and ascetic practices like living on fruits and roots.

> Les natifs de Sīhala virent de leurs yeux, et remplis de foi . . .
> (Srīsradhārāja) cūlāmuni plaça sur le sommet de la colline . . . fit
> de bonnes œuvres. Les natifs . . . adorer . . . un . . . sculpté . . . aller
> construire . . . cetiya à . . . rayons de six couleurs.[72]

The Singhalese customs of decorating the avenues, worshipping sacred religious objects, constructing and inaugurating *chedi* thus predated the Sukhothai customs, which were recorded in later Inscriptions Nos. 4 and 8, quoted earlier. It would not be too far-fetched therefore to assume that the Sukhothai performing arts, chiefly music and dancing, might have also been directly influenced by the same source. In a description of the dance of drums by the gods and goddesses in Indra's heaven in the *Trai Phum Phra Ruang,* one cannot help comparing it with the *Kandyan* dance of Ceylon, in which a variety of drums are played in different rhythmic patterns and the dancers dance to the drum beats.

There are four *khonthap* (musicians)[73] who play big drums and one-faced drums at the four corners of the Mount of the Universe. The words for dancing, *fon, ram,* and *rabam*, are sometimes used together, sometimes separate or in pairs such as *rabam ram*, indicating that they are three distinct types of dancing. *Ram* and *fon* may also be used as verbs meaning dancing in general. *Ram* and *rabam* may have derived from Khmer dancing, as the etymology indicates. *Fon* (*rabam* from "Ramam") is a Thai term indicating a slow dance like in the North where dancers wear long, curved, metal fingernails.

The "Panja Sikhon Thewada" is later described as a handsome god wearing white garments and five knotted hair strands (from which his name derives).[74] In his past life on earth he had earned great merit, which caused him to be reborn as a god in "Chatumaharachika" heaven. He is richly clad in jewels and perfumed with sweet scented herbs. He is the most favoured *khonthap* of all the gods. Thai musicians and dancers worship him as a god of music. In the legend concerning the origin of *nora chatri* dance-drama in southern Thailand, the first *nora* dancer who learned the art from the divine messenger Phran Bun (Hunter Bun) is called "Phra Thep Singhon," a derivative of "Phra Thep Sikhon" or "Panja Sikhon Thewada." The divine musician "Panja Sikhon" is said to be the same *khonthap* who neglected his duty of entertaining Indra and therefore had to assume the existence of an ogre named Viradha in the *Ramayana* epic. The ogre Viradha, or Phirap in Thai, is worshipped as the master of dance and is highly revered by Thai dancers and musicians.[75] The *Trai Phum Phra Ruang* also tells about a Brahmin who disguised himself as "Panja Sikhon" and preached the Dharma to the gods.[76]

Another grand occasion mentioned in the *Trai Phum Phra Ruang* is one in which the divine guardians of the four corners of the world (Chatulokaban) bring their entourages to pay homage to Indra. There, the twenty-eight Phraya Yaksa (kings of the ogres), all carrying their weapons, are present. Indra is beautifully dressed and decorated. The gods and goddesses in countless numbers come from all over the universe to worship him. The god's twenty-four million goddess-wives, each bearing royal decorative items, such as *chatra* (umbrellas, a symbol of royalty), fans, etc., surround the god. There is also two hundred and forty million *khonthap* dancers who play music and dance on the mountain walls of the four corners of the universe. Indra then bathes in the Great Pond. He descends from the Erawan Elephant and amuses himself with the multitude of goddesses in the Garden of Pleasure.[77]

This grand occasion may possibly be a precedent to the *Phra Ratchaphithi Inthraphisek* (the royal ceremony of Indra's coronation) mentioned in the *Phra Ratcha Phongsawadan* (Royal chronicle of Ayudhaya) and held in A.D. 1496 to celebrate King Ramathibodi II's twenty-fifth anniversary and again in 1638 during the reign of King Prasat-thong. In this particular ceremony there was a religious performance, called *kan len chak nak duk dam ban* or *len kan duk dam ban*, in which officers dressed as the gods Siva, Vishnu, Indra, Vishvakam, and others are on one side with Phali (Vali), Sukhrip (Sugriva), and Thao Maha Chomphu (Chumbuvara), the monkey kings from the *Ramayana*. On the other side are the *asura*s (demons). The two sides pull the Great Naga (snake), which curls itself around Mount Sumeru in the process of churning the ocean to create the Fountain of Immortality (Amarita). This religious event derived from a Sanskrit drama performed at the foot of the Himalaya mountains in India. It is believed to be the origin of the Thai *khon* drama, in which dancers wear masks and dress as gods, monkeys, and demons. H.R.H. Prince Damrong Rajanubhab has stated, "The performance in the royal *Indraphisek* ceremony is about a legend based on superstition, performed for the auspices [of the king and the people]. It came from the same source as the *khon* performance of the *Ramakien*."[78]

This particular Hindu mythological event is depicted on the sculptured relief of Angkor Wat done by Khmers, from whom the Sukhothai artists might have adopted the dramatic performance. Though the *Trai Phum Phra Ruang* is fictional literature, the writer might have painted these scenes either from wall sculptured reliefs of actual dances performed by the Khmers or by the Hindu Brahmins, who also served at the court of Sukhothai kings. Since the terms *ram* and *rabam* are derived from Khmer, it is more probable that the Sukhothai people learned the arts from the Khmer and incorporate them into their own indigenous dance, the *fon* (a Northern Thai term). Both the Hindu Brahmins and the Buddhist Singhalese provided the overall inspiration and models.

The inscriptions and the *Trai Phum Phra Ruang* do not clearly state the sexes of the dancers in *ram, rabam,* and *fon*. However, it seems that both men and women performed *ram* and *rabam*. The *fon,* however, might have been restricted to either men or women, probably mostly to women as in the "*fon* Chiengmai" today. On the other hand, the "*fon* Ngieo" of the Ngieo hill tribe is performed by both men and women.

Evidence in the *Prachum Phongsawadan Phak Nung*

Another interesting literary source of an uncertain date which informs us about the dance and music culture of the northern Thai people in comparatively the same period is the *Phongsawadan Lan Chang* (Chronicle of Lan Chang kingdom). In the preface to the *Prachum Phongsawadan* (Collected chronicles; Part 1), H.R.H. Prince Damrong Rajanubhab gives a brief historical background to these Northern chronicles. They were written in the Ayudhaya period and were edited by Phra Wichienpricha under the royal commission of King Rama II in A.D. 1807. They were first published by King Chulalongkorn in 1869 together with the legend of the Emerald Buddha.[79]

In the legend of the origin of the Lan Chang kingdom it is said that the god Phraya Thaen taught the people to cultivate all the arts. He sent Sikhan-thapa Thewada (Srigandava Deva), the god of the music and dance, to teach them to play different musical instruments: gongs, drums, castanets, lutes, oboe, *che waeng,* and *phin phia.* He also taught them to compose sonnets and dance the *rameng lamang,* so that they could entertain themselves.[80]

The *Memoirs of Nang Nophamat,* or *Tamrap Thao Si Chulalak*

The final literary source concerning the Sukhothai performing arts is the *Memoirs of Nang Nophamat,* otherwise known as the *Tamrap Thao Si Chulalak.* Scholars have long debated the historical existence of this famous lady who served as a consort to a certain King Phra Ruang of Sukhothai. Prince Damrong has expressed his doubts about the authenticity of the authoress as well as her origins.[81] King Chulalongkorn, though in agreement with the prince on this subject, believed that the present versions, which are much more modern in both language and style than the Sukhothai inscrip-tions, were later creations by Ratanakosin writers based on an original Sukhothai work.[82] In comparing these various versions, Prince Damrong later came to the conclusion that the *Memoirs of Nang Nophamat* must have originally come from Brahmin texts written in Old Thai before the Ayudhaya period, due to the fact that it records traditional ceremonies performed in the Sukhothai and pre-Ayudhaya periods.[83]

Prince Damrong stated that the traditional ceremonies described by Nang Nophamat in her *Memoirs* might have derived from the ceremonial books of the Brahmins (who played an important role at the Sukhothai court) written in Thai. Some of these books are now kept in Wachirayan Library. Some court writers during the reigns of Rama II or Rama III might have rewritten the *Memoirs,*[84] hence the more modern language and style. King Vajiravudh had another theory that the name of the Lady "Nophamat" (meaning nine months) was symbolic of the nine months ceremonies and was not a proper name.[85] Whichever the case may be, the book is considered one of the most important records of Thai customs and ceremonies of the past, and one to which King Chulalongkorn referred in many instances in his *Phra Ratcha-phithi Sip Song Duan* (The royal ceremonies of twelve months).

The *Memoirs* lists all the royal ceremonies over twelve months that were revived by King Chulalongkorn as an important asset to the Thai monarchy.

Nang Nophamat described the *mahorasop* (festivities, entertainment) on the full moon day of the twelfth month, in which the king and the courtiers worshipped the Buddha's footprints and performed the *Phra Ratchaphithi Chong Priang* (royal ceremony of candle light and lanterns). On this particu-lar occasion, Nang Nophamat invented a lantern in the shape of a lotus and floated it down the river, which set the precedent to the custom of *Loi Krathong* (floating lotus lanterns). The *mahorasop*[86] was performed over three nights and included song contests (in which young men and women competed in singing and rhyme-making in boats), dancing, music of all types, contests for decorating altars and boats, and of course fireworks. The king and queen cruised down the river in the royal barge followed by beautifully dressed courtisans. The king gave prizes to the costume contestants, thus starting another tradition in this occasion.[87]

In the first month of the lunar year (December), there was a royal Hinduistic ceremony called *Triyampawai* or *Tripawai,* in which the king attended a Brahmanistic ceremony at the royal temple. In the evening, the Brahmins carried the idols of the god Siva and the god Vishnu in a procession around the city. One phrase describes three kinds of entertainment relating to the religious occasion, *du kwai nang kradan sat nam ram saneng. Kwai nang kradan* may be the swinging of plank on which a lady or a group of ladies sat, similar to the Giant Swing of Bangkok. It may also be a doll on a miniature swing. *Sat nam* is water throwing, possibly similar to what happens on Songkran day (Thai New Year's Day), symbolic of cleansing and blessing. *Ram saneng* is unclear as to which type of dancing it refers to. However, it may also have originally been connected with the worship of the Hindu gods Siva and Vishnu and then later lost its religious function.

In the third lunar month, there was a rice-threshing ceremony called *Phra Ratchaphithi Than Dǫ*, in which rice stalks were brought to the threshing ground to be processed by sacred oxen. Court ladies dressed in Malay costumes pulled golden and silver carts filled with the rice stalks and beautifully decorated with flowers, banners, and flags to the ground. The king observed the ceremony from the royal pavilion. The Brahmins read the sacred scriptures, blew conch-shells and set a sacred fire using straw (a symbolic gesture of burning the fields). The *mahorasop* were varied.[88] They included *rabeng, rabam, chiri thaeng ken, nang kra-ua phua thaeng kwai, hok khamen, tai luat, lot buang, ram phaen,* all of which are described in the later Ayudhaya chronicles. One more dance other than *rabeng* and *rabam* was *ram phaen,* which may be of Laotian origin. The rest of the *mahorasop* were *kan lalen* (lit., entertainment), which were performed in dance steps and movements, some to accompanying percussion music, and some purely games and acrobatics.

In the fourth lunar month the king performed the *Phra Ratchaphithi Samphatcharachin,* a Buddhist celebration lasting three days and three nights during the Thai New Year. The people worshipped the image of the Buddha and the god-protectors of the four corners of the world. They also attended Buddhist sermons, gave alms and observed the five moral precepts (*panja silas*). Guns and cannons[89] were fired 108 times to drive away evil spirits. There was a grand procession of five colourful troupes of soldiers leading chariots carrying the Buddha image, the patriarch, and other Mahatheras (senior monks) around the city. The *mahorasop* consisted of music, singing, and dancing appropriate to worshipping the Buddha image, as well as merry-making to celebrate the New Year.[90] The description of the procession is similar to that contained in the Inscription of Wat Prayun.[91]

In the fifth lunar month, there was a grand royal ceremony called *Phra Ratchaphithi Sanan Yai,* which was held in the Ayudhaya and Ratanakosin periods and is mentioned in the *Trai Phum Phra Ruang.* The king appeared at the Indraphisek Hall to accept the homage and tribute of all the lords, vassals, high officials, leaders of the community, merchants, and heads of important families. The court dancers and musicians entertained these royal attendants after the king took his leave.[92] It is mentioned here that the court dancers were called *"rabeng* officers.*"* It is more probable that they were men, since women court dancers performed strictly for the king in the Inner Court.

In the afternoon, there was a procession of elephants called *Phithi Kachenthara Rassawa Sanan* followed by a procession of horses. The festive ceremony lasted three days. The grand procession was led by Brahmins and soldiers dressed in colourful costumes carrying banners, flags, and umbrellas. They blew conch-shells and beat gongs and drums, as described also in the *Trai Phum Phra Ruang.* The parallel with the mythology is obvious here. In the *Phra Ratchaphithi Sanan Yai* the king presided as the god Indra, the king-god, surrounded by gods and goddessess, his subjects and vassals who pledged their loyalty.

In the afternoon and evening, the court entertainers performed dances, songs, and a shadow dance, then lit fireworks in worship of the gods in front of the royal temple for three nights in a row.[93]

On New Year's Day, the royal officials, members of the royal family, court ladies, pages, and officers of all ranks inside and outside the city took the oath of fealty and drank the sacred water, *nam phiphat.* This is a ceremony which continues to the present reign.

It is interesting to note that while there were performances of *nang ram* (shadow dance) in the Sukhothai period as stated here in the *Memoirs,* there was no mention of the words *khon* or *lakhon.* This has led some scholars to believe that *nang* (lit., puppets made of cow hide) preceded *khon* and *lakhon.* It might have been performed as a religious ceremony to please the spirits of the gods and ancestors, since these shadows are also symbols of the spirits as in Javanese or Malay *wayang.* The Thai *nang ram* might have been performed as a sacred ritual and then may later have developed into a form of public entertainment. The huge puppets depict scenes from the great epics, notably the *Ramakien.* Since the figures in the scenes are static, having no movable parts like the Javanese or Malay puppets, they have to be held up by performers who dance to the accompanying music. Prince Dhaninivat, a well-known Thai scholar, was of the opinion that *nang* was an older form of dramatic art and was the possible prototype of *khon.*[94] In other words, *khon* might have been a later development in which the performers danced without puppets and instead wore masks and costumes representing the different characters in the *Ramakien*.

This writer, however, is of another opinion that *nang* and *khon* are sister arts which could have developed simultaneously, thus influencing one another. Since they were simultaneously performed in great festivals, either separately or on the same programme (in which case it is called *nang tit tua khon* [shadow play with *khon* dancers]),[95] it does not necessary follow that one should have derived from the other. *Nang* characters and scenes were taken from wall paintings or illustrations in old manuscripts, while *khon* masks and costumes might have originated from the *Chak Nak Dukdamban* (churning the ocean with the snake) in the *Indraphisek* pageant as mentioned earlier. The dance steps and movements might have been influenced by the martial dance and procession to the rhythm of a percussion orchestra and the fighting dance based the martial art, *Ram Krabi Krabong* (dance of swords and batons).[96]

As *nang* figures were held up for display, music was performed and the narrator sang from a dramatic text, called the *kham phak*. The dance movements might have been introduced later to make the figures move with the music and the narrative. *Khon* dancers with their colourful masks and costumes may also perform the same scenes simultaneously to vivify and give life to the characters.

Since there is no mentionining of either *nang* or *khon* in the Sukhothai inscriptions and the date of the *Memoirs* is uncertain, most scholars agree that these two dramatic forms were created during the Ayudhaya period. However, since there are the terms *ten* and *ram* referring to the natural artistic expressions of the Sukhothai people in all festive occasions, it could be assumed that these arts were known to the Thai as early as this first kingdom. The names *nang* and *khon,* however, might have entered the Thai vocabulary in the Ayudhaya period. Khun Dhanit Yupho, former Director of the Krom Silapakon, has suggested that the Thai might have received the art of *khon* dance-drama from the Khmer, since the term is derived from the Khmer term *khol*. It is also well known that in both A.D. 1352 and 1431, Thai kings conquered the Kambhuja empire and brought back as hostages Khmer dancers and artists to Ayudhaya.[97]

The *mahorasop* in the sixth lunar month described by Nang Nophamat on the occasion of the Hindu ploughing ceremony, *Phithi Raek Na*, included *rabeng, rabam, hok khamen, tai luat, lot buang, ram phaen, thaeng wisai, kai pa cha hong*.[98] All these dances and entertainment are mentioned in the Ayudhaya chronicles. They were revived in the Ratanakosin period.

On Wisakhabucha (Visakapuja) day, there were religious ceremonies and civil celebrations for three days and three nights. People gave alms, listened to Buddhist sermons and lit candles and fireworks. The streets were decorated with colourful banners, flags, and flowers. Music was performed to worship the images of the Buddha throughout the city: Phra Chinasri, Phra Chinarat, Phra Loknatsattharot. Had it not been for the more modern language and style in the writing of the *Memoirs*, one would assume that this text had recaptured the same festive, religious atmosphere as described in the Sukhothai inscriptions (Nos. 4, 8, and Inscription of Wat Prayun).

In the seventh lunar month the Brahmins performed the *Phithi Khentha*, in which a giant top was spun to predict the future of the kingdom.[99] If the top should spin well and produce beautiful sounds, prosperity and peace were assured. The assembling Brahmins, noblemen, and the people then danced and sang in great joy and spread good tidings.[100] It seems that dancing and singing were the natural expressions of the Sukhothai people, since they were performed on all occasions. *Ten ram* here may be a general term meaning dancing, and not necessarily indicating separate art forms.

During the Lent season, or *Khao Phansa* (entering a monastery during the months of the rainy season), Nang Nophamat describes the religious activities of the Sukhothai people of all classes. Both Hindu and Buddhist ceremonies were simultaneously performed with no contradiction between them. There were processions on land and on water. Members of leading families in their beautiful attires carried their *phansa* candles around the temples and placed them on the altars, where they remained lit for the whole Lent season lasting three months. Music was heard from these processions everywhere.[101] The spirit is the same as described in the Sukhothai inscriptions.

There was a three-day-long Hindu rite of fertility, called the *Phra Ratchaphithi Pharunasat* (*Varuna Sastra*), to pray to the god Siva for rain in the ninth month. Except for the religious procession of the Brahmins, there was no mention of any other ceremony or entertainment.

In the next month (tenth), there was a harvest ceremony called *Phra Ratchaphithi Phatarabot,* which incorporated Hindu, Buddhist, and magical aspects. The Brahmins made sacrificial offerings to give thanks to the goddess of grain, Phra Phaisop, and purified themselves at the river for three days, while the Buddhists gave food to the monks. Two queens led a group of court ladies to stir the sacred rice, *khao thip* (a pudding made of rice, honey, sugarcane syrup, and milk). There was *mahorasop,* music and dancing for the occasion as well.[102] Here *rabeng* and *rabam* were performed exclusively by women.

The Buddhist monks and the Hindu Brahmins were given food and the sacred pudding. The atmosphere was of joy and celebration.[103] The people did good deeds to help the dead, whose spirits existed in the other worlds. The religious piety and the belief in the different worlds as described in the *Trai Phum Phra Ruang* indicate a close relationship between the *Memoirs* and Sukhothai literature. The religious preoccupation of the Thai people, which is mentioned as early as the inscription of King Ramkhamhaeng, continues to be a very important characteristic even today.

In the eleventh month, the Brahmins worshipped the god Vishnu and his consort, goddess Laksmi. There was a race between the royal barges. The images of Vishnu and Laksmi were placed in these two barges. If the barge of Vishnu won, it was predicted that the glory of the king would spread to all directions and foreign relations would prosper, but the fertility of the land would diminish. On the contrary, if the barge of Laksmi should win, fertility and prosperity would be assured, while foreign trade would decline.

Music orchestras were placed in the barges and performed during the procession. On the banks of the river, the merchants and rich families who attended the race were described as dancing and cheering the oarsmen on.[104] The term *ram fon* in the *Memoirs* here again may be a general term to describe the joyful mood and expression of the spectators.

It was in this way that Nang Nophamat concludes the twelve months of ceremonies as she remembered them from childhood. On each of these occasions she boasted of her ingenious inventions and creative undertakings, such as arranging flowers, costumes, or participating for the first time as a woman in these ceremonies, which had originally been restricted to men. Her creativity set precedents for new court and general social customs. Here more than in any other of her many roles does she represent the free and democratic spirit of the Thai woman, and this spirit continues to play a major role in Thai literature and society. The ready acceptance of her initiatives by the male-dominated society of the time is a strong indication of the Thai liberalism and permissiveness which existed since the Sukhothai period, in contrast to other countries where womens' liberation became necessary as a revolt against male chauvinism.

Another memorable and significant work of Nang Nophamat is her "Advice to the Ladies of the Court,"[105] in which she criticizes the behaviour and manners of ill-bred ladies and warns that physical beauty and worldly knowledge were not essential elements. They should not only serve the king with great loyalty, but also be enlightened in the Dharma of Lord Buddha and make merit in order to attain a higher level of existence in heaven. In one passage on the art of dancing and singing, she states that some court ladies professed excellence in playing various musical instruments, singing, and dancing, but some had bad morals and behaviour. If they did not repent in their early lives and became attached to the worldly pleasure of dancing, they would suffer in hell, in the world of sin called *loha kumphi*. Furthermore, if they should continue to teach their pupils to dance they were also committing a great sin. Therefore, it would be wise to follow the teaching of the Buddha and study the Three Gems. In the *samsara vatta* (cycle of existence), dancing and singing were considered worldly pleasures and therefore causes of human suffering. It is clearly stated in this particular essay that despite the wealth and pleasure on earth that the king and his entourage seemed to enjoy, the highest aim in the life of a devout Buddhist is to discard these worldly entrapments and attain spiritual happiness in heaven.[106]

In dreading future association in the next life with immoral court ladies, whose behaviour would be a thousand times worse than in this life, she tried to make merit in order to be born into *thewa lok* (the world of the gods). In serving the king with unwavering loyalty, she hoped to set an example for the future generation.[107] It seems that the highest goal is not to attain *nirvana,* but the heavenly world, which is customary for any ending to such a literary work. Out of modesty perhaps, or the realization that they are still bound by craving and desires, most Thai poets and writers only wish and pray to attain heavenly bliss in the world of the gods.

From these various historic inscriptions and the fictional *Trai Phum Phra Ruang,* which were evidently written in the Sukhothai period, we learn that the Sukhothai people professed great freedom in entertaining themselves and that their entertainments were closely related to Buddhist celebrations and occasions. It is very clear that the variety of musical instruments far exceeded that of dancing. The dance forms mentioned were of a general nature in the categories of *rabam, ram, fon,* and *ten.* As time progressed from the reign of King Ramkhamhaeng (1277–1317) to that of King Thammaracha I (Luthai) (1318–54), we can see a definite development in both dance and music, from the vague physical expressions of joy, *len* and *hua* poetic singing, *luen* and *khab,* and a few music instruments, drums, lute (*phin*), percussion (*phat*), to more definite dance forms, *rabam* and *ten,* and a full orchestra, *duriyaphat* (including *phin, khong, klong*). There were also during King Luthai's reign frequent celebrations for temples, Buddhist relics, and Buddha images and footprints. The roads were decorated with flowers, banners, and candles in the Ceylonese tradition. The height of the Sukhothai culture was definitely achieved during the period of King Maha Thammarachathirat (Lithai) (1354–76), as vividly described in the inscriptions and reflected in the *Trai Phum Phra Ruang* (1345). Here the religious celebrations incorporated more Hindu festivities. There was a greater variety of musical instruments associated with Hindu rites and influenced by the Brahmins, such as conch-shells, horns, oboes, and a vast variety of drums and percussion instruments (*morathong,* etc). The five sections of the orchestra, *panchanka duriya,* were completed during this time. Dances also had more definite forms and titles, such as *rabeng;* and in the celestial dance of gods and goddesses the god Indra played a great role in patronizing these celestial dancers and musicians. Indra's pageant in heaven might also reflect that of the royal pageant procession in King Lithai's reign.

These Sukhothai forms of entertainment became highly elaborate in the *Memoirs of Nang Nophamat.* The word *mahorasop* was mentioned for the first time.[108] It usually lasted three days and three nights, whereas the merry-making and entertainment in other Sukhothai inscriptions were not specified as to duration. Besides *rabam, ram, fon,* and *rabeng*[109] which appeared in the inscriptions, the *mahorasop* of Nang Nophamat's time included *nang ram* (shadow dance), *ram saneng, ram phaen,* and other forms of entertainment: *chiri thaeng khen, nang kra-oa phua thaeng kwai, hok khamen, tai luat, lot buang.* The Brahmin influence was predominant. Belonging to a Brahmin family, Nang Nophamat frequently emphasized the importance of the Brahmin role in the royal court. They were the leaders and strict observers of the Hindu religious rites and state ceremonies. As the Thai court became more sophisticated, the functions of these Brahmins increased. However, it is interesting to note the perfect harmony between the Buddhist and Hindu aspects in all these ceremonies, which still exists today. Both the Buddhist monks and Hindu Brahmins dutifully do their share in securing prosperity, wealth, happiness, and glory for the Thai rulers and people.

The grand scales to which these ceremonies, pageants, and entertainment were carried out in the *Memoirs of Nang Nophamat* lead us to believe that the account was written either at the end of the Sukhothai period or the beginning of Ayudhaya. The detailed description of the *Phra Ratchaphithi Sanan Yai* ceremony is closer to that of the later Ayudhaya reigns from the fifteenth to the seventeenth century.

In all these early literary works, there was no mention of drama or dramatic performance, except *nang ram,* which again is a dramatic dance form. It may be concluded that drama did not evolve until the Ayudhaya period. Since dancing, singing, and music are still the dominant artistic forms of the Northern Thai people as well as the Laotians, it is possible that drama culture was a later development in the central region under Hindu influence transmitted by the Khmer. The native Singhalese might also have contributed to the dancing and music, but not the drama. Though the *Ramayana* and the *Jataka* tales were known in their oral forms, dramatic texts were not written until Ayudhaya. The origin and development of the Southern *nora chatri* dance-drama is another debatable subject as discussed earlier.

The Thai synthesis of Indian civilization in this early period was a gradual and natural process. Through the Singhalese Buddhist elements were reinforced, while through the Brahmins more sophisticated court culture and Hindu myths penetrated into the life of the ruling class, and the Thai were able to develop their unique civilization from this synthesis. As Coedès has pointed out, "Les pays conquis militairement par la Chine ont dû adopter ou copier ses institutions, ses mœurs, ses religions, sa langue et son écriture. Au contraire, ceux que l'Inde a conquis pacifiquement, par le prestige de sa culture, ont conservé l'essentiel de leurs caractères individuels et les ont développés, chacun suivant son génie propre."[110]

COURT DANCE AND DANCE-DRAMA IN THE AYUDHAYA PERIOD

While there is a large body of scholarly literature on the historical, political, economic, and social development of the Ayudhaya kingdom, very little serious work has been written or published about the Ayudhaya performing arts. The current textbooks on Ayudhaya dramatic literature and theatre arts are generally based on a single source, *Tamnan Lakhon Inao* by Prince Damrong, which contains only his speculations and assumptions, most of them lacking historical proof. Many later scholars have criticized Prince Damrong's theories. Among these are Prince Dhaninivat and Dhanit Yupho. Mom Ratchawong Kukrit Pramoj, in his writing about Ayudhaya society, also contributed some new concepts, particularly on the religious and political aspects of theatrical and dramatic literature.

The major cultural and artistic differences between Sukhothai and Ayudhaya society are characterized first by their political systems. While Sukhothai kings ruled their subjects in a patriarchal system, the Ayudhaya kings from the very beginning adopted the Hindu system of *deva-raja,* which deified the king and placed him above the common people. Special royal language, customs, and ceremonies were used to glorify his god-like position.

Secondly, the Sukhothai kings ruled by a family line of succession within the same dynasty, while the Ayudhaya kings used military power to usurp the throne whenever it was possible. Consequently, the history of Ayudhaya kingship is full of civil wars, violent battles, and treacherous power struggles, which resulted in frequent dynastic changes. The successful and prosperous kings were those who had strong control over the military.

Thirdly, the Ayudhaya court ceremonies, dance, and dance-drama, both *khon luang* and *lakhon luang*, are forms of tribute to the divine kingship, and hence excluded commoners and other members of the nobility. They were created to assure the king's position as the sole, absolute god-king. On the other hand, the Sukhothai kings did not have any formal court traditions or ceremonies. Their residences were more humble. The people had the right of access to the kings to petition their grievances by beating a bronze gong (*kangsadan*) or a bell (*krading*), which was hung in front of the palace.

Fourthly, there were only two classes of people in the Sukhothai kingdom: the *luk chao luk khun* (members of the royal family and aristocrats) and *phrai fa* (ordinary citizens). They were both legally equal. Buddhist monks, the Sangha, were a special group separated from the citizenry. In contrast, the social classes of the Ayudhaya kingdom were more complicated under a feudal system in which each class was designated by *sakdina* (social status based on land) similar to Western feudalism. However, the Thai *sakdina* served only as a measure for social stratification. They may have originally been connected with actual land-ownership, later to become only a social class indicator without any relation to the land. The lowest *sakdina* was 5 rai for a slave. A commoner, *phrai rap,* had a *sakdina* of 20 rai. People with a *sakdina* of more than 400 rai were *phu di* (gentry, i.e., upper class). The highest *sakdina* for noblemen was 10,000 rai. The theatre master had a *sakdina* of 40 rai.[111] However, there was always flexibility in this social system which allowed for considerable social mobility.

Finally, the Ayudhaya royal court was governed by a strict Law of the Palace, *Kot Monthienban,* which dictated the lives of the members of the royal family and courtiers including the court dancers. While the Sukhothai court had no royal dance troupe, the Ayudhaya kings from the seventeenth century onward, or even from earlier on, had their royal dance troupe to perform *khon* and *lakhon* for royal functions and ceremonies.

The *Punowat Kham Chan* of Phra Mahanak, written during the reign of King Boromakot (1732–58), is the first record to mention *lakhon nai* performing *Anirut* and *Inao* by female court dancers. Scholars agree that *lakhon nai* (an abbreviation of *lakhon nang nai,* dance-drama by ladies of the Inner Court) was created during this reign, while *lakhon nok* was performed by men outside the royal court. The stories for *lakhon nok* came from *Jataka* tales. The most popular *lakhon nok* plays of the Ayudhaya period were *Manohra and Phra Suthon, Khawi, Maniphichai, Sangthong, Sangsinchai, Suwannahong,* and *Chaiyachet.*

While the Sukhothai performing arts were for both the king and the people, there was in Ayudhaya a clear division between court and folk dances, drama, and other performing arts. The oldest form of folk dance drama is *nora chatri* of southern Thailand, which developed during the Ayudhaya period. Its off-shoots were *lakhon nok* and *lakhon chatri.* There are still debates about the origin of *nora chatri.* Prince Damrong's theory is that it originally came from Ayudhaya and was brought to Nakhon Sithammarat by Khun Sattha, who taught the dance-drama to the local people. Other scholars disagree with Prince Damrong, contending that it was brought directly to the south by Indian settlers, who taught it to the Thai natives, since the movements are closer to Indian or Sri Lankan dances than to classical Thai dance.

There are no historical records of *lakhon* before the seventeenth century. When the French diplomat De La Loubère reported in his *Du Royaume de Siam* in the reign of King Narai the Great (1656–88), there were already *khon, lakhon,* and *rabam* (dance). The *Kot Monthienban* of the Ayudhaya royal court also prescribed a variety of performing arts for the royal *mahorasop* (entertainment), including *rabam, lakhon, rabeng,* and *kula ti mai.* It could be assumed that *lakhon ram* developed in its earliest form before the seventeenth century, possibly in the fifteenth or sixteenth century, or even earlier. By the eighteenth century, during the reign of King Boromakot, it developed into its fullest form in *lakhon nai* of the royal court, which dramatized only three sacred myths about kingship: the *Ramakien, Unarut,* and *Inao. Lakhon nok* (the term *nok* means outside or provincial) remained popular among the common folk.

Towards the end of the Ayudhaya dynasty, court dance-drama declined. It is mentioned in the chronicles that King Ekathat (1758–67), the last king of Ayudhaya, had to hire a *lakhon phuchai* (male dance troupe) to perform for him at court. This was probably due to the absence of female *lakhon nai* performers. After the fall of Ayudhaya, two princesses, Kunthon and Mongkut, who wrote the two versions of *Inao, Dalang* (or *Inao Yai*) and *Inao Lek,* continued to teach classical dance to young girls at the royal court of the Ratanakosin kingdom.

Classical *khon* was also developed to its fullest form in the Ayudhaya period. It derived from the ritual dance *Chak Nak Dukdamban* in the *Indraphisek* ceremony, where royal pages and military officers dressed as characters in the *Ramakien* and pulled the great serpent Anandha Nakharat, in a tug-of-war between the gods and demons (*yak*) to decide who would get the sacred water of immortality. The Ayudhayans probably adopted this ceremony from the Khmer, since there are sculptures depicting this scene at Angkor Wat. There is a record of the *Chak Nak Dukdamban* in the 1496 chronicle of King Ramathibodi II.

All these performing arts were related to Hindu culture and religious cults, particularly the cult of Vishnu-Rama, the righteous king in the *Ramakien.* The *thosaphit ratchatham* (ten kingly virtues) upheld by Rama represented a model for the Ayudhaya kings. The *Jataka* tales in *lakhon nok* also emphasize these kingly virtues of the heroes, who are Bodhisattvas. The romance of *Inao* in *lakhon nai* portrays the hero as a great lover and fighter, who suffers the consequences of his misbehaviour, spoiled character, arrogance, pride, and bad judgement. After a long period of trial and suffering, he finally attains happiness together with his true love, Busba.

As a whole, the dance-drama of the Ayudhaya period was closely related to the political institution of the monarchy, as well as to Buddhism and Brahmanistic Hinduism. It inherited these elements from the Indian *Natayasastra* and combined them with Thai indigenous culture. The Ayudhaya kings and members of the royal family of the later period from the eighteenth century on contributed significantly to the development and refinement of *khon* and *lakhon,* which became models for Thonburi and Ratanakosin drama and theatre. After the fall of Ayudhaya in 1767, court dancers were taken to Burma to teach the court dancers there. They settled down there in a village called Yodia (i.e., Ayudhaya). Hence, the Burmese-Thai dance and dance-drama were called *rabam yodia* and *lakhon yodia.*

The First Revival of Traditional Dance-Drama: The Reign of King Taksin

After the fall of Ayudhaya in 1767, King Taksin, having reunified the country to a large extent and having established himself as the king in the new capital of Thonburi, made the first attempt to restore traditional *khon* and *lakhon* within the royal court, with both the cultural aim of continuing the tradition of Ayudhaya classical dance-drama and a political aim of establishing himself as the rightful successor to the throne and a legitimate founder of a new dynasty. Socially, it was also necessary for him to set up his own royal court complete with its Lakhon Luang (royal *lakhon* troupe) in the tradition of the Ayudhaya kings; for to have possession of such a royal troupe, particularly an all-female (*lakhon phuying*) one, was a privilege appertaining only to the monarch. The Lakhon Luang and Khon Luang, royal *lakhon* and *khon* institutions, were therefore indispensable royal prerogatives, which would support his status equalling that of the great Ayudhaya kings in times of peace and prosperity. More precisely, the comparison was meant to be made with King Boromakot, who was associated with the origin of royal *lakhon* (*lakhon nai*) at the court of Ayudhaya before the period of decline.

Written evidence of *lakhon phuying* at the Ayudhaya royal court is first found in the *Bunnowat Kham Chan* of Phra Maha Nak of Wat Tha Sai in the reign of King Boromakot. It is therefore assumed by most authorities on Thai literature that it was in this reign that *lakhon phuying,* or *lakhon nang nai khong luang* (abbrev., *lakhon nai*), was first developed. There is, however, the possibility that it may have been initiated even earlier, after the reign of King Narai, probably in the Ban Phlu Luang dynasty, starting with King Phra Phetracha (1688–1703)[112] and culminating in the reign of King Boromakot, who usurped the throne, deprived Chaofa Aphai of his right to succession after King Phra Chao Thaisa in 1732, and proclaimed himself King Somdet Phra Borom Rachathirat III.[113] The reign of King Boromakot was apparently the last reign to have enjoyed such cultural richness, for it is recorded that in the following reign, that of King Ekathat (Somdet Phra Chao Yu Hua Phra Thinang Suriyat Amarin), there was no *lakhon phuying* available to the royal court. When the king, during his illness, wished to see *lakhon,* a *lakhon phuchai* (male dance-drama) troupe had to be brought from outside the Royal Palace to perform for him.[114]

Lakhon nai was therefore an essential attribute to the personal glory of King Taksin, as in the case of King Boromakot, who similarly may have developed *lakhon nang nai* at his court in order to show his divine majesty, comparable to that of a *deva-raja* surrounded by celestial female dancers. As one historian has stated, King Boromakot and the Ban Phlu Luang dynasty had many political reasons for justifying their ascension to the Ayudhaya throne.

> The Ban Phlu Luang dynasty began its history with the usurpation
> of a commoner so that there was a strong need for the justification
> of their position. . . . Doubts as to the Ban Phlu Luang kings' right
> to kingship prevailed throughout the history of the dynasty. The
> doctrine of *karma,* which was supposed to give the explanation
> which would lead to the acceptance of one's condition in the present
> existence was used to justify the struggle for the throne.
>   The Ban Phlu Luang political means of consolidating power was
> to curb the power of the *khunnang* by balancing it with the *krom*
> of the *chao.* The first three Ban Phlu Luang kings materialized this
> policy by creating very few but large *krom* of the *chao.* . . . In order
> to remain on the throne, Somdet Phra Chao Boromakot found it
> necessary to readjust the policy of distribution of power. The
> balance of the control of manpower between the *khunnang* on the
> one hand and the *chao* on the other had to be maintained.[115]

To establish the royal court in the most glorious fashion possible was
therefore an effective means to show the royal *barami* (glory and fortune
accumulated from past merits according to one's *karma*) of the king and to
place him above both the *khunnang* (nobility) and other *chao* (members of the
royal family). The parallelism between the legitimization of the Ban Phlu
Luang dynasty and that of the Thonburi dynasty of King Taksin, a commoner
by origin, is self-evident.

Moreover, in reconstructing the court ceremonies and traditions during the
reigns of King Taksin and his successor, King Rama I of the Chakri dynasty,
the royal court of King Boromakot was also followed as model, since it was
a long and relatively peaceful reign[116] and has been regarded as the golden era
of Ayudhaya court culture.

Soon after his *Prapdaphisek* (bathing or lustration on the occasion of his
investiture), King Taksin ordered the assembly of *lakhon* and *khon* dancers
under the Ayudhaya kingdom, who had been scattered all over the country
after the fall of the old capital. Many troupes and dancers had died in the war.
After the sack of the capital, many dancers were, with another thirty thousand
Thai captives, taken to Burma. They settled down in Sagaing[117] and taught
and performed dance-drama in the Burmese royal court.[118] Later when the
Burmese capital moved to Mandalay, they were taken there, where they
resided in an area which came to be known as "Yodhayase" (Ayodhaya
market). They taught the Burmese court dancers and children. The plays they
performed most frequently in the Burmese festivals and royal functions were
Inao, known as *Eenaung* in Burmese, and *Ramakien.* They also performed
Sangthong and *Nang Keson* (*Sangsinchai*), known in Burmese as *Kesasiri.*[119]

Despite this drain of dancers, there did remain behind some authorities on
royal *lakhon nai* of the Ayudhaya court, namely, Princess Phinthawadi,

daughter of King Boromakot. There were also Lakhon Luang dancers who had escaped to the provinces. One of these, known for her role as Nang Usa in *Unarut,* and hence nicknamed "Chan Usa," became a dance teacher at the court of King Taksin.

In 1769, two years after his ascension, King Taksin took over the city of Nakhon Sithammarat, an important centre for *lakhon phuying* in the Ayudhaya style. He confiscated the *lakhon phuying* troupe of the Chao Nakhon and brought it to his court to set up, with other dancers, a new Lakhon Luang troupe in the tradition of Ayudhaya. Some of the principal teachers of the Chao Nakhon troupe had originally been dancers in the Lakhon Luang of the Ayudhaya royal court. According to King Chulalong- korn in his commentary on the memoirs of Krom Luang Narinthrathewi, *Phra Ratchawichan Chotmaihet Khwam Song Cham Krom Luang Narinthrathewi,*[120] the *lakhon* troupe of Chao Nakhon seemed to hold higher prestige over other *lakhon* troupes. Since they had not been affected by the sack of Ayudhaya, they were able to maintain their traditional art, while the Lakhon Luang at the court of Thonburi was just newly organized and probably, therefore, had to depend on the knowledge and instruction of the teachers of the Chao Nakhon troupe. Later in the reign, King Taksin restored Chao Nakhon to his original position as a royal vassal lord. He was proclaimed "Phra Chao Phaendin Muang Nakhon Sithammarat" (sovereign of the city of Nakhon Sithammarat) with the status of "Phra Chao Prathetsarat" (vassal lord), and was given a *lakhon phuying* troupe as *khruang pradap*[121] (i.e., a royal possession befitting the honour of a monarch). To grant him such a royal privilege meant that he could hold *lakhon phuying* performances of his own. It was said that the king wished to honour Chao Nakhon, since two daughters of Chao Nakhon were major royal consorts.

The Chao Nakhon troupe was often called to the capital to perform in competition with the Lakhon Luang at *somphot* (celebration) functions, such as the *somphot* of the Emerald Buddha.

King Taksin was extremely fond of *lakhon* and was said to have punished singers and dancers who could not perform to his liking.[122] Towards the end of his reign, when the king became mentally deranged, it was reported that he was so emotionally involved in a *lakhon* performance of *Inao* (in the scene when Queen Madewi tried to talk Busba into saying a prayer in the temple to make a prediction about her rightful husband) that he ordered the dancer who performed the role of Queen Madewi to be whipped for having been "such a busybody" (*chao ki chao kan*) in the play.[123] The Lakhon Phuying Khong Luang (royal female dance troupe) of King Taksin was known to perform the *Ramakien, Inao,* and *Unarut.*[124]

The king contributed quite significantly to the composition and reconstruc- tion of the dramatic texts, which had been missing or incomplete from the Ayudhaya times. His works, which appear in four *smut thai dam* (Thai black books), a total of 2,012 *kham klon* (verses), include the following episodes from the *Ramakien:* Phra Mongkut episodes, Hanuman's courting of Nang Warin to the arrival of Thao Maliwarat, the judgement of Thao Maliwarat to Thosakan's entering the city, and Thosakan's making the *sai krot* (magic sand), Phra Lak's being hit by Kabinlaphat's spear, and Nang Montho and Thosakan being tied up by the hair by Hanuman.

However, Prince Dhani raised doubts about the authenticity of the king's compositions, since the king had not shown any talent in literary creativity elsewhere. It may have been more likely that the king merely supervised the reconstruction of the texts from scattered fragments, or sections of the texts which had remained from the Ayudhaya period and had been collected for this purpose.

The urgency with which King Taksin developed court dramatic activities lends support to the theory that the king needed all the necessary attributes to establish a firm foundation for his position as the new nucleus for the reunification of the country and to endorse claims to a cultural lineage from the old kingdom of Ayudhaya. Conscious of the natural tendency of the Ayudhayans to look down upon any new culture as inferior to the glorious past of Ayudhaya, both King Taksin and King Rama I, who continued this difficult task of cultural reconstruction, tried to measure up to the royal standard of the Ayudhaya kings in their re-establishment of court customs and ceremonies. For this very reason, authorities and courtiers who had lived and witnessed the grandeur of the court of King Boromakot and of the last kings of the Ban Phlu Luang dynasty were constantly consulted, especially during the next reign, that of King Rama I, who wished to preserve all the physical aspects of Ayudhaya to the last detail (even the bricks used in the reconstruction of some temples and the Royal Palace were brought down from the old city). The re-establishment of the Lakhon Luang and Khon Luang troupes within the royal court served therefore as a cultural cement to fill any gaps within court life. It also provided some much-needed glitter for the new monarchy.

During the reign of King Taksin, there were both Lakhon Phuchai Khong Luang (royal male court dance-drama) and Lakhon Phuying Khong Luang (royal female court dance-drama) who competed in their performances at most royal *somphot* occasions. It was recorded that at the *somphot* of the Emerald Buddha, the royal pavilion was flanked by the Lakhon Phuying (female troupe) on one side and the Lakhon Phuchai (male troupe) on the other.[125] However, the style of performance of the Lakhon Phuchai was not clearly indicated as being either popular *lakhon nok* or royal *lakhon nai* in character. Basing their judgement on the collection of fourteen scripts, *bot lakhon nok* (scripts of popular dance-drama) of Ayudhaya in the National Library,[126] some authorities have concluded that it was more likely that this Lakhon Phuchai performed *lakhon nok* rather than *lakhon nai,* which, in any case, as a general rule, was restricted to the Lakhon Phuying Khong Luang troupe. There are also five *bot lakhon nok* of an unidentifiable period[127] which are assumed to have been written either in Ayudhaya or Thonburi times, or even during the reign of King Rama I.

Beside the Lakhon Luang troupe, there were many private *lakhon* troupes in the Thonburi period, some of which were recorded in the royal decree issued for the *somphot* of the Emerald Buddha. They were the Luang Wichitnarong, Mun Sanophuban, and Mun Wohanphirom troupes. The last two troupes were said to have been transported in barges in the river procession for the Emerald Buddha. There was also a barge for the *lakhon khamem* (Cambodian dance-drama) of Luang Phiphitwathi. All these private troupes are assumed by authorities to be made up of male performers.[128]

There were also *lakhon* troupes in the provinces, since some of the dancers from the capital of Ayudhaya made their way to different parts of the country after the fall of the city. Two incidents connected with the *lakhon* circle are mentioned in the chronicles. The first is an account of Nakhon Ratchasima where Chao Phraya Sisuriyawong, acting governor of Phra Chao Phimai (Krom Mun Thep-phiphit), and his two sons killed their rival, Luang Phaeng (Chao Nakhon Ratchasima), and his followers while they were watching a *lakhon* performance. The second incident concerns King Taksin being rescued by two *lakhon* dancers, Nai Ket and Nai Chu, when the king's boat capsized during his trip from Tak to Khai Luang at Ban Rahaeng after his conquest of Chiengmai in A.D. 1774.[129]

RECONSTRUCTING THE DRAMATIC ARTS: THE REIGN OF KING RAMA I

Despite the effort of King Taksin to restore Ayudhaya culture during the fifteen years of his reign, his mental breakdown and abnormal behaviour towards the end of his rule worked against all the previous good deeds he had accomplished for the country. Finally, the self-appointed monarch, who did so much to reunify Siam from the scattered remnants of a country ravaged by the Burmese, was executed in the most honourable manner befitting a king, by being put in a red cloth sack and clubbed to death with batons of sandalwood. Somdet Chao Phraya Maha Kasatsuk (formerly Chao Phraya Chakri), his right-hand general, who had fought side by side with him in numerous battles and had shared similar dreams and anxieties in the work of reconstructing the country, was, by the consent of the Council of the Lords of the Realm,[130] proclaimed king.

Somdet Chao Phraya was established as Phrabat Somdet Phra Phuttha Yotfa Chulalok, the founder of a new dynasty, the Chakri dynasty in 1782. Also born a commoner in the sense that he was not descended from the Ayudhaya royal family, the new king had an advantage over King Taksin, however, in being associated with a long line of *khunnang* (aristocrats) who had served the kings of Ayudhaya. He himself had also been in the royal service since childhood as a page during the reign of King Suriyat-Amarin.[131] His heroic deeds in the battles during his service under King Taksin had not only earned him the country's highest title and position, Somdet Chao Phraya, second only to the king, but these accomplishments also gained for him the admiration and respect of the Thai, who were at the time in great need of a national hero in whom they could place their hopes and aspirations for the restoration of the glorious past.

King Rama I realized the necessity for continuing the reconstruction of Siamese traditional culture, court customs, and ceremonies on the model of the Ayudhaya royal court. Though this had been started by King Taksin, King Rama I, being a more cautious traditionalist, made a careful study and enquiry into all court etiquette and national ceremonies before taking any important steps to revive them. For example, before his own coronation, in 1783 he appointed a royal commission headed by Chao Phraya Phetphichai to study the forms of the ceremony as practised in the days of Ayudhaya. Chao Phraya Phetphichai was a former high court officer of Ayudhaya. The commission, which included three other former Ayudhaya officials, based their report on the coronation of King Uthumphon, who ascended the throne in 1758 and remained king for only one year before abdicating to his brother, Krom Khun Anurakmontri, who became King Phra Thinang Suriyat-Amarin, the last king of Ayudhaya. One historian suggested that the reason why this commission referred to the coronation of King Uthumphon and not that of King Suriyat-Amarin, which they had also witnessed, was due to the fact that the memories of the sack of Ayudhaya were too shattering an experience, and that they did not wish to recognize the last reign which had brought the old kingdom to its fall and destruction.[132]

To the Ayudhayans who had lost their *khwan* (spiritual essence or courage) in the fall of the old kingdom, this cultural reconstruction led by King Rama I stimulated a sense of national identity and unity. It also created an image of prestige for the new kingdom of Ratanakosin (lit., the jewel city built by the god Indra) and the new dynasty which would eventually gain recognition and respect from neighbouring countries, particularly Burma, its arch-enemy. It would prove to them the indestructibility of the Thai people and their civilization, which had been uninterrupted for many centuries despite the ravages of many wars.

Though Ayudhaya was the model of this new state, King Rama I was determined to show that the final results of his reconstruction would even surpass Ayudhaya, both in the external physical appearance of the city, complete with its royal palace, and royal temples, and in the richness of its culture and arts, more specifically of literature and drama.

Upon the completion of each important construction, there was a grand *somphot* (celebration) with festivities, dance, drama, and other entertainment of the best possible kind. The glorification of Krung Thep—the "city of the gods" as the new city was named—and of the Royal Palace and royal temples appear purposefully in all the major literary works of this reign, such as in the *Ramakien, Inao, Dalang,* and *Unarut.* The *bot chom muang* (narratives describing the beauty of a city) in the *lakhon* scripts written during this reign followed the literary convention of Ayudhaya. They are, however, richer and more elaborate in their detailed descriptions. Thus, evidence indicates either that the new capital was glorious in reality, or that the authors intended that it surpass all the descriptions that had gone before. The latter interpretation is more convincing.

One other important point to be noted concerns the name of this newly founded dynasty, the "Chakri" dynasty (deriving from the former title of Chao Phraya Chakri). It is symbolically associated with the god Vishnu, the bearer of the *chakra* (discus), which became the crest of the dynasty. King Rama I was to personify Vishnu Incarnate, the Great Preserver, who saved the world of Siam from its evil enemies and who restored peace and prosperity to the land. The cult of Rama, the ideal king, the incarnation of Vishnu most significant in its association with monarchy and warfare, was made alive by the monumental composition of the *Ramakien* and its dramatic performances in *khon, nang,* and *lakhon,* which were given frequently during this reign. Both the Royal Palace (Wang Luang) and the Palace of the Front (Wang Na, belonging to the second king, brother of King Rama I) had their own *khon* and *lakhon* troupes. In the grand *somphot,* the *khon* troupes of both parties would perform together, representing opposite camps: the Wang Luang troupe on Phra Ram's side and the Wang Na on Thosakan's. One historical incident was recorded of such a performance in 1796,[133] which turned into a real gun battle between the *khon* dancers of the two parties, and which caused their royal patrons, the king and the second king, to become angry with each other for a long period of time until their sisters[134] brought about a reconciliation.

Rivalry between the two palaces often caused bitterness between the king and his brother. The latter became extremely resentful in his old age as he lost hope in the succession to the throne for himself and his own children, despite the fact that he had fought side by side with his brother and had supported him all through their younger days to see him finally installed on the throne. The dramatic battles between Phra Ram and Thosakan, ending always with the defeat of Thosakan, who was represented by the *khon* troupe of his Wang Na, itself spoke clearly, though symbolically, of the perpetual conflict between the two leaders with the Krom Phra Ratchawang Bowon (the second king) always on the losing side as Thosakan. The defeat was hard to accept, since he had proven on many occasions on the real battlefield to be a greater fighter than the king.

This incident of the gun battle, then, though it may have come about due to a mixture of chance and circumstance, shows how the epic of the *Ramakien* and its dramatic performance were closely intertwined with political and social institutions at the highest level, and how the dance-drama was so realistically presented that it lost its original entertaining purpose and turned into a political battle. Incidentally, the performance of *khon* on this particular occasion was done in the style of *khon klang plaeng* (*khon* in an open-air field) on the royal festival ground between the two palaces, which is now called the Pramane Ground. The physical setting of the field with the two palaces as the background enhanced further the realistic effects of the whole dramatic performance. The final battle scene between the two troupes must have been a shattering experience for the spectators, as real cannons were fired at each other, causing serious casualties and deaths on both sides.

This performance of *khon klang plaeng,* following the tradition of Ayudhaya, had been deliberately revived by King Rama I in order to continue the cultural heritage and establish ties to the glorious past as he remembered it, without, of course, the intention to make it a political affair. The unforeseen consequences merely add a new dimension to the seriousness of the king's intent in reconstructing the traditional culture and arts of Ayudhaya.

The writer wishes to concentrate here only on the reconstruction of dramatic literature and classical dance-drama during the First Reign. Other aspects of reconstruction have been dealt with by historians.[135]

The first step King Rama I took in restoring the dramatic arts to the royal court was to commission the court poets to reconstruct all the *lakhon* and *khon* scripts which had remained from the Ayudhaya period and to complete the missing parts (even to the point of including some passages which may not have existed in original texts), in order to establish complete versions of royal standard texts for posterity and for the glory of the new kingdom. These texts, upon their completion, were presented to the king for his final revision and approval, whereupon they were officially stamped as *bot phra ratchaniphon* (royal manuscripts). In most cases the king acted as the supervisor of the projects rather than the composer or a direct contributor to the compositions. It does not appear in his *Phra Rachanukit* (Daily personal activities of the king) that he was directly engaged in such literary and dramatic activities.[136] The phrases constantly used when referring to the king's commission for the writing of these dramatic texts and in the training of the court dancers are that he *kho raeng* (asked the assistance of the other poets and courtiers) to accomplish the tasks, or that he *prot hai hat* (commissioned the training of) all types of entertainment in the Royal Palace, namely, *khon, nang, lakhon, hun,* and other minor *mahorasop* (royal entertainment) both in the Wang Luang and Wang Na. The term *prot hai hat* indicates that the task of training and directing was in the hands of other authorities in the field rather than in the king's hand, unlike the case of his son, King Rama II, who was personally involved, as recorded in his daily schedule. When referring to the dramatic activities of King Rama II, another term is used: *song hat,* to train them (the dancers), himself.

As to the *phra ratchaniphon bot lakhon* (royal *lakhon* manuscripts) of King Rama I, there were four major texts of *lakhon nai* reconstructed during his reign: *Ramakien,* in 116 *smut thai* (books); *Unarut,* in 18 *smut thai; Dalang,* 32 *smut thai; Inao,* 38 *smut thai.* According to authorities on Thai literature, the first two *lakhon* scripts (*Ramakien* and *Unarut*) were composed during the First Reign, while the last two (*Dalang* and *Inao*) were revised from original texts of Ayudhaya, since they contain many passages written in the *klon* poetic style of that period, which differs considerably from the poetic style of the First Reign. They also lack the coherence of the first two works.

As to the works of the king himself, there seems to be only one: *Phra Ratchaniphon Klon Phleng Yao Ruang Rop Phama Thi Tha Din Daeng* (Royal manuscript in *klon phleng yao* verse on the battle with Burma at Tha Din Daeng), or *Nirat Tha Din Daeng* for short. It was said that he also composed two other short poems, which were inscribed in the stone plates on the wall behind the Phra Lokanat Buddha image in the Ubosot (chapel) of Wat Phra Chetuphon, as well as many *phra ratchaputcha* (religious questions, i.e., discussions) on Buddhism.[137]

King Rama I revived all the *kan mahorasop* (entertainment), which had been known in the Ayudhaya period, as well as *khruang mahorasop* (entertainment properties) of various kinds. In the chronicles and dramatic texts, there are several references to festivities which took place frequently and at which these various *mahorasop* were performed in order to make this "Krung Thep Maha Nakhon" (the great city of the gods, i.e., Bangkok) the cultural centre of Siam, equal to Ayudhaya at its height in times of peace and prosperity as remembered by its survivors, or even, if possible, surpassing the old capital in grandeur.

There were many *lakhon* troupes outside the Royal Palace during the First Reign. They must have all been *lakhon phuchai* (male dance-drama), since the *lakhon phuying* (female dance-drama) were restricted to the royal court by the royal command of King Rama I. Even the royal princes of the rank of Chaofa (children of the king born of the queens) were not permitted to keep a *lakhon phuying,* or *lakhon nang nai.* (The case of Chaofa Krom Luang Isarasunthon—later King Rama II—and his training of young girl dancers, which had infuriated the king and was discontinued, is a most frequently quoted example of this restriction.)

The two best-known troupes in the royal circle in this reign were the Lakhon Phuying Khong Luang troupe (female dance-drama troupe of the royal court) which performed only *lakhon nai,* and the troupe of Chaofa Krom Luang Thep-harirak (head of the Thephatsadin family, nephew of the king, son of Somdet Chaofa Krom Phra Sisudarak, sister of the king) which performed both *lakhon phuying* and *lakhon phuchai* in the style of *lakhon nai* and was well known for its *Inao* production. After the death of the Chaofa in 1805, his brother, Chaofa Krom Luang Phithakmontri (head of the

Montrikun family) inherited the troupe. He also became the most highly respected choreographer and teacher of *lakhon* in the Second Reign. Among the *lakhon* troupes outside the Royal Palace, the Lakhon Nai Bunyang troupe was the best known for its performances of *lakhon nok*.

The leading dancers of these above-mentioned troupes became masters of *lakhon nai* and *lakhon nok* and taught many generations of dancers in the following reigns. Some remained teachers even until the Fifth Reign. To cite some of the more famous ones:

1) Chaofa Krom Luang Phithakmontri, who became head master of the Khon Luang and Lakhon Luang in the Second Reign and is worshipped even today as a patron spirit of *lakhon*.
2) Nai (mister) Thongyu, who is known for his performance of *Inao* in the troupe of Chaofa Krom Luang Phithakmontri, became the advisor who directed the choreography of Chaofa Krom Luang Phithakmontri in the training of the Lakhon Luang dancers in the Second Reign and taught dancers in most of the troupes outside the Royal Palace in the Third Reign when the Lakhon Luang was discontinued at the royal command of King Rama III. He was also teacher of *sepha* (a poetic narrative form).
3) Nai Rung, who played the role of *nang ek* (heroine, leading female role) in the *lakhon* of the Chaofa, became a teacher of the *nang* (female role) in the Second and Third Reigns and worked closely with Nai Thongyu.
4) Nai Bunyang, who was master of his own *lakhon nok* troupe and taught *lakhon nok* in the following reigns. His troupe was so successful that he managed to build a temple with the money collected from his earnings. The temple was called Wat Lakhon Tham (temple constructed by the *lakhon* troupe).
5) Nai Bunmi, the brother of Nai Bunyang, who became teacher of the *nang* role in *lakhon nok* and worked together with his brother.

In the prayer of the worshipping of the spirits of teachers (*wai khru*) recited by the *khon* and *lakhon* dancers, the names of these teachers (*khru*) are mentioned, since many generations of dancers owe to them the principles and training of Thai classical dancing. Some of the female dancers of the Lakhon Phuying Khong Luang in this reign also became famous teachers in the following reigns.[138] Among them Chao Chom Manda Ampha is often referred to in connection with the influence of Thai classical dance-drama upon that of the Cambodian royal court. Her *lakhon* troupe was brought over by her daughter, Chawiwat, to the court of the Cambodian king in the Fifth Reign.

The Lakhon Luang (royal dance-drama troupe) of the Cambodian court was first developed in the First Reign with the assistance of a group of dancers from the Thai royal court. They were granted permission by King Rama I, towards the end of the reign, to help form the Cambodian Lakhon Luang troupe, upon the request of King Uthairacha (Nak Phra-ong Chan) when King

Rama I invested him with the name and title of King of Cambodia in 1806. However, they were allowed to perform and train in *lakhon nok* only (since *lakhon nai* was exclusively the royal prerogative of Thai monarchs). It was not until the Third Reign that the Thai-style *lakhon phuying* was introduced into the court of King Harirak (Nak-ong Duang) of Cambodia (see p. 66).

The foundation laid by King Taksin and built upon by King Rama I in the reconstruction of Thai dramatic literature and classical dance-drama provided a firm base for expansion to the highest degree by King Rama II, who proved to be both a great poet and a creative dramatist. Under his initiative and leadership Ratanakosin culture, as it reached the height of a golden era in artistic refinement, creative ingenuity, and sophistication, was no longer dependent on the Ayudhaya model. It succeeded in establishing its own identity and served as a model and a standard for generations to come.

THE GOLDEN ERA OF CLASSICAL DANCE-DRAMA: THE REIGN OF KING RAMA II

The reign of King Rama II (1809–24) is lauded by Thai scholars as "the golden era" of that country's dramatic literature and classical dance-drama due to both the creation and training of the Lakhon Luang and Khon Luang troupes, which set a standard for the following generations of Thai classical dancers, teachers, choreographers, composers of dramatic texts, music and songs up to the present day.[139] The flourish of court arts and culture was directly due to the king's personal interest and involvement in all types and genres of artistic creation. The king was an all-round artist: a poet, musician, composer, choreographer, dramatist, and sculptor. His natural talents and artistic flare are evident in all of his works, which became models for later artists and dramatists.

In his early days during the reign of his father,[140] the king also took part in warfare and undertook administrative responsibilities laid upon him by his father. However, his major inclination had always been in the fields of art, literature, and drama. As crown prince he was one of the court poets who contributed to the writing of major *bot lakhon,* namely, the *Unarut, Ramakien, Inao,* and *Dalang* which are together called *Chabap Phra Rachaniphon Nai Ratchakan Thi 1* (The royal literary works of King Rama I). He also started training young female court dancers and secretly formed his own *lakhon phuying* troupe, which was a sole prerogative of the king. Upon learning of this, King Rama I was infuriated, and the crown prince's *lakhon phuying* was therefore discontinued until his coronation.

When King Rama II ascended the throne after his father's death in 1809, the country was at peace. Owing to the capable hands of his assistants in state affairs and administration,[141] the king was able to spend most of his leisure time creating artistic works, not only in dramatic literature and dance-drama, but also in the fine arts, such as sculpture, carving, painting, and decorating.

In the *Phra Rachanukit,* it is written that each day he spent a considerable amount of time rehearsing *khon* and *lakhon* and writing the dramatic texts along with a group of court poets and dance teachers.

Unlike the *Phra Rachanukit* of his father and his son, King Rama III, the full detail of the administrative sessions in King Rama II's daily schedule is not given. Rather, his personal recreations are given more attention.[142] This is clear evidence of the peace and prosperity which his reign seemed to have enjoyed after the heavy task of reconstruction, restoration, and reunification of the country accomplished by his father. He was fortunate to reap the fruits of that hard labour and to be able to turn to art and culture to bring this important area of Thai civilization to perfection. This he did with the help of his poet and dramatist colleagues, namely, Prince Phithakmontri, Prince Surinthararak, Prince Chetsadabodin (later King Rama III), Khun Sunthon Wohan (Phu, or known as Sunthon Phu), and Phraya Wichaiwichit (Chamun Waiworanat). Their poetic collaboration with the king included two *bot lakhon nai,* the *Ramakien* and *Inao,* and six *bot lakhon nok,* the *Sangthong, Chaiyachet, Maniphichai, Kraithong, Khawi,* and *Sangsinchai.* However, some scholars contend that *Sangsinchai* is the work of Prince Chetsadabodin, composed also during this reign.

All these *bot lakhon* were created for the actual performances by the Lakhon Luang, both in the *lakhon phuchai* and *lakhon phuying* styles. However, it seems that the king concentrated his attention more on the *lakhon phuying* due to his interest in training young female dancers since his crown prince days. Being a romantic person and known for his passionate love affairs, and also being endowed with such refined artistic taste and talent, it was natural for him to favour the *lakhon phuying,* or the *lakhon nang nai,* especially when it was performed by his own consorts and female attendants.

The first evidence of the performance of the Lakhon Nai Khong Luang was at the *somphot* of the first white elephant in 1812 during the fourth year of the reign. The dancers were young female performers whom he had secretly trained during the First Reign. Through striving for perfection both for his own sake and for Prince Phithakmontri, the chief choreographer, the king was able to establish a standard of *khon* and *lakhon* at the royal court, both in the dramatic text and performance, which has been retained until the present day. However, it was not until the reign of King Rama III that this standard was extended outside the Royal Palace. Even the royal princes and the Palace of the Front, according to authorities on Thai drama, did not dare to imitate the royal style nor train a *lakhon phuying* during the first two reigns.[143]

The reign of King Rama III was indeed a contrast in terms of court dramatic activities. For example, the inactivity, or rather the discontinuation, of the Lakhon Luang troupe turned out to be a direct stimulus for expansion of the *lakhon* circle outside the Royal Palace. It gave rise to the revival and modernization in the Fourth Reign.

The dancers of the Lakhon Luang troupe became teachers of most leading troupes in the following reigns. Chao Chom Manda Yaem, famous for her role of Inao, became the teacher of that role until the Fifth Reign. Khun Malai (Thao Worachan in the Fourth Reign, grandmother of Prince Dhaninivat, and Thao Worakhananan in the Fifth Reign) was the director of the Lakhon Luang during the Fourth and Fifth Reigns. Khun Phan, famous for her role of Inthrachit in the *Ramakien,* was a teacher in the Lakhon Luang during the Fourth Reign and director of the performance of the *Ramakien.* Khun Phu (known for her role as Hanuman) became a teacher in the Lakhon Luang during the Fourth Reign. Khun A-ngun (famous for her role as Sida) taught in the Lakhon Luang during the Fourth and Fifth Reigns.[144]

King Rama II's own compositions for *lakhon nai* are:

1) *Inao,* the complete story about 20,520 *kham klon* (verses), first published in three volumes by the National Library in 1921.
2) *Ramakien,* from the episode of Hanuman giving the ring to Sida to Thosakan's death, and from the episode of killing Sida to the wedding at Mount Krailat, about 14,300 *kham klon,* first published in 1913 in three volumes.

His five compositions for *lakhon nok* are *Kraithong,* about 888 *kham klon; Khawi,* about 1,808 *kham klon; Chaiyachet,* about 1,426 *kham klon; Sangthong,* about 3,256 *kham klon;* and *Maniphichai,* about 500 *kham klon.*

These dramatic texts were composed for actual dance performances and not literary texts for reading or narrating as those commissioned by King Rama I. Each section of the scripts was choreographed and rehearsed under the king's direction and supervision with the chief choreographer and master teacher, Prince Phithakmontri, and leading court dancers. Being an accomplished poet-dramatist-musician-dancer, King Rama II was able to develop classical dramatic texts and dance movements to the highest standard. His dramatic works as well as music and songs are models for later artists. They are used today in schools and universities as standard textbooks and compositions.

PREPARATIONS FOR NEW DEVELOPMENTS: THE REIGN OF KING RAMA III

The reign of King Rama III (1824–51) has often been regarded by many scholars as the "dark age" for classical dance-drama, in comparison with the "golden age" of his father, King Rama II. This is due to the long period of restriction and suppression of dramatic activities within the royal court. Consequently, private troupes patronized by members of the royal family and noblemen discontinued their public performances for fear of creating displeasure to the king.

There are many reasons given for King Rama III's prohibition of dramatic activities within the Royal Palace. Firstly, the king, being a serious and pious Buddhist, regarded dramatic activities as frivolous entertainment, that often led to immoral practices and behaviour within the royal court and among aristocratic society. Unlike his father, who indulged in artistic, dramatic, and romantic activities, King Rama III spent most of his hours of relaxation in supervising religious works and constructing temples. Secondly, external political threats and warfare with neighbouring countries like Burma, Vietnam, and the southern states and the threat of aggression by the Western powers preoccupied most of his time. It would not be appropriate to have *sanuk* (fun) activities within the Royal Palace during such a crucial period.

During the reign of his father when still Prince Chetsadabodin, he did participate in the customary court practice of writing dramatic literature in the poetry circle. His dramatic work is contained in two books on *lakhon nok, Sangsinchai,*[145] and two episodes in *Khun Chang Khun Phaen.*[146] However, he was probably not very enthusiastic about this type of artistic activity. Moreover, his unpleasant experience with Sunthon Phu, the favourite protégé of his father, in poetic competitions composing the texts of *Inao* and *Sangthong,* was probably a blow to his pride, since he was criticized by the poet in front of his father. Sunthon Phu immediately left the court when King Rama III succeeded to the throne.

King Rama III's displeasure with *lakhon* performances may also have been due to the fact that *lakhon* was (and still is) a worldly pleasure which, more often than not, could lead, and has been known to have led, its ardent devotees astray. Furthermore, the irregular behaviour and way of life of the *lakhon* people (with probably the exception of those in the Lakhon Luang troupe who were under strict rules laid down by the Royal Palace) have always been viewed suspiciously. The scandal of Krom Luang Rakronnaret involving his affairs with the *lakhon* dancers in his troupe was said to have influenced him in rendering unfair verdicts and in bungling many court cases under his jurisdiction. In addition, it was an obvious practice of the Krom Luang to measure himself against the king. His plot to usurp the throne caused King Rama III to rid him of his royal title, reduce him to the status of Mom Kraison, and finally execute him in 1848.[147]

The Lakhon Luang dancers, particularly those in the *lakhon nang nai,* were, in most cases, consorts of kings in the past who entertained the monarchs in their hours of leisure. It was therefore natural for King Rama III, an extremely devout Buddhist, to shun all these worldly pleasures and to seek other more pious forms of leisure. In his *Phra Rachanukit,* it is stated that the king's private activities were mainly religious, military, artistic, and literary. His favourite hours of relaxation were spent in reading, writing, and playing games with three close members of the royal family: Krom Luang Woraset, Somdet Phra Thepsirinthon, and Somdet Phra Nang Somanat (who later, during the reign of King Mongkut, trained young girl dancers in the *lakhon nai*). This period of relaxation was called the *len phra chaliang* (playing on the porch).[148] There is no mention of any musical or dramatic entertainment. It was recorded towards the end of the Third Reign,

> His Majesty [Rama III] respected Buddhist religion and the members of the royal family to a high degree. He always carried out administrative responsibilities, major and minor, without any failings, from his hour of rising to his hour of retiring. *He never listened to any singing or watched any dancing.* He remained [in his old age] within the Royal Palace and did not make any visits [outside the Royal Palace], except during the *kathin* [presentation of robes to the monks at the end of the rainy season].[149]

King Rama III considered *khon* and *lakhon* wasteful luxuries, which a country in difficult times could not afford and which created temptations to indulge in worldly pleasure and obstacles to a religious life. He therefore resented any performances within his royal court, despite the fact that he had patronized a *khon* troupe before becoming king. It is stated in the Royal Decree of King Mongkut written by Phraya Woraphongphiphat in 1855, "In the reign of King Phra Nang Klao, the King disliked *lakhon*. He cursed and reprimanded those [who performed it] in order to prevent them from continuing it."[150] And again in the Royal Decree on the taxation of the *mahorasop* of King Mongkut in 1861,

> When it came to the reign of King Phra Nang Klao, the King considered his patronage of *lakhon* would be an act of heedlessness without any value to the royal charity work and to the service of the country. He therefore shunned *lakhon* all through his reign. There was no longer the *lakhon khang nai*, but only a few plays secretly performed in the court by the *chao chom* [consorts]. When the King knew about this, he was angry and the activity was discontinued.[151]

However, the *lakhon* performances, taken as a whole, were not too greatly diminished. On the contrary, the restriction gave rise to many private troupes outside the court, who secretly performed in the palaces of princes and princesses and in aristocratic households. The same Royal Decree of 1861 states,

> The *lakhon khaek* [Malay dance-drama] troupe started therefore to train female dancers. The leading dancer, the *nai rong* [master of the theatre], was male, and some *nang* [female roles] were female. Some other troupes [following their example] wanted also to train a whole troupe of female dances for *lakhon khaek*. Later, senior and junior officials secretly trained female *lakhon* dancers and performed many stories in various theatres. But the training was

carried out at home and they were not performed openly as they used to be at great social functions as this might cause too much gossip. They performed only secretly within the company of close friends and any information about the performances was hidden from the king.[152]

Since the royal dance troupe was inactive, these private troupes began to adopt the court style of dancing from *lakhon nok* and *lakhon nai* and used dramatic texts written by King Rama II, which had been performed exclusively at court and had become favourite plays there. This was a rather daring undertaking and had never been attempted before. Indeed, the suppression of dramatic activities by King Rama III yielded just the opposite results. That is to say, the classical dance-drama of the court was expanded to a wider sphere outside the court and was even exposed to the general public. The restriction was therefore effective only within the court itself.

At first, these dramatic activities outside the royal court were secretly sponsored by members of the royal family and aristocratic families for fear of the king's displeasure. Later, they were more publicly shown. In defending and justifying King Rama III, Prince Damrong explained,

> When I now examine the situation, I begin to see the reason why the king [Rama III] did not abolish *lakhon* altogether. Because King Phra Nang Klao had a personal dislike of the *lakhon* performance, he therefore suppressed the Lakhon Luang. When he knew that there were some who still kept up their involvement with *lakhon* training and performance, naturally he had to criticize them, but he did not intend to abolish the *lakhon* altogether, as *lakhon* had been entertainment in the country from the old days. Whenever there were *mahorasop khong luang* [royal entertainments], there was still *lakhon* as in the tradition. The only prejudice the king had was against the people with *bandasak* [titles] training others or themselves being trained in *lakhon*.[153]

Towards the end of his reign, the king denied that he had ever been against *lakhon* and had never used his power to stop it. He even left bequeathed funds for the restoration of temples for the performance of *lakhon*.[154] In many royal temples constructed during his reign, some of which were under his personal supervision (notably Wat Phra Chetuphon, commonly known as Wat Pho), there are paintings and sculpture depicting well-known scenes from *khon* and *lakhon*. The best example is the 152 bas-reliefs on the outer wall of the gallery of the Phra Ubosot (main chapel) of Wat Phra Chetuphon, representing episodes from the *Ramakien* (including that of Nang Loi). These bas-reliefs are generally accepted as being made to the order of King Rama III during the restoration of the temple in 1826.

Another example from a different temple is the four pairs of sculptured figures (in the round), also of the same reign, at the four corners of the Temple of the Emerald Buddha. They are famous pas-de-deux dances of major characters in the classical *khon, lakhon nok,* and *lakhon nai.* They are Chao Ngo and Rotchana from *Sangthong* (*lakhon nok*), Hanuman and Nang Suwannamatcha from *Ramakien* (*khon* and *lakhon nai*), Phra Suthon and Manohra from *Manohra* (*lakhon nok*), and Kraithong and Wimala from *Kraithong* (*lakhon nok*). (These sculptures are now in the Wat Phra Keow Museum.)

These works of art are evidence of King Rama III's interest in the classical dance-drama as represented in other art forms. Prince Naris explained to Prince Damrong, in one of his letters, the importance of these four pairs of figures in relation to King Rama III,

> These four sculptures are of considerable importance. From the point of view of the idea of selecting these particular scenes and characters, they were created with the utmost intelligence, i.e., so as to present different types of characters which could be identified by the viewers themselves without having to be told by others. For instance, if the figures of Phra Chaiyachet and Nang Suwincha were ordered to be made, there would be endless query as to who they are [because the story is less well known to the general public]. . . . I think that this original idea could belong to no other person than King Phra Nang Klao [Rama III] himself. . . . The sizes of the stones are quite big. The only person who had the power to order them to be transported from the provinces to the city could be the king. To have this accomplished, it had to be by royal command. Finally, these works of sculpture are not merely figures. They were created in the most beautiful style of Thai sculpture in the Third Reign. They must be the work of teachers, and not of any inferior crafts-men. From my observation of the style, they are very close to the work of Achan [master] Chai, who was Luang Phromphichit. This Achan Chai was an artist who created the *nang phra nakhon wai* [big leather puppet depicting a city scene] which were very famous, and the stone bas-reliefs of the *Ramakien* on the wall around the Ubosot of Wat Phra Chetuphon; these were supervised by this Achan Chai. I presumed that Achan Chai himself drew the figures for the leather carvers to make them into *nang* figures. But this particular work [i.e., the four pairs of sculptures] was a combina-tion of half-drawing and half-carving. . . . Before the execution of the sculptures, the artist had to draw the figures and present them to the king for approval. If the king was pleased with them, they would be sent as models to the *chang hun* [puppet makers, carvers of puppet heads, sculptors] to make them.[155]

This statement suggests the king's personal involvement in the creation of these *khon* and *lakhon* figures. His prejudice against the royal dramatic entertainment was therefore oriented more towards stage performance within the royal court, which he possibly regarded as a senseless, time-consuming pleasure of very little value. It should be noted that the development of literature, including that of dramatic literature, during this reign was not in the least insignificant. The two great poets of the Second Reign, Prince Poramanuchitchinorot and Sunthon Phu, lived on to the Fourth Reign, and they both created many important works during the Third Reign. It is true, however, that the poets belonging to the generation of the Third Reign itself could hardly match their predecessors of the Second Reign. Their shortcomings were obvious to the extent that King Rama III strongly criticized their inferior qualities in his *phleng yao* (a long poem, usually of a country nature or personal opinions). It was also during this same reign that printing technology was introduced, which later helped to expand the sphere and scope of dramatic literature itself. Taking all these factors into consideration, the Third Reign was far from being a "dark age" of dance-drama, as it has generally been labelled by students of Thai literature. On the contrary, it was this reign that paved the way to the modernization efforts that took place in the following era under King Mongkut.

The patrons of private *lakhon* troupes outside the royal court during the Third Reign were in most cases nobles of high *bandasak*. They wished to carry on *lakhon* and claimed their justification in the hope that the tradition of the Lakhon Luang troupe would be preserved for later generations. In particular, they insisted that the plays written and choreographed by King Rama II, which were considered incomparable dramatic masterpieces, should be rehearsed and performed in order to maintain the standard of royal dancing and to prevent them from going into extinction. For these latter reasons, they began to train their dancers in *lakhon* in the pattern and tradition of the Lakhon Luang troupe. Some very senior members of the royal family, both with and without *krom* rank,[156] such as Krom Phra Ratchawang Bowon Mahasakdipholasep, the second king (of King Rama II's reign), and other *senabodi* (high officials), who patronized *khon* troupes, began to train them also in *lakhon*. Krom Phra Ratchawang Bowon, Chao Phraya Bodindecha (of the Singhaseni family), and Chao Phraya Nakhon Sithammarat (of the Na Nakhon family) even dared to train *lakhon phuying* dancers in the style of the *lakhon nai khong luang,* which had been restricted to the Royal Palace for the king's pleasure only. There is no evidence that the King Rama III showed any strong disapproval of them or ordered them to stop their activities.[157]

The training in *lakhon* after the pattern of the Lakhon Luang troupe of King Rama II was therefore a status symbol, *khruang pradap kiatiyot* (lit., decorations marking a bestowed title of honour), for the aristocrats. They would hire teachers, who had been in the Royal Troupe of King Rama II, to train their dancers. The most popular teachers were Khru (master) Thongyu and Khru Ruang, who finally earned considerable fortunes from training all these private troupes in both the *lakhon nai* and *lakhon nok* traditions of King Rama II. *Inao* was the most popular.[158]

Among the well-known private *lakhon* troupes which trained female dancers in the style of the royal *lakhon phuying,* or more formally called the *lakhon nang nai* (dance-drama of the Inner Court ladies), were that of the Front Palace under the patronage of Krom Phra Ratchawang Bowon Mahasakdipholasep, Chao Phraya Bodindecha, Chao Phraya Nakhon Sithammarat, Prince Thinnakon (later Prince Phuwanetnarinrit), Prince Isaretrangsan (later the second king, Phra Pin Klao, in the reign of King Mongkut), Prince Rakronnaret, Prince Phiphitphokphuben, Prince Phithakthewet, Prince Lakkananukhun, Prince Phumintharaphakdi, and Phraya Siphiphat (later Chao Phraya Borom Maha Phichaiyat of the Bunnag family).[159]

Most of the plays for *lakhon nai* and *lakhon nok* were those of King Rama II. New plays were also written for these private theatres. Krom Phra Ratchawang Bowon himself wrote a number of episodes for *lakhon nok:*

1) *Ramakien:* Episode of the jealous quarrel between the two wives of Hanuman, Benyakai and Suwankanyuma, in the *lakhon nok* style, as in the play *Kraithong* of King Rama II.
2) *Kaki:* Episode of Khrut (Garuda) abducting Kaki.
3) *Phra Lo:* Episode of Phra Lo's madness.
4) *Khun Chang Khun Phaen:* Episodes of the confrontation between Nang Wanthong and Nang Laothong, Khun Phaen breaking into the house of Khun Chang, and Wanthong preventing the war between Phra Wai and Khun Phaen.

Prince Thinnakon trained his female dancers in the court style, but only to perform *lakhon nok.* He composed three *lakhon nok* plays: *Suwannahong, Nang Kaeo Na Ma,* and *Nang Kula.* They became very popular and were regarded as second only to the plays by King Rama II. *Suwannahong* and *Nang Kaeo Na Ma* have been produced by the Silapakon Theatre with great success from the 1950s to the present.[160]

The troupe of Prince Rakronnaret performed the *Inao* of King Rama I, which was a rather rare event, for it has never been as popular as the *Inao* of King Rama II.

Another important development of *lakhon* in this period was the extension of *lakhon phuying* to the courts of vassal lords and kings, more precisely to the courts of Nakhon Sithammarat and Cambodia. Chao Phraya Nakhon Sithammarat in this reign started with the training of male dancers for *khon* in his palace. Later, he inherited the *lakhon phuying* from Krom Phra Ratchawang Bowon, a relative.[161] He then began training female dancers. According to historical records, the *lakhon phuying* of Chao Nakhon Sithammarat could be traced as far back as the reign of King Taksin, when in 1769 King Taksin suppressed the rebellious Chao Nakhon and brought him as a captive to Bangkok, the king also confiscated his *lakhon phuying* troupe. Later the king restored him his position and granted him the prestige of possessing a *lakhon phuying* troupe as an honour conferred upon a vassal lord (as it was usually restricted to the Siamese royal court). At the celebrations for the Emerald Buddha in 1780, Chao Nakhon brought his *lakhon phuying* troupe to perform in competition with the Lakhon Luang performers and was very successful.[162] During the reign of King Rama III, in 1832, dancers were brought to Bangkok together with artisans and other artists from Nakhon Sithammarat, Phatthalung, and Songkhla. They settled down in the capital and performed *lakhon chatri,* which began as an all male cast but later became a mixed cast and, probably after the reign of King Chulalongkorn, adopted the style of *lakhon nok* and *liké* as they appear today.[163]

Siamese *lakhon phuying* went to the royal court of King Harirak (Nak Phra Ong Duang) of Cambodia for the first time through the introduction of Chao Phraya Bodindecha, who brought a *lakhon phuying* troupe to Udongmichai.[164] Later, the dancers from this troupe became teachers at the royal court of King Harirak of Cambodia. This adoption of *lakhon nai* by the Cambodian monarch, a foreign vassal of Siam, was the first time that the Thai royal tradition was broken. During the reign of King Rama I, only the *lakhon nok* dancers were taken to the court of King Uthairacha of Cambodia, since *lakhon nai* was then still restricted only to the Siamese royal court and prohibited to foreign vassals. An incident illustrative of the exclusive nature of *lakhon nai* is found in the Thai chronicles[165] and recounted by Mom Ratchawong Kukrit Pramoj in his *Khrong Kraduk Nai Tu (Skeletons in the closet* [*sic.*], Kukrit Pramoj's own translation of the title).[166] When Chao Anuwong of Vientiane asked permission from King Rama III at the royal cremation of Rama II to take some *lakhon nai* dancers to train dancers in his court at Vientiane, the king, probably out of suspicion that the Lao vassal had an ambition to measure up to his Siamese suzerain, refused him. This hurt his pride and made him vengeful towards the Siamese king. This may have been one of the reasons which later caused him to attack the border cities in Siam. This incident proves that *lakhon nai* had been regarded as the exclusive property of the Siamese royal court until these new developments later in the reign of King Rama III (viz., the cases of King Harirak of Cambodia and Chao Phraya Nakhon Sithammarat, both vassals of the Siamese king). It therefore marks the end of any restrictions imposed by the king himself.

Lakhon nok was also developed further during this reign. As a flourishing drama, it became widespread during the reign of King Mongkut. The most well-known *lakhon nok* troupes were that of Chao Chom Manda Ampha (consort of King Rama II) and Chao Krap. Chao Chom Manda Ampha was famous in the role of Nang Kanchana in the *Inao* of King Rama I. She became a very highly respected dance teacher to many private troupes and set up her own troupe of female dancers to perform *lakhon nok* in the classical style of royal *lakhon phuying.* Whereas Chao Krap (a commoner; though the prefix Chao [pronouncing with an extended vowel "Chāo"] means a member of the royal family, it can also mean "master" or "mister" [when pronounced with a short vowel sound "Chao"] and was usually given to masters of dance troupes)[167] had only male dancers in his *lakhon nok* in the traditional style, until the reign of King Mongkut. When the king gave official permission to train female dancers outside the court, Chao Krap started to train girls with the intention of having a mixed cast in his *lakhon nok.* However, he did not succeed in this, as the dancers, once well-trained, were more often than not asked to become teachers in other troupes belonging to members of the royal family or the aristocracy.

In 1854 during the celebration of the new city canal Chao Krap volunteered to give *lakhon nok* performances in seven theatres. The folk version of *lakhon nok,* however, still used traditional style and texts, since they dared not perform the royal texts of King Rama II.

Since the Khon Luang and Lakhon Luang troupes did not serve the court throughout the reign of King Rama III, the principal dancers, both male and female, became teachers to private troupes or the royal troupe which was revived in the following reigns of King Mongkut and King Chulalongkorn.[168]

Incidentally another remarkable, new genre of dramatic literature developed during the reign of King Rama III in the form of a parody of *lakhon nai.* The piece is called *Raden Landai* and was written by a very witty poet, Phra Mahamontri (Sap). It is a hilarious parody of *Inao.* The hero, Landai, is satirically called "Raden (i.e., Javanese prince) Landai" (like "Raden Inao"), and instead of being a royal prince is a poor beggar who lives in a shabby hut near the Giant Swing in front of Wat Suthat. The descriptions of his hut, character, habits, and romance are direct parodies of those in *Inao.* "The comic essence of the story was to pair off things of high and low nature [or qualities], such as 'His [Raden Landai's] palace and pillars were slender [weather-worn] poles without spires.'"[169]

The heroine, Nang Pradae, is the Malay wife of an Indian cow-man. In this clever parody, the poet portrays also the society and way of life of the lower class of people. Though the dramatic piece was never peformed as a play during these early Bangkok reigns and was simply read for entertainment, it was produced on stage later in the twentieth century as a short comic piece by amateur groups. The daring act of satirizing the *Inao,* which was a most highly respected and well-loved dramatic masterpiece and a work of King Rama II, could be regarded as the development of a new liberal spirit under the cover of comedy.

Most authorities on Thai literature would regard this dramatic work only as a comedy for sheer entertainment, yet during the socialist-Marxist movement after the students' uprising in 1973, *Raden Landai* was lauded as the "literature of the people," and its hero hailed as the "champion of the proletariat" by leftist literary critics, as the work portrays the life of a beggar and his association with underprivileged social groups in satirizing the decadent aristocracy. Many feel, however, that such claims are too far-fetched.

In comparison with the glorious age of dramatic literature and dance-drama in the preceding reign, King Rama III strongly criticized the poor quality of poetry and lack of creative originality during his own reign. In his poem *Phleng Yao Klon Suphap Ruang Phra Ratchaprarop* expressing the king's opinions, written in *phleng yao* form in the *klon* metre and composed on the occasion of the restoration of Wat Phra Chetuphon (Wat Pho), the king explained his purpose in setting standard models for all types of Thai poetry,

> In the olden days, children in the families of scholars
> And descendants of aristocrats and noblemen
> Were usually taught and trained in the way of the court scribes.
> They knew the principles of dialogue, speech, [and] games of poetry.
> Today, there are only hooligans of lowly nature,
> Who behave sinfully and create a bad reputation all over the land.
> True scholars are well-nigh absent from the whole city.
> We therefore ask for the blessings of the three Buddhist virtues,
> That the good children, our descendants in the future,
> Be well-rounded in knowledge and happy, [and that] every *mun* and
>   *khun* [officials]
> May set his mind to charity and to making merit.[170]

He went on to admonish officials against opium-smoking, drinking, and indulging in worldly entertainment and love poems. He emphasized that love of the body ruins the soul and "is poisonous to diminishing and whittling away worldly desires; that is, it obstructs any renunciation of worldly existence by way of entering the monkhood."[171] Finally, he dedicated the poem as a religious offering in place of the *sangkhit* (Sanskrit, *Sam-gita;* meaning, in Thai, music, dance, song) and expressed his ultimate desire to attain enlightenment.

This *Phleng Yao* explains his reasons for suppressing all worldly entertainment in his court. His criticism of contemporary literature was valid to a large extent. Nevertheless, it may not be an exaggeration to state that the above-mentioned dramatic parody of *Raden Landai* by Phra Mahamontri, though not considered a masterpiece by conservative authorities of Thai literature, opened up a new dimension in Thai dramatic literature, which was to be more fully explored and developed in the next two reigns. Moreover, the dancers of both *lakhon nok* and *lakhon phuying* in private troupes[172] during this reign set up new styles of dancing which became the tradition for later *khon* and *lakhon* dancers down to the present.[173]

With the expansion and development of *lakhon* outside the royal court all through the Third Reign, the situation was ripe for the revival of the Khon Luang and Lakhon Luang when King Mongkut ascended the throne in 1851.

Chapter II
Westernization and Revival of Classical Dance-drama

The Reign of King Mongkut, Rama IV

THE BEGINNING OF WESTERNIZATION

King Mongkut ascended the throne in 1851, rather late in life at the age of forty-seven, after having spent twenty-seven years in a Buddhist monastery leading an austere religious life in the Thammayutika sect (Thammayut Nikai), a new monastic order that he himself had established in order to reform the state religion of Siam. These formative years in the monastery, while detaching him from political and administrative responsibilities, were valuable as a long period of preparation for his eventual succession to the throne. It enabled him to travel freely as a monk among his subjects without any distinction of rank, to learn about them from first-hand experience, and to establish close ties with them, something that other Siamese monarchs in the past, and even those after him, were not able to do. He was also able to view state affairs with greater objectivity. His scholarly pursuit of knowledge, particularly in astronomy, philosophy, religion, literature, and language, led him to establish personal contacts with Westerners who shared the same interests.

It was partly through these relationships and mainly from his own observation and study that King Mongkut came to know more about Western civilization and to realize the approaching danger of Western imperialism, which at that period was rapidly making headway into the neighbouring states of Burma, the Malay Peninsula, and Indochina. The rivalries between France and England over these and other territories in Asia became increasingly threatening to the independence of Siam.

Unlike his half-brother, King Rama III, who had mistrusted and feared the aggression of the Western powers and therefore developed a negative policy in dealing with them, King Mongkut came to the throne with the readiness and determination to deal with the West, not as an inferior but as an equal. To establish Siam on the same par with the great powers of the West was not an easy task. However, in the comparatively short period of his reign, which lasted only seventeen years, through his wise planning and methods for gradual modernization and Westernization, he was able to put Siam on the map and to receive the recognition, and at times even respect, from the Western aggressors through treaties and diplomatic ties. Since these subjects have been amply dealt with in numerous publications and theses,[1] the writer will discuss here only the influence of this movement for Westernization and modernization on the development of Thai classical dance-drama, both at the royal court and among the general public.

Western Education and the Role of Christian Missionaries

The first policy that King Mongkut employed in coping with the Western threat was the introduction of Western education within the court, with the purpose of educating in the ways of the West the royal children who would become future leaders. Through this learning they would be able to negotiate with the Western powers on more equal and dignified terms and to maintain Siamese sovereignty. English teachers were hired to instruct the royal children at the Royal Palace, and ex-officers of the British Army were employed to reorganize the Siamese army and to train personnel in modern military science and technology. The ultimate purpose was, in truth, to defend the country more efficiently against these same English and the French. American and European missionaries both Protestant and Catholic became close associates to the inner circle of the royal court and the Siamese aristocracy.

Prince Mongkut, while residing at the monastery before his ascension to the throne, learned Latin from and exchanged knowledge of the classical languages (Latin and Pali) with Bishop Pallegoix of the Catholic mission. He also received assistance from Protestant missionaries in his English language studies and astrology. Prince Isaretrangsan, his brother, who had been before the Fourth Reign in charge of the royal artillery corps, sought instruction from the missionaries in the Western art of warfare. Luang Nai Sit, the eldest son of the Phra Khlang, Minister of Finance, learned the Western method of ship building also from these missionaries.

With the founding of the Fourth Reign Prince Mongkut became King Rama IV, Prince Isaretrangsan the second king, and Luang Nai Sit the Kalahom, or Minister of Defence. Chief Physician Prince Wongsa, half-brother of King Mongkut, who was deeply interested in modern medicine and who had received instruction from Dr. D. B. Bradley, an American missionary, became head of the royal commissioners who signed the Anglo-Siamese treaty with Sir John Bowring in 1855, which, according to historians on Siam, paved the way for the official opening of the country to the West.[2]

While these missionaries did fail in their primary mission to convert the Thai to Christianity,[3] they had, incidentally, succeeded in introducing modern Western science, medicine, technology, and education to the Thai people to their great benefit.

The Thai felt that their Buddhist religion was by far superior to the religion of the *farang* (white Westerners), but they readily accepted other aspects of Western civilization from these missionaries for their own progress and modernization. So long as they did not contradict the Thai way of life, religious beliefs, and philosophy, and they were practical and contributed to the well-being of the people, foreign influences were, and still are, assimilated without much obstruction. Though objections were raised by the traditionalists, they served as "checks and balances" to neutralize and assimilate foreign influences and to prevent them from becoming dominant.

The most significant contribution of the American missionaries to the development of modern Thai literature and drama was printing technology and the publication of journals, periodicals, literary works, and dramatic literature. Dr. D. B. Bradley has usually been given the credit for introducing printing and publishing to the Siam of King Mongkut. But according to his great grandson, Dr. William J. Bradley, the true pioneers were J. T. Jones and Robinson.[4] Dr. D. B. Bradley, however, was the first American to scientifically study the Thai language and alphabet. He and his American associate designed the first Thai movable type for printing, which was widely used by both foreigners and Thais for many generations.

As a missionary, Bradley started off with the aim of converting the so-called "heathens," but he soon realized the fruitlessness of such missionary efforts, especially among the elite society, whom he befriended in order to gain social status and recognition among the Thai nobility. He then concentrated his efforts on publishing newspapers, journals, translations of Chinese tales, and even worldly dramatic literature, which became a subject of controversy among the moralistic missionaries. Through his publications, which helped to stimulate Thai literary interests, the American missionary was given more recognition and credit by Thai scholars and historians than his predecessors, Jones and Robinson, who were more interested in translating and printing the Bible and were driven by a strong conviction that Siam would eventually become a colony of the United States or England through Christian efforts.

The Rise of Modern Thai Literature

We will not discuss here the details of Bradley's publications, which can be found in other theses and documents, but will only cite a few significant works which had direct effects on the later literary activities of the Thai intellectuals. In this respects the two most important contributions made by Bradley were the development of Thai journalism and the publication and circulation of Thai literature to a wider reading public. Both of these contributions helped to increase the rate of literacy, develop critical thinking and a sense of artistic appreciation, and to stimulate literary creativity. In one sense, therefore, he helped to extend to the public both formal and informal kinds of education.

The first Thai language newspaper, *The Recorder,* was published by Bradley in 1843, followed by *The Bangkok Recorder* (also published by Bradley) in 1865. *The Recorder* appeared fortnightly until his death in 1873,[5] but *The Bangkok Recorder* lasted only one year. Following Bradley's initiative, four English language newspapers came into existence: the *Siam Times* (1864), the *Bangkok Press* (1864),[6] the *Siam Weekly Monitor* (1866–68), and the *Bangkok Summary* (1868). Though most of these newspapers were short-lived, they paved the way for the development of journalism in Siam, both in English and Thai.

Through journalism Dr. Bradley has also been given the credit for having introduced to the Thai press the Western idea of "freedom of the press" and journalistic objectivity and responsibility.[7] However, taking historical, political, and social factors into consideration, King Mongkut should be congratulated and given credit for having allowed such freedom of expression, especially for foreigners, during a period when absolute monarchy was still a sacred institution in Siam. In response to the critical reviews and articles in these foreign newspapers, the king ordered the publication of the *Ratchakitchanubeksa,* or the *Royal Gazette,*[8] in 1858 and had it circulated among the members of the royal court as well as the general public.

The long-standing *Ratchakitchanubeksa* is regarded as the first Thai language journal proper, since it was published by Thais. It is still in existence today. The main objectives of the journal were to inform the people of important laws, decrees, announcements, and news within the royal court and throughout the country. It also gave commentaries on articles published in other journals by Dr. Bradley and another English missionary, Dr. Smith, who published three periodicals following Bradley: two in English, including *The Siam Weekly Advertiser* (1869), and one in Thai, the *Chotmaihet Sayam Samai* (1882–86). Through its objective reporting of news and airing of critical opinion, and through its prose writings and un-selfconscious periodical format, the *Ratchakitchanubeksa* also marked the beginning of modern Thai literature by relating directly to the reality of contemporary Thai society. Today, after having undergone many alterations, it serves only as the official means of promulgating laws and no longer attempts to provide intellectual stimulation.

Dramatic Literature and Prose Publications

Other contributions by Bradley to Thai literary publication included the *Thai Annual Almanac,* the *Bangkok Calendar,* the *Journal of the Siamese Embassy to London* (1857) and *Nirat London* (1861–65) by Mom Rachothai, *Kotmai Tra Sam Duang* (Laws of the Three Seals) published in 1863, and popular chronicles: the *Samkok* (*The Three Kingdoms,* a 1865 Thai translation by Chao Phraya Phra Khlang Hon of the well-known Chinese historical tale) and the *Rachathirat* (a chronical tale of the Mon people, 1880), which later became a popular story for the *lakhon phan thang* production in the Fifth

Reign (see Chap. 3). Bradley also published the first Thai primer, the *Chinda Mani,* in 1861 as a means of educating the people and increasing the rate of literacy. The primer had been written for the royal children in verse by Prince Wongsathiratsanit in 1849 under the royal command of King Rama III. It followed the original primer, the *Chinda Mani* of Phra Horathibodi, written during the reign of King Narai (1656–88) of Ayudhaya, but was simplified and modernized to suit the practical needs of King Mongkut's Bangkok period. The primer not only gives lessons in the Thai language and its usage, but also includes moral teachings as well, particularly on the subjects of duty and loyalty to the throne and to society.

Dr. Smith is another Western missionary who may be considered a significant contributor to the expansion of Thai drama through the publication of classical dramatic texts. Smith came to Siam as a young boy of thirteen during the reign of King Rama III. He later, through his excellent knowledge of both the Thai and English languages and close association with Phra Pin Klao, the second king and brother of King Mongkut, became his personal secretary. In 1865, Smith started a publishing house and began to print Christian writings and Buddhist sermons commissioned by Chao Phraya Thiphakorawong. He soon ventured into the publishing of periodicals and Thai secular literature. This included the great masterpiece, *Khun Chang Khun Phaen,* a long romance composed in verse by the poets in the court of Kings Rama II and Rama III, and in parts avowedly sensuous. He also published *Phra Aphaimani* by Sunthon Phu, a long poetic tale of adventure and romance, in which fantasy reaches the extremes of human imagination and passion. Both of these tales were incorporated into classical dance-drama during the reign of King Chulalongkorn in the modernized version of *lakhon nok* and *lakhon nai* called *lakhon phan thang* (to be discussed in detail in Chap. 3). They were published in short sequences and sold at one *salung* a piece.[9] Being exciting and romantic stories, they instantly became bestsellers. Smith gained both wealth and a questionable reputation among conservative Europeans for publishing such sensual and worldly literature. He was later prohibited by the English Consular Court from carrying on further publication. The work was, however, taken over by Thai publishers.

The publication of these dramatic works and tales from Thai and foreign chronicles helped to spread Thai literature to the common people outside the royal and aristocratic milieu. By the end of the reign of King Chulalongkorn, these romances and tales had become very popular and well known among the public, which explains the great success of the *lakhon phan thang* when it produced episodes from *Khun Chang Khun Phaen, Phra Aphaimani,* and *Rachathirat.* They provided exciting material for a phase of presenting both Thai classical and folk dance-drama. The classical form was mainly the *lakhon phan thang,* and the folk forms constituted the *hun krabok* (puppets on bamboo rods) and the *liké* (a modernized version of *lakhon nok* and *lakhon chatri*).

These Western missionaries, though unsuccessful in their primary religious endeavours, contributed both knowledge and technical experience to the sciences and humanities. Through their initiatives taken in journalism and literary publishing, Thai poetic prose and dramatic masterpieces became widely read by the people. It was through periodicals, both English and Thai, that social and political conditions and criticism were presented to a wider public for the first time in the history of Thai literature. Travelogues, news reports, critical essays, and scholarly commentaries and articles in these journals introduced the concepts of objectivity and realism to Thai writers.

King Mongkut's greatest achievement and contribution to Thai modern prose were his *Phra Ratchahatthalekha* (Personal letters), which were written to his ministers and advisors and set the tradition for later Thai monarchs, together with his *Phra Ratchaphongsawadan Chabap Phra Ratchahattha-lekha,* the royal manuscripts of Thai chronicles from the Sukhothai period to the reign of King Rama I in 1790. The latter is regarded as the first standard history of Siam.[10] His effort to compile and rewrite documents on Thai history, culture, archaeology, art, and language for educational purposes not only extended the horizon of Thai prose but also laid the first foundation stone for the institution of public education.[11] Prose writing began to flourish from this period onward and eventually assumed the dominant role in Thai literature. Sophistication in literary, political, and social criticism is still far from being attained in Thai journalism and prose literature. Nevertheless, this starting point, as modest as it was, deserves to be recorded as the origin of modern Thai literature.

REVIVAL OF ROYAL TRADITIONS, CEREMONIES, AND FESTIVITIES

Though King Mongkut was very keen on introducing the ways of the West, its scientific knowledge and technology, aspects which he realized were vital to the development of the country, his deep involvement in religious activities closely related to Thai culture and life style ingrained in him a great appreciation for the Thai cultural heritage, and thereby struck a harmonious balance with his eager interest in Western civilization. This Fourth Reign was therefore a period of synthesizing Western culture with Thai civilization.

One of King Mongkut's ideas was to propagate an atmosphere of grandeur and pomp to surround the Siamese monarchy in the eyes of the Thai as well as the foreigners, or more precisely the Westerners, who were accustomed to looking down on Asian monarchs, whom they sometimes labelled as "barbarian despots of the Orient."[12] The king started to revive many royal customs and the pageantry of the Ayudhaya period as described in the *Kot Monthienban* (Palatine Laws) of King Boromatrailokanat.[13] He must have also remembered from his childhood the glorious days during the reign of his father, King Rama II, when the royal court flourished in cultural, artistic, dramatic, and literary activities and the grandeur of the royal festivities and entertainment, such as those at his own tonsure ceremony, and other *ngan somphot* (celebrations). He therefore emphasized in his 1855 decree (see p. 61) permitting the performance of *lakhon* outside the Royal Palace that entertainment and festivity were attributes glorifying the country.[14]

King Mongkut also made a point of being present at all royal ceremonies, many of which he himself had revived, such as the *Triyampawai Tripawai* ceremony in which the Brahmans celebrated their New Year and swung the Giant Swing in front of Wat Suthat. King Mongkut with his royal children and consorts dressed in traditional costumes would ride on elephants in a grand procession.[15] King Chulalongkorn recalls how he, as a child, suffered from the chill of the cool season, being bare-chested and covered with perfumed powder. He adds, "The purpose of King Chom Klao [Mongkut] in riding on elephants in a grand procession was to engage anew in the customs and ceremonies as in the old days. To use the present expression, it could be said that he was *ee* [extremely enthusiastic, and fond of, royal ceremonies]."[16]

However, in his daily activities, King Mongkut concentrated on administrative work and religious activities. It should be noted that in the latter portion of his reign his habits changed in accordance with the introduction of Western architecture and altered ways of living in the Royal Palace. King Chulalongkorn describes the changes, made under Western influence, in the New Year banquet in Western style given to members of the royal family, high officials, diplomats, missionaries, leading merchants, and foreign dignitaries.

> In the reign of King Chom Klao Chao Yu Hua [Mongkut], the King sought examples of royal ceremonies which are in the *Kot Monthian Ban* to combine with new customs and established them, in condensed forms, as models. But concerning this banquet, which was originated from the *somphot* [celebration] to give a feast to the *luk khun* [judicial officials, high officials] and which appeared in many old royal ceremonies, such as the coronation, the King saw that the idea was the same as the *farang* [Western] banquet and thought it would be a good thing to experiment with it because it would include both the old and the new and would create unity among all who gathered there at the same time.[17]

In the morning, there was a religious ceremony to worship Phra Sayam Thewathirat (patron god of Siam) and other deities. A temporary outdoor theatre was set up in the Royal Palace for the Lakhon Luang troupe to perform various dances and short episodes of the *Ramakien* in the *boek rong* style (i.e., short prelude pieces)—such as "Phra Ram Entering the Garden of Phra Phirap" and "Narai Prap Nonthuk" (God Narai defeating the ogre Nonthuk).[18]

From these various accounts, we can see clearly how King Mongkut attempted to bridge the old and the new within the royal traditions and ceremonies. One of his very first decrees was to have all male courtiers wear upper garments and not to go bare-chested in the Royal Audience Hall and at official assemblies. It is recorded in the chronicles of the Fourth Reign.

> One day the royal officials were gathering together for the royal audience at the Royal Armoury Pavilion. At that time, there had not yet been the custom wearing a top garment to the audience. The King [Mongkut] then said, "People who do not wear shirts are like naked people. Their bodies may show skin diseases or sweat, all of which are very dirty. In other countries, which are great countries, of all languages, they all wear shirts [upper garments], except the Lawa [Mon-Khmer], Lao, and Chao Pa [jungle people], who do not have clothes as they are lowly human beings. But Siam is a great country. We know many customs and traditions, we should not follow the ancient customs of the primitives in the past. Let all of you wear shirts when you come to the Royal Audience Hall, every one of you." From then on all members of the royal family and royal officials wore at least shirts [jackets] in the royal audience.[19]

This new custom of dressing obviously came about under Western influence. During the previous reign, King Rama III allowed officials to wear top garments only in the cool season and was displeased to see anyone who wore them in warm weather or in the summer.[20]

THE RENAISSANCE IN COURT DANCE-DRAMA

Two of the most important steps taken by King Mongkut through the advice of his court were to revive the Khon Luang and Lakhon Luang troupes and their performances in the royal court and to officially permit private *lakhon* troupes to give public performances outside the Royal Palace after a long period of restriction and suppression during the reign of his half-brother, King Rama III. As mentioned earlier, in the previous reign dramatic activities within the Royal Palace were prohibited due to the religious piety of the king and his personal dislike of such frivolous entertainment. Furthermore, state affairs and warfare with the neighbouring countries of Burma, Vietnam, and the southern states and the threat of aggression from Western powers had preoccupied most of his time.

On the other hand, the private *lakhon* troupes patronized by other princes, princesses, and noblemen flourished outside the royal court in discretion. With the expansion and development of the *lakhon* outside the court all through the Third Reign, the situation was ripe for the revival of the Khon Luang and Lakhon Luang troupes when King Mongkut ascended the throne in 1851. As the country was officially open to contacts with the West, it became necessary to provide social activities within the royal court, with which to entertain foreign royal visitors.

The far-sighted king saw the importance of Siamese culture, especially the refined and highly cultivated arts of the royal court, as both political and social means to convince any Western aggressors of the rich heritage of the Siamese people, the stability and glory of the Siamese monarchy, and its political and social superiority of Siam over other neighbouring countries in the peninsula.

One authority on Thai history states,

> In their [Westerners'] eyes, King Mongkut propounded his theory in his inimitable style, the country and people of Asia were no better than animals and vegetables destined for human consumption, the Westerners considering themselves alone as human beings. Since in the policy of divided spheres of influence they had found a new way of satisfying their appetite without getting in each other's way, the Asian nations, unable any longer to rely for their safety on the mutual jealousies of these Western bullies, must turn to work instead on their vanity. In King Mongkut's opinion the aggression of a Western nation could only be halted by moral strictures from its equals, namely, other Western powers—hence his policy of bringing Siam, as it were, into the limelight, for if she remained tucked away in the far corner of the earth she would fall a sure prey to the dark deeds of one or the other of the greedy powers. The treaties of commerce and friendship with the West were only the first step of the policy which aimed at establishing contact through which if need be Siam could bring her grievances to the attentions of the civilized world.[21]

Dramatic and musical activities could therefore create a respectable image of a civilized, peaceful, culture-rich country in the eyes of the Western powers.

Moreover, on the practical and realistic side of the matter, since private *lakhon* troupes outside the court were becoming more active and popular in their indiscrete performances of the *lakhon phuying* (female court dance-drama) in the styles of royal *lakhon nai* and *lakhon nok,* the royal court would not only lose face if it remained silent and inactive on the matter. More realistically, the court was also in danger of suffering a drain of talented dancers, who continued to leave the royal court to teach in these private troupes. The traditional role and prestige of the royal court as the "great patron of the arts" would then be diminished.

In this new social atmosphere, and in the liberal attitude of the monarch towards dance and drama within the court, the royal *lakhon phuying* began its renaissance, first under the guidance of Princess Somanat, who began to train young female dancers and form a troupe of the *lakhon phuying* at court. Unfortunately, the princess died of a rather mysterious illness[22] before the troupe had an opportunity to perform before a royal audience.

The event that prompted the king to officially revive the Lakhon Luang troupe was the capture of two white elephants, Phra Sawet Wisutratana Kirini in 1853 and Phra Wimonratana Kirini the following year. To have two white elephants coming in quick succession into the reign at such an early stage (only the third and fourth years of his reign) was a sacred omen, predicting a "great and glorious" reign for this scholar-king, who had spent twenty-seven years leading an ascetic religious life and had reformed the rules and practices for Thai monks to restore them back to good order and high prestige.[23] This auspicious occasion presented members of the royal family and the court with the opportunity to encourage the new monarch to celebrate the acquisition of the white elephants in the grand style with all types of *mahorasop* (entertainment) as in the tradition of past kings. In the Royal Decree on the taxation of *khon, lakhon,* and other entertainment of 1861,[24] the justification was given for this revival of dramatic activities in that they were glorifying tributes to the monarchy. There was also an indirect criticism of King Rama III for having suppressed court dance-drama. An association between the absence of the Lakhon Luang troupe and white elephants in the Third Reign indicates clearly the political, religious, and social role of the royal *mahorasop* and its close relationship with the Siamese monarchy, which still continues to the present day, though having undergone some modern transformation.[25]

In the same Royal Decree, there is an explanation at the beginning on the subject of the restriction placed on the possession of the *lakhon phuying*. It was indeed exclusive to the royal court, and the Royal Decree criticizes the practice of past kings in recruiting young children by force for *lakhon* training in the royal court, which caused suffering to the people up to the point that they would hide their good-looking children or make them physically disabled by various clandestine means.[26] In this way King Mongkut was convinced that he should revive the Lakhon Luang troupe for the white elephant celebration, starting with the forming of a new royal dance troupe with dancers remaining from the court of King Rama II and girl dancers newly trained by Princess Somanat. Among these girl dancers there was one Khien, who was famous in the role of Inao and who later became Chao Chom Manda Khien, mother of Prince Narathip, founder of the Pridalai Theatre and *lakhon rong* in the reign of King Chulalongkorn. She was responsible for the training of the many greatly admired dancers during the Fifth Reign, and in particular those of the Lakhon Luang Narumit which developed into the *lakhon rong* of Prince Narathip.

In 1854, there was held the first *Phithi Khrop* (ceremony of initiation for *khon* and *lakhon* dancers) for this new royal dance troupe.[27] King Mongkut also had the text of the *Wai Khru* (invocation ceremony) edited and established it as the *Phra Tamra Khrop Khon Lakhon Chabap Luang* (royal standard text of the *khon* and *lakhon* initiation ceremony; see Appendix A on p. 89).[28] This occasion especially marked a "renaissance" in court dance-drama of the middle Bangkok period.[29]

As soon as the Lakhon Luang troupe was functioning again, other private troupes, out of fear of competing with the royal court, refrained from their dramatic activities. This caused great concern to the king. He therefore made another announcement in the following year, permitting and encouraging them to continue with their activities: to entertain the people and to glorify the country, without forgetting to remind them not to force children into training. He also promised to give his royal patronage and rewards to private troupes to come and perform in the Royal Palace. The main restriction concerning costumes, decorations, and ceremony imposed by King Mongkut was the use of *rat klao yot* (a special head-dress for a royal princess), enamelled decorations, gold trays and boxes (symbols of royal ranks), and the conch-shell in the *Bot Tham Khwan* (auspicious rite for royal children to pacify or please the *khwan,* the vital essence of an individual).[30]

From the Royal Decree of 1861, we also learn that King Rama II, when he was invested with the rank and title of Krom Phra Ratchawang Bowon, deputy king, started to train young girl dancers for the *lakhon phuying* in his palace. However, before the whole troupe was complete, he was crowned king after the death of his father. Prince Damrong elaborates further in his *Tamnan Lakhon Inao* that the *lakhon phuying* of King Rama II when still Prince Isarasunthon had to be discontinued when it became known to King Rama I infuriating him.[31] This incident reaffirms the restriction that the *lakhon phuying* be the property of the king only. Not even the Uparat (deputy king, or in some cases second king, such as Phra Pin Klao in the Fourth Reign) of the Bowon Palace, or the Palace of the Front, was allowed to have *lakhon phuying* right up to the reign of King Rama III. However, *lakhon phuying* was secretly performed in the Bowon court, as well as in private troupes outside the Royal Palace as mentioned earlier. There are contradicting reports in the Royal Decree of 1861 of King Mongkut and the *Tamnan Lakhon Inao* of Prince Damrong on this subject. In the Royal Decree, it is stated, "In the reign of Phra Phuttha Loetla Naphalai [Rama II], the Krom Phra Ratchawang Bowon later trained *lakhon phuying* and *ngiu phuying* [female Chinese opera], which became widely known and is so today."[32] Prince Damrong denied this in saying, "But in the Second Reign, the dance form and dramatic texts which the king newly created at that time were performed only by the Lakhon Luang [of the royal court]. No other persons dared to imitate the royal dance troupe. The princes of different *krom,* for example, Krom Phra Ratchawang Bowon, apparently trained only the *ngiu phuying.*"[33]

In the same Royal Decree of 1861, King Mongkut, after allowing *lakhon* to be freely performed, made one reservation: he limited the use of the royal dramatic texts of the *Ramakien, Inao,* and *Unarut* exclusively to the Lakhon Luang troupe as they were created by kings, royal princes, and princesses and had been performed traditionally in the royal court by the *lakhon khang nai* (dance-drama of the Inner Court) from Ayudhaya times to his own reign. It was known to King Mongkut that other private troupes had been secretly performing them. He therefore made this public decree to discontinue the activity, thus making it a punishable act to imitate the king. However, the king did not prescribe any forms of punishment. It is interesting to note that he grouped the use of these dramatic texts along with other royal prerogatives, such as rhino horns, cardamom, gamboge, tin, pepper, opium, and gambling. His justification of the restriction was given as follows:

A Royal Decree [permitting the performance of *lakhon phuying* of the Year of the Tiger, in the *cho sok* (1854)]. At present, royal officials, high and low, in the city and provinces, are training more *lakhon phuying,* with two or three troupes in addition. Some are big troupes, some send only the *nai rong* [leading male dancers, masters of troupes] and *nang ek* [leading female dancers, performing the roles of heroine] to join others in a *kumpanni* [company] as is known to all. Then in the first month, Year of the Snake, *nopha sok* [1857], there was a royal celebration of Buddha images at Prathumwan. The King gave his royal explanation, concerning the [*lakhon*] tradition, to royal officials that the *lakhon* of *Ramakien* and *Unarut* which are stories of the incarnation of God Narai [Vishnu] had been performed by and trained for by the Lakhon Luang of the kings from the time of the old capital of Ayudhaya onward. But the *Lakhon Inao* had been that of the *chao fa* [royal princes and princesses born of queens] and *phra ong chao* [children of royal consorts] who were royal children of the Inner Court, and who were trained to perform it in the old days. In the reign of King Phra Phuttha Yotfa Chulalok [Rama I], at the beginning of the reign, the King ordered the training of the *lakhon khang nai* to be carried out, to perform the *Ramakien* and *Unarut* as in the past tradition. Later, he ordered them to train [dancers] for the performance of *Inao* and other stories. Then at the beginning of the reign of King Phra Phuttha Loetla Naphalai [Rama II], the King trained dancers for the *Lakhon Inao* and other stories. Later, he considered that the *Ramakien* was a story about the incarnation of God Narai, which all kings had performed previously. Even if he did not much favour it, it should be performed so as not to break with the royal tradition. He therefore made a new adaptation of the *Ramakien* and trained the *lakhon khang nai* to perform the *Ramakien* for the royal court. Since he had heard the words of his royal father [King Rama I] in the past and had remembered them, he trained the *Lakhon Ramakien* following the tradition of past kings, in order to preserve royal honour in keeping the *lakhon* of the incarnation of God Narai as the Lakhon Luang. . . .

The King [Mongkut] therefore commanded that *lakhon* performances of the *Ramakien, Inao, Unarut,* as [in the past] they had been performed only for *ngan luang* [royal occasions], should be *khong tong ham* [royal prerogatives] as rhino horns, elephant tusks, wild cardamom, cardamom, gamboge, tin, pepper,[34] and the promoting of cockfights, bird-fanciers' contests, fighting-fish contests, and other gambling, and the purchase, sale, and smoking of opium, which have been *khong tong ham* in this land, and will all henceforth be so.[35]

With this official confirmation of the exclusive nature of these plays, the sacredness of *lakhon khang nai* to the royal court is demonstrated. The dramas, as well as their performance, show close association with the Thai monarchy, with the Hinduistic concept of the *deva-raja,* the god-king, as an incarnation of Vishnu, and, in particular, with the identification of the Chakri dynasty of the Ratanakosin era with the cult of Rama, Narai (Vishnu) Incarnate. It also made clear a distinction between *lakhon nai* and *lakhon nok.* This tradition continued up to the Revolution of 1932, after which the absolute monarchy lost its sanctity and power to the new democratic system, which became a constitutional monarchy. Consequently *lakhon khang nai,* or *lakhon nai,* was no longer a high and sacred property of the king, or a royal prerogative. It became one of the treasures that belong to the people under the supervision of the Krom Silapakon established in 1933.

The new freedom granted by King Mongkut and his revival of court entertainment led to another period of efflorescence in dance, drama, and music. The king also reorganized the different departments which were responsible for royal entertainment, namely, the Krom Khon (Khon Department), Krom Hun (Department of Royal Puppetry), Krom Hok Khamen Ram Khom (Acrobatics and Lantern Dance Department), Krom Piphat (Department of Royal Orchestra), and Krom Mahorasop (Royal Entertainment Department).[36]

With *lakhon phuying* no longer restricted to the royal court, most dance troupes began to use female dancers in all types of dance-drama. Thus, they were found not only in the *lakhon nai* style, but also in *lakhon nok, lakhon khaek* (Malay dance-drama in *makyong* style, with Thai dialogue),[37] and later in *lakhon chatri* as well.

Lakhon chatri, in particular, from its origin as the *nora chatri* of the south up to this Fourth Reign, had been exclusively an all male dance-drama. The *nora chatri* dance troupe was brought up to Thonburi by King Taksin in 1769 and later to Bangkok in 1844 during the reign of King Rama III. After they settled down permanently in Bangkok on land granted by the king at Tambon Sanam Khwai (now Lan Luang Street and Nang Loeng Market), the *nora chatri* troupes began to adopt and adapt the style of *lakhon nok* and gradually develop it into *lakhon chatri,* first with an all male cast and then later, during the reign of King Mongkut, with a mixed cast. At present, *lakhon chatri* is performed by female dancers, with the exception that the roles of clowns, ogres, and animal characters are still performed by men comedians. The most famous *lakhon chatri* troupes during the Fourth Reign were Nai Nu, performing in the traditional style of Nakhon Sithammarat with a mixed cast, larger than that of the *nora chatri,* and the Lakhon Chatri Khong Luang (of the royal court), which was trained at Nakhon Sithammarat by Princess Patthamarat, daughter of Krom Phra Ratchawang Bowon Surasinghanat (the second king in the reign of King Rama I). It was later presented to King Mongkut, and hence became another Lakhon Luang troupe.[38] The *khon* troupes also began to train in *lakhon.* Some merely incorporated *lakhon phuying* and some completely changed their performances to *lakhon phuying.* Some patrons who had women *mahori* orchestras (consisting mostly of string instruments) also developed their troupes into *lakhon phuying* companies.

It is also recorded in the Royal Decree of 1861 that Chao Phraya Sisuriya-wong Samantaphong Phisutha Maha Burutratanodom "Samuha Phra Kala-hom" (Minister of Defence) greatly supported the king in his promotion of *lakhon phuying* for the practical reason that girls and women, being the weaker sex, were by tradition not registered in groups (*sak mai mu;* lit., tattooed with the number of the group to which they belonged under the supervision of a master) and therefore were not liable for royal service. Being *nang lakhon* (dancers, actresses) would enable them to make a living and earn a considerable income. Whereas men, according to the Chao Phraya, were unsuitable for this profession, since they would take the opportunity of becoming dancers to avoid corvée labour, military service, or entering other scheduled artisan professions which would be useful to the country. The king agreed with the Chao Phraya and commanded that his arguments be recorded in the decree.[39]

Economically speaking, the maintenance expenses of a *lakhon phuying* troupe were lower than that of *lakhon phuchai* (male dance-drama), the super-vision of women easier, and the physical attraction of female dancers greater, hence more profitable. Moreover, a large aristocratic and middle-class house-hold would normally have a large number of girls and women dependants, who would in any case have been helping with making costumes, doing the make-up, stage work, singing, and playing music. Being already available and more obedient and submissive, they were easier to train as dancers. The income from the performances would help to pay off daily household expenses. For these practical reasons, most troupes would eventually present only female dancers, since they were in greater demand, particularly in gambling halls to attract customers. This phenomenon brought a large increase in income for both the proprietors of the gambling halls and dance troupes, which led to the promulgation of the decree in 1861, which explained the reasons for the taxation of all types of *mahorasop*. However, according to Prince Damrong, the official decree on taxation of *lakhon* had been announced two years earlier in 1859.[40] The decree of 1861 may have been issued as a justification. (The details of the rates of taxation for each type of *mahorasop* are given in Appendix B to this chapter.)

The decree of King Mongkut of 1861 led to a new development in Thai dance-drama in that the *lakhon,* which had traditionally been associated with social status or had been a status symbol of the aristocrats and noblemen, moved towards being a commercial profession even among the private troupes under the patronage of the members of the royal family and high royal officials, since they were a means to increase the family income of its patrons. The entertainment taxation did not much affect them at the beginning, since they could add it on to the admission charge for any performance. The highest amount of entertainment tax income 4,400 baht per year was recorded during the reign of King Mongkut, and revenues averaged 36,000 baht per year during the reign of King Chulalongkorn.[41] These figures were almost eight times the original revenue. In 1892 King Chulalongkorn revised the decree and called this category of taxation the entertainment revenue (*akon mahorasop*) and put it under the direct control of the royal government instead of going through the Chinese custom and tax collectors as in the previous reigns.[42] With the new addition to the types of taxable *mahorasop* and the revision of the tax rates, the *mahorasop* tax income increased to 167,828 baht per year in 1904.[43]

The change in the nature of *lakhon* through its close association with gambling circles caused both economic prosperity and cultural decline to the dance form. As the gambling halls gained more customers due to the *lakhon* entertainment attraction, the *lakhon* troupes prospered accordingly. Later, in the reign of King Chulalongkorn, it was the policy of the king to abolish gambling altogether, starting in 1888, through a gradual process of illegalization, so as not to affect the Chinese community. Gambling was restricted to only 76 *tambon* (districts) and later to the 13 *tambon* where Chinese earned their living from it. The tax income from gambling and the entertainment associated with it therefore decreased, as the gambling halls diminished in number and no longer could afford to hire *lakhon* performers. Consequently, many *lakhon* troupes were forced out of business, leading to its decline during the Fifth Reign. Hence, another decree was promulgated by King Chulalongkorn in 1907, exempting *mahorasop* from tax when not connected with gambling halls. When King Vajiravudh, Rama VI abolished all gambling in 1917, all entertainment taxes were thereby suspended.[44] As for the taxation on gambling during the Fourth and Fifth Reigns, see Appendix C.

From the point of view of society, it is interesting to note the change in the social function of the *mahorasop* at the beginning of this so-called "age of modernization" starting in the reign of King Mongkut (a subject which will be further discussed in Chapters 3 and 4). Another important aspect in this new development is the role of the Chinese in their association with *lakhon* as the proprietors of gambling halls, clients, and the *mahorasop* tax collectors. It was the Chinese who introduced all the types of gambling into Siam, including the *huai, thua, po, bia,* and they made a living from them. Tax collection was also controlled by the Chinese until the reign of King Chulalongkorn.[45] In such a non-respectable environment as the gambling hall, the social status and the profession of *nang lakhon* (female dancers), which had always been regarded with some traditional prejudice as being an unacceptable profession for women of good families (with the exception of the secluded court dancers and those under princely and noble patronage), was further degraded and became comparable to cabaret or casino dancers.

As to the development of dramatic literature during the reign of King Mongkut, there was a new trend in creating separate playscripts for individual productions following the practice of King Rama II, who introduced this method for the first time in the history of Thai dance-drama. Traditionally, each play had been memorized or written in a long continuous sequence to be recited or read, and later to be performed by extracting certain sequences from the whole text. King Rama II set a new tradition in his adaptation of the *Ramakien* and his composition of the *Inao* and *lakhon nok* in selecting only the parts that were suitable for dramatic performance. However, his royal manuscripts were restricted only to the Lakhon Luang and Khon Luang. Other private troupes outside the court continued to use the traditional method and dramatic texts handed down from the time of Ayudhaya, either through memorization or in written form. During the reign of King Rama III, private troupes began secretly to use the playscripts of King Rama II and adopt his method of adapting and modernizing dramatic texts by condensing and dramatizing certain selected parts for not only enhanced dramatic effect, but also to suit practical time limits of performance. Plays so edited include the works of Krom Phra Ratchawang Bowon Mahasakdipholasep, *Ramakien* ("Episode of the Hanuman Volunteers"), *Kaki, Phra Lo,* and *Khun Chang Khun Phaen;* and those of Prince Phuwanetnarinrit, *Suwannahong, Nang Kaeo Na Ma,* and *Nang Kula.* This practice became more widespread during the reign of King Mongkut after the promulgation of the Decree of 1855, granting freedom to all *lakhon* performances. In competing with one another, these *lakhon* troupes created many new plays with exciting and romantic stories, plots, and characters to attract audiences. Consequently, dramatic literature flourished both within and outside the royal court.[46]

King Mongkut himself, though more adept in prose, proved his poetic ability in his adaptation of the *Ramakien* in the episode of "Phra Ram Doen Dong" (King Rama wandering in the forest). This particular episode, written in 4 *smut thai* books and consisting of 1,664 *kham klon,*[47] is a symbolic play representing his own renunciation of worldly existence and kingship to make way for the crowning of his half-brother, King Rama III, and to lead a long period of religious asceticism as a Buddhist monk helping him to prepare for his eventual succession to the throne as the rightful heir to his father King Rama II after the death of Rama III.[48] King Mongkut also recomposed the episode of "Narai Prap Nonthuk" (God Narai defeating the ogre Nonthuk) from the *Ramakien* to be performed as a separate *bot boek rong* (opening or prelude dance piece). This episode, which leads to the whole story of the *Ramakien,* depicts the triumph of good over evil, the birth-origin of Thosakan, the villain in the *Ramakien,* and the challenge of Nonthuk to the god Narai to fight with him on earth not as a god but as a human being. It became a favourite *boek rong* dance. The most important part in it is the dance of the god Narai disguised as a woman. The dance goes through all the basic steps and movements, which are imitated by Nonthuk. In the final movement of the *Nakha Muan Hang Wong* (Serpent curling its tail), Narai duly points his index finger at his leg, and Nonthuk, in imitating Narai, points his own deadly "diamond finger" at his leg and falls. This particular dance of Narai, an equivalent of the dance of Siva-Nataraj, which outlines the basic dance movements and gestures of Indian classical dance, is regarded as a *ram mae bot* (dance of basic movements) of Siamese classical dance. Instead of the god Siva the Siamese place Narai (Vishnu) in this episode as the "master of the dance." This indicates the greater influence of the cult of Vishnu over the cult of Siva in the history of Siamese civilization. It is necessary to emphasize here also that among the stories concerning the incarnations of Vishnu, the story of Rama and the cult of Rama in its association with the Thai monarchy are the most influential, whereas the cult of Krishna and recourse to *Mahabharata* have had very little importance in Thai culture, religious beliefs, customs, tradition, art, and literature.

Among other minor dramatic texts of King Mongkut are

1) *Bot boek rong* (opening dance piece): *Ramakien* ("Episode of Phra Ram entering the garden of the ogre Phirap"). Another dance of good conquering evil.

2) *Rabam boek rong* (opening dance): *Ram Ton Mai Thong Ngun* (Dance of gold and silver trees, a tribute to the king) and *Bot Phra Rusi* (The hermit).

3) *Lakhon nai* (dance-drama of the Inner Court, an adaptation of the episode of Unakan in the *Inao.*

4) A new dance-drama: *Yukhanlikhit,* based on a Persian tale, written in the style of *Inao.* Some authorities said that it was the work of King Rama II, but Prince Damrong, judging from its poetic style, thought it might have been the work of poets who helped create the texts of King Rama I.[49]

In comparing the dramatic texts of King Rama I and King Mongkut in the episode of "Narai Prap Nonthuk" in the *Ramakien,* it is quite clear that King Mongkut maintained most of the essential texts, condensed only a few sections or lines and omitted some minor parts for more dramatic effect and economy of performance time. The *bot boek rong* of the episode of "Narai Prap Nonthuk," in particular, shows the vivid dramatization of actions in rapid succession towards the end of the dance piece and a moralistic conclusion in the finale. There are also some changes in the musical tunes. The overall aspects of the adaptations are those of rapidity, unity, and conciseness. His poetic refinement of the original text of Rama I, though effective in many places, does not equal that of King Rama II in its eloquence, literary imagery, or dramatic sophistication.

As mentioned earlier, there were many new plays written during King Mongkut's reign. Among the more unique ones are *Aphainurat* of Sunthon Phu and *Maniphichai,* assumed to be the work of Prince Phuwanetnarinrit. Sunthon Phu, after his exile and Buddhist ordination, came under the patronage of Prince Isaretrangsan and Princess Apsonsuda, daughter of King Rama III. Prince Isaretrangsan later became Phra Pin Klao, the second king in the reign of King Mongkut. He granted Sunthon Phu the title of Phra Sunthonwohan, chief of scribes of the Palace of the Front. Sunthon Phu wrote *Aphainurat* in two playscripts for Princess Duangprapha, daughter of Phra Pin Klao. The play is not as popular as his *Phra Aphaimani* and is not known to have been performed in a later period. Similarly, *Maniphichai* by Prince Phuwanetnarinrit was not performed by other theatre troupes in this reign, whereas his *Suwannahong* enjoyed great popularity.

The entertainment tax caused a new type of *lakhon nok* plays to be developed, imitating the story of the *Ramakien*. Since the tax on the *Ramakien* performance was the highest (20 baht per day), compared to the *lakhon nok* tax of only 2 baht per day, many new *lakhon nok* plays were written with *Ramakien*-like characters (specifically ogres and monkeys) and plots, such as the *Thip Sangwan* (Magic necklace) and the episode of King Sophin abducting Nang Thep Lila in *Khawi.*

Other popular *lakhon nok* consisted of episodes taken from *Phra Aphaimani, Laksanawong,* and *Chanthakhorop* by Sunthon Phu, and *Phra Samut* (anonymous). They were performed by women. There was also the dramatization of extracts from the *sepha,* for mixed casts, such as the episodes of Khun Chang assisting in the wedding of Phra Wai in *Khun Chang Khun Phaen.*[50]

This Fourth Reign also produced a unique woman dramatist, Khun Suwan, who was regarded to be insane by her contemporaries, but who is now praised by Thai modern scholars for her ingenuity as a witty satirist-poetess. Her two unusual pieces of dramatic literature are *Phra Malé Thé Thai* and *Unarut Roi Ruang.* Both are parodies of Thai classical romance, similar to *Raden Landai* of Phra Mahamontri in the Third Reign, but more absurd in the language, rhymes, and plots. While maintaining the form and structure of *lakhon nai,* the stories are comic and confusing. The alliterations are abundant but senseless, especially in *Phra Malé Thé Thai.* The unintelligible rhyming sounds produce instant comic effects in their absurdity, yet readers are able to follow the ideas and plots. *Unarut Roi Ruang* (A hundred stories of Unarut), as its title indicates, is a conglomeration of adventure stories in illogical sequence. The ingenious creativity, sense of humour, and witticism of Khun Suwan in these parodies and in *Mom Pet Sawan,* a poem criticizing lesbian practices in the royal court, are evidence of Thai women's critical minds and freedom of expression (in satirizing royal dramatic texts and criticizing the royal court). Examples of this have enjoyed a prolonged success in the world of Thai literature from the early history of Siam to the present (the earliest example being Nang Nophamat, allegedly a consort of a Sukhothai king).

The masters and dancers of major troupes in the Fourth Reign inherited both an art, the skill of dancing *khon* and *lakhon,* and also theatrical appurtenances and concrete artistic materials, such as musical instruments and costumes, from forerunners in the Second and Third Reigns. They, in turn, maintained the tradition of handing the heritage down to the next generation in the Fifth Reign. To name a few significant cases:

1) The Prince Mahesuan Siwawilat Troupe (Fourth Reign) inherited many leading dance teachers from the Prince Rakronaret Troupe (Third Reign). (Prince Rakronnaret, or Prince Kraison, was executed in 1848 for his immoral relationships with his dancers and for his plot to usurp the throne.)
2) The Princess Duangphrapha Troupe had dance teachers in *lakhon nai* and *lakhon nok* from the Second Reign and performed through the next reign of King Chulalongkorn (Fifth Reign).
3) The Somdet Chao Phraya Borom Maha Sisuriyawong Troupe was formed with dancers left from the Chao Phraya Bodindecha Troupe (Third Reign) and performed in the style of the Lakhon Luang troupe of the Second Reign.

The troupes of Prince Mahesuan and Somdet Chao Phraya were both major ones and were presented to the royal court of King Mongkut. Leading dancers, both male and female, of many other troupes became dance teachers in the royal court of King Chulalongkorn or in private troupes outside the court during his reign.[51]

Other individual dancers, who joined together occasionally in a *lakhon kumpani* (company) to perform in the palaces and villas of the aristocratic members of the *kumpani,* continued also to form major troupes in the Fifth Reign. Each of these *kumpani* dancers had their own singers and assistants. They, together with the *piphat* (orchestra) provided by the owner of the house, formed a temporary theatre on location. The costumes of the *lakhon kumpani* were less elaborate, which possibly led to a new style of costume in the next reign, particularly in *lakhon phan thang* and *lakhon rong.*

It is necessary to emphasize here that the availability of the court dance-drama to the general public through private troupes outside the royal court during the reign of King Rama III, the re-emergence, comparable to a renaissance in the royal court of dramatic entertainment under the support and patronization of King Mongkut, and the new creations and adaptations of dramatic literature during both reigns formed a broad and firm foundation for the forthcoming "age of Westernization and modernization" during the reign of King Chulalongkorn, in which a new generation of the elite, the future leaders of modern Siam, who had been intellectually and emotionally prepared by the future-oriented generation of King Mongkut, were readily receptive to new ideas, systems, methods, and experiments in the "way of the West" in all aspects of society and culture. While new avenues for challenging innovation were opened to these enthusiastic young aristocrats, the deeply rooted traditional cultural heritage persisted through a continual process of transformation at the well-trained hands of creative artists and dramatists.

Appendix A

Copy of the Royal Command in the Fourth Reign Concerning the Invocation Ceremony of the Teachers of the Royal *Lakhon* Troupe in the Year of the Tiger (1854)[52]

Phraya Bamroephak has received the royal command that the *Mom Lakhon* [king's consorts who were *lakhon* dancers] in the Royal Palace will come out to perform the ceremony of *Khrop Wai Khru Lakhon* [Initiation of dancers and invocation to the dance teachers of *lakhon*] at the raised platform of Dusit Mahaprasat Hall, and that seven monks will chant the Buddhist prayers at the Thim Dap Khot site in the palace on Wednesday, the 14th day of the waning moon, the fifth month, in the afternoon. On the next day, Thursday, the first day of the rising moon, sixth month, in the morning, after the monks have taken their meal, the [dance] teachers will initiate the *Mom Lakhon* by putting over their heads the sacred masks and head-dresses: that of the Bharata Rishi,[53] Phra Phirap,[54] and the *soet* head-dress of *nora chatri*.[55]

The rest of the text describes in detail the preparation and arrangement of the ceremony, not the ceremony itself.

There is a second version of the text with the detail of the ceremony in Dhanit Yupho, *Silapa Lakhon Ram,* pp. 309–22. This text is said to have been used as the royal standard text of the initiation of *khon* and *lakhon* dancers (*Phra Tamra Khrop Khon Lakhon Chabap Luang*). According to Dhanit Yupho, the text may have been collected and edited by a group of teachers and scholars and presented to King Mongkut for his approval. Since the style of writing is different from that of the king, Dhanit Yupho did not believe that King Mongkut had actually revised the text himself.[56] In the Sixth Reign, King Vajiravudh had this text revised for the grand ceremony of the initiation of the royal dancers and musicians. He also included among the collection of *khon* masks in the ceremony masks of characters taken from the *Ramayana* of Valmiki, which had not appeared in the ceremony before, namely, Khun Prahat, Chomphumali, and Chomphu, the bear-king.[57]

APPENDIX B

Rates of Taxation on *Mahorasop* in the Royal Decree of King Mongkut (1859)[58]

1. *Lakhon nai* performed by *lakhon rong yai* (big theatres or troupes)
   Ramakien   1 day and 1 evening, or 1 day

                                                tax rate 20 baht

   Inao   1 day and 1 evening, or 1 day   16 baht

   Unarut   1 day and 1 evening, or 1 day   12 baht

   (*Later, in the Royal Decree of 1861, these three plays were restricted to the Lakhon Luang.)

2. *Lakhon nok*
   kumpani (company), i.e., selected dancers joined together in a
      company   1 day   4 baht
   ordinary *lakhon* in *ngan plik* (individual occasions)
                            1 day and 1 evening   3 baht
                            1 day   3 baht
                            1 evening   1 baht
   lakhon in *ngan mao* (charged as a whole)
                            1 day and 1 evening   1.50 baht
                            1 day   1 baht
                            1 evening   .50 baht
   Exceptions: The Lakhon Luang and *lakhon* recruited for the *ngan luang* (royal occasions) were tax-exempted.

3. Other entertainment
   khon   1 day   4 baht
   lakhon na cho nang (dance-drama performed in front of the screen of shadow-play), performing the *Ramakien* with ten dancers
        and over   1 evening   20 baht
   lakhon na cho nang with fewer than ten dancers   2.50 baht
   lakhon chatri and *lakhon khaek* (Malay dance-drama) 1 day .50 baht
   phleng (songs)   1 day   1 baht
   khaen (northeastern panpipes), *mon ram* (Mon dance), *thawai ram* (Thawai dance)   1.50 baht
   klong yao (long drums)   1 day   12.5 satang or 1 fuang
   hun thai (Thai puppets)   1 day   1 baht
   nang thai (Thai shadow-play)   1 evening   .50 baht
   ngiu (Chinese opera)   1 day   4 baht
   hun chin (Chinese puppets) 1 day   1 baht
   nang chin (Chinese shadow-play) 1 day   .50 baht

Additional Categories in the Revised Rates of Taxation on the *Mahorasop* **in the Reign of King Chulalongkorn (1892)**[59]

1. *Lakhon chatri* imitating *lakhon nok*   1 day   4 baht
   (This addition affirms the fact that *lakhon chatri* later adopted the style of *lakhon nok* as it appears today.)

2. *Nang talung*   1 evening   .50 baht
   (There is no mention of *nang talung* until this reign. It is assumed therefore that this type of shadow-play was introduced from the south into Bangkok during the reign of King Chulalongkorn.)[60]

3. *Sakkawa* (improvised poetry contests between two or more persons)
                                          1 evening   1 baht

4. *Sepha* (recital or narration of dramatic stories such as *Khun Chang Khun Phaen*)   1 evening   .50 baht

5. *Liké* (folk dance-drama)   1 evening   2 baht
   (another type of folk dance-drama which originated during this reign.)[61]

6. *Piphat,* or *mahori* orchestra, or *klong khaek khruang yai* (Malay drums with a large orchestra)   1 day   1 baht

7. *Piphat,* or *mahori* orchestra, or *klong khaek khruang lek* (Malay drums with a small orchestra)   1 day   .50 baht

8. *Cham uat suat sop* (comedians chanting mock prayers for the dead)
                                          1 evening   2 baht

APPENDIX C

A Note on Gambling and its Taxation in the Fourth and Fifth Reigns

It is explained in the chronicles and *Phra Ratchaprarop* (Royal pronouncements) of King Chulalongkorn on the abolition of gambling that the Chinese had brought *thua, po, huai,* and the like into Siam from the Ayudhaya period. They became widespread in the Ratanakosin period. The royal government in the beginning collected *kha thamnian* (duty) from the owners of the *bon kan phanan* (gambling houses) by way of allowing some middlemen (Chinese) to hold a monopoly over the tax collection (*phuk khat akon*) for each town throughout the country (i.e., the collectors would give the government a lump sum each year, then they would subsequently be free to gain as much profit as they could). These collections were called *akon bon bia* (tax on gambling houses). Each town had a *nai akon* (Chinese tax collector). Bangkok was divided up among many *nai akon* according to district. In the Third Reign, the total annual collection was as high as 400,000 baht.

In the Fourth Reign, due to the trade agreement with foreigners, chiefly with Western countries, many tax monopolies had to be discontinued, resulting in a fall in state revenues. King Mongkut then issued the Royal Decree on the Taxation on Gambling in addition to the *akon bon bia* among many other new taxes. The government was able then to gain as mush as 500,000 baht per year from this particular area. However, King Mongkut later realized the ill effects of gambling on the whole population, after his visit to Phetchaburi and Ayudhaya, where he saw how the people indulged in gambling and became poorer. He then abolished gambling in these two cities, while other cities were allowed to continue the practice.

In the Fifth Reign, due to a great increase in gambling and crime connected with gambling houses, Prince Damrong, then Minister of Interior, proposed to the king that gambling be abolished in Nakhon Sithammarat and Chumphon. The king gave his total support and ordered further restraint on gambling in other cities as well. In 1888, gambling was restricted to only 76 *tambon* (districts), where Chinese earned their living from it. The numbers of gambling centres were gradually reduced and were finally abolished altogether during the Sixth Reign in 1917.[62]

Chapter III
Modern Transformations in
Thai Dance-drama

The Reign of King Chulalongkorn, Rama V

Under the influences of the West, the social, political, and cultural modernization introduced by King Chulalongkorn had great impact on the development and transformation of Thai drama and the theatrical milieu, both classical and folk. Prince Damrong states,

> In examining the historical development of *kan len lakhon* [dance-drama performance], the Fifth Reign [i.e., King Chulalongkorn's reign] should be considered to contain the turning point of the *kan len lakhon ram* [dance-drama performance; *ram,* a dance], since that reign lasted as long as forty-two years. At the beginning of the reign, *kan len lakhon ram* was widespread. . . . But later, when all the affairs in Thailand changed because of the progress and prosperity of the country, *kan len lakhon* also changed for various reasons.[1]

The writer wishes to examine here the changes that took place in the world of theatre and drama in Thailand within this span of forty-two years in terms of three aspects:

1) The revival and continuation of traditional dance, namely, *khon* and *lakhon* of all types, and the modern adaptations of traditional dramatic literature.
2) The growth and modern transformation of dance-drama and the new creations of dramatic literature.
3) The introduction of a new form of dramatic literature and theatre under Western influence.

Since the subjects of modernization of dramatic techniques, theatre arts, and theatre construction will be dealt with in detail in later chapters, the writer will concentrate here only on the dramatic tradition, its performance, and its literature.

REVIVAL AND CONTINUATION OF TRADITIONAL DANCE-DRAMA

During the first five years of the Fifth Reign (1868–1873) under the powerful direction and supervision of Somdet Chao Phraya Borom Maha Sisuriyawong, the regent, King Chulalongkorn did not have much freedom in state administration or in his private life for that matter. This is revealed in his numerous personal writings reflecting upon this period of frustration and conflict between the old power group under the regent and the new modern elite led by the king.[2] In the *Phra Rachanukit* (Personal activities of the king), during the first period, the king had to submit to the personal daily schedule of the Inner Court (Fai Nai) in the pattern of King Rama III, which was imposed on him by Thao Chao Chom Manda Ung during the Third Reign, and to the activities of the Outer Court (Fai Na), which was supervised by Prince Bamrapporapak.[3] It was after his trip to Singapore and Batavia that the king revised many customs of the Inner and Outer Courts.[4] After the coronation ceremony marking the king's assumption of full royal power (he had been a minor at the time of his succession) in 1873, he was able to gain full control of his administration and of the royal court and succeeded in introducing new political and administrative institutions which provided a firm foundation for modern Siam.

Revival and Modernization of the Royal Court Dance-drama

The cultural activities within the royal court during this early period followed the tradition of the previous reign. All dancers belonging to the Khon Luang and Lakhon Luang troupes were those remaining from the Second, Third, and Fourth Reigns. When there were royal grand occasions (*mahorasop*), these former dancers would be commissioned to perform in the traditional style of King Rama II. The first royal celebration in the Fifth Reign was to mark the acquisition of two royal elephants[5] in 1870. In the first evening, there was a performance by the Lakhon Luang at the Rong Lakhon (Royal Theatre) behind the Temple of the Emerald Buddha. During the same performance, there was also a comic *rabam,* the "Rain-making Dance of Orachun, Mekkhala, and Ramasun."[6] The text of the *rabam* was composed by the king himself during the Fourth Reign while he was still crown prince and living at Suan Kulap Palace. It was said that the performance was very funny, but unfortunately the manuscript has not been found. Fragments of it have been recalled from memory by some of the dancers.[7] The dancers were all male comedians selected from the royal troupes of the Second and Third Reigns.[8] On the next day, the king asked the royal Lakhon Phuying (female dance troupe) of the Second Reign to perform *Sangthong,*[9] with dancers from the Lakhon Luang of the Fourth Reign as substitutes and in minor characters.

In 1872, when another white elephant (later named Phra Sawet Suwapha-phan as a royal elephant) was captured in Muang Suwannaphum and was presented to the king, he held a *Somphot Chang Phuak* (Celebration of a

White Elephant) with the traditional Lakhon Luang performing the *Inao* by the dancers of the Fourth Reign. This Lakhon Luang troupe of the former reign, however, performed only for the *Somphot Chang Phuak* and not for other ceremonies or occasions, such as the *Sokan* (Royal Tonsure Ceremony) of royal children, where other *lakhon* troupes were commissioned to perform the *lakhon* of Phraya Ratchasuphawadi (later Chao Phraya Mahintharasakdithamrong, producer-director-owner of the Prince Theatre) and that of Phra Intharathep (later Phraya Phichaisongkhram).[10]

During the first thirteen years of the Fifth Reign, there was no training of a new troupe of Lakhon Luang dancers. According to Dhanit Yupho, "In a period when a king had many other important administrative duties, such as in the Fifth Reign, he would delegate to other senior members of the royal family or high officials the supervision [of the entertainment activities of the royal court] for him,"[11] and

> The reign of King Chulalongkorn was longer than any other reign, and there were many events and changes, both in state affairs and in the area of art and culture, particularly in the art of dancing *khon* and *lakhon*. The king, though a *khattiya kawi* [royal poet] who had written beautiful and lyrical *kap, klon, khlong,* and *chan* poetry, had composed very few *bot rabam* [texts for dance] and *bot lakhon* [texts for a *lakhon*], for example, *Ngo Pa* [a *lakhon*]. In the field of *lakhon,* it seems that the king preferred to support other members of the royal family and private individuals to set up their own troupes. As it happened, when new troupes were formed, the king would encourage them, for example, by attending the performances at their theatres or commissioning them to perform in the Royal Palace. Thus, during this reign, there were many famous *lakhon* theatres.[12]

In the opinion of this writer, it seems that this intelligent monarch, in supporting and encouraging both the former dancers of the previous reigns and those of private troupes, was able to create a sense of unity within the circle of artist-aristocrats and members of the royal court, while at the same time winning their respect, devotion, and loyalty to the throne. Being brought up since childhood in close relationship with these elder members of the royal court, King Chulalongkorn probably had, on the one hand, admiration of and appreciation for these dancers of the previous reigns and felt, on the other hand, that it would not be wise and diplomatic to begin training new dancers when many old ones were still available. In Thai tradition, performances by the dance teachers were both to honour the teachers themselves and to set an example for their disciples.

It was not until the fourteenth year of the Fifth Reign, in 1882, at the *Somphot Phra Nakhon* (Celebration of the City) on the occasion of the centennial anniversary of Bangkok that a new group of royal *lakhon phuying* dancers were trained. For such a great event of national importance, new training was therefore appropriate.

Another reason for the absence of Lakhon Luang training in the early year of the reign was the king's preoccupation with learning and administering state affairs, which may have prevented him from taking active charge of entertainment within the royal court.[13] However, he had shown great talent and interest in the art of writing the *bot rabam* (dance script) of the "Rain-making Dance of Orachun, Mekkhala, and Ramasun," the *bot lakhon* of *Ngo Pa* and *Wongthewarat,* and *bot cheracha* (dialogues) for the *Inao* (all of which are to be discussed later). It may be concluded here that during the first thirteen years of his reign, King Chulalongkorn only played the role of patron in preserving, continuing, and encouraging the traditional forms of dance-drama.

While introducing new Western ideas, style of living, customs, sports, and entertainment, starting first among the courtiers and later to be spread more widely to the outer circle of aristocrats and upper middle class, King Chulalongkorn also continued his father's policy of reviving traditional royal customs and ceremonies. The mixture of Westernization and Siamization created rather curiously harmonious hybrids, probably comparable to those of Japan's Meiji era. Many new buildings constructed in this reign reflect this phenomenon, such as the Chakri Hall in the Royal Palace. Other obvious examples were the dressing habits and Thai conversation with touches of *farang* (foreign) technical terms and expressions in Siamese pronunciation, such as *talaepkaep* (telegraph), *polit* (police), and *ratchapataen* (royal pattern). It was not until the next reign that this modern terminology was Sanskritized and Siamized.

The Fifth Reign reflected the attempt of a modern monarch to have the best of two worlds, the old and the new, the *farang* and the Thai. Siam was to be the modern leader of the peninsula and the dignified, respectable "East" in the eyes of the West. It was a state of independence, prestige, and long traditions that were to be viewed with great respect by neighbouring countries, all of whom by then had lost their independence to the Western powers. Siam was therefore to retain links with its glorious past, with all the living royal traditions and ceremonies to prove it, and at the same time to keep in step with modern advancement in the international world, just as the kingdom of Ayudhaya at its height had been a centre of Southeast Asia. Krung Ratanakosin of the "Sayam Mai" (New Siam) under King Chulalongkorn was to attain the same position in all its grandeur and prosperity in a wider sphere. This story in itself is a *lakhon* (drama) with very challenging and difficult roles to play. The king, being the *nai rong* (master of the theatre and leading actor), performed this drama for forty-two years through the process of trial and error. He successfully held the troupe together until the finale when the curtain fell to applause from the world at large.

The following are some of the royal ceremonies during the Fifth Reign in which traditional dance-drama and entertainment were performed. A few can be described in detail. Most of them are referred to only as traditional entertainment mentioned in the chronicles. Fortunately, photography, which had been introduced in the Fourth Reign, provides vivid pictorial witness of this atmosphere of festivity and grandeur in many of these royal occasions, such as the Royal Tonsure Ceremony, the Investiture of the Crown Prince (both of Prince Wachirunahit and Prince Vajiravudh), Royal Cremations, and the Centennial Celebration of the City of Ratanakosin.[14] In the *Phra Ratchaphithi Sip Song Duan* (Royal ceremonies of the twelve months) written by King Chulalongkorn in 1888 for the *Wachirayan Journal,* there are also paintings of these ceremonies and entertainment.[15]

Up to 1880, the male Lakhon Luang or the female Lakhon Phuying Khong Luang were made up of former dancers of the Second and Fourth Reigns (pl. 19). The following year, the fourteenth year of King Chulalongkorn's reign, the king asked these dancers to train a new group of younger dancers to perform the *Inao* for the grand *Somphot Phra Nakhon* (Centennial Celebration of the City of Ratanakosin) in 1882. The king supervised the adaptation and modernization of the text himself together with some of his brothers including Prince Phichitprichakon. He also composed a new set of 68 *bot cheracha* (dialogues) (pl. 20).

In this new adaptation of the *Inao* and the *bot cheracha,* the personal effort and interest of the king in modernizing the classical dance-drama of the royal court are clearly shown. His personal choice and preference of the *Inao* over the *Ramakien,* and his selection of the episodes from "Inao Khao Fao Thao Daha" (Inao at the royal audience of King Daha) to "Lom Hop Nang Busba" (The wind sweeping away Busba), rather than the war episodes, reflect his personal taste for romanticism and lyricism, since the story of *Inao* itself is a romance and the episodes selected the most romantic ones in the play. Here emotional conflict, passionate love, anxiety, and deep emotion of royal adolescents are portrayed with great sophistication, subtlety, and refinement, both in the literary and dramatic aspect, befitting the highest class, the royal "elite" of traditional society under the Thai absolute monarchy.

For such an important national event as the Centennial Celebration of the City of Ratanakosin, it would have been more logical to perform the *Ramakien,* since it is the national myth associated, in general, with Thai history and the monarchy, in particular relating to the Chakri dynasty. Being a modern and Westernized monarch and known to have a romantic disposition himself, the king may have chosen the *Inao* simply for his own personal pleasure and enjoyment. It can be assumed that on such a national occasion, the *Ramakien* would also be performed in *khon* by the Khon Luang troupe within as well as outside the palace. (There were also grand parades of elephants, horses, and the military.) The *Inao* production was exclusively for the Inner Court and the close royal family circle. On the other hand, the traditional status of *Inao* as the jewel of *lakhon nai,* which had been regarded as a major attribute to a golden era of the Thai royal court since the reign of King Boromakot (1732–58) in the last Ayudhaya period and had been refined and elevated to the highest form of Thai classical dance-drama during the reign of King Rama II (1809–24), lent great prestige to the royal court of King Chulalongkorn. To have a new troupe of Lakhon Phuying Khong Luang perform such a sophisticated and refined *lakhon nai* as the *Inao* in those most difficult and challenging episodes was undoubtedly a status symbol for the new reign, representing the beginning of another golden era of an enlightened monarchy. The *Somphot Phra Nakhon* celebration in 1882 marked therefore a new period of development for the court dance-drama leading towards the age of modernization.

Prior to this event, there had been a few new experiments with *lakhon ram* and the introduction of a new type of drama, *lakhon phut,* which was spoken, usually without dancing. These new experiments in drama may have also influenced the modernization of *lakhon nai* in its texts, *bot cheracha,* and stage techniques.

However, according to Prince Damrong, this new Lakhon Phuying Khong Luang, consisting of ninety-two dancers, performed only once for the *Somphot Phra Nakhon.* After the event, it was discontinued.[16] It is most likely that the king was too preoccupied with state affairs (see also pp. 99–100). Many new dancers who had been trained on this occasion had therefore no opportunity to perform. The *Inao* production was given at a newly erected theatre in front of Phra Thinang Aphonphimok Hall. The theatre was built for the *Chaloem Phra Ratcha Monthian* (Celebration of the Royal Palace) at Phra Thinang Chakri Maha Prasat Hall on the same occasion as the *Somphot Phra Nakhon.*[17]

The administration of the various departments of royal entertainment in this reign was under the supervision of many princes and high officials of the court, as was the case in the Fourth Reign. The most important director in the previous reign who continued to serve during this reign was Prince Singhanat Ratchadurongrit, son of Prince Phithakthewet (head of the Kunchon family). Prince Singhanat inherited from his father the *khon* and *lakhon* troupes who were trained in the Third Reign. He was also head of the Krom Mahorasop (Department of Royal Entertainment) and Krom Hun (Department of Royal Puppetry). In 1880, after the death of Prince Singhanat, King Chulalongkorn handed over the responsibilities to the prince's heir, Chao Phraya Thewetwongwiwat (shortly Chao Phraya Thewet; Mom Ratchawong Lan Kunchon, father of "Dok Mai Sot," the famous woman novelist). Later in 1893, the king assigned to him the administration of three other departments of royal entertainment: Krom Khon (Khon Department), Krom Ram Khom (Lantern Dance Department), and Krom Piphat (Department of Royal

Orchestra). Chao Phraya Thewet, having control over these five departments, was thereby the most powerful authority over the royal dance and drama. Moreover, his own troupe, which he inherited from his father, was considered the best in the city. Later in the reign, it was also Chao Phraya Thewet together with Prince Naris who initiated a new type of classical dance-drama, the *lakhon dukdamban* (see pp. 124–38).

The success of the Chao Phraya Thewet troupe was due not only to the creative innovations of its master and Prince Naris, but also to the fact that the Chao Phraya, in his position, had access to the leading dance teachers and dancers of the Khon Luang and Lakhon Luang and from the *khon* troupe of the Wang Na (Palace of the Front), such as Khru Khum (role of Phra Ram), Khru Phaen (Hanuman) (both from the Khon Luang troupe), and Khru Khong (Thosakan) from the *khon* troupe of Wang Na.[18] Since these teachers and dancers only registered with their departments and did not have to report to work every day, they were allowed to teach or perform independently of other troupes to earn a living, and were occasionally called upon to perform in the Royal Palace for special social functions.[19] According to Prince Damrong, the troupe of Chao Phraya Thewet was the most frequently commissioned to perform for royal functions and ceremonies than any other troupe in the same reign.[20]

There have been no reports or historical records of any performances by either the Khon Luang or the Lakhon Phuying Khong Luang after the grand celebration of the centennial anniversary of Ratanakosin in 1882. The private troupes became more active. Some leading ones, such as that of Chao Phraya Thewet and Prince Narathip, were commissioned to perform in the Royal Palace in place of the royal troupes. This may have been due to the king's policy to encourage private enterprise as a way to develop and expand the art, or more possibly for the more practical reason that the country in the period following the Centennial Celebration of Ratanakosin had to face both international crises, wars, and an overall reformation of its political, economic, and social structures. King Chulalongkorn launched a complete programme of reforms for government administration, both at the central and provincial levels, starting in around 1888. He had experimented with a reform policy from the time of his second coronation in 1863 and had already prepared for three great changes prior to 1888.

From the late 1880s onward, there was an acceleration in establishing new administrative, economic, social, educational, cultural, and religious organizations to modernize and develop the country. It was also a period of struggle and conflict with Western powers and a period of war. The rising of the Ho tribe in the Northeast in 1874 started a series of wars occurring in 1875, 1883, 1885, and 1887. The later ones led to complications, conflict, and finally quarrels with France, which resulted in heavy losses to France on Siam's Indochina border territories.[21] Two years later in 1908, Siam lost the four southern states, Kalantan, Tranganun, Perlis, and Saiburi (Kedah), to England in exchange for England's surrender of judicial rights.

These internal reform and external political conflicts were the most probable causes of the discontinuation of dramatic activities within the royal court. It was not until the return of the king from his first grand tour of Europe in 1897 that the Lakhon Phuying Khong Luang had another opportunity to perform again to welcome the monarch, this time under the direct and close supervision and sponsorship of Her Majesty the Queen, Somdet Phra Siphatcharin. It should be stated here that from 1883 to 1896, i.e., from after the Centennial Celebration of Ratanakosin to before the king's first grand tour of Europe, the court dance-drama was not in full function. This inactivity in the royal court, therefore, gave rise to the development of dance-drama outside the Royal Palace among private troupes, similar to the situation and consequent developments in the Third Reign.

In 1897, at the grand *somphot* of the king's return from Europe, the Inner Court officials of the Fourth Reign wished to perform the *Inao* as in the past. According to Prince Damrong, prior to this event "there had been no training of the Lakhon Luang as before."[22] This statement could be interpreted as either that there had been a total lack of any training of the Lakhon Luang at all since the Centennial Celebration in 1882, or that the existing Lakhon Luang had not been trained specifically for the *Inao* performance. Whichever the case may be, these elderly Inner Court ladies who had been dancers in the Lakhon Luang during the last reign wished to "pay their homage and gratitude to the king" by dancing the *Inao* for him. When they proposed the idea to the queen, she readily supported them and financed the whole production, including the design of new type of light costume for the elderly dancers. The queen had a new temporary theatre constructed in the Sivalai Garden, near Thalaengkit Gate. She also frequently watched the rehearsals. The performance presented the story from the episode of "Inao Khao Fao Thao Daha" (Inao at the royal audience of King Daha) to the episode "Buang Suang" (The sacrifice to the gods). It was given on 7 February 1897 for a very select audience consisting of close members of the royal family and children and grandchildren of the dancers. Though many people wished to see this special production, since the dancers were highly respected teachers and had been the leading dancers of their day, King Chulalongkorn restricted the audience, stating, "All dancers are ladies of high *bandasak* rank and positions. They are the *chao chom manda* [mothers] of many princes of high position in the land. Therefore, only their children and grandchildren should be allowed to see their performance."[23]

The cast for this *Inao* production included *chao chom manda, thao* (high-ranking Inner Court officials), *thao kae* (senior officials), some of whom were over fifty years old.[24] There were also new, young trainees, children and grandchildren in the royal family, such as Prince Dhaninivat (in the role of

Siyatra), and others who played animals for the sacrifice dance. Prince Damrong states, "The Lakhon Luang of the Fourth Reign performed on this occasion for the last time in the Fifth Reign."[25]

Modern Development in Private Dance-drama Troupes

During the Fifth Reign there were more *lakhon phuying* troupes belonging to the aristocrats than in the previous reign since *lakhon* was now performed widely throughout the country. Prince Damrong in his *Tamnan Lakhon Inao* listed as many as twenty well-known troupes both in Bangkok and in the provinces.[26] The most famous were those of Prince Singhanat Ratchadurongrit (later inherited by Chao Phraya Thewet), Chao Khun Chom Manda Em (mother of Krom Phra Ratchawang Bowon Wichaichan), Chao Phraya Mahintharasakdithamrong, and Prince Narathip Praphanphong.

The *Lakhon* Troupe of Chao Phraya Thewet Chao Phraya Thewet had the best teachers and dancers from the Khon Luang and Lakhon Luang troupes and performed most frequently for the king in the Royal Palace on state and social occasions. Chao Phraya Thewet first maintained the *lakhon nai* style of the Second Reign, since there were teachers who had been dancers in the *lakhon phuying* troupe of his father, Prince Phithakthewet in the Second and Third Reigns. Later Chao Phraya Thewet produced such *lakhon nok* as *Phra Aphaimani* and, while chief of the Krom Mahorasop, he trained Khon Luang male dancers to perform the *lakhon ram,* for the first time since the Third Reign, in the *Ramakien* and *Inao*. It was considered the first *lakhon phuchai* (male dance-drama) in the style of the royal court in this reign. The leading dancers (male) who later became teachers in the Khon Luang and Lakhon Luang of the Sixth Reign were Phraya Phromaphiban (famous for the role of Thosakan, and teacher of the *yak* roles) and Phraya Natakanurak (famous for the role of Phra Ram, teacher of the *phra* [refined or royal male] roles and master of dance, initiator of the Royal Khon and Lakhon in the Sixth Reign). The wife of the latter, Khun Ying Natakanurak, known for her *yak* role in the *lakhon phuying* of the same troupe, also became a teacher in the Krom Mahorasop during the next reign.

The *lakhon* troupe of Chao Khun Chom Manda Em belonged to the Palace of the Front and performed in the style of the Lakhon Luang. Her son, Krom Phra Ratchawang Bowon Wichaichan, the *uparat* (deputy or second king), composed some *lakhon nok* plays for the troupe. A most interesting fact is that two leading dancers of this troupe became teachers of *lakhon* at the royal court of King Sisawat of Cambodia. They were Phring (known for her role of Inao) and Lek (known for the role of Sankhamarata).[27]

Lakhon Chao Phraya Mahin and Lakhon Pridalai Chao Phraya Mahin had previously produced *lakhon* in the Fourth Reign, but set up in the Fifth Reign for the first time in the history of Thai theatre a permanent public theatre, the "Prince

Theatre," and collected admission fees. At the beginning this troupe performed the *Dalang* of King Rama I and other *lakhon nai* and *lakhon nok*. Later Chao Phraya Mahin began to improvise by introducing new stories taken from Thai and foreign chronicles, for example, *Rachathirat* from the Mon chronicles, and other popular dramatic literature, such as *Phra Aphaimani*. To make the settings and movements more realistic, he adopted national costumes, mannerisms, music, and dance styles from the stories. This is why the dance-drama is termed the *lakhon phan thang* (drama of a thousand ways). The dance movements were also simplified, and the plots and movements made more rapid. These creative innovations, together with spectacular and exotic set designs and costumes, created instant attractions for Thai audiences, who were beginning to grow tired of the old classical style of *lakhon nai* and *lakhon nok* and were seeking new exciting dramatic entertainment. Hence, the Lakhon Chao Khun Mahin, as it was widely known, gained great popularity and success.

After the death of the Chao Khun, his son Chao Mun Waiworanat (But), carried on the business and even took the troupe, then called the "Lakhon But Mahin" (dance-drama of Mahin's son) to perform in Europe for the first time.[28] The troupe later became the "Lakhon Phasom Samakkhi" under Khunying Luanrit Thephatsadin Na Krungthep, who took over the company after the Chao Mun Waiworanat. (The style and conventions of *lakhon phan thang* will be discussed in further detail later in the next section.)

It is necessary to mention here that Sa-ngiam, a leading dancer of the Lakhon Chao Phraya Mahin, became a dance teacher in the court of Chao Inthawarorot Suriyawong of Chiengmai, and a few others in the *lakhon* troupe of Chao Khun Chom Manda Phae, who continued the style of the Lakhon Chao Khun Mahin.

Prince Narathip (head of the Worawan family) started to train dancers in his palace towards the end of the reign both in *lakhon nai* and *lakhon nok* and performed for the king on several royal occasions. Later he experimented with *lakhon phan thang* and a new form of dance-drama-operetta, known later as the *lakhon rong,* which became the model for the popular *lakhon rong* in the Sixth and Seventh Reigns (to be discussed in detail in the next section, pp. 119–24, 138–47). The prince also opened a permanent theatre following that of Chao Phraya Mahin, called the "Lakhon Pridalai" Theatre. Hence, the new *lakhon rong* was also named after the theatre, the "Lakhon Pridalai."

It is interesting to note other innovations among the *lakhon phuying* troupes in Bangkok, that of Phraya Phisanphonphanit, "Chin Su," who used the fighting style of Chinese opera in his *lakhon*. This is also true of the Lakhon Chao Phraya Mahin in the battle scenes depicting Chinese characters, such as the fight between Saming Phra Ram (a Mon hero) and Kamani, his Chinese challenger, in the *Rachathirat*. The influence of Chinese opera had been present in the circle of Thai drama since at least the Second Reign, for example, in the *ngiu phuying* (female Chinese opera) of Krom Phra Ratcha-wang Bowon Mahasakdipholasep of the Second Reign. A few dancers of this *ngiu phuying* lived on till the Fifth Reign, one of whom worked in the Royal Palace and entertained the royal children with *ngiu* songs.[29] Phra Pin Klao, the second king in the Fourth Reign, also patronized a male Chinese opera troupe (with Chinese dancer) in his Wang Na Palace. Most royal princes in the early reigns of Ratanakosin had private Chinese opera troupes in their retinue, probably as status symbols, in the same manner as having *lakhon* troupes of their own.

The *lakhon nai,* which had been restricted to within the Royal Palace in the Fourth Reign as decreed by the king, later spread out into Bangkok and the provinces. This reflected the new freedom granted by the modern and open-minded King Chulalongkorn. In Chiengmai and Lampang in the North, there were the royal troupes of Phra Chao Inthawitchayanon, ruler of Chiengmai, Chao Inthawarorot, Prince of Chiengmai City, and Chao Bun Thawat Wong-manit, Prince of Lampang City. In the South, the best-known troupes were those of Chao Phraya Suraphanphisut (Petchaburi), Chao Phraya Sutham-montri (Nakhon Sithammarat), Phraya Wichitsongkhram (Phuket), Phraya Senanuchit (Takua Pa), and Khun Kulap (Songkhla). In the East, the *lakhon* of Chao Phraya Khathathon Thoranin of Pratalong, which had been trained since the Fourth Reign, was the most popular.[30]

As to the new dramatic texts written in the traditional style of classical *lakhon,* there was none that we know of for the *lakhon nai* in this reign, and only a few in the style of *lakhon nok,* namely, *Phra Samut* in three *samut thai* (volumes) by Krom Phra Ratchawang Bowon Wichaichan of the Front Palace and some episodes of *Narai Sip Pang* (The ten incarnations of the god Narai, i.e., Vishnu), *Phra Aphaimani,* and *Phra Lọ* by Chao Phraya Thewet. Prince Narathip and Chao Phraya Mahin adapted many new versions of popular dramatic literature for their new styles of *lakhon ram.* They are sometimes labelled *lakhon nok* and often *lakhon phan thang.* They were versions of *Kraithong, Phra Lọ,* and *Khun Chang Khun Phaen* by Prince Narathip, for example. At the beginning, Chao Phraya Mahin hired two playwrights, Nai Wan and Nai Thim, to adapt the *Dalang* of King Rama I and the *Sepha Khun Chang Khun Phaen.* He later extended techniques of adaptation to new historical plays taken from Mon and Chinese chronicles and tales. These were written by Khun Chopphonlarak (later Luang Phatthanaphongphakdi) (to be discussed in the next section).

There were several *bot lakhon* written in serialized form mainly for pleasure reading and not to be performed, such as *Chanthakhorop* (later a very popular story for *liké*), *Thinawong, Manisuriwong, Laksanawong, Phra Samut, Singhatraiphop, Suriyawong Phromet,* which are later grouped as the *ruang chak chak wong wong* (stories about fantastic adventures of kings and princes genre).[31]

King Chulalongkorn's Innovations in Drama and Theatre

King Chulalongkorn once wrote a satire in the style of the nonsensical play called *Wongthewarat* (Dynasty of the deva-raja, god-king), in which he mocked some of the courtiers and wittily criticized the society in his time. The play was written while the king was taken ill in 1884 and had asked for some new plays to be read to him. One of them was the *Wongthewarat* of Khun Chopphonlarak, a playwright of Chao Phraya Mahin. The king found the story and plot so absurd and the knowledge of royal ceremonies of the playwright so incorrect (for example, having the king mounting from a *koei* [mounting platform] at all times) that he wished to try his hand at satirizing the play by using real personalities in the royal court as characters. The play is as long as 14 *samut thai* (volumes) and was first published in 1926. In the preface, Prince Damrong explained,

> I [Prince Damrong] had often expressed my wish to publish this play, but had seen some difficulties in it. This *bot lakhon* was written by the King to satirize others, both the original playwright of *Wongthewarat* [Khun Chop] and various persons existing at the time of its writing, many of whom had comic personalities and life histories. These were the people the King discreetly treated as characters in his *Wongthewarat*. Therefore, only those who knew the motive of its composition and who knew the individuals hidden within the play would enjoy reading it. Now that forty years have passed, the author of the original *Wongthewarat* and persons satirized by the King in his play have, for the most part, long passed away. There may be only one or two of them left today. If the play is published, most readers would fail to understand the funny points in the play. . . . But I have come to the conclusion that if the play is not published, it will later be lost. Furthermore, there are still many princes and princesses who do understand the funny points in the play. If any interested readers wish to know about them, they can still ask.[32]

King Chulalongkorn also showed his creative innovations in writing two other dramatic works, *Lilit Nithra Chakhrit* in 1878, adapted from the *Arabian Nights* in the *lilit* form, and *Ngo Pa* in 1905 as a *bot lakhon* for pleasure reading, both of which have been lauded for their poetic and dramatic qualities and were later performed as *lakhon phut* (spoken drama) and *lakhon ram* (dance-drama) in the same reign. They have often been produced from that time up to the present. Since both plays exhibit many new characteristics in literary style, dramatic aspect, and social implications, they will be discussed in the next section in detail, and not be grouped under traditional classical drama (see pp. 109–17).

Another new phenomenon of this reign concerning dramatic literature was the publication of play texts for reading. This was initiated by Dr. Smith, who first published the *Ramakien* of King Rama I from the version of Somdet Chao Phraya Sisuriyawong in serial instalments and sold them at 25 *satang* per copy. It can be considered the first introduction of plays to be the reading public by mass production. Since his first publication gained rapid popularity and success, Dr. Smith then published *Inao* in 1874 (also for the first time). From then on other publishers followed suit. Play publications became the most effective means to extend a knowledge of Thai dramatic literature to people of all classes and to break the former barrier set up to reserve dramatic texts exclusively for the aristocracy. As a result, a new type of *bot lakhon* written purely for pleasure reading and not to be performed on stage was thus developed on a commercial scale. Many publishers hired playwrights to produce this type of work. The consequences of such commercial enterprise were both positive and negative. On the one hand, it helped to expand the sphere of Thai dramatic literature and to encourage new playwrights to create new *bot lakhon*. On the other hand, the rapid growth and demand affected the qualities of the plays, since many of these playwrights were not true dramatists and did not have any dramatic experience. Their works were written for commercial publishing purposes and were not suitable for stage production.

Towards the end of the reign, the decline of the classical *lakhon ram* (dance-drama) was generally felt. The abolition of slavery decreed by King Chulalongkorn had direct effects on theatrical circles. Since freed slaves were not longer bound to the aristocrat masters, it became more difficult to maintain large dance troupes. Moreover, the king's policy of reducing gambling houses, which had been the money-earning centres for the *lakhon* troupes, hurt the *lakhon* profession in general.

Since most big *lakhon* companies thereafter performed in permanent theatres, they had to depend on large audiences. The producers had to find new ways to attract customers, and this led to the development of new dramatic forms towards the end of the Fifth Reign, namely, the *lakhon dukdamban* of Chao Phraya Thewet and Prince Naris, the *lakhon rong* of Prince Narathip and others, the *lakhon phan thang* of Chao Phraya Mahin, all of which still maintain some major traditional aspects of *lakhon ram*. There were also new folk forms: *lakhon chatri* (a mixture of *nora chatri* and *lakhon nok*) and *liké* (developed from *lakhon nok* and *lakhon chatri*) with some indications of Malay and Indian sources in music, singing, costumes and the opening piece called "Ok Khaek" (Entrance of an Indian), in which a comedian dressed usually in white with a cap, like an Indian "Babu," dances, sings and parodies an Indian accent. These new dramatic creations gained rapid popularity over the more conventional styles of *lakhon nai* and *lakhon nok*.

Lakhon nai, such as *Inao,* which was originally composed and performed for sophisticated aristocracy with artistic and literary refinement far above the understanding and appreciation of the common people, lacked the popular comic and melodramatic features and the rapidity of dance movements and popular musical tunes to attract the public. Moreover, dancers in *lakhon nai* and *lakhon nok* had to spend long periods of training to polish their skills, unlike those in *lakhon rong* and *liké,* who could learn the art in comparatively short time since their dance forms did not require such artistic refinement. As the cost of stage properties increased, the less elaborate costumes of *liké* and *lakhon rong* had economic advantages over the classical ones (pls. 11, 12). These factors together with the introduction of films imported from Japan, China, and the West added further causes for the decline of the classical *lakhon ram.* Prince Damrong concluded his *Tamnan Lakhon Inao,*

> Due to these various factors, most of those who had *lakhon ram* troupes went out of business. . . . Traditional *lakhon nok* declined with *lakhon nai.* . . . Whereas *liké* and *lakhon rong* . . . did not have to invest so much as *lakhon ram,* because *liké* only per-forms to amuse the audiences and *lakhon rong* to move their emotions [with melodramatic stories] and to please them. They therefore secure large enough audiences to make a profit and maintain their existence. Not only that, there were also foreign entertainments, that is, the films shown in theatres, which were another audience stealer. For these reasons, *kan len lakhon ram* in the traditional styles went into a gradual decline. At present, in the Sixth Reign, except for the Lakhon Luang of the Krom Mahorasop and the *lakhon* troupe of the Suan Kulap Palace, there is hardly any *lakhon* troupe performing the *Ramakien, Unarut,* or *Inao* in the tradition of *lakhon nai.*[33]

Crown Prince Vajiravudh's Contribution to Classical Dance-drama

Towards the end of the reign, Crown Prince Vajiravudh, while residing at the Sranrom Palace, made an attempt to preserve Thai classical dance-drama in the traditional style by training his pages and the sons of aristocratic families and high officials under his patronage in the art of *khon.* Leading teachers came from the troupe of Chao Phraya Thewet, namely, Khun Rabamphasa (later Phraya Phromaphiban), teacher of *yak* (ogres) roles, Khun Natakanurak (later Phraya Natakanurak), teacher of *phra* (heroes or male roles) and *nang* (heroines or female roles), and Khun Phamnaknatnikon (later Phra Dukdambanprachong), teacher of *ling* (monkeys) roles.[34] This new troupe was known as the Khon Samak Len (amateur *khon* troupe) under the direction of the crown prince himself. The crown prince also adapted many episodes of the *Ramakien* for his productions which were performed on several important occasions at the end of the Fifth Reign. The purposes of the Khon Samak Len were explained by the crown prince in the programme of the performance for the Royal Military Cadets Academy on Saturday, 25 December 1909 (one year before the end of the Fifth Reign),

> This *khon* troupe is called the "Khon Samak Len" because the performers volunteer to perform, not because they are recruited or because they want money as remuneration. The purpose is to entertain friends of the same class and not to let them forget that it is not necessary to see only the *farang* (Western) art of dancing. We still have old Thai traditions which should not be left to decline. This *khon* troupe usually performs in the Sranrom Palace. However, on this occasion, as we consider cadets as belonging to the same class as ours and hope that they will become the strength of our nation in the future, the *khon* dancers are therefore willing to entertain them, to help the occasion to be all the more enjoyable. If the audience feels that it is entertaining and that genuine Thai entertainment should still be seen, the performers who spend energy and effort in this will receive more satisfaction than by being given any other reward.[35]

Among the amateur *khon* dancers in this programme were some who became very high officials and close associates of King Vajiravudh, Rama VI, in the next reign, namely, Mom Luang Fua Phungbun (later Chao Phraya Ramrakhop, chief of the Royal Pages, favourite protégé closest to the king) in the role of Phra Orachun (Arjuna); Mom Luang Fun Phungbun, his brother (later Phraya Udomratchaphakdi), Intharachit; Nai Ut (later Phraya Sucharitthamrong), monkey officer; Mom Ratchawong Po (later Phraya Chatdet-udom), Phiphek.

By means of dramatic activities, King Vajiravudh made an attempt to implant at this early stage, that is, while he was still crown prince, a sense of pride, unity, and comradeship among those men who were to become the "King's clique" and the much-needed strong support for his monarchy. The Khon Samak Len was not therefore intended only for entertainment, but more seriously as a political instrument. These particular politico-dramatic endeavours of the crown prince were more clearly and extensively developed during his own reign. For the period of the Fifth Reign, however, they may have been regarded by outsiders only as the prince's efforts to preserve and promote traditional Thai classical dance-drama for cultural and entertainment purposes.

It should be noted that the crown prince emphasized in the introduction of the *khon* programme the concept of the "same class," i.e., that of the "elite," which included the courtiers, high officials, and military officers—the backbone of the monarchy. His message also expresses some criticism of those who preferred *farang* art and culture to Thai heritage, a common phenomenon among the "elite" of the Fifth and Sixth Reigns. Despite his own educational background in the West, King Vajiravudh made continuous efforts to uplift Thai cultural traditions as national symbols to counteract the influx of Westernization. At this turning point of Thai modern history he saw the necessity of establishing a social and cultural balance in Thai society, particularly among the "leading class."

THE GROWTH AND MODERN TRANSFORMATION OF DANCE-DRAMA

The extended period of inactivity of the royal *lakhon nai* during the Fifth Reign, as mentioned in the last section, reflected not only the social changes and political crises which must have affected its development, but also the changes in dramatic interest and taste of a newly modernized generation exposed for the first time to Western civilization. The influences of Western culture and ideas are most clearly shown in the literature of the period, as briefly discussed earlier. In drama, or more precisely, *khon* and *lakhon,* Western influences became apparent towards the end of the reign in the development and expansion of *lakhon ram* into new forms of *lakhon dukdamban, lakhon phan thang, lakhon rong,* in the classical tradition, and *lakhon chatri* and *liké* in the folk tradition.

It is evident that King Chulalongkorn was seeking new ways to modernize *lakhon ram* to suit his own personal taste and that of his contemporaries. His criticism of the lengthiness and repetition of the classical *lakhon ram* is often found in his personal letters, for example, in his letter to Prince Narathip written after having seen *Krung Phan Chom Thawip,* a *lakhon dukdamban* of Prince Naris at the Dukdamban Theatre of Chao Phraya Thewet performed for Prince Altenbert, the king's royal visitor. In the play there were several traditional dances and entertainment, such as *rabeng, kula ti mai, khon chon prop kai.* The king commented:

> The *farang* [Westerners], who come to see a *lakhon,* have different tastes. Those who have studied the traditions of other countries like to see the genuine forms of [entertainment of] that country. Nevertheless, they should be short and should always appear exotic [i.e., interesting] for those who do not know the language. In performing traditional forms of entertainment, there should be short pieces, not like the "O La Pho" [in the *rabeng* dance] performed in front of the royal audience for Prince Altenbert in the *Khrung Phan* at the Lakhon Dukdamban Theatre. Even though it is said to be very old, when the dancers repeatedly danced the same steps, I could not tolerate it.[36]

The new *bot cheracha* for the *Inao* (1882) was the king's first attempt to modernize *lakhon nai* in order to make it more lively and realistic. According to Somphop Chanthraprapha, an authority on Thai drama, the dialogue in this *bot cheracha* imitates very closely the witticisms of the *chao wang* (courtiers), especially those of the court ladies.[37] The comic satire of *lakhon nok* in his *Wongthewarat* (1884) could be considered the first known dramatic satire in which real personalities of the royal court are impersonated and satirized. Though the *Raden Landai* of Phra Mahamontri in the Third Reign, *Phra Malé Thé Thai* and *Unarut Roi Ruang* of Khun Suwan in the Fourth Reign preceded this type of comic satire, they do not portray real individuals in the highest circle of society. On the other hand, the king in his exalted position could enjoy complete freedom to criticize his own courtiers more openly and wittily, a privilege belonging only to an absolute monarch.

It should be remarked also that those characteristics of *lakhon nok* approximating popular comedy and farce are appropriate for this type of comic satire. Usually there are some royal characters in the plays who have idiotic personalities and who behave absurdly. They are often the kings in the stories. This particular feature could be interpreted either as a means whereby the common people could criticize and satirize the aristocracy and monarchy, or as self-criticism by the aristocrats themselves, since most dramatic texts of *lakhon nok* were composed by kings and their court poets of other members of the royal family. King Chulalongkorn in his *Wongthewarat* developed it further by using real individuals as characters in the play as well as some actual social and political events.

Lilit Nithra Chakhrit

Lilit Nithra Chakhrit (1878) is a remarkable innovation of King Chulalongkorn's in adopting and adapting for the first time the *Arabian Nights,* but through the medium of the West, that is, through English translation. Exotic tales and foreign chronicles had been adapted into Thai ever since the First Reign of the Ratanakosin period. However, they were all from the East: India, China, Mon, Burma, and Java, such as *Samkok* and *Rachathirat* in the First Reign by Chao Phraya Phra Khlang Hon (respectively, from Chinese and Mon chronicles), and *Dalang* and *Inao* from Java in the First and Second Reigns. It is needless to mention Indian tales, which are abundant in Thai literature from the greatest epics of *Ramayana* and *Mahabharata* to comic tales in *lakhon nok, lakhon nora chatri, lakhon chatri,* and *liké.* However, to the knowledge of this writer, these had not been any tales from the West published before the *Lilit Nithra Chakhrit.*

The king's two purposes in composing and publishing this tale, which he adapted from *The Tale of the Sleeper Awakened* in English in the *Arabian Nights Entertainment,* a collection of tales from countries west of Siam (i.e., India, Arabia, and Africa), were, first, to give it as a personal gift to members of the royal family on New Year's Day in 1879 to be read for pleasure,[38] as he wrote in the introduction and conclusion of the *Lilit Nithra Chakhrit.*

Introduction: I will tell a tale, found in Arabian stories, translated and adapted from the English version, presented in the Siamese version. There are many of its like, but they have not been found [in Siam] before. It is for the New Year, intended to give pleasure to all members of the royal family. I therefore copied the text and composed it in *klon lilit,* in a concise form, only to make known the story.

Conclusion: To give in place of gifts to all the members of the
  royal family,
Everyone of whom has gathered together
On this New Year's Day,[39]
I offer this story to them to fill their minds with delicate images,
Which may cause their hearts to rejoice.

Secondly, as the tale has moral lessons as well as entertaining qualities, it was an appropriate gift for the occasion. The king explained the message of the tale at the end.[40]

Here's the story's meaning: Hassan
Could number, say, a hundred people as his friends.
But when he fell on hard times, they all turned away.
So making friends with even a single person who is worthless brings
  great danger.

But to become friends with a mighty ruler, the lord of the land,
Might even lead to being lord of the land oneself, as one desires.
To hit upon the right man for a friend is as good as having a
  hundred of the other sort.
So, in making friends, one has to choose and choose again, many
  times over.

When one has great happiness, one often indulges in it,
And lets one's heart go, thinking that everything will be perfect.
When suffering comes, one is struck down, and one's life lies
  wasted.
To indulge too much usually leads quickly to great danger.

Having learned the lesson, one should discard pride.
Then good will reappear,
[And] one will attain fortune lasting till death.
One should remain ever cautious and aware, never being over-
  excited by good fortune.

That much is the value [of this tale] which I recommend to you.
The rest is full of nonsense.

I have adapted the story following the original version to this end,
For the singers of poetry to read and amuse themselves.

Through the tale the king introduced new knowledge of Persia, its customs,
language, and culture, and explained them in the footnotes of the book. By
virtue of these moral messages and information, the tale was prescribed as a
text for the Royal Pages School in the same reign, and after the Revolution
of 1932, for students in the last years of secondary school up to the present,
by order of the Ministry of Education.

On the same occasion of the New Year in 1879, the king wished to present
the tale as *lakhon phut* (spoken drama) in the production of the Royal Magical
Society, an entertainers' club founded along with his brothers for the members
of the royal court and officials. The Society annually performed magic or
spoken drama or organized fancy dress parties as New Year's entertainment.
The king ordered a temporary theatre to be set up on the west platform of
Phra Thi Nang Phiman Rataya Hall and cast his brothers and sons of high
officials as characters in the play (pl. 21). He also composed songs for the
production. The lyrics were either newly written in *klon paet* or extracted from
the *khlong* in the *Lilit Nithra Chakhrit*. The king often watched the rehearsals
and gave directions. However, not having recovered from illness on New
Year's Day, he postponed the production to the Songkran Day on the seventh
and eighth days of the waning moon in the fifth month of the same year. The
episodes performed were from when Abu Hassan loses consciousness in the
palace to the end of the story. It was divided into two evenings (the first
evening, to when the Caliph brought Abu back to his home; and the second,
from Abu Hassan's madness to the end of the story). The king also gave prizes
to the three best actors, namely, Prince Kasemsi Suphayok (head of the
Kasemsi family), first prize, Prince Damrong (head of the Diskul family),
second prize, and Prince Prachak Silapakhom, third prize.

It should be remarked here that *lakhon phut,* which is often misunderstood
as having been initiated by King Vajiravudh in the Sixth Reign, in fact finds
its origin in the Fifth Reign long before the birth of Prince Vajiravudh.[41] In
1892, thirteen years later, Prince Vajiravudh himself, when still a child of
twelve, made his stage debut in the same play, in the children's production
with royal children from the Rongrian Ratchakuman (School for Royal
Children) as cast (pls. 22, 23).

It may possibly have been this childhood exposure to *lakhon phut* and
followed later by his dramatic activities in England that set the prince off on
the course of a dramatic form which he later developed to its maturity in his
own reign. King Chulalongkorn should therefore be given the credit of being
a true pioneer and the "father of spoken drama" in Siam. Despite the dramatic forms in general, it is an accepted fact that the quality of his creativity,
originality, innovative character, and artistic talents as dramatist-poet and also

prose writer is far more significant than the quantity of his works. Being much more deeply rooted in Thai culture and having known his people better through his extended reign, his plays appeal more to the Thai people in general, both to the aristocracy and to commoners, than could those of King Vajiravudh. King Chulalongkorn also had the advantage of being able to communicate and express his ideas, sentiments, and emotions with natural ease and simplicity, which are often lacking in the works of his son. To a certain extent, Western intellectual and cultural influences may be blamed for Vajiravudh's laboured and pedantic style and Victorian moral conscience, unfamiliar to the Thais of that period. Even in later times up to the present, except to fervent admirers of King Vajiravudh's works, they are, when compared with those of his father, inferior in literary style and over-selfconscious in expression. However, his literary translations and adaptations of Western plays are often remarkable.

One practice of King Chulalongkorn following the tradition of previous kings in composing dramatic texts, which was not fully practised by the Westernized and individualistic King Vajiravudh, was his collaboration with other court poets and talented members of the royal family in editing and correcting the verses he wrote. As he explained in the conclusion of *Lilit Nithra Chakhrit*,[42]

> Prince Phichit[43] made a great effort
> In condensing, adding, extending some of the verses,
> And improving the rhymes of the *klon*
> To make them more beautiful and meaningful.

> Later, it was given to Phra Sri-Sunthonwohan, named Noi,
> To revise once more in case there were still mistakes,
> And to examine and polish the *klon* verses to perfection.

Moreover, the proofreading of each section of the publication was done separately by seven editors,[44] whose corrections were gathered together on a single sheet for each reprint. The king often expressed modesty in not being experienced or gifted in poetry and excused himself for his unconventional style.

> A thought came to me that scholars who may happen to see this
>   work
> May criticize me for being carried away
> [And] for not having followed the forms and conventions their ears
>   have always been accustomed to;
> So that my verse sounds very funny from beginning to end.

> Concerning the poetic styles of *chan, klon,* and *kap,* there were
>   many difficulties.

I was ashamed and afraid of my inadequacy.

I [therefore] asked people to help me out of shame for my ignorance.

But not finding any assistance, I had to try my awkward hand at writing it with such limited ability, only for fun.[45]

Readers should not deem these excuses to be false modesty, but rather to be expressions of his great care over poetic creation, while manifesting his inclination towards the *ni baep* (escape from a model), i.e., the unconventional, which reflects his modern and revolutionary spirit. He also indicated the original source of the tale, the English version. This was a rather new practice for Thai writers to acknowledge the sources of their works instead of the usual habit of plagiarizing and giving credit to themselves. (Plagiarism has been and still is an incurable disease among Thai writers even today.) In this respect, King Chulalongkorn referred to *Phra Aphaimani* by Sunthon Phu which is a pure creation of fantasy. The poet even advised those who could read English to find the complete original version and explained that his work was only an adaptation in a concise form, not a faithful translation. All these explanations show liberalism and integrity, which are the great qualities of King Chulalongkorn as a poet as well as a monarch.

Later, the king gave permission to Chao Phraya Mahin to produce *Nithra Chakhrit* as *lakhon ram*. A new dramatic text for this production was written by Khun Chopphonlarak (Thim), taking only the end of the story from when Abu Hassan gave the second feast to the Caliph. After that, the play was performed in this *lakhon ram* style at other theatres.

Another *lakhon phut* production of the play was given in 1892, at Sichang Island, by the Ratchakuman Katanukon Society (Society of Activities for Royal Children), in which the royal children, including the crown prince, who were pupils of the Ratchakuman School, performed for the king (pls. 22, 23).

The writer wishes briefly to remark here that the costumes in these two royal productions, in 1879 and 1892, following closely the national style of the Persians, mark a new step towards both realism and exoticism in Thai drama (a subject which will be elaborated in Chapter 7). There are also photographs of other productions of the same play by female actress-dancers dressed in more elaborate Thai-Persian costumes (pl. 10). These were taken from the *lakhon phan thang* production of the *Arabian Nights* of Prince Narathip. They show considerable differences from those of *lakhon phut phuchai* (male spoken drama) productions given in the Royal Palace (pl. 21).

The play was later adapted also in the form of *sepha* by royal command to be recited at the *song khruang yai* (the king's hair cutting). This continued the royal tradition of King Mongkut, who commissioned court poets to compose a *sepha* from the Thai chronicles. There were eleven poets who contributed to the *Sepha Nithra Chakhrit*.[46]

With all these dramatic and literary innovations and creations, it can be concluded that the *Lilit Nithra Chakhrit* of King Chulalongkorn holds a very important place in the "new era" of Thai drama and literature.

Ngo Pa

It is generally agreed that the best dramatic work of King Chulalongkorn and one of the foremost dramas in Thai history is *Ngo Pa,* written in a total of three *smut thai* (books) in eight days during the king's illness in 1905. It is a romantic tragedy dealing with a love triangle of three Ngo, or forest-dwellers in southern Thailand. It has great dramatic intensity equal to that of *Phra Lo,* an epic which has a similar heroic-tragic ending when the three lovers courage-ously meet their deaths. Many aspects of the play are inspired by *Inao,* such as the situation of Somphla, the hero, being in love with Nang Lamhap, the heroine, who is already betrothed to Hanao; the abduction of Lamhap by Somphla on her wedding day; and the dual between Somphla and Hanao. The poet-king maintained some dramatic conventions of the traditional *bot lakhon* as follows:

1) The introduction of the characters with the terms *mua nan* ("at that moment"), *ma cha klao bot pai* ("now to tell about [name of character]"), *bat nan* ("then . . . "; usually referring to a character of less importance).

2) The literary and dramatic conventions of *bot long song* (bathing) and *bot song khruang* (dressing) of the main characters (male and female), *bot chom dong* (admiring nature), *bot khao phra khao nang* (the love scene), *bot chom chom* (admiring the beauty of a woman), *bot sok* (a scene of sadness, melancholy, love parting, death), and *bot rop* (a fight scene).

3) The *Bot Lakhon Ngo Pa* was written in the traditional forms of *klon* and *rai.*

4) The music both for singing and for the accompaniment and responses are prescribed for each section.

5) There are interludes of *bot cheracha* (not published, only indicated) and comic relief, such as the love scene of an old couple, Ta Wang Song (a widower of sixty-five) and Nang Thing (a widow of fifty-four), who are teased by two Ngo children.

However, this revolutionary dramatist king broke away from tradition by introducing a completely new theme, unprecedented by any writers in the past, that of an aborigine tribe in southern Siam in place of kings, queens, princes, and princesses in *lakhon nai* and *lakhon nok.* In the Third Reign Phra Mahamontri did write a parody of *lakhon nai* in his *Raden Landai,* in which he depicted the lives of the lower class. However, the work is a comic satire with an unrealistic plot, exaggerated setting, and absurd actions. *Ngo Pa,* however, is a serious romance and tragedy in the style of *Inao* and *Phra Lọ,* but with jungle people as characters in the play. The author explains,

> This book was written without the intention of its being performed as *lakhon,* and I did not think that it was going to be good, because it is a story of the *chao pa* (jungle people), who are extremely deprived. It was like setting a table with only coconut shells, most of which had no stands or legs. It was therefore difficult to make it beautiful. But when it was finished, it looked quite pretty, more like blue, red, or purple colour chinaware. I have discarded all the "high" words and created a new story by my own imagination, while mixing in facts in some parts to make it more interesting.[47]

It was his curiosity about the Ngo tribe, their customs, and the Goi language that had prompted him during a trip to the south in 1905 to adopt a Ngo boy from Phatthalung. Khanang, the Ngo boy, became a favourite of the king and the royal court (pl. 24). He was raised by Princess-consort Saisawaliphirom, who treated him almost as her own. The king patiently learned the customs and the Goi language of the Ngo from Khanang and collected them in the glossary appended for the information of his readers. King Chulalongkorn also explained the physical appearance, way of life, religious beliefs, eating habits, merry-making, dressing, hunting, and courting of the Ngo. Their ceremonies of birth, marriage, and burial are described both in the Preface and in the play. Their songs, dances, and music, introduced for the first time in the history of Thai *lakhon ram,* are not intended only for dramatic novelty, but more seriously as a new step towards the use of primitive culture as material for classical dance-drama, a "revolution" in itself. In portraying the dignity, courage, passionate love, honour, and self-sacrifice of these so-called "barbarians," King Chulalongkorn succeeded in elevating the status of these jungle people to a level equal that of royal princes and princesses and kings and queens in traditional *lakhon nai* and *lakhon nok.* When comparing the texts of *Inao, Phra Lọ,* and *Ngo Pa,* it is clear that, in contrasting the primitive culture and customs of the Ngo with those of the Javanese-Thai and Lao-Thai royal courts, the king wishes to show the similarities of basic human elements and values existing in all societies and social classes. This concept of *le noble sauvage* is not unlike that of the Western romantic novelists during the eighteenth and nineteenth centuries, namely, Chateaubriand, Jean-Jacques Rousseau, Bernardin de Saint-Pierre, and Fenimore Cooper. King Chulalongkorn states, "Their [the Ngo's] thinking is quite intelligent. They have an excellent memory, which is natural for people without a written literature. Rather shy [easily frightened, on the side of being cowardly], but not ferocious by nature."[48] And in the Prologue, he makes his intention quite clear.

I will begin the story as if I were going on a pleasure trip to the
  jungle,
Up to Songkhla, as intended
Then embarking on a big *mat* barge[49] to Phatthalung. . . .
Visiting Thai villages.
They told me about the Ngo in particular.
I therefore asked them to bring me to their huts.
They [the Ngo] gave me a grand welcome and I had great pleasure
  [in meeting with them].
I met Grandma Lamut, an old woman of the jungle. . . .
Nai Sin-nui helped me in conversing with her in the Ngo language,
Which sounded like *farang* [Western] language, loud and clear.
Grandma Lamut told me a story,
Like a romance, very clever, not at all boring.
I therefore jotted it down in *klon* verse,
Hoping not to forget the narrative.
Whosoever reads this may misunderstand, as they usually do, that
These are only primitive Ngo; so when I praised them as being
  beautiful, it seemed ridiculous to them.
I write this with the intention to use the Ngo language,
Because I find it beautiful and suitable to their nature.
Whosoever wishes to hear this, *please listen with care,*
Imagine yourself as a Ngo, and do not mock them.[50]

The Goi terms and customs were supplied by Khanang, whom the king
questioned daily. However, the king commented that he could only learn very
limited vocabulary from the boy, since Khanang was still a child, "They are
mostly names of animals, birds, trees, and fruits."[51] In the Preface, the
king writes, "The spoken language is genuinely Goi, very distantly related to
Thai and Malay. The endings sound somewhat like English and German. It
does not have all the sounds [of Thai]. It seems that the genuine Goi language
has a very small vocabulary. They therefore have to use some Thai and
Malay words.[52]

The royal poet-dramatist also expressed his desire to be "unconventional"
in not following the literary and dramatic models.

This book was not intended to be written in the correct way. And
I did not intend to follow the set model. I wrote it following the
promptings of my heart; whatever I wished to do, I did. This is because when I write, it is a time when I want to open myself up and
not have any restraint to control me. . . . [This book] is suitable for
reading only for people who like to read strange books and who do
not choose merely the "conventional" models, or are tired of those
models.[53]

The "unconventional" qualities of this play are not only found in the theme, the plot with the tragic deaths of the three main characters instead of the conventional happy ending of *lakhon,* and in the use of Ngo language and customs, but also in the introduction of new ways of including indigenous Ngo songs and having them sung by the dancers themselves, as in the wedding and burial scenes. This type of singing by dancers was a new phenomenon initiated during this reign which became a main feature of new forms of classical dance-drama-operetta, namely, *lakhon dukdamban* of Prince Naris and Chao Phraya Thewet and *lakhon rong* of Prince Narathip. It is also used in the folk forms, *liké* and *lakhon chatri.*

According to Chao Chom Mom Ratchawong Sadap (consort of King Chulalongkorn), a leading singer and an assistant to the king in selecting musical tunes for the play, the king wrote the play in sections and from time to time had them sung out by the court ladies, who contributed also to the composition of the music and songs. Leading music teachers were also consulted at times. "Most of the musical tunes follow the pattern. But the king did not like the *khaek* (Malay, Javanese) tunes, because the Ngo were jungle people, not *khaek.* Any other tunes which were suitable could be used."[54]

It is evident that many parts of the *Ngo Pa* story imitate those of *Inao* and *Phra Lọ.* The most striking dramatic scene is the final scene, when Somphla, having been hit with an arrow by Ramkaeo, Hanao's brother, and dying, expresses his love to Lamhap, his wife, and his forgiveness to Hanao, his rival whom he asks to take care of Lamhap. This is followed dramatically by the suicides of Lamhap and Hanao. The mourning of their deaths and praise by their relatives and parents of their love, sacrifice, and courage, echo *Lilit Phra Lọ* (The romance of Prince Lọ).[55]

Nithra Chakhrit and *Ngo Pa* by King Chulalongkorn are very illuminating examples of the inquiring and pioneering spirit of the aristocratic dramatists of the age, who were searching for new ways of entertaining themselves and their contemporaries with new dramatic materials and styles of presentation.

The foremost innovative directors-producers-dramatists in this reign were Chao Phraya Mahin, Prince Naris, and Prince Narathip. However, it would be hard to state definitely when each began his work, as there are no historical records describing most of their works. In terms of popularity and success, Chao Phraya Mahin and Prince Narathip had the advantage over Prince Naris, whose works were appreciated mostly by the upper class, the elite. Those of the former two appealed to wider audiences from the royal court to the common people, since their plays were taken from popular romances, adventurous historical tales, and contemporary melodramatic and domestic stories. Yet among the authorities of Thai drama, Prince Naris is regarded as the most sophisticated, artistic, talented, and creative dramatist of the age. His work is a milestone in the development of Thai classical dance-drama and music. His *lakhon dukdamban* introduced many modern features which were later followed by other troupes, including those of Chao Phraya Mahin and Prince Narathip. However, since *lakhon dukdamban* contained only performances of classical stories and still maintained the artistic refinement of *lakhon nai,* it could be fully appreciated only by the *savants* and *connaisseurs.* Even King Chulalongkorn remarked on its slowness and repetition of movement, as quoted earlier. The competition between the major *lakhon* companies stimulated the other troupes to rival them in creating more exciting plays and to "steal" star dancers to perform for them.

The three most important modernized forms of *lakhon ram* which are associated with the three aforementioned innovators are *lakhon phan thang, lakhon dukdamban,* and *lakhon rong.*

Lakhon Phan Thang

As its name indicates, *lakhon phan thang* (*phan thang,* a thousand ways) is a deviation from traditional *lakhon nai* and *lakhon nok.* It introduced many new types of story from Thai and foreign tales and chronicles in order to give exotic flavours to the *lakhon* form. As has already been mentioned previously in the first section to this chapter, these tales gave ample opportunity to create attractive costumes, set designs, and exciting dance movements accompanied by foreign orchestration, including Burmese, Mon, Lao, Chinese, Indian, Cambodian, Malay, Javanese, and *farang* (Western). This improvisation in combining Thai and foreign elements in music and dance is called *ok phasa tang tang.* The lyrics and dialogues are also enriched with a few vocabulary items of the languages of the foreign characters, mixed with Thai so as to create an appropriate atmosphere in each play, sometimes extending even to an admixture of foreign-type scenery.

The dance movements in general are simplified with fewer *ram na phat* (specific dances for special actions in *khon* and *lakhon*), but with more *ram chai bot* (interpretative dance connected to the text) and less complicated gestures.

As for the costumes, there is no longer the *yun khruang* characters (i.e., those dressed in tightly fitting traditional dance costumes), since this required expensive, richly embroidered fabrics and elaborate head-dresses. The dancers in *lakhon phan thang* usually wear realistic period costumes or national costume as indicated within the plays.

Chao Phraya Mahin was the first to experiment with this new form of *lakhon phan thang* at his "Prince Theatre," the first permanent theatre which charged admission. His most successful productions were that of *Phra Aphaimani, Rachathirat,* the episode of *Phlai Phet Phlai Bua* in *Khun Chang Khun Phaen, Samkok,* and other Chinese chronicle tales, such as *Hong Sin, Tang Han, Ngo To, Sui Thang, Buai Huai Lao.*[56] He was also the first to introduce foreign dance movements in his plays; for example, the Chinese war dance in *Rachathirat* and Chinese dance steps in other Chinese tales, which were taught directly by Chinese opera dancers, and the *farang* mannerisms, gestures, and military procedures in *Phra Aphaimani* taught by Westerners.

Prince Narathip Praphanphong's Contribution to *Lakhon Phan Thang* The most important contributor to the further development of *lakhon phan thang* was Prince Narathip Praphanphong, the king's brother. Prince Narathip started his dramatic productions at the Rong Lakhon Wiman Narumit ("Magic Palace" Theatre) in Wat Saket.[57] Hence they were called Lakhon Narumit. Apparently, Lakhon Narumit, which performed stories from the chronicle tales and romances, was very popular not only among the elite and the courtiers, but also middle-class audiences. King Chulalongkorn is said to have frequented the Rong Lakhon Wiman Narumit himself and invited the troupe to perform at the royal court on several social occasions for royal guests and foreign dignitaries, such as Duke Johann Albrecht, the Regent of Brunswick.[58]

At the beginning, Prince Natathip adapted Thai historical tales and chronicles with patriotic themes such as *Wira Satri Thalang* (The heroines of Thalang [Ayudhaya period]), *Khun Ying Mo* (Lady Mo, another heroine in the Ayudhaya period), and *Kabot Thammathian* (The Thammathian rebellion). Later, the audiences became tired of chronicle plays. King Chulalongkorn gave a witty criticism of the *farang*-oriented Thai in his personal letter to the prince,

> The reason they don't like the *phongsawadan* [chronicles] is because they don't know them and have never read them. They don't like the "old things" because they are afraid to be old-fashioned. They want to be chic in preferring *farang* things. And another thing, the *farang* themselves have been over-enthusiastic about them [modern Western plays]. If the story is new, they can understand it. If it is old, it seems too far from the smell of butter and milk and they don't appreciate it.[59]

Prince Narathip's experimentation with dramatic adaptations of Thai chronicles was a very courageous step. It may also have provoked negative reactions from some Thai conservatives, since the plays involved true historical personalities and events, which may have been controversial subjects, because most unsophisticated Thai people regarded their national history as something sacred, to be highly revered and not to be performed as *lakhon* entertainment. King Chulalongkorn was very wise in observing these reactions and controversies. As he wrote to the prince in an understanding and encouraging tone,

> I must admit that the *phongsawadan* [chronicles] are difficult to perform [as *lakhon*] because the stories are ancient and longwinded.

But to speak the truth, your performances are less exaggerated than those of the *farang*. Their productions are so exaggerated that they become different, a second and distinctly different version, in order that they could emphasize easily the points of the tales. But you [Prince Narathip] are not the type to do such a thing for many reasons.

First, Thai people cannot distinguish between a tale and a true story. If you try to tickle their senses by stimulating them with an emotional tale, then there is no response. But once they do get stimulated, then anything and everything will tickle them.

Another reason is the damage done by "Ta Ku" [Ko So Ro Kulap, a self-made historian who was criticized for distorting the *phongsawadan* and whose plagiarism and criticism raised a court case].[60] People know only Ta Ku, whose "objective" view is different [from ours]. ... It is therefore very difficult.[61]

The prince later turned to romantic and adventurous tales that became instantly very successful, particularly those with melodramatic and tragic themes. The most popular among these was the tragic romance of *Phra Lo,* which the prince adapted from the *Lilit Phra Lo* into *lakhon phan thang*. It should be classified as *lakhon phan thang* because the story is of northern Lao kingdoms and the dancers dress in Lao-Thai costumes, dance and sing to Lao-type musical tunes, and speak with touches of Northern dialect (col. pl. 1).

It seems that the whole royal court was involved in one way or another in the creation and production of *Phra Lo*. The king himself helped to correct the manuscript of the *bot lakhon* of Prince Narathip and sent the copies to Chao Chom Dararatsami, one of his favourite consorts, to read in her spare time. "Chao Dara," as she was called, was one of Prince Narathip's ardent theatre patrons. In his personal letter to the princess-consort, the king wrote, "Krom Narathip sent me the last part of the *Bot Lakhon Phra Lo*. There are still some mistakes which I told him to correct. As I see that you are lonely and have nothing to do, I collected the beginning and two books of the middle part for you to read for relaxation."[62]

The king also attended the rehearsals of the play and criticized the conservatives who were against innovations and modernization. As he wrote to Chao Dara,

My efforts in trying to rehearse the *lakhon* to perform *Phra Lo* and to create even a barely "passable" production demanded a lot of courage on my part. People who can create successful *lakhon* have to be able to control the production and to choreograph, and they have to create new stories to suit the dancers who happen to be available. Therefore, those who succeeded in *lakhon* in the past [Phra Phuttha Loetla (King Rama II), Ta Chao Krap, Nai Net, Nai

Tao, Chao Phraya Mahin] created it themselves. With *lakhon* performances, if there are always people who criticize, "This must be done this way; that must be done that way, if you want to be correct," then whichever way we perform it, it will never equal what it was in the past, that is, it will never measure up to the standard of those who performed it at the beginning.[63]

This statement, or rather complaint of the king, reveals his impatience with the narrow-mindedness of his contemporaries, who thought themselves authorities on Thai dance and drama. It also shows how the king made an effort to encourage new dramatic creations and modernization.

King Chulalongkorn was the first king of Siam to set a new tradition of going to see performances at private theatres outside the royal court. As he wrote in one of his letters to Prince Narathip to ask him to reserve seats his entourage,

> Krom Narathip,
>
>   As I first told you that there would be twenty of us coming to see your *lakhon,* we now have to increase the number to twenty-five persons to include the children, but the ladies and the men are in a separate group of about ten. For those who will sit in the box, there are only three or four. I am therefore writing to you to reserve these seats for us.
>
> Sayamin [literally, "Indra of Siam,"
i.e., King of Siam][64]

The king admitted that this "democratic" gesture and practice had been influenced by Western theatre customs. As he wrote to the prince on the next day after the performance, "My going to see the play at the theatre is rather *rang rang* [i.e., *farang* (Western)]."[65] However, he continued that despite the *farang* practice, he was still Thai in maintaining the tradition of rewarding the dancers (which was customarily done while the dancers were performing on the stage). Realizing that the traditional practice was awkward for the modern theatre, he sent the reward to them later through the prince after the performance. He writes,

> But I am still Thai at heart, and am a *chao nai* [a royal person]. When I like the performance, I am used to giving rewards. But to give them there would be distracting. I am therefore sending 300 baht to you to reward them [the dancers] as you consider appropriate, not only for the two performances I saw, but for your having trained them so well.
>
> Sayamin[66]

Also for the first time in the history of the Thai theatre, King Chulalong-korn granted official patronage to a private theatre troupe, the Lakhon Narumit troupe of Prince Narathip, following the concept of a Western "royal theatre" or "royal company" open to the public. Hence, the original, private Lakhon Narumit became the Lakhon Luang Narumit (Royal Lakhon Narumit). The company served both the royal court (at social functions) and the public, from whom admission fees were collected. It was this very freedom and encouragement bestowed by the king that enabled *lakhon* in the Fifth Reign to flourish and attain a "golden age." *Lakhon* of good quality was no longer restricted to contexts where royal ceremonies (whether calendrical or particular) were usually involved. The modern liberal and democratically minded king had made it "entertainment for the poeple," in which the king mingled with his own subjects of all classes.

The grant of royal patronage to companies for royal service was initiated by King Chulalongkorn after the Western model. It was an effective means of relating private enterprises to the service of the king and of compensating them with royal honour and prestige. In this way, the king was able to create a deep sense of loyalty to the throne among the leaders of society.

As for Prince Narathip, the creative dramatist, his innovation and modernization further developed in his experimentation with another form of dance-drama-operetta, *lakhon rong,* which became an even greater success at the end of the Fifth Reign and was continued with other private troupes into the Seventh Reign (to be discussed in the following section).

According to several authorities on the *lakhon* of Prince Narathip, its success and popularity were due to the creative artistic abilities of the prince himself and his colleagues, in the same manner as the combined talents of the Chao Phraya Thewet and Prince Naris company in creating *lakhon dukdamban*. The lyrics and dialogue were composed by the prince, who is considered one of the most gifted poets and prose writers. Among his best-known plays are *Phra Lǫ, Sao Khrua Fa* (adapted from *Madame Butterfly*), *Khrua Narong, Tukata Yot Rak* (adapted from *The Enchanted Doll*), *Si Po Min Khotrabong* (a Burmese chronicle), and *Siharat Decho* (a Thai historical play). The dancers were trained by Chao Chom Manda Khien, mother of the prince, a leading dancer in the Royal Lakhon troupe of the Fourth Reign, known for her role as Inao. She was later a dance teacher in the Royal Lakhon of the Fifth Reign. The songs and musical tunes were composed by Mom Luang Tuan Worawan, one of the prince's consorts and great-granddaughter of Chaofa Krom Luang Phithakmontri (brother of Queen Srisuriyentharamat of King Rama II), the most important dancer-teacher and choreographer in the First and Second Reigns, whose choreography of *lakhon nai* forms the basic tradition that has been carried on until the present day. Prince Phithakmontri is respected as a great *khru* (guru) of *lakhon* and is worshipped at the Invocation Ceremony of classical Thai dancers. "Mom Tuan" is known for her beautiful songs, especially songs of love and sadness. She often assisted King Chulalongkorn in composing *lakhon* songs and music for his productions and was given money (from 40, 60, to 80 baht) as gifts from the king for her moving songs, the best of which was her tragic song for *Phra Lo* called the "Kroen Anat" or "Kroen Sok" depicting the longing passion of the hero and the extreme grief of his mother, the queen. For this particular melody and song she was given 100 baht from the king (a very big sum at the time).

The last important element contributing to the success of this *lakhon* company was the talented, creative, and modern direction of Prince Narathip himself, who introduced many new and exciting features, some adopted from the West and other foreign countries. To demonstrate the creative modernization of Prince Narathip in his *lakhon phan thang,* let us look at one of his most popular and well-loved plays, *Phra Lo.*

When comparing *Ruang Phra Lo* of Prince Narathip with the original *Lilit Phra Lo,* the *Bot Lakhon Ruang Phra Lo Norarak* of Krom-Phra Ratchawang Bowon Mahasakdipholasep, and the *Bot Lakhon Ruang Phra Lo* of Chao Phraya Thewet, it is very clear how the prince revolutionized the form, structure, dialogue, lyrics, and music. While Krom Phra Ratchawang Bowon and Chao Phraya Thewet still maintain the form and structure of the *khon bot lakhon,* the prince, following the model of Western plays, introduces a division into the acts and scenes, alternations of poetic narration sung by the chorus, prose or poetic prose dialogue spoken by the actor-dancers, and lyrics sung by the actor-dancers themselves as in Western operetta. There are also folk songs sung by minor characters, exchanging (between men and women) witty remarks often concerning Thai fashionable people who try to imitate the *farang.*

As mentioned earlier, two major features of *lakhon phan thang* are the music and dancing imitating the national cultures of the countries represented in the play. In the *Phra Lo* of Prince Narathip, there are many Lao-type tunes to create the local colour for this northern Thai-Lao story.

The most modern element is the stage directions for actions and movements of the actors, replacing omitted pieces of the text or narrative. Technically, this provides more dynamic and dramatic effects for the production instead of the traditional lengthy dancing as in *lakhon nai.*

The final dance, "Thawai Phra Phon" (Salutation and blessings to the king), though rather common of most *khon* and *lakhon* performances for the king, exhibits an interesting features in describing the various good deeds of King Chulalongkorn and praising him as the leader of modern Siam. The dance ends with the "Sansoen Phra Barami" (the royal anthem) which concludes each part of the play as a separate performance. The concept of playing the royal anthem at the end of performance is definitely a Western import. It was first introduced in *lakhon dukdamban* by Prince Naris.

It is interesting to note also the absence of the detailed description of the erotic *bot atsachan* (love-making scene), which is famous in the *Lilit Phra Lo*. As mentioned in the analysis of *Ngo Pa* of King Chulalongkorn, the absence of such a scene became a common feature in the plays of this period, probably due to the influence of Western (Victorian) morality, since some *farang* dignitaries attended these performances and the king may not have wished to have such scenes presented on stage for fear of criticism. It may have been due also to the king's personal distaste for such eroticism. On the other hand, this type of scene in Thai literature (for example, in *Inao* and *Khun Chang Khun Phaen*) is written mostly for reading and not for actual performance. It would, in any case, be next to impossible on stage. It should be noted that the *bot atsachan* began to appear less and less in Thai literature from this reign onward. (It has also been a subject of strong criticism by Marxist-Maoist literary critics as representing the decadence and immorality of Thai aristocracy.)

Lakhon Dukdamban

Two names have been associated with the new form called of *lakhon dukdamban* since its origin in 1891: Prince Narisaranuwattiwong, brother of King Chulalongkorn, and Chao Phraya Thewetwongwiwat, chief of the Krom Mahorasop (Department of Royal Entertainment). These two had joined together in experimenting with many ways of modernizing Thai classical music and entertainment before their great success in the creation of *lakhon dukdamban*.

Prince Naris and His Dramatic Innovations   Prince Naris, being an all-round artist, endowed with extraordinary talents in literature, music, art, architecture, design, and decoration, was one of King Chulalongkorn's avant-garde young men. These enthusiastic royal princes, mostly brothers of the young king, formed a "clique" of their own, with the king as their leader, and experimented with new, modern ideas in literature, art, music, and entertainment, and later turned their attention to political and social reforms as well. The group started a club, called the "Magical Society," with Prince Phanurangsi Sawangwong as president. The Society introduced modern forms of entertainment, mostly imported from the West, at the New Year for the king and his royal court. One of their most talked of productions was the king's *Lilit Nithra Chakhrit* mentioned earlier. It was probably the first stage debut for Prince Naris at the age of sixteen in the role of Nang Natasol (pl. 21). However, his love was more for music, in which he acquired versatility in most types of instruments. When the prince was granted a private residence by the king at Wang Tha Phra Palace, he formed his own orchestra, with Luang Praditphairo (later Phra Praditphairo) as chief instructor for training young pages under the prince's patronage.

In 1888, the king asked Prince Naris and Prince Phanuphan Wongworadet, Chief Commander of the Krom Yuthanathikan (War Office), to help form a Thai classical orchestra made up of military personnel. The Royal Army-Navy Orchestra performed for the first time before the king at his royal birthday anniversary in September of the same year. The concert was the innovation of Prince Naris based on the model of a Western "royal command concert." For this special occasion, the prince composed a song for the king describing the natural beauty of the Saiyok waterfall, which the king had visited in 1878 with the prince in attendance as his personal guard. The musical tune for this song is "Khamen Klom Luk" (a Cambodian lullaby). The song has been a great success and is one of the most popular among Thai classical music lovers even today. It has been called "Khamen Saiyok" ever since.

One innovation of Prince Naris in this concert was the mixed chorus, in which the prince had female singers from the troupe of Chao Phraya Thewet singing with the male officer singers in his orchestra. Chao Phraya Thewet was most impressed with the prince's musical ingenuity and creativity. It was their first collaboration. From that time onward Chao Phraya Thewet invited the prince to be consultant in all his dramatic and musical activities. The prince frequented Ban Mọ Palace of Chao Phraya Thewet and often performed with the Wang Ban Mọ orchestra either in concert or at *lakhon* performance.

Another innovation introduced by Prince Naris in Thai classical music leading to the development of *lakhon dukdamban* is the dramatic musical suite. The lyrics are taken from classical *lakhon* stories, namely, *Ramakien* and *Inao,* and are connected together in short episodes to be performed as complete units in themselves, each within an hour or so. The prince called this new type of dramatic musical suite *lakhon mut* (drama in the dark), since the listeners had to see the story "in the dark," i.e., in their imagination. These innovative compositions were performed several times for foreign royal visitors at the royal palaces. Each suite was composed in many versions to suit the type and time limits of social occasions, for example, in the *Tap Nang Loi* (Floating Lady Suite), the final part (*ban plai*) was composed first as a concert piece for the reception of foreign royal visitors. Later the prince composed the first part (*ban ton*) to lengthen the performance for Thai audiences (since Thai social occasions are usually longer).

In 1894 Prince Naris experimented with another type of musical drama, imitating the "tableau vivant" of the Western theatre. He composed short musical suites for different scenes taken from tales, foreign and Thai, and presented them on stage with live characters in still poses. There were altogether eight suites. One, for instance, portrayed a scene from *Samkok* (now called the *Chulong Suite* after the main character in the scene); another told the story of Cinderella, which is called in Thai, *Nang Sin*. These were composed for Crown Prince Maha Wachirunahit to perform with his younger brothers and relatives.[67]

In modernizing classical *lakhon,* the prince first rewrote stage scripts of *lakhon nok* and *khon* by condensing the original texts and presenting short episodes with just a few characters. These were to be performed in small salons or on porches, i.e., in confined spaces. They included the episode of "Narai Prap Nonthuk" (God Narai defeating the ogre Nonthuk) from the *Ramakien,* performed on deck of the royal ship, and an episode from *Maniphichai* (*lakhon nok*) to welcome Prince Phisanulok on his brief return from Europe in 1899 at the Palace of Somdet Chao Phraya Thewawongwaropakon.[68]

In the same year the king asked Chao Phraya Thewet to entertain foreign royal visitors at Nong Bua, Saraburi. Prince Naris presented *Maniphichai* again, this time in the open air and natural setting of the forest with only one constructed pavilion. He also used torches as lighting, which lent very realistic effects. The play was preceded by a *fon* (Northern dance) and *aeo khaen* (Northeastern pipe music and songs) to create local colour for the performance. This innovative use of natural setting may have also been a result of Western influence, that of the open-air theatre. The production created quite a favourable reaction and excitement among the courtiers. It was also a practical way to reduce production expenses, while creating natural and realistic effects in the classical dance-drama for the first time in the history of Thai theatre. Though there had been *lakhon* troupes performing in the open air before, natural surroundings had not been used to their full advantage to enhance the productions. It is this style of presentation that the revival productions of *lakhon dukdamban* are modelled after today by the descendants of Prince Naris at the Wang Plai Noen Palace at Khlongtoei.

An important year for this new development was 1891. An idea imported from the West was planted in the creative mind of Prince Naris when Chao Phraya Thewet, upon his return from Europe, told him about the *farang* opera. It had so captured the attention and interest of the Chao Phraya that he wished to apply the form and technique to Thai classical music and *lakhon,* i.e., using Thai *lakhon* stories and classical music and presenting them in the form of an opera combined with ballet, having the dancers sing their parts as well as dance them. The prince, being an ardent experimentalist, immediately agreed to try his hand in composing a new stage script for this innovation. Chao Phraya Thewet built a theatre for this purpose at his Ban Mǫ Palace and prepared the costumes for the production. The prince started to rewrite the classical *lakhon* texts, trying them out with new musical tunes with the help of Luang (later Phra) Praditphairo and the musicians of the Wang Ban Mǫ orchestra. Since Chao Phraya Thewet had direct access to the Lakhon Luang and Khon Luang troupes, their dance teachers and leading dancers, the best in the country, participated in this new creation, which was to become a historic event in the development of Thai dance-drama.

The new theatre was finished and was given the name Rong Lakhon Dukdamban. With the ingenious design of Prince Naris, whose architectural and artistic work represents the best synthesis of Western and Thai art and architecture,[69] the theatre was by itself the most exciting, modern theatre of the period. (See further discussion on the modernization of theatre construction and stage design, Chapter 7.)

The new dance-drama-opera production is believed to be first presented at the Rong Lakhon Dukdamban on 27 December 1899 to welcome the royal visit of Prince Henry, brother of the King of Prussia. It later became a practice of the king to entertain his foreign royal visitors at the Rong Lakhon Dukdamban following the Western royal custom. The new form of *lakhon* performed at this theatre was hence named after the theatre, the *lakhon dukdamban*. When not commissioned by the king, the company gave public performance and collected admission fees in the same fashion as other theatres.

The *lakhon dukdamban* was performed for only ten years, until 1909, one year before the end of the Fifth Reign. Ailing in his old age, Chao Phraya Thewet asked the king permission to leave the royal service. With that the *lakhon dukdamban* ended its run at its first theatre. However, it continued to be performed by other troupes. The new dramatic form was taken up by later dramatists including King Vajiravudh, who adapted a few classical plays in the style of *lakhon dukdamban,* such as *Phra Khanet Sia Nga* (Lord Ganesha losing his tusks), *Orachun kap Thosakan* (Arjuna and Ravana).[70] King Vajiravudh, when still crown prince, also permitted Chao Phraya Thewet to produce his play, *Phra Nala,* for the first time at the Rong Lakhon Dukdamban in 1905 to celebrate his twenty-fifth birthday as crown prince. It was also the first Thai play of the crown prince to be performed in Siam.[71]

The most important features of *lakhon dukdamban,* which mark a very significant step in the modernization of Thai classical dance-drama, are as follows.

Firstly, there is the complete absence of narration sung by a chorus, or *luk khu* (lit., "companions" in singing), and the discarding of the convention of announcing or introducing a character on stage, starting with the words *"Mua nan . . ."* (At that moment . . .) for a royal character, or *"Bat nan . . ."* (Then, or Suddenly . . .) for a person of a lower status or a non-human character as in *lakhon nok, lakhon nai,* and *khon.* Prince Naris explained that since the character was already physically apparent on stage, it was rather redundant and a waste of time to tell the audiences. This absence is also applied to the description of actions or narration of the story, which traditionally precedes the actions themselves and has to be repeated again when the dancers enact the passage. It seemed rather ridiculous to the prince that the dancers had to repeat the movements and gestures at least twice, once when the narration is sung and again in dancing it to the music. Some actions seemed unrealistic and even comic, such as when Norasing was kicked by Thosamuk in *Unarut,* the dancer had to lie on the floor waiting for the narration to describe his fall and then he would rise to perform the movement again.

Secondly, with the absence of the chorus, the dancers in the *lakhon dukdamban* dance and sing their parts by themselves. The lyrics are usually taken from the *bot lakhon nai* and *bot lakhon nok,* but are presented in very condensed forms, to shorten the performance time.

Thirdly, as in the *Bot Cheracha Inao* of King Chulalongkorn, the *cheracha* (dialogues) in *lakhon dukdamban* are also mostly written in prose and in colloquial everyday language. The texts of the *cheracha* were usually written out in the way that they were spoken, in realistic manner with tonal sound marks and slang. This element of realism renders more human such noble and royal characters as Phra Ram, Sida, Inao, and Busba. They are more down to earth than they had ever been portrayed in the classical *lakhon* and *khon.* They speak like the aristocrats of the period and even swear like them, especially when talking to their servants. This could sound a bit vulgar to the ears of the middle-class, so-called "conservatives" at present who idealize the heroes and heroines in classical stories, particularly those in *lakhon nai,* such as *Ramakien* and *Inao* where extreme refinement is expected in all aspects: behaviour, speech, actions, and reactions.

In the *lakhon* playbooks of the past, the *cheracha* is usually unwritten, with only an indication where it should occur at the end of the passages. The actors improvise at will, and therefore depends largely on the wit and humour of the performers. In general, the refined characters speak poetically, using noble language, while the comedians and villains of lowly character speak vulgar, colloquial language to create a contrast. Prince Naris wrote all the *cheracha* with spelling imitating the actual sounds which appear as misspellings in written language. (This element is also found in the *Bot Cheracha Inao* of King Chulalongkorn.) Sometimes, he would start the play with a *cheracha* preceding the sung lyrics, a reverse of the normal convention. In some action scenes, the lyrics and *cheracha* are altogether absent, since the audiences can understand the story from the acting and dancing movements on stage. This modern technique not only helps to shorten the performance time, but more significantly, it excites the attention of the audiences and creates a much-needed liveliness and realism in Thai classical dance-drama.

Fourthly, there are, in most plays, interludes of folk dances and songs, especially those written for performances before foreign dignitaries, such as *Krung Phan Chom Thawip.* In this particular play, taken from an episode in the *Ramakien* which had been performed as a *khon boek rong* (opening dance in *khon*), the prince starts with a grand festive occasion, in which Krung Phan orders various types of Thai traditional folk entertainment to be performed, namely, *rabeng, kula ti mai, ram lae ti dap dang* (swords dance), Thai boxing, and *prop kai,* all of which are military sports and games (*yutha kritha*). This innovation set a precedent for later productions up to that of the Silapakon today.

Fifthly, Prince Naris and his musician colleagues experimented with many new musical tunes, most of which were traditional tunes that had rarely been used (according to Montri Tramote, there are ever five hundred tunes in Thai classical music). The musicians also used tunes imitating the music of other nationalities, the *ok phasa tang tang*.[72] In his first collection of "tableaux vivants," each scene represents a culture with tunes sounding somewhat like the music of that particular country, or, to be exact, what the Thai believe to be the music of that country. They are as follows:

Tableau No. 1: Invocation to the Hindu Trinity, Narai (Vishnu), Isuan (Siva), and Phrom (Brahma), and dance teachers.

Tableau No. 2: "Episode of Saming Phra Ram" from *Rachathirat,* from the Mon-Burmese chronicles.
Musical tunes: Phama He (Burmese), *Mon Ram Dap*, *Tanao* (Mon), *Mon Rong Hai* (Mon).

Tableau No. 3: "The Wedding of Abu Hassan and Nosater Uadat" from *Nithra Chakhrit,* an adaptation of the *Arabian Nights.*
Musical tunes: Khaek Klom Chao, Khaek Thon Sai Bua, Khaek Nang, Khaek Toi Mo, Khaek Chao Sen, Phram Dit Nam Tao, all of which represent the *khaek* (meaning Indian; Arabs as well as Malays are also classified as *khaek*).

Tableau No. 4: *Cinderella* (Western).
Musical tunes: Wilanda Ot (Dutch), *Farang Choraka* (black *farang,* i.e, dark-skinned Westerners), *Khrop Chakrawan* (universal), *Farang Ram Thao* (lit., Westerners dancing with their feet), *Wesukam* (god of art and architecture similar to the *farang* fairy, godmother who creates beautiful things by magic).

Tableau No. 5: "Lao Pi Taek Thap Cho-cho," an episode from *Samkok,* Chinese chronicles.
Musical tunes: Chin Hu Yin, Chin Sia Phi, Chin Khim Lok, Chin Chuan (*chin* = Chinese).

Tableau No. 6: "Khom Dam Din" (Khmer), an episode from *Phra Ruang.*
Musical tunes: Khamen Phuang, Khamen Khao Khiao, Khamen Pao Bai Mai, Khamen Eo Bang (*khamen* means Khmer or Cambodian).

Tableau No. 7: *Phra Lọ* (Lao), Episode of the "Kai Kaeo" (the crystal pheasant).
Musical tunes: Lao Choi.

Tableau No. 8: *Unarut* (Thai), Episode of Unarut being abducted to Nang Usa.
Musical tunes: Krabok Ngun, Blim, Tuang Phra That.

This principle was carried on in his composition of *lakhon dukdamban* and has been followed by later dramatists and musicians, as in *lakhon phan thang,* mentioned earlier. Most of Prince Naris' lyrics and musical tunes are now used in the *bot khon* and *bot lakhon* scripts of the Krom Silapakon (Department of Fine Arts), in addition to his musical suites. They are regarded as the best among the masterpieces of Thai classical music and songs for *lakhon* and *khon.* This introduction of special songs and music is one of the most important aspects of the modernization of Thai classical dance-drama.

Prince Naris also learned the Western system of musical notation and applied it to Thai music, probably for the first time in its history. In the past as well as at present, Thai music has been for the most part learned from memory. Each musician can also improvise at will according to his musical ability once he has mastered the basic tunes. (This practice is similar to that of modern jazz musicians.) The quality of the musician is judged by both his mastery of technique and creativity in improvisation and variation.

The lyrics in *lakhon dukdamban* constitute the most outstanding feature in the play, as they express deep and strong human feelings and passions, particularly in scenes depicting love, sadness, anger, violence, jealousy, heroism, and religious piety. Prince Naris modernized both the melodies and rhythms to make them more appealing to the senses. In violent or passionate scenes, he uses *rai dan* and *rai rut* as poetic forms for the lyrics to accelerate the rhythm, whereas in scenes of love and sadness, the melodies are sweet, lyrical, and soft, with the *uan* (elongating of each syllable in singing) shortened. He was a master at the most complex combination of contrasting feelings. For example, there is a scene in expressing both extreme sadness and fright in *Sangsinchai,* where Nang Kraison sees her son collapse in front of her. Here Prince Naris used the traditional *ot* tune but had it sung in the *don* style. The result is the expression of both sadness and shock.

For more dramatic effect, Prince Narathip changed the order of the plot and movements, starting the play with "Pu Chao," the old wizard-cum-demon coming to lure Phra Lo to Muang Song (City of Song). This is in contrast to the usual beginning, which introduces Phra Lo and praises his beauty (sung by a bard to the two princesses), as in the original version of the *Lilit Phra Lo.* Here, in the new version, Phra Lo, the main character, enters in the third scene and is immediately presented as having gone mad as a result of Pu Chao's black magic. He then departs for the two princesses, ending Part I of the play. This part, though constituting only one third of the story, is an entity in itself, with the introduction of main characters, development of plot, climax (i.e., Phra Lo's madness), and a denouement (his departure).

Part II also has a building up of tension in Phra Lo's "Siang Nam" and the suffering of Phra Phuan and Phra Phaeng, a climax in the scene of "Kai Kaeo" (the crystal pheasant) luring Phra Lo to the garden of Muang Song, and a denouement in Phra Lǫ entering the garden. This part is the most popular of the whole play and has been performed most frequently up to the present day, especially the *chui chai* dance exhibiting the beauty of Phra Lǫ and the aforementioned "Kai Kaeo" dance.

Another Western influence is the prince's new composition of *phleng cha prasom,* in which male and female vocalists sing in harmony in a manner similar to the Western chorus. This is a totally modern, Western feature which had never existed in Thai music and song. Traditionally, only the melody is sung either by a solo singer or chorus, or both, singing only the melody lines. However, since Thai music is very different from Western music both in tonal scale and form, Prince Naris had to adapt the harmony pattern to the Thai special musical elements. He writes,

> I have heard singing by mixed male and female voices in the concert arranged by Chao Phraya Thewet in the Royal Palace, but it was not successful. Sometimes only the women's voices were heard, sometimes only the male voices, because men have low voices and women high ones. If they sing the same melody, it has to be arranged in octaves. When the music plays in low keys, the women's voices are piercing, and the men's mumbling and disappearing; when it is in high keys, the men's voices are deafening, the women's voices unable to reach them are lowered to that of the men's and murmuring into nothingness. I saw this defect and therefore thought how to correct it. I use the *farang* method of singing in "split" voices [i.e., in harmony], having the male part lower than that of the female, only in fourths and fifths and not quite in octaves. It was more successful.[73]

Another musical creation of Prince Naris was that of a special type of orchestra to suit the small space of the Rong Lakhon Dukdamban, using a full orchestra in which all the beating sticks are cushioned (*piphat mai nuam khruang yai*) and omitting loud sounding instruments, such as the bronze xylophon (*ranat thong*) and small gong (*khong lek*), because of their piercing sounds. He also added a set of muted gongs (*khong hui thao*) at long intervals to add some low resonant sounds to the music. This new orchestral arrangement came to be known later as the *piphat dukdamban.*

Next, there are fewer *na phat* dance-pieces so as to accelerate the performance. Traditionally, the *na phat* dances enabled the leading dancers to exhibit their artistic technical ability and creativity in improvising dance movements. However, they appear repetitious to untrained eyes, especially to the *farang* and modern generations, as King Chulalongkorn often complained. *Lakhon dukdamban* concentrates more on action and a faster development of the story in a similar manner to storytelling ballet of the West. The dancing therefore is mostly *ram chai bot* (dancing to the narratives or lyrics). Only in important scenes are exquisite dances performed, such as when Nang Rotchana chooses Chao Ngo as her husband in *Sangthong*.

In the "finale" of each play, there is always a spectacular "ensemble" of the whole cast, or most of them, and a grand finale dance, ending with the royal anthem "Sansoen Phra Barami." Each play starts also with the *ram boek rong* (overture dance). During the Fifth Reign, the national anthem of the visiting foreign dignitary who attended the performance was played at the beginning, as indicated in the *bot lakhon dukdamban* of *Krung Phan Chom Thawip*. This feature of having the "overture," "finale," and royal anthem is clearly a result of the direct influence of Western opera, concerts, and ballet performances in the grand style.

A very significant point in terms of Western influence in Thai music and dramatic performance is that the music of the royal anthem is a Thai adaptation of a Western anthem written during the reign of King Chulalongkorn. In his personal letter to Phraya Anuman Rajadhon, Prince Naris explains,

> As to the melody of the "Phleng Sansoen Phra Barami" [royal anthem], I have heard many theories. Krom Mun Thiwakon was heard saying that Luang Praditphairo [Mi] was the composer and that he had adapted it from our Thai "Phleng Trae Farang" [Western fanfare]. This Luang Pradit [Mi] is clever at music. In the Fourth Reign, he composed the "Thep Banthom" and "Phirom Surang" songs, for instance. But I am afraid this may have been an assumption. . . . But I have also compared both [i.e., the melodies of the "Phleng Sansoen Phra Barami" and our "Phleng Trae Farang"] . . . there is no similarity to the "Phleng Sansoen Phra Barami" at all. Another theory was heard from Krom Luang Chumphon that we had purchased the "Phleng Sansoen Phra Barami" from a *farang* in Yaho [in Malaya] when His Majesty [King Chulalongkorn] visited Singapore and India. The music was composed for sale. There were then people who spread the information [as if they knew the truth] that the royal anthem of some country is the same as ours, because the music was bought from the same source. But the king doubted the theory, as there is a lot of Thai music in the melody of "Phleng Sansoen Phra Barami." If the *farang* had composed it, the melody had to be *farang*. I agree with him. I only remember that in the past we played the English royal anthem, then we changed it to the "Phleng Sansoen Phra Barami." But I cannot remember when we did it. . . . As to the melody of "Phleng Sansoen Phra Barami," I don't know who composed it or from where it came. But I composed the lyric to be sung in the *lakhon dukdamban* for the first time. Then, His Majesty [King Vajiravudh] revised it later.[74]

Last but not least, another aspect of modernization by Prince Naris in *lakhon dukdamban* is his artistic, three-dimensional, and realistic set designs. This again was directly influenced by the Western theatre. In the past, *lakhon* and *khon* had been performed on a very simple stage without any decoration other than a long bench which was used as a throne, a seat, or even a log or a stone platform in the forest. Later probably starting in the Fifth Reign, painted backdrops were used depicting scenes of palaces, forests, sea, or heaven (pl. 20). It was Prince Naris who introduced for the first time in the history of Thai theatre architectural set designs in three-dimensional perspectives following Western models, yet with elaborate and exquisite Thai decorative designs (pl. 25). Natural settings were also used to heighten realism, and special effects in lighting and sound increased the theatrical attraction of the production, to the point that many people came to see the plays only for these exciting and delightful theatrical effects. (See a more detailed discussion in Chapter 7.)

The artistic talent of the prince also helped to improve the style of make-up, changing it from the mask-like appearance to a more realistic, human style. (See the discussion in Chapter 7.) Only the *lakhon* costumes remained the same as the traditional style with leading characters wearing elaborate, tightly sewn costumes fitted to their bodies.

Prince Naris' musical and dramatic works represent in themselves the appearance of Western influence in Thai drama and music and the Thai assimilation and application of that influence into the existing Thai culture and arts. The following is a collection of his published works, some of which were especially written for foreign dignitaries, and some of which remained unfinished. Many of them contain remarks by the author revealing his purposes and methods of modernization.

1894   Musical suites for eight "tableaux vivants" for Crown Prince Maha Wachirunahit's (Fifth Reign) production with young royal princes and princesses in the Royal Palace.[75]

1898–99   *Bot Mahori,*[76] music and lyrics for *mahori* orchestra for concert performances to entertain foreign royal guests:

1) *Nang Loi* ("ban plai"). Episode of the Floating Lady, i.e., Sida (the final part), from the *Ramakien*. To welcome the Count of Turin from Italy at the Chakri Hall at the Royal Palace on 13 December 1898.[77]

2) *Phromat* from the *Ramakien*. Episode of the battle between Inthrachit and Phra Ram, Phra Lak, in which Inthrachit uses the magic arrow, Phromat. To welcome Prince Henry of Prussia, scheduled for the end of 1898, but the prince did not arrive as planned. The suite was later performed on 17 April 1899 for M. Paul Doumer, the Governor-General of Indochina, at the Chakri Hall.[78]

3) *Nakhabat* from the *Ramakien*. Episode of the battle between Inthrachit and Phra Ram, Phra Lak, in which Inthrachit uses the magic arrow, Nakhabat. To welcome Prince Henry of Prussia. However, according to Prince Naris' memoirs, the concert given for Prince Henry in December 1899 was instead the episode of "Buang Suang" (The sacrifice to the gods) from *Inao,* and not the *Nakhabat* as originally planned.

Later, Prince Naris added another suite to the *Nang Loi* and *Nakhabat* to lengthen the performance to two or three hours for Thai audiences, depicting the first part of each episode (the previous suites are a little over one hour long). Hence, they are called the *Nang Loi Ban Ton* (*Nang Loi,* first part) and *Phromat Ton Ton* (*Phromat,* first act), and the former ones, *Nang Loi Ban Plai* (*Nang Loi,* last part) and *Phromat Ton Plai* (*Phromat,* last part).

In Prince Naris' collected plays and songs (*Chumnum Bot Lakhon Lae Bot Khap Rong*), there are eight *bot lakhon dukdamban*. Unfortunately, the dates are not available. They are:

1) *Sangthong:* from the episode of "Luak Khu" (Choosing a mate) to the "Ti Khli" (Polo match); three acts and six scenes.
2) *Khawi:* from the episode of Khawi being tricked by the old Thao Thatprasat to that of "Khanthamali Khun Hung" (Khanthamali being jealous) when her old husband, Thao Sannurat, wants to rejuvenate himself, a trick of Honwichai; three acts, seven scenes.
3) *Inao:* from the episode of "Tat Dokmai Chai Krit" (Cutting the flower and flashing the kris) to that of "Wai Phra" (Worshipping the gods), and "Buang Suang" (The sacrifice to the gods); three acts and five scenes.
4) *Sangsinchai,* Part 1: from the episode of Sangsinchai being pushed over the cliff by Sisan with the intention of killing him, to when Nang Pathuma starts out to look for her lost son (Sangsinchai), ending with the search (for Sangsinchai) by the Vietnamese[79] sailors carrying lanterns of different colours and singing a Vietnamese song (in Vietnamese); three acts, six scenes.
5) *Sangsinchai,* Part 2: from when Thao Senakut prepares a grand reception with various kinds of entertainment to welcome the return of his six children, and Nang Kesonsumontho tells him the truth about the good deeds of Sangsinchai and the evil deeds of his six children, to when the god Indra revives Sangsinchai and saves his life; three acts, six scenes.
6) *Unarut:* the episode of "Krung Phan Chom Thawip"; four scenes, especially written for a foreign dignitary on a state visit. The prince explained,

"This *Bot Lakhon Dukdamban Ruang Unarut,* I composed for a production to welcome a *farang* state visitor. But which one, I cannot recall. . . . I adapted it especially, having many characters dressed in different costumes, and choreographing beautiful movements, making them more rapid, playing beautiful songs, but having the least numbers of words [lyrics] as possible, because the *farang* could not understand them. This version of *Unarut* was not performed, either because the guest who was scheduled to come did not appear, or because the king did not ask for it, I could not remember."[80]

7) *Surapanakha* episode from the *Ramakien* written for a production at the Ante Parikathurin Club in the Royal Palace during King Chulalongkorn's second tour of Europe in 1906. During the eight months of the king's absence, the high officials assembled together at the Royal Palace for administrative meetings, followed by a high tea or a dinner sponsored by members of the royal family and high-ranking officials who took turns. The gatherings became a club with members from inside and outside the palace. A clubhouse was built for the purpose and was called "Samoson Ante Parikathurin." There were also various kinds of entertainment provided by the sponsors. At the turn of Phraya Prasoet Suphakit, Prince Naris was requested by the Phraya to write a *lakhon* for the performance. The prince chose this episode from the *Ramakien* and explained,

"I chose the story of Surapanakha, which had been in my mind, and wrote the stage script for the performance because it is a short episode. Thus there is very little script. It has never been performed again elsewhere since then.

I arranged a small stage, using two parallel Cantonese monks' seats as the stage floor, and produced many types of entertainment, one of which was a *lakhon dukdamban* [the episode of Surapanakha]."[81]

The most interesting point about this particular *bot lakhon* is that it was taken from the *Ramayana* of Valmiki which the prince had read in English. It was probably the first time in the history of Thai classical theatre and dramatic literature that the original version of the *Ramayana* was used as a source. It should also be noted that King Vajiravudh, who is often given the credit for being the first person to introduce the *Ramayana* of Valmiki, was not, in actual fact, the pioneer. Prince Naris should be credited with his first creative venture along this line. It was not until 1909 that Crown Prince Vajiravudh wrote and produced his versions of the *Ramakien* for his amateur *khon* troupe, the "Khon Samak Len." Later, he adapted many episodes from

Valmiki's *Ramayana,* again indirectly through the English translation, in the form of the *bot lakhon dukdamban* following the model of Prince Naris. Prince Naris was therefore his predecessor and guru, whom he consulted on *khon* and *lakhon.*

Another interesting aspect of this production of Prince Naris is the use of natural make-up for the *yak* (ogres) character of Surapanakha, instead of the traditional *khon* mask. (See the discussion in Chapter 7.)

In the prince's personal note to his niece, Princess Phatthanayu Diskul, he explained his use of the Sanskrit names as they appear in the original Indian version instead of the Thai names: for example, Ram (for Phra Ram), Laksamana in the dialogue pronounced "Laksman" (Phra Lak), Surapanakha (Samanakha), Raphana or Ravana (Thosakan), Wiphesana or Wiphisana (Phiphek).[82]

8) Episode of "Pisat Nang Adun" (The ghost of Adun) from the *Ramakien* (not existing in Valmiki's version). In this episode the demoness Nang Adun provokes Phra Ram's jealousy and causes Sida to be banished after her short return to Ayodhya. There are six scenes. The names of the characters here are Sanskrit.

9) *Inao:* Episode of "Phao Muang" (Setting the city on fire). Unfinished; three scenes.

10) *Khun Chang Khun Phaen:* Episode of "Wanthong Hung" (The jealous Wanthong). Unfinished; six scenes.

These last three *bot lakhon dukdamban* (nos. 8–10) were written for the production of Chao Phraya Thewet, but remained unfinished, and hence not produced. They contain some of the best examples of his use of colloquial language and slang with deliberate misspellings to represent the phonetics of the spoken language. This same technique had been used in the *Bot Cheracha Ruang Inao* of King Chulalongkorn, but not to this great extent.

Prince Naris also composed *bot lakhon nok:*

1) *Maniphichai* adapted from the *bot lakhon nok* of King Rama II, using natural setting and torches. To welcome the Count of Turin from Italy at Nong Bua, Saraburi in 1898. There were also performances of Northeastern dances and songs such as "Aeo Khaen," and "Soeng." Later, Chao Phraya Thewet asked Phraya Kaset to add to the last part of the story the performance of his *lakhon dukdamban,* which appears in the National Library version.[83]

2) *Unarut:* Episode of "Som Usa" (Usa's night of love): *Unarut* is usually performed as *lakhon nai.* This episode was written as *lakhon nok* for the tonsure ceremony of Mom Luang Wong Kamalat (Kunjara) around 1904. Prince Naris composed this *bot lakhon* especially for the eight-year-old daughter of Chao Phraya Thewet to perform in the role of the

infant Thosamuk. She could dance beautifully and had danced for the king to his great pleasure in the role of Nang Maeo, the cat in *Chaiyachet*.

3) *Sangthong:* Episode of "Thuang Sang" (Drowning the conch): Written for the tonsure ceremony of Mom Luang Wong Kamalat, again with Chao Phraya Thewet's daughter performing as the infant Phra Sang. In this *bot lakhon* there was also a scene with an elephant which is forced to stamp on Phra Sang. There was a very clever elephant in the house of Chao Phraya Thewet called "Phlai Mongkhon" that was trained to perform in *lakhon*.

These three *bot lakhon nok* of Prince Naris differ from tradition in that they are shorter and more action-oriented. The *cheracha* (dialogue) is also very modern and realistic, and the music more varied in tunes.

This extensive collection of Prince Naris' dramatic and musical works demonstrates clearly how the creative prince was a daring pioneer in experimenting with various types of dramatic forms and music in order to modernize Thai classical dance-drama and to adapt it to the taste and mentality of his contemporaries. The modernism of his work still achieves successful results today. The lyricism of his poetic texts and musical tunes, and the witticism of his dialogues, has hardly been matched by later works. His pioneer spirit represented this age of modernization and Westernization, in which the intellectual and artistic elite competed in their experiments, be they political, social, literary, or artistic. Following generations have been fortunate to gather the fruits from trees which had been planted by their forerunners of the Fifth Reign. Princess Duangchit Chitraphong, daughter of Prince Naris, concluded in her Preface to the *Chumnum Bot Lakhon Lae Bot Khap Rong,*

> Somdet Chao Fa Krom Phraya Naris is thus praised by people who like unusual things and things which change to suit changing taste, in as much as he had great ability in devising and arranging things to appear at their best. These are things that are still liked by many people today. However, there are also a number of conservatives, who like to preserve very strictly the traditions and thus criticize him as being *nok khru* (deviating from the footsteps of the teachers, i.e., revolutionary) and that he destroyed the traditions of Thai art, music, and literature. Prince Naris used to say that if we hold on only to the principles taught by the teachers and do not think of any improvements, knowledge will gradually become "thinner." But if we adapt and correct something, using the proper principles and methods, it can only improve. But if we have not studied it seriously first and try to adapt it, not knowing really what we are getting into, it will lead only to destruction.[84]

The princess also added that if her father had lived today he would surely experiment with modern media, those new scientific devices and techniques such as television, tape-recorders, electrical appliances, and rotating stages. When he saw the later productions of his own *lakhon dukdamban,* he complained that they were outdated and too slow. If there was an opportunity, he said he would produce a new kind of *lakhon* and would get a lot of fun (*sanuk*) out of it.[85]

The most frequently quoted saying of Prince Naris is:

> Among people who act, sing, dance and play music, I see that there are three types. I will nickname them "pupils," "teachers," and the "mad men." The "pupils" will do only what they are taught to do. . . . The "teachers" have much more knowledge than the former group and have the wisdom to choose only the good models following the traditions. As for the "mad men," even if they have the knowledge they will depart from it and do what they feel like doing.[86]

He then classified himself among the last group. Yet most people who know his works and achievements would not deny that his "madness" was in truth his creative genius, kindled by the fire of his innovative spirit, which set the Thai classical drama on a new and exciting path leading to the present day.

Lakhon Rong

Prince Narathip is also accredited with having originated *lakhon rong* (singing dance-drama) towards the end of the Fifth Reign. There is still a debate among authorities on Thai drama about its origin. King Chulalongkorn in his letter to Chao Dararatsami stated that the prince imitated *farang* opera, in adapting *Madame Butterfly* into *Sao Khrua Fa,* the most popular and well-known *lakhon rong* of the period. He expalined:

> *Ruang Khrua Fa* [The story of Khrua Fa] is the story of *Madam Butterfly,* which I mentioned in my *Nangsu Ruang Klai Ban* [*Letters Far from Home* by King Chulalongkorn written on his first royal tour of Europe] about Paris. The Japanese is changed to Lao, and *farang* to Thai, that's all. The reason he [the prince] composed the lyrics imitating *farang* opera in this way was because he had heard a Khmer prince singing it.[87]

However, according to Prince Damrong, Prince Narathip was influenced by the "Malay opera" called Lakhon Bangsawan Malayu which was performed for King Chulalongkorn at Saiburi on his royal tour of the Malay Peninsula. In his *San Somdet* (correspondence between Prince Damrong and Prince Naris), Prince Damrong explained:

In *rọ sọ* 109 [A.D. 1891], Somdet Phra Phutthachao Luang [King Chulalongkorn] toured the Malay Peninsula. When he was at Muang Saiburi, Chao Phraya Sai arranged for a *lakhon malayu* (Malay dance-drama), which had been newly created. It was called *bangsawan* and translated into English. Many years after, the Lakhon Bangsawan troupe came up to perform in Bangkok at a theatre near the Burapha Palace, near my old house. . . . and it was this Lakhon Bangsawan that Krom Phra Narathip adapted into *lakhon rong* and had it performed at the Pridalai Theatre. Later, others, such as Mae Bunnak, followed the example. However, everyone, even Sir Josiah Crosby, the English minister, in his speech at the Rotary Club recently, praised Krom Phra Nara for having originated *lakhon rong*. Nobody knows that he received the idea from the Lakhon Bangsawan Malayu.[88]

According to other authorities, Chao Phraya Thewet was the first to introduce, after his tour of Europe, the idea of Western "opera-ballet" into Thai classical theatre in his creation, together with Prince Naris' *lakhon dukdamban.*

The *lakhon rong* of Prince Narathip was first performed at the Wiman Narumit Theatre, or Rong Lakhon Narumit. When the theatre burned down, the prince constructed a new one at his palace at Phraeng Nara (see Chapter 7). The new theatre was called the Rong Lakhon Pridalai, and this type of *lakhon rong* became known as *lakhon pridalai,* in the same manner as *lakhon dukdamban.*

In the beginning, the plays were about current events and domestic problems. Since the idea and form were totally new and rather foreign, *lakhon rong* at first did not gain much popularity with Thai audiences, who were used to *lakhon ram* (dance-drama). As King Chulalongkorn wrote to Chao Dararatsami,

For the *lakhon* performance to celebrate the new house of Princess Soi [Princess Phuangsoisa-ang] and Khun Mot [Chao Chom Manda Mot], Prince Narathip had already sent me the playscript, which I have enclosed in this envelope for you to read. The story is *Khuat Kaeo Chiaranai* [The crystal bottle] which he performed at the Wiman Narumit at Wat Saket. . . . "Lakhon Krom Nara" seems to be gaining a little more success. Even so, there are still such small audiences that the elite rarely see it, *because it is a new thing. They don't understand it. They have to do a lot of listening and watching* [i.e., to concentrate] *and cannot look other ways, as they will not be able to follow the story.* Usually, people who go to see a play like to sit and talk with each other. Only to see the dancers moving about here and there, to hear a little singing and some sounds from the *phinphat* orchestra, that's enough. *They only want to talk, that's why they don't like it.* [89]

It seems that this comment could still be applied to Thai audiences in general who prefer dance-drama to serious play-acting. Spoken drama with lengthy speeches is only appreciated by a very select group of intellectuals, who are accustomed to Western drama.

Later, as Prince Narathip introduced more exotic tales adapted from the *Arabian Nights* and other romantic, tragic, melodramatic, and adventure stories, the *lakhon rong* became very popular, especially that which had first been performed in the Royal Palace. King Chulalongkorn commented on this newly acquired success of the prince and his plays:

> Talking about "madness," the courtiers are now "mad" about "Lakhon Krom Nara," every person, every name, from the masters to the servants. Since you left, there have been many more performances, and from the time that you set up the rule not to allow men to come in and see it, there has not been one single male in the audience. The consequence is that the men who did not see it became very frustrated. It's up to Krom Nara, whether he will perform the play again after having performed it in the royal court at the Pridalai Theatre. If he does, the audience will be large. In the past, I went to the theatre of Krom Nara, and there were not more than 500 present. But since he has performed in the Royal Palace, there are not enough seats. This happens only to the plays which have been performed in the palace and are later performed outside. The money collected from the outside performances is over 10,000 baht. Krom Nara exclaimed that it was due to the "the glorious virtue of the king."[90]

This statement proves that the king's patronage was a most effective stimulus to the development and expansion of drama. The king also rewarded the best actors and actresses, some with as much as 100 baht: for example, Nang Phrom, who performed the role of Sao Khrua Fa (the Thai version of Madame Butterfly), was rewarded with 100 baht for her suicide scene,[91] and some comedians received as much as 200 baht each.[92]

The greatest success in the *lakhon rong* genre of Prince Narathip was *Sao Khrua Fa,* the adaptation of *Madame Butterfly* set in the scenery of Chiengmai. The hero is an army officer from Bangkok and the heroine a northern beauty of Chiengmai. The adaptation is very successful even today, because it is still a practice of the Bangkok "playboys" to flirt with Chiengmai girls, who are renowned for their innocence and beauty, and to leave them heart-broken, often with fatherless children. The story has been produced repeatedly on stage and screen. The most recent film of it was made in the late 1960s.

The reason for the success of *Sao Khrua Fa* in the Fifth Reign was not only because it was a moving, tragic romance, but also probably because the king talked favourably of *Madame Butterfly* in his *Klai Ban* (Far from home) letters when he visited Paris on his first royal tour of Europe, as the king commented,

> In observing the preference of the people in these later dates, they seem to like *Sao Khrua Fa* more than any other play, to the point that there have been letters sent by mail asking for repeat performance at a particular *wik* (theatre)[93] because it is a *lakhon farang* story. Another is because they think the king likes it since he mentioned it in the *Nangsu Klai Ban* [Letters far from home]. But the most imortant reason is E Nang Phrom, who played the role of the heroine. When she came in to perform at Wang Tha Palace, she was given as much as 100 baht at one time for cutting her throat [in the suicide scene]. Some people suggested that there should be a *lakhon somphot* [dance-drama for a special royal celebration] for three days when you return [from Chiengmai]. I am afraid that we shall have to repeat the plays because you have missed seeing many of them. They are guessing that you will ask for a repeat performance of this *Sao Khrua Fa*.[94]

This particular play should have had great personal appeal to the princess consort of Chiengmai, Chao Dararatsami, since the romance between the Chiengmai heroine and the Bangkok hero relates directly to that of hers and the king's in reality, without of course the tragic in the story. However, it is known that the princess had gone through some difficulties while residing at the Royal Palace due to the domineering role of Queen Saowaphaphongsri and to jealousy among certain consorts and their entourages. Being of the Northern royal family, whose kingdom was a vassal and subject to the king of Siam, the kingdom of Chiengmai was very sensitive politically. It was a common political practice of the kings of Siam to take royal princesses of Chiengmai as consorts to ensure and exemplify the nature of the relations between the two states. However, King Chulalongkorn was famous for having mastered the art of being the perfect lover, who could convince each of his many queens and numerous consorts that she was very dear to his heart, as if she was the one and only wife he had. His personal correspondence with them, probably the biggest collection of all Thai kings on this subject, conveys sincerely his feelings, his thoughtfulness, and his tenderness. His letters to Chao Dararatsami, in particular, are counted among the most celebrated love letters in Thai literature.

There are certain similarities between *lakhon rong, lakhon dukdamban,* and *lakhon phan thang.* The first similarity is the division into acts and scenes following the model of Western plays. A special feature in *lakhon rong* is the thematic title for each act. The last word of each title rhymes with the first or second word of the next, and together they tell the plot and the themes of the story. For example,

Act 1: "Thon Man" (Calling off the engagement)
Act 2: "Khan Mangmi" (Competing in wealth)
Act 3: "Sethi Lom" (False millionaire)
Act 4: "Lom Lalai" (Bankruptcy)

This can perhaps be not directly a result of Western influence. The idea may have come from the Western vaudeville or scenes in melodrama, in which there are placards on stage or notes in theatre programmes announcing the acts. However, the rhyming of the titles is purely Thai.

The second similarity is the singing and speaking of lyrics and dialogues by the actor-dancers themselves, with a chorus, or *luk khu,* in certain parts in the case of *lakhon rong* and *lakhon phan thang,* while *lakhon dukdamban* omits narrative completely.

The third point of similarity is the simplification of movements in *lakhon phan thang* and the bare minimum of dancing in *lakhon rong,* to the point that King Chulalongkorn referred jokingly to them as the *lakhon kam kam bae bae*[95] (dance-drama in which dancers only open and close their hands). In *lakhon rong* the female performers only sway their bodies to the music and gesture with their hands; whereas *lakhon dukdamban* still maintains the refinement of dancing, as in *lakhon nai,* with a certain amount of modernization in rapid and action-oriented movements, as earlier discussed.

The fourth point is the use of a great variety of musical tunes, both old and new, Thai and foreign, which express emotions and actions. The musical rhythms are also faster in most of these plays, and the singing has less *uan* (slurring and elongating of each syllable). Folk songs and tunes are also a new feature common to these three forms, found predominantly in *lakhon phan thang* and *lakhon rong,* since the stories in *lakhon dukdamban* are mostly classical.

The main differences between *lakhon rong,* on the one hand, and *lakhon phan thang* and *lakhon dukdamban* are in the stories, the dialogue, the dancing, the musical accompaniment, the costumes, and the set designs.

As mentioned earlier, stories in *lakhon rong* are mostly concerned with everyday domestic problems in a contemporary setting, or are adaptations of foreign tales, the most popular being either from the *Arabian Nights* or Western comedies, melodramas, and tragic romances. On the other hand, *lakhon dukdamban* depicted classical tales taken from *lakhon nai* and *lakhon nok,* while *lakhon phan thang* depended largely on Thai and foreign (i.e., Asian) chronicles and historical tales. The favourite themes in *lakhon rong* are that of the love triangle, *yua phua yua mia* (provoking the husband, irritating the wife), major wife vs. minor wife, interchanges of identities, false identities, evil or goodness in disguise, unrequited love, or happy romance ending in marriage and fortune. During the Sixth Reign, patriotic themes became fashionable following the political campaigns of King Vajiravudh, particularly during the First World War when the king announced the Thai alliance with the West. Many plays praising the allies as the righteous powers standing against the evil power of Germany were written and widely performed.

The dialogue in *lakhon rong* can be either in prose, poetic-prose, or poetry. It is spoken or sung by the actors. The language is modern and colloquial, with a less strict rhyming pattern.

Since the stories were all new, all the lyrics and dialogues had to be original creations set to either popular or traditional musical tunes already existing at the time, adaptations of classical and folk tunes, or a brand-new score. The music accompaniment is simpler than that of *lakhon ram.* In the first period, the orchestra consisted of the *phinphat mai nuam* (xylophone with cushioned beating stickes), the *so u* (two-stringed fiddle), and *krap phuang* (a bundle of castanets). In the later period a four-piece modern band replaced the traditional orchestra.

The most important feature that contributed to the great success and popularity of Prince Narathip's *lakhon rong* was the choice of musical tunes and lyrics expressing great emotion, particularly in scenes of sadness, love, anger, violence, or jealousy. According to some authorities on *lakhon rong,* the choice of emotion-charged lyrics appropriate to the actions and situations in the plays is essential to this type of drama, as music and songs are the main features in the plays. They have to be sung with deep feeling, the singer reaching the highest notes to move the audience to tears. Often the wish to heighten emotional tension seems false and exaggerated, as in many Western melodramas.

Most of the musical tunes in *lakhon rong* are dual-level (*song chan*). The word "level" (*chan*) here, however, refers to the degree of elaboration of musical figures and grace notes, i.e., the higher the *chan,* the greater the elaboration. In extending the musical notes, each syllable of the lyric is sung in a moderately slow *uan* (slurring and elongating of the syllable), which requires great singing ability. At first, there was still a chorus (*luk khu*) singing the narration with a lot of *uan.* Later, the *uan* parts became shorter and were sung by the actors themselves to quicken the pace of the production. In *lakhon rong* of the last period in the reign of King Prajadhipok, Rama VII (1925–35), even the musical accompaniment, the "Phleng Reo," which used to be played by the orchestra alone, was filled with lyrics and sung by the actors. When the actors sing their parts, there are usually responses by the chorus in unison to supply emotional support. In some parts, when the actors are performing very important actions, such as committing suicide, the chorus will sing a narration until the actors pick up their cues again.

Unlike in *lakhon ram,* the costumes and settings of *lakhon rong* are as contemporary as the situations in the plays: for example, the men wear *pha muang* (a silk sarong pulled up at the back to look like pantaloons), the white *ratchapataen* (royal pattern) jackets with high collars, and Panama hats, or military uniforms. Women wore long silk *phanung* (skirts) and lace blouses, with fancy ribbons, sometimes hats, and silk stockings and high-heeled shoes. Informal male attire for the *phu di* (aristocrats) consisted of *kang keng phrae* (Chinese silk trousers worn very high up above the waist in the fashionable style of the Fifth and Sixth Reigns), round-necked shirts without collars made of thin fabric, and long hanging silk hankerchiefs. In Western, Chinese, or Arabian stories, national costumes in Thai adaptations were used.

As to the set designs, there were changes of sets, usually four, according to the division into acts and scenes, as in *lakhon dukdamban* and *lakhon phan thang.* The stage was a proscenium stage facing the audience as in Western plays. There were three bells, the first to announce the beginning of the performance, the second for the entrance of musicians and singers, and the third the beginning of the action. At intervals between scenes and acts, there were usually dancers or comedians performing in front of the curtain for about fifteen minutes. These comedians, as in all *lakhon,* were indispensable. They were usually companions or servants of the leading characters, the heroes and heroines, as in Elizabethan plays. They were always men, while the main characters, both male and female roles, were performed by women as in *lakhon nai.* Many leading stars of *lakhon rong* were those cast in the hero roles. The most popular were Mae Bunnak, Mae Luan, Mae Chamoi, and Mae Sinuan, who dressed like men even in their off-stage lives. Their admirers were mostly women and young girls, as is the case with the celebrated Japanese female dancer-singers of the Shochiku and Takarazuka companies, who perform as men. They were usually more attractive than those performing the female roles, being both handsome as men and strikingly pretty as women, too.

At present, there are over seven hundred *bot lakhon rong* in the collection of the National Library, probably the biggest collection of any single type of play in the corpus of Thai drama. These playbooks were published mostly in the Sixth and Seventh Reigns, when *lakhon rong* enjoyed great popularity. They were sold at the theatres for 50 *satang* each. Following the Pridalai Theatre of Prince Narathip there were several other *lakhon rong* companies. Among the more successful of these were the Pramothai, Nakhon Banthoeng, Phatthanalai, and Chantharophat (in a later period) companies. Others were the Thep Banthoeng, Banthoeng Ruam Mit, San Banthoeng, Pramot Muang, Pramot Nakhon, Pramot Banthoeng, Pramothai Banthoeng, Duriyang Bamroe, Banthoeng Sayam, Banthoeng Narumit, Kasem Narumit,

Ratri Phirom, Charoen Thai, Chaloem Krung, Thatsanalai, Mano Samai, Busba Natasala, Ratri Phatthana, Seri Samroeng, Prathuang Thai. It is quite obvious that some of the companies names were taken after one another.[96]

These numerous theatres and troupes were not only in Bangkok; there were also many more travelling troupes, or *lakhon re,* all over the country up to the Revolution of 1932 and shortly after. Then *lakhon chai ching ying thae* (plays in which real men and women perform their own roles) and talking pictures (the cinema) began to "steal" audiences from the original *lakhon rong.* It soon went into decline and finally into extinction. It was briefly revived again on television by some old "pros" left over from the Seventh Reign. The revival was more or less educational in purpose, to show the present generation the art of *lakhon rong.* It was an exhibition of a historical museum piece rather than a true revival. It therefore faded quickly away again and did not catch the attention of a permanent audience. Again, for educational purposes, Thammasat University presented another exhibition, with this same group of actresses and male comedians, for the public in the "Dance, Drama, and Music Festival" of 1971. This was probably one of the last efforts to demonstrate a dramatic genre which has now become a monument to the theatre's recent past.

Quoting from a statement by an authority of Thai drama, Princess Duangchit Chitraphong, daughter of Prince Naris, comparing the approaches of the two dramatists, Prince Naris and Prince Narathip, "Prince Naris applied the *farang* techniques to Thai *lakhon,* whereas Prince Narathip made Thai *lakhon* to appear like the *lakhon farang.*"[97] That is to say, the former tried to modernize the Thai classical *lakhon* by applying Western theatre techniques, yet maintaining the Thai classical character, such as in the art of dancing, music, costume, and poetry, while the latter tried to bring Thai *lakhon* closer to the Western forms in simplifying the dancing, using modern costumes, and composing modern songs and music after Western models of operetta and ballet.

Judging from the numerous personal notes and letters written to Prince Narathip towards the end of his reign, King Chulalongkorn seemed to prefer the Lakhon Luang Narumit (later Lakhon Pridalai, i.e., *lakhon phan thang* and *lakhon rong*) of Prince Narathip to the Lakhon Dukdamban of Prince Naris. Though in earlier times, the Lakhon Dukdamban Company of Chao Phraya Thewet, with Prince Naris as the main creative form behind it, had officially served the king in entertaining many foreign royal visitors (as mentioned earlier), it did not seem to receive as much personal attention from His Majesty as that of Prince Narathip's works. The king even spent time editing the *bot lakhon* of Prince Narathip and frequently gave constructive criticism, whereas he seemed to treat *lakhon dukdamban* with due respect and at times was even critical of its slow, repetitious performances, which he found utterly unnecessary.

The king once wrote to Prince Narathip to consider how to modernize the *Ramakien* in the better way.

> . . . on such an occasion the Lakhon Luang [Royal Lakhon Troupe] would join in the performance [of the *Ramakien*]. There are some young dancers who could dance the roles well. But to perform it now in the traditional way is no longer satisfactory.
>
> The audience would be bored with it. The story is rather bland. You could improve it in which every way you like. But if it is too dragging and not *sanuk* (fun), we don't need it.[98]

The king seemed to be very concerned how best to entertain his foreign guests so that they, who did not understand the language, could get the most enjoyment out of it. The attempt of Prince Naris to show very old traditional entertainment, such as *rabeng, kula ti mai, khon chon prop kai* in the *Krung Phan Chom Thawip,* though it had cultural value, was boring to the king because of the length and repetition of these dances. However, he approved of the choice of Prince Narathip to perform *Phra Lo* for the Duke of Brunswick, as it had *Lao khaen* bamboo pipes, wind instrument dances and music of the Northeast, which would be exotic and interesting to foreigners. He comments,

> Concerning the *lakhon* to receive the Duke of Brunswick, *Phra Lo* is good. It has both fun and tragic qualities for those who do not understand the language . . . the quiet garden scene later in the play, wouldn't it be boring to those who do not know the language? . . .
>
> We have to imagine ourselves as if we don't know the language. Be careful about the later scenes, which will be performed late in the evening, try not to make the audience sleepy. The *Lao khaen* and *lakhon ram* [dance-drama] should be fun, but in three hours, I'm afraid is too long. If it could be two hours, it would be perfect. . . .
>
> When you rehearse it until it is satisfactory, bring the *Lao khaen* to perform for us here one day, because it is a new thing. I think after I have completed the arrangement at the Royal Hall [i.e., Dusit Palace], we should have a rehearsal one day, to practise the women [dancers] so that they would not be awkward. When it is ready for a real performance, please let me know.
>
> Sayamin[99]

Some authorities said that during this period the king was very much in favour of the Northerners, since Chao Dararatsami, Princess of Chiengmai, was then one of his favourite consorts. The plays of Prince Narathip which had northern Thai-Lao flavours, such as *Phra Lo* and *Sao Khrua Fa,* received therefore His Majesty's special attention. However, even without this reason, it is rather evident that King Chulalongkorn had an inclination towards the romantic and the exotic, as seen in his own compositions of *Ngo Pa* and *Nithra Chakhrit,* as well as his personal love letters to his queens and consorts. He was also in favour of the *farang* way of doing things and was impressed by *farang* theatre while touring Europe. However, he always cautioned his close associates not to blindly imitate them, and even mocked those who were over-enthusiastic about the *farang* culture. He once commented about sending Thai students to learn the art of Western opera with an Italian professor.

> About the opera, I think it is impossible, if we still sing and have our orchestra in this way. The *farang,* they can sing with twenty or more violins, because they bay like dogs. But the way we sing is like mumbling, the *phinphat* orchestra will overpower the voice. . . . if they [the Thai students] go for training, when they return, I am afraid they would not be able to do much except bay like dogs. Actually, the important thing is the student himself. If the student has the ability to adapt it to Thai, not to imitate it directly and sing it in Thai, with a *sala luk khun* face [face of a lawyer in the court house, i.e., expressionless]. He has to be able to adapt it well as in the case of the temple of Wat Benchamabophit [the Marble Temple, designed by Prince Naris].[100]

The Role of Women in the Modernization of Traditional Dance-drama

As mentioned earlier, the other two persons responsible for the success of the Lakhon Luang Narumit or Lakhon Pridalai of Prince Narathip were Chao Chom Manda Khien, his mother, and Mom Luang Tuan Worawan, his consort. Both came from long lines of families of dancers and musicians. Chao Chom Manda Khien was a relative of Somdet Phra Nang Chao Somanat Watthanawadi, the first queen of King Mongkut. Queen Somanat was the first to revive the training of young dancers to perform *lakhon nai* in the Royal Palace.[101] However, she suffered an untimely death of a rather mysterious cause in 1852,[102] before her *lakhon phuying* (female *lakhon*) could perform for the court. She had inherited the art of *lakhon nai* dancing from her father, Phra Chao Boromawongthoe (3d grade) Phra-ong Chao Lakhananukun, the owner of well-known *lakhon nai* troupe in the reign of King Rama II. After the death of her mother, King Rama III adopted her and treated her as his own.

Khien Siriwan was trained since the age of eight in the queen's palace by the teachers of the Royal Lakhon Nai troupe of the Second Reign. After the death of Queen Somanat, Khun Khien stayed on with the queen's mother, Chao Chom Manda Ngiu, who gave her further training with the assistance of Khru Bua, a male *lakhon nok* teacher (as Khun Khien performed the role of Phra, i.e., the male part). Khru Bua came from the troupe of Krom Phra Phiphitphokphuben.[103] She also trained many other female *lakhon nai* teachers of the Second Reign. Khun Khien was therefore adept in both *lakhon nai* and *lakhon nok.* When still young, she performed the role of Siyatra, Busba's younger brother, in *Inao.* Later, she was promoted to more major roles and finally to that of Inao himself, which brought her fame and success and gave her the pseudonym "Khun Khien Inao."

When King Mongkut revived the Lakhon Luang in the Royal Palace, Chao Chom Manda Ngiu presented to the king all her female dancers. Many of them, including Khun Khien, became his consorts and gave birth to many royal princes of the rank of Phra-ong Chao. The consorts were therefore promoted and given the title of "Chao Chom Manda."

When Khun Khien gave birth to Phra-ong Chao Worawannakon (later Krom Phra Narathip Praphanphong), King Mongkut gave his royal swords to be put in the child's cradle, following the tradition of initiating a royal prince. In addition, the king sent as a symbolic gift a *kris* (which is Inao's personal weapon in the Javanese royal custom) saying, "He is Inao's son" (i.e., son of "Khun Khien Inao," the dancer-consort).[104]

Chao Chom Manda Khien held a highly respected position in the royal court, not only because of her own fame as a prima-dancer since the Fourth Reign, but further for her training activities in the Lakhon Luang of King Chulalongkorn, and later for her choreography and direction in the Lakhon Luang Narumit Company of her son, Prince Narathip. King Chulalongkorn once commented on the great influence she had on the *chao wang* (lady courtiers), most of whom had learned *lakhon* dancing from her, "You [Prince Narathip] know that Mae Khien has all the *chao wang* as her disciples. If she complains about anything, her disciples will always side with her."[105] This letter referred to the crisis concerning the objection of Chao Chom Manda Khien to the king asking the teachers of the *lakhon* company of Chao Phraya Mahin to perform and teach in the royal court. The *chao wang* dancers considered this particular troupe inferior and below their standard, because of their simplified style of dancing.

It was the intention of the king to join together these separate groups of *lakhon* dancers, and he asked Prince Narathip to act as mediator.

> My personal preference is to have them perform together. She accepts that their [Chao Phraya Mahin Company] ideas, stories, role playing, and stage decoration are very good. She has nothing to do with it or against it. The only thing she refuses to give in is the dancing and to have the *lakhon* of Chao Phraya Mahin be considered *khru* [teacher]. In this she cannot join with them. It would be rather degrading to her honour and prestige.
>
> Therefore, if you could make way for a royal diplomacy to be established between the two parties, I would be very happy. If this should be an obstacle, because of the conflict between the *nai* [Inner Court] and the *nok* [outside the royal court] [i.e., the *lakhon nai* of

Chao Chom Manda Khien and the *lakhon nok* of Chao Phraya Mahin], we could cancel the performance of *phongsawadan* [the chronicle play of Chao Phraya Mahin Company] and perform the *Inao* for one day. When there is a performance of *phongsawadan* at the theatre, I would go myself to see it, because there are probably not many women who understand it. . . . Moreover, as Mae Khien is so dominant, the disciples in the palace will follow her example in refusing to accept it.[106]

This crisis is an example to show how the tradition of *lakhon nai* in the time of the absolute monarchy was jealously guarded by the *chao wang* and those related to the royal family. Though both Prince Narathip and Chao Phraya Mahin produced *lakhon phan thang* and *lakhon phongsawadan* (chronicle plays), the *lakhon* of the former was better accepted by the *chao wang* than that of the latter, as Chao Chom Manda Khien was the main force in directing, training, and choreographing for the prince's company.

As to the other important personality in the Lakhon Pridalai (Lakhon Luang Narumit) Company, Mom Luang Tuan Worawan, her "Montrikun Na Ayudhaya" family had produced as many as four generations of dancers and musicians since the reign of King Rama I. Her great grandfather was Chaofa Krom Phra Phithakmontri, the head master of the Lakhon Luang troupe of the First Reign and the creator of the *lakhon nai* style of dancing in the Ratanakosin period. He has been worshipped among the great teachers in the Invocation Ceremony by Thai classical dancers and musicians until this day. His dance movements and gestures in *lakhon nai* have been the foundation of Thai classical dance. Prince Phitakmontri inherited the *lakhon nai* troupe from his brother, Chaofa Krom Luang Thep-harirak, after the latter's death. In the reign of King Rama II, he choreographed for all the *lakhon* of the king. His son Mom Chao Baen and his grandson Mom Ratchawong Tap (father of Mom Tuan) continued the family's line of musicians and dancers. According to an authority on the Lakhon Pridalai, Mom Tuan "genetically speaking received the inheritance of music—the 'seeds'—from her ancestors."[107] As shown in her musical compositions, variations, and adaptations of traditional tunes and songs to suit new plays, such as the Lao-type songs in *Phra Lo,* which are still very popular today, it is evident that Mom Tuan had inherited the creative talent of her great grandfather. Her songs are among the most important for Thai musicians and singers to learn. After the Revolution, when Princess Laksami, daughter of Prince Narathip, started a *lakhon* company, she continued to give advice on the dancing and music. In her old age, she was often consulted by many groups who wished to revive traditional *lakhon ram,* such as the family of Prince Naris in reviving *lakhon dukdamban* and Somphop Chantharaprapha in his *lakhon phan thang* and *lakhon phongsawadan.* (Though he called them *lakhon dukdamban,* it is not accepted as such by other authorities.) At present, many disciples of both Mom Tuan and Chao Chom Manda Khien are teaching in the circles of Thai classical dance and music.

In this rather lengthy discussion on the two personalities of the Lakhon Luang Narumit or Lakhon Pridalai Company, Chao Chom Manda Khien and Mom Luang Tuan, the writer would like to show how and why the Company attained such great success and popularity with its rare combination of three geniuses at work together: i.e., Prince Narathip in the *bot lakhon* and production, Chao Chom Manda Khien in the choreography and training of dancers, and Mom Luang Tuan in the music and songs. It is also revealing that King Chulalongkorn, during the last years of his reign, was more personally involved in *lakhon* production, particularly that of the Lakhon Luang Narumit Company. They received more of his personal attention and concern than did other troupes or companies. Lastly, in tracing the long family lines of Chao Chom Manda Khien and Mom Luang Tuan, it is shown that the inheritance of Thai classical music and dance is usually continued without interruption by old families for many generations from the beginning of the Ratanakosin period to the present through the successive reigns of the Chakri dynasty.

NEW CREATIONS IN DRAMATIC LITERATURE AND THEATRE

Lakhon Phut (Spoken Drama)

As in other Asian countries, the traditional form of Thai drama has always been and will continue to be that of dance-drama. The spoken dialogue, or the *cheracha,* only plays a supporting part at the intervals of dance and lyrics. In *khon,* the *cheracha* is always in poetic *rai* with rhyming words in an irregular pattern. In *lakhon nai,* it was traditionally poetic prose or spoken lyrics. It was probably Prince Naris and his contemporaries including King Chulalongkorn, who wrote the *cheracha* in the *lakhon nai* in contemporary colloquial prose, as shown in the *cheracha* of *Inao* by King Chulalongkorn and in the *lakhon dukdamban* of Prince Naris. While in the *lakhon nok* as performed by folk troupes, the *cheracha* is mostly in prose or poetic prose with much more slang, earthy, often obscene humour, comic expressions, and vulgar allusions to the subject of sex. However, in the *lakhon nok* performed by the royal troupe, these characteristics are understandably toned down, as in the *bot lakhon nok* of King Rama II and Prince Naris.

It was not until this Fifth Reign that spoken prose drama, or "straight plays," as it is referred to in the West, was first introduced in the Royal Palace, again by King Chulalongkorn, and not by his son King Vajiravudh, as it is generally thought.

The first production of *lakhon phut,* or the spoken drama, was an experiment of the king after the Western model. Prince Damrong recorded in his *Tamnan Lakhon Inao.*

Sometimes there were parties for the New Year. The king had *lakhon* performed by amateur actors, the *lakhon smak len* [voluntary *lakhon*]. The performers were members of the royal family, and some were *khunnang* [noblemen, high officials, aristocrats], whosoever volunteered. But the performance was that of *lakhon phut*. It is considered that the spoken drama in Thai first originated then.[108]

The plays were taken from *lakhon ram* (dance-drama), such as *Sangsinchai,* originally *lakhon nok,* or tales. The last play performed in this new style was *Nithra Chakhrit* by King Chulalongkorn in 1879. Crown Prince Vajiravudh had his stage debut in the same play in a children's production in 1892. It was probably his first exposure to this type of drama, which later continued to be his favourite pastime while studying in England and remained so after his return to Siam.

The fact that this modern genre of drama, a direct import from the West, enjoyed only a short period of experiment for only a few years and did not continue after 1879 until Crown Prince Vajiravudh revived it again in a more complete form after his return from England reveals the distant relationship between this type of Western entertainment and the Thai audiences who much prefer dance-drama in all forms, traditional and modernized, albeit *khon, lakhon nai, lakhon nok.* Even their variations and new diversions in *lakhon dukdamban, lakhon phan thang,* and *lakhon rong* were successful because they maintained many aspects of *lakhon ram.* They all represent to the Thai the concept of "total theatre," which is able to entertain them with a variety of audio-visual attractions.

Despite the efforts of Kings Chulalongkorn, Vajiravudh, and their successors, *lakhon phut,* ever since its origin in Siam until the present day, has not seemed to catch on with Thai audiences, except among the intellectual and Westernized elite. *Lakhon phut* therefore has to incorporate dance, songs, and music to secure any success among general Thai audiences. Serious social and political plays, though attracting intellectuals, have very little chance even in the contemporary theatre, whereas melodramatic, historical, domestic, and straight-forward patriotic plays with songs and dances gain favourable responses.

Towards the end of the Fifth Reign, *lakhon phut* made its timid and modest debut within a close circle of the elite and courtiers. Crown Prince Vajiravudh was a major force behind its development. One of his first literary and cultural activities two years after his return from England was to establish on 30 March 1904 the Thawi Panya Smoson (lit., "increasing wisdom") Club to promote literary, dramatic, and cultural activities among the educated elite. The Club had as its members young members of the royal family, mostly Western-educated, and young noblemen friends of the crown prince. A clubhouse was built with a small theatre attached to it for meetings and entertainment. According to Mom Luang Pin Malakul, it was probably the first theatre for "straight plays" in the country.[109] The Club published a literary magazine called *Thawi Panya,* with articles on political, economic, literary, social, and cultural subjects, to which the crown prince was a major contributor, using different pen names. In 1904, in one of the *Thawi Panya* magazines, Crown Prince Vajiravudh stated the purpose of promoting dramatic activities at the theatre of the Club.

> I have consulted with some committee members, and we are of the same opinion that we can stage plays in the new theatre for members of the club and their relatives and friends. Tickets will be sold at a moderate price.
>
> There will be approximately a hundred seats. Quite a number of club members have heard of my plan, and they are quite enthusiastic.
>
> We hope to produce an entertainment better than *liké.*[110]

The first production of *lakhon phut* presented on 30 March 1904 by this Club was *Som Pho Som Luk* (Like father like son). The event was reported by the crown prince in *Thawi Panya* five weeks later, as quoted above. However, since the proper theatre was not yet finished at the time, the play had to be performed at the clubhouse.

On 1 May 1905 at the farewell party for Prince Asadang Dechawut, the librarian of the Club, the crown prince himself produced another *lakhon phut,* this time at the newly completed theatre. From then on, the Thawi Panya Smoson company gave many public performances of *lakhon phut,* many of which were written by the crown prince himself. Among the better-known *lakhon phut* written by the crown prince for this theatre is *Hen Kae Luk* (For his child) which, according to Mom Luang Pin, "brought tears from the actors on the stage, as well as from those in the audience."[111] As its title suggests, the play is a melodramatic, domestic drama, a genre which always wins over the hearts of Thai audiences.

Among the plays of Crown Prince Vajiravudh during his first period after his return to Siam from 1904 to 1910 (at the end of the Fifth Reign) are included *Ching Nang* (Stealing the lady), *Nintha Smoson* (Gossip Club), *Koen Tong Kan* (Too much of a good thing), *Hen Kae Luk, Khwam Di Mi Chai* (Victory of goodness), *Noi Inthasen* (The Earl of Claverhouse), and *Ha Lo* (The shield).[112] The first three are translations: *Ching Nang* from *The Rivals* by Richard Brinsley Sheridan, *Nintha Smoson* from *The School for Scandal* by Sheridan, and *Koen Tong Kan* from a French play by M. Tristan Bernard. The last four were original.[113] For a pen name, the crown prince used "Phra Khan Phet" (diamond dagger), the weapon of Hanuman in the *Ramakien* (hence the name is also given to Hanuman). It may also be symbolic of wit and wisdom, both of which are also attributes of Hanuman. Other pen names during this first period were "Sri Ayudhya," or simply "Nayok To Po So" (president of the Thawi Panya Club). These plays were written during his residence at the Sranrom Palace for his men to perform, hence the troupe was called the Lakhon Sranrom. They were presented usually at the Rong Lakhon Thawi Panya Smoson theatre, which was also situated in the compound of the Sranrom Palace. It therefore became later a customary practice of King Vajiravudh in his own reign to have a theatre in the palace or wherever he resided. It could be considered an effective means to promote theatre activities throughout the country. However, the theatres were in general restricted to the "inner clique" of the king or the upper class and were not open to the public, even in the productions to raise public funds for worthy causes.

On 5 October 1905, Crown Prince Vajiravudh invited the members of the "Samakhayachan Club" to see a play at the Thawi Panya Club theatre and gave them a special reduction on admission fees.

Following the example of the Thawi Panya Smoson, the "Samakhayachan Smoson" (Teachers' Club, which had been founded by the Ministry of Education in 1903) presented a *lakhon phut* for the public in its annual festival on 24 December 1905 and collected admission fees (1–3 baht for members, 2–4 baht for the general public).[114] It seemed that *lakhon phut* began to spread among the educated in Bangkok, or as Mom Luang Pin stated, it was "the beginning of a new era."[115]

The above statement could refer to the development of drama in the Fifth Reign as a whole. With the new creations of *lakhon phan thang, lakhon dukdamban, lakhon rong, lakhon phut,* and the modernization of the traditional classical dance-drama, the foundation of the modern Thai theatre was laid. At this historical junction, the old and the new merged. Though undergoing many awkward hybrid-cultural defects and weaknesses, these first attempts exhibited the enthusiasm, unbound creative energy, receptiveness to foreign (i.e., Western) influences, hard-working effort, and open-mindedness of these "modern leaders of society," which certainly led Thai drama to attain another "golden age" and set standards and models for many generations to come.

This progress was not without controversy and obstacles. One of these was the very Abolition of Slavery Act issued by King Chulalongkorn himself. On the one hand, the Act gave freedom to all Thai citizens, and on the other hand, it effected the manpower and free labour of many enterprises. The private *lakhon* troupes began to suffer from this problem. Many eventually went out of business. The few which remained were either the royal troupe or those sponsored by wealthy noblemen and members of the royal family. This drastic change led to the gradual decline of the classical theatre, more precisely *lakhon ram*. It was directly and indirectly forced to take other modern forms, either *lakhon rong, lakhon dukdamban,* or *lakhon phut,* which in a way helped to extend modern Thai drama in a more secure path. Among these three genres, *lakhon rong* seemed to achieve the greatest success (as mentioned earlier), whereas *lakhon dukdamban* declined after a decade, despite the attempt to recreate it in the later period, and *lakhon phut* still had a long way to go in proving its social and dramatic value among the less sophisticated audiences.

Despite these obstacles, the Fifth Reign in all its aspects, albeit political, social, economic, and cultural, is one of the most important turning points in the history of Thai theatre, as well as in the history of modern Siam as a whole.

Appendix

Synopsis of *Ngo Pa*[116]

Prologue   King Chulalongkorn invents a situation in which he makes a royal tour of the south of Siam and visits a Ngo village in Phatthalung, where he hears this story from an old woman. He also states here his purpose in composing the story as a play in *klon* verse.

Scene 1   Khanang, a Ngo orphan, and Mai Phai, his close friend, enjoy their childhood hunting in the jungle. Here the poet describes different wild animals, birds, trees, plants, and flowers in the Thai literary convention of admiring nature. The two boys sing a folk song in the Goi language.[117]

Scene 2   Somphla, a young Ngo man, in love with Lamhap, sister of Mai Phai, suffers from his desire to marry Lamhap and from fears of being disappointed, for his social position is inferior to hers and to that of her betrothed suitor, Hanao. He joins Khanang and Mai Phai hunting in the jungle. Somphla bravely kills a tiger to the praise and admiration of the two boys. Mai Phai encourages him to send a love message to Lamhap and promises to arrange their meeting. Somphla sends wild flowers and a tiger's claws as a love message to tell Lamhap that he will fight his rival for her hand and abduct her if her parents refuse him.

Scene 3   Lamhap, unhappy at her parents' marriage arrangement with Hanao, for whom she has no love, receives from Mai Phai, her brother, the love message from Somphla. Being afraid of conflict and danger, she keeps silent so as not to give him further encouragement. She goes to gather flowers and roots in the jungle. Mai Phai informs Somphla, who comes secretly to admire her beauty. A snake is about to bite her, but Somphla kills it instantly. Lamhap faints. Somphla embraces her and brings her back to consciousness. Lamhap, being grateful to him, accepts his love.

Scene 4   A comic interlude of an old couple, Ta Wang Song and Nang Thing, whose courting is teased by Khanang and Mai Phai.

Scene 5   Yo Pan, Hanao's father, arranges the wedding for his son. Here the author describes in detail the preparation for the wedding. Hanao, in his best bridegroom costume, dances gracefully. The Ngo rhythmic dance and procession of maidens add vivid, picturesque, and exotic touches to the scene.

Lamhap cries her heart out. Mai Phai quickly informs Somphla, who sends a secret message to his beloved that he will take her away on the night of the wedding.

Scene 6 The wedding is performed in a grand style with a religious ceremony and the parents' blessing. When left alone Hanao tries to make love to Lamhap who refuses him. The Ngo children help Somphla in throwing stones at the nuptial hut, driving Hanao out to chase them and leaving Lamhap alone to be abducted by Somphla.

Scene 7 The two lovers, Somphla and Lamhap, spend a blissful time hiding in a cave. Hanao is enraged. He searches for them. Somphla has a nightmare that a big rhinoceros and a tiger kill him. Both lovers fear for their lives. Somphla, despite his beloved's warning, goes out to hunt for food and meets Hanao. They fight each other in a duel. Somphla is shot with an arrow by Hanao's brother, Ramkaeo. Lamhap runs to her husband's side and bewails his tragic end. Somphla, before he dies, forgives Hanao and asks him to take care of his wife. Lamhap kills herself with Somphla's hunting knife, followed by the suicide of Hanao. Ramkaeo buries the three lovers and informs their parents and the villagers. The play ends with a religious funeral ceremony, the last comments and mourning songs of the parents, and the moral of the story.

Chapter IV
Modern Thai Drama and Western Influence

The Reign of King Vajiravudh, Rama VI

King Vajiravudh and Modern Thai Theatre

Many Thai scholars regard the reign of King Vajiravudh, Rama VI (1910–25), as a "golden age" of Thai drama. Under his leadership and personal effort, modern Thai drama and theatre arts evolved and took a new educational, social, and political role. Having participated in drama since childhood (pl. 23) and having been educated in England and exposed to Western theatre from childhood when he was crown prince, the king introduced Western dramatic literature and new theatre techniques in acting, directing, script writing, and set and costume design to the modern generation.

The king was a very versatile dramatist who tried his hand in almost all forms of theatre. In classical dance-drama he introduced new political ideas in *khon* (masked dance-drama), *lakhon nok,* and *lakhon nai* and new social concepts in *lakhon rong* and *lakhon dukdamban*. Within the form of *lakhon phut* (spoken drama), he experimented with different styles of writing: poetry, poetic prose, prose with songs and dances, and historical and social plays. According to the record, the total collection of his plays consists of approximately 180 plays, 143 of which are in Thai and 37 in English, written within a span of twenty years from the time he was crown prince to the end of his reign (1905–25). This is undoubtedly the largest collection of plays by a single author in the history of Thai drama, an average of about one play every two months. The king wrote daily with amazing ease. One time at Bang Pa-in summer palace, during a twenty-day stay, he wrote, produced and directed ten short plays a night. Most of the plays written during his short reign are *lakhon phut* in verse and prose, some of which were adapted for performance as *lakhon rong*.

The young king realized that Siam was entering a very difficult time, politically, economically, and socially. While the Western-educated military and civil officials increasingly demanded democracy to replace absolute monarchy, the majority of the people were uneducated and underdeveloped.

He was deeply concerned that they would easily become victims of power-hungry leaders who tried to introduce socialism as a means to create political disturbances among the poor. The king saw an oncoming danger and therefore tried to use drama as a tool to educate, inform and prepare his people for the modern world.

Western Influence in the Introduction of Modern Theatre

Western civilization and culture, which came into Siam during the reigns of Kings Rama III, Rama IV, and Rama V, was a gradual, assimilating, and synthesizing process. In the areas of theatre and dramatic literature, King Vajiravudh, from the time of his education in England, followed by his return as the crown prince, introduced many new ideas, concepts, modern theatrical forms, and techniques through his writing and producing of Western plays first in direct translation and adaptation, and then eventually in the creation of his own plays.

The king translated and adapted many English and French plays including those of Shakespeare, Sheridan, Molière, and Gilbert and Sullivan. Most of these plays are comedies to suit the *sanuk* (fun-loving) character of the Thai. The plays usually end happily, with all problems solved, conflicts reconciled, wrong-doers reformed and forgiven, and the righteous, virtuous heroes and heroines rewarded with love, marriage, and fortune. This is all in the tradition of Thai drama.

A few of his plays are tragedies, mostly translations or adaptations of Western great masterpieces, such as Shakespeare's *Romeo and Juliet* and *Othello* (adapted into *Phya Ratchawangsan*). The king remarked that Thai audiences did not like plays with tragic endings. There is also a superstitious belief that the death of a king or a royal person of great stature on the stage would cause misfortune and calamity to the theatre and performers. However, the Westernized king vowed that he would introduce a new kind of comedy of greater value than the local *liké* (folk dance-drama in the style of low comedy full of sexual insinuation). As he noted in the journal of the Thawi Panya Smoson (Club for Intellectual Development), which he founded in 1904 two years after his return from Europe,

> I consulted with some committee members. We agreed to produce a play in the new theatre and invite members and relatives to see it. We would not charge them much for each seat. Estimating the seating capacity, we think that 100 seats could be arranged. I have talked with some members who came to the party on the first of this month, they seemed happy to come to the play. I believe that our performance will be much more fun than *yiké* [*liké*].[1]

Among the Western comedies chosen by the king were Shakespeare's *As You Like It* (translated into *Tam Chai Than*), Sheridan's *The Rivals* and

The School for Scandal (adapted into *Ching Nang* and *Nintha Smoson,* respectively), Molière's *Le médecin malgré lui* (adapted into *Mo Cham Pen*), and *Mikado,* a comic opera by Gilbert and Sullivan, adapted into *Wang Ti* with Thai songs and music composed by the king himself. In some other plays he merely took the stories from Western or Asian (mainly Sanskrit through English translations) sources. He would then write new Thai scripts and lyrics. This experience led him into writing his own plays, such as *Noi Inthasen* (a farcical comedy in three acts), which may well be his first Thai play in prose without depending on any foreign sources.[2] He later wrote another version of the play in English under the title, *The Earl of Claverhouse.* It was also translated into French under the title *Le Duc d'Erretchagay* by M. René Pradère-Niguet, a French legal advisor to the Ministry of Justice.

Beside introducing Western plays to the Thai audience, the king also applied Western theatre techniques in directing, acting, stage management, and set and costume design. He himself tried his hand in every department of the production and taught the courtiers the new methods and techniques of modern realistic theatre. In the genre of classical and historical plays, he was the first Thai playwright to study the archaeological and geographical evidence for social, economic, and political accuracy. All these were new to the Thai, particularly the research methodology which the king acquired from his education at Oxford University. For educational purposes, he made a habit of writing an informative introduction to each of his plays and published his writings for circulation among his peers and the educated middle class. Many of his writings and plays are still being used as standard textbooks in schools and universities today.

In relating drama to the education of the people and the socio-political development of the country, King Vajiravudh deserves the title, "father of modern Thai theatre." The themes and subjects of King Vajiravudh's plays are usually about domestic and social values and political issues concerning duty, responsibility, and loyalty to the nation and to the king. Each play ends with a moral lesson or a speech by a main character emphasizing moral virtues, national obligations, and sacrifice for the country and the monarchy.

A New Political Approach to Classical Dance-drama: *Khon* and *Lakhon Ram*

King Vajiravudh found great significance in the *Ramayana* of Valmiki, which supports the concept of ideal kingship and loyalty to the monarchy. He therefore adopted and propagated this new political concept in the Thai *Ramakien* to make it the most important national myth of Siam, in which the figure of the ideal king, Rama, or Phra Ram, is magnified and fully projected.

It is noteworthy that the king's personal selection of the particular episodes of the *Ramakien* from traditional *bot khon* (scripts for masked dance-drama) and *bot lakhon ram* (scripts for dance-drama), which he recomposed or adapted or revised for the *khon* and *lakhon ram* performances were, in most cases, filled with either political, social, or cultural significance. In rewriting the *bot cheracha* (dialogue) in these classical dance-dramas, he was able to communicate his ideas to audiences who, on most of these theatre occasions, were the new leaders of society. The episodes from the *Ramakien* chosen for his productions were therefore usually those showing the deep loyalty of the soldiers and generals of Phra Ram to the monarch, or the concept of the right ruler overcoming the wrong and amply rewarding his supporters and assistants according to their dues.

Among his new adaptations of the classical dance-drama, there are six *kham phak khon* (narratives for masked dance-drama) and *bot rong* (lyrics) of various episodes in the *Ramakien*.[3] However, they follow the story-line in Valmiki's *Ramayana*. He also wrote nine *bot boek rong* (prelude pieces),[4] seven *bot lakhon dukdamban*,[5] seven *bot lakhon ram*,[6] and three literary texts in which the king attempted to trace from the Sanskrit sources the origins of myths directly related to Thai *lakhon ram* dance-drama. They are *Bọ Koet Ramakien* (Origin of *Ramakien*), *Phra Non Kham Luang* (The story of Nala told in the *kham luang* style, narrative of mixed versification and formal, courtly language), and *Lilit Narai Sip Pang* (The ten incarnations of the god Narai in *lilit* poetry). Among his adaptations of *lakhon phan thang* is the episode of "Taeng Ngan Phra Wai" in *Khun Chang Khun Phaen*. With such a large collection and a great variety of dramatic texts, and because of his efforts to promote Thai classical dance-drama and its dancers, and to relate traditional Thai dance-drama to contemporary social and political contexts, King Vajiravudh came to be worshipped by Thai classical dancers as the father of *lakhon* in modern times.

In his *lakhon ram,* such as the allegorical *lakhon, Thammathamma Songkhram* (War of righteousness) written in 1919 after World War I had ended, the king explicitly expressed his views in support of the Allies, personified by Thamma Thewabut (God of dharma), and condemning their enemies, personified by A-thamma Thewabut (God of evil). This play derived from a *thamma chadok* which was told by Patriarch Wachirayan in a sermon for the king. (Thamma Thewabut was a Bodhisattva in his former life, and A-thamma Thewabut was Thewathat, his antagonist.)

The king composed other ballet pieces, called *rabam* or *lakhon ram* (in some editions they are also referred to as *lakhon rong*), on a similar theme of good conquering evil: for example, *Thamma Mi Chai* (lit., victory of dharma) and *Mit Mi Chai* (lit., victory of friends), which the king translated as "The Triumph of Friendship" and had both of them performed for Sir Edward Brockman, High Commissioner of the Confederation of Malaya[7] in 1917. In the finale dance of the *thewada* and *nang fa* celebrating the victory of Mit, god of friendship, over Phalasun, the villain who wanted to steal the rays of the sun from the gods, the dancers waved national flags of the Allied countries. This type of political manifestation in a dance was repeated again during

19 Royal dancers (all male) during the reign of King Mongkut. The middle group (*seated*) are dancers in *lakhon nok, Sangthong,* with Chao Ngo wearing a mask.

20 Royal dancers (all female) during the reign of King Chulalongkorn, possibly performing a dance of gods and goddesses in *Inao* play. Female characters are wearing *rat klao yot* head-dresses; male characters are wearing *chada* royal crowns.

21 King Chulalongkorn (*centre seated*) and his brothers in *Nithra Chakhrit* (*Arabian Nights*), a spoken drama in poetic prose with songs. Prince Naris is seated on the right.

22 Royal children's production of *Nithra Chakhrit* in the Fifth Reign. H.R.H. Prince Vajiravudh (*centre seated*) as the heroine Princess Sobide.

23 H.R.H. Prince Vajiravudh in the role of Princess Sobide in the royal children's production of *Nithra Chakhrit* in the Fifth Reign.

24 Khanang, the adopted Ngo boy in the court of King Chulalongkorn, in a Thai classical dance costume as Chao Ngo in *Sangthong,* a *lakhon nok.*

25 Prince Naris' Javanese-Thai style temple setting designed in three-dimensional perspective for *Inao* in the *lakhon dukdamban* style in the Fifth Reign.

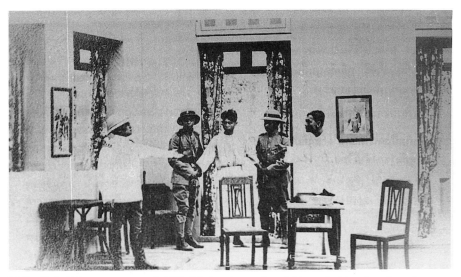

26 Realistic living room set and 1920s Thai costumes in a *lakhon phut* (spoken drama), *Huachai Nak Rop,* by King Vajiravudh.

27 Drawing of Phra Ruang after the costume design by King Vajiravudh for his play, *Phra Ruang,* a *lakhon* in verse with music and songs.

28 King Vajiravudh playing the role of Nai Man Pun Yao, a forest scout, in *Phra Ruang*, 1917.

29 King Vajiravudh (*centre,* pointing his finger) in the role of Nai Man Pun Yao on the stage in *Phra Ruang*, 1917.

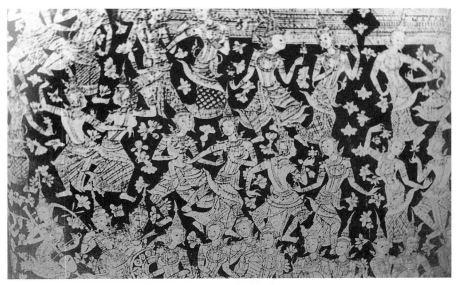

30 Painting depicting a dance scene. Male and female dancers are wearing traditional classical dance costumes of the Ayudhaya, Thonburi, and early Ratanakosin periods.

31 Classical *lakhon* dancers of the Silapakon (Department of Fine Arts) demonstrating a dance movement.

32 Mixed male and female dancers playing the *phra* and *nang* roles in the *Ramakien,* a classical dance-drama, in the 1950s.

33 Training young female dancers in front of the royal chapel of the Palace of the Front, where the College of Dance and Music, Silapakon is located. Late 1980s.

34 Khunying Phaeo, head dance mistress of the Silapakon, demonstrating a movement to a leading dancer in a *lakhon* rehearsal, possibly in the 1950s.

35 Dance of the ghost of Nang Wanthong and wood nymphs in *Khun Chang Khun Phaen.* The costumes and choreography by Khunying Phaeo were inspired by the Western ballet, *Les Sylphides,* in the 1950s.

the Marshal Phibunsongkhram regime in the 1940s and 1950s to promote international and diplomatic relations with neighbouring countries, either Japan or the Western powers, depending on the specific occasion and purpose of the performances attended by the particular foreign dignitaries and guests of the government. The style of the finale dance was developed by Prince Naris in the Lakhon Dukdamban Company in the Fifth Reign. However, in the Sixth Reign it was put into full use for political purposes.

King Vajiravudh also composed and produced short *lakhon boek rong* (dance-drama for the opening of the theatre, i.e., prelude pieces) in the style of the *dukdamban* (i.e., ancient) tradition, that is, the traditional religious dance-drama about the gods, principally Vishnu and his different incarnations, which he had also translated and composed in his *Lilit Narai Sip Pang*. Among these *lakhon boek rong* are "Maha Phali," "Rusi Siang Luk," "Phra Norasinghawatan," "Phra Khanet Sia Nga," "Sudawatan" (or "Narai Prap Nonthuk"). In "Maha Phali" there is a message for government officials and civil servants about their duties and responsibilities to the country and to the king. In "Rusi Siang Luk" (an episode from the *Ramakien*) the hermit throws his three children into the water and prays that the ones who are his true children return to him and those who are not to turn into animals. Nang Sawaha is the only one to swim back in her original human form, while the other two become monkeys and run into the jungle. (They are Phali and Sukhrip, the two leading generals of Phra Ram.) Phali is the son of the god Indra and Sukhrip, son of Phra A-thit, the sun god. Hence in the Thai *khon*, Phali is green and Sukhrip red, as the colours of their fathers, while in other Asian countries they are identical, and usually red in colour (in India, Indonesia, Malaysia, etc.). The king's theme of the selection of the faithful and true among his followers, whom he often referred to as his children, is very obvious here.

The New Role of *Lakhon Phut* in Politics and Society

It was through *lakhon phut* (spoken drama) that the political and social ideas of King Vajiravudh found more effective means of expression.[8] The three best examples are *Huachai Nak Rop* (Heart of a warrior, 1914; pl. 26) *Phra Ruang* (*lakhon phut kham klon* version, 1917; *lakhon rong* version, 1924; pl. 27), and *Chuai Amnat* (*Coup d'état*, 1923). *Phra Ruang* was probably the first attempt to create a national myth from the legendary figure of Phra Ruang who fought against the Khmer rulers and who finally became king of Sukhothai (pl. 28). King Vajiravudh had originally composed the text of this play for *lakhon ram* (dance-drama) performance, but later adapted it to spoken drama in *klon* verse for the Wild Tigers Corps. As he explained in the Preface,

> This *Bot Lakhon Kham Klon Ruang Phra Ruang* I have composed because the members of the Wild Tigers wished to perform the story of "Phra Ruang," since it is a good story to stimulate a

sense of nationalism for the Thais. But the *klon* text which I had originally composed was for a *lakhon ram* performance in the traditional style. It would therefore be difficult for the members of the Wild Tigers to perform, because it requires *lakhon* dancing and movements which are difficult for those who have never been trained in them. For this reason, I have composed a new text in the form of *lakhon phut kham klon* to make it convenient so that those, who have never received training in *lakhon* dancing in the traditional style, could perform it.[9]

As the Thai theatre began to change the character of dramatic entertainment from quasi-religious, courtly to quasi-political, social ones under the influence of modern trends and pressures, the *lakhon ram* in the traditional style was no longer adequate and effective for communicating these new concepts and ideas to the modern public, since what was needed was immediate and direct verbal expression rather than a lengthy display of beautiful dance movements and refined gestures. The performers of *lakhon phut* and *lakhon rong* do not have to undergo strenuous and long periods of training as do classical *lakhon ram* dancers. Most of those who performed in this reign were amateurs. This is still true at present, even among the so-called professional *lakhon phut* actors, who are in actual fact amateurs with long experience on stage, rather than true professionals with good formal training in their trade.

The political themes of patriotism and sacrifice for the nation in *Huachai Nak Rop,* of nationalism in *Phra Ruang,* and justification for the system of absolute monarchy against socialist revolution in *Chuai Amnat* would have been lost, or only vaguely suggested, if the three plays had been performed as traditional *lakhon ram.* In the realistic style of these *lakhon phut,* the messages seem more convincing and show direct relevance to the audiences of that time. However, at present, these *lakhon phut* plays of King Vajiravudh seem outmoded, since the language used in them is no longer current and the style of presentation old-fashioned and unnatural. This explains the failure of the revival by his admirers in modern times of the king's plays on stage and television.

In the Fifth Reign, King Chulalongkorn gave royal patronage to private *lakhon* troupes outside the Royal Palace. In the Sixth Reign, King Vajiravudh put this into full practice and followed a Western model of conferring the word "royal," or *nai phra rachupatham* (under royal patronage), upon the theatres, troupes, productions, and any activities deemed appropriate. He also elevated the social status and position of dancers and actors by granting the leading ones noble titles. This again was adopted from the practice of Western monarchs (more precisely the English kings and queens), who confer titles of "Lord," "Lady," "Dame," etc., upon leading actors and dancers. One has only to look at the cast lists of the royal *lakhon* and *khon* performances under the direction of King Vajiravudh to see that the majority, if not all, were titled

"Phraya," "Phra," "Luang," and "Khun," especially among the dancers of the Khon Samak Len troupe. It is often said that the quickest way to obtain these noble titles was to join the troupe and perform well in it. These noble titles were so abundant in the Khon Samak Len (either because the dancers were originally titled nobles, high officials, and royal pages, or because they had earned them through their performances in the troupe), that the troupe was referred to as the Khon Chaloeisak (*khon* dancers who were not registered with any organization, i.e., private troupes outside the Royal Palace).

This sytem of compensating with titles the officials and leading professionals for their service to the king was a diplomatic and political scheme to win loyalty to the person of the king himself. Many Western monarchs were known to have used the same method in widening the sphere of royalist supporters of the monarchy. However, it was practised on such an extravagant scale by King Vajiravudh that it aroused strong prejudice and provoked criticism among outsiders, especially among the older aristocrats of the previous reign, members of the royal family, and the military officers who had been against the king because they had been mistreated by him when he was still crown prince. (There was the case of whipping officers in public to punish them for having a fight with his pages, which was one of the causes of their attempted *coup d'état* to overthrow him in 1911, and which led him to write the play *Chuai Amnat* [*Coup d'état*] in 1923 to reprimand them.) The king's personal military project called in the Wild Tigers Corps, which was independent of the military administration but imitated it in practice, competed with the military rather than supported it. It also received the king's full personal attention and rewards as well as promotion.

These personal activities of the king therefore aggravated their negative attitudes towards him and his men and widened the undercurrent conflicts between the monarchical institution and the military, which led a showdown in the following reign. Though fully aware of this danger, as shown in many of his writings and plays, the king continued to create and strengthen his royal court entourage and the Wild Tigers Corps, in order to counterbalance the military and other power groups. It is true that the Wild Tigers Corps was established as a mechanism of defence for the nation. However, its political significance concerning the security of the monarchy and its dramatic role in propagating the king's policies and political ideas should also seriously be considered.

The personal life style of King Vajiravudh had a strong effect on the development of the court dance-drama. The king remained a bachelor until rather late in his reign and surrounded himself with male courtiers, some of whom were especially close to him and were involved in his personal affairs, namely, Chao Phraya Ramrakhop and Phraya Anirut-thewa, the two brothers of the Phungbun family. They gained enormous wealth and high positions through their service to the king. With the absence of the Fai Nai (Inner Court, i.e., lady courtiers), who had traditionally been in charge of the training and the performance of the Lakhon Phuying Khong Luang, dramatic activities were in the hands of the Khon Samak Len, who were royal pages and close male associates and companions of the king. The training was carried out by teachers and dancers of the Khon Luang (as mentioned earlier). Moreover, the king preferred to reside at his different private residences outside the old Royal Palace. He disliked the depressing atmosphere of the Royal Palace, and he had adopted the style of life of English aristocrats in changing his residence at different seasons. He also had many personal activities at his provincial palaces, such as the military manoeuvres of the Wild Tigers Corps.

The Grand Royal Palace became a museum-like residence of old court ladies, and Inner Court life began to degenerate. Many princesses and consorts of previous kings and their dependants moved out to other private residences. Those who were left behind were either too old or too poor to make other arrangements. The king only came to the Royal Palace on special state occasions and had slept there only twice, once during his coronation and another time near his death, when he insisted upon sleeping in the Royal Chamber in the tradition of his ancestors.

Wherever the king resided, the Khon Luang and the Khon Samak Len went with him to entertain the court daily in the evening, when the king dined with his men and had his new plays read aloud by royal pages at the royal dinner table. After dinner, there would be impromptu plays, games, rehearsals, play reading, music, and other entertainment to keep the court alive until the early hours of the morning. The proportion of the time which King Vajiravudh spent in dramatic activities in his private life was very much the same as that of King Rama II. However, there are two major differences between the two dramatist-monarchs.

Firstly, King Rama II worked on the dramatic texts, rehearsals, and performances with the close collaboration of other court poets, musicians, and dancers, who contributed their efforts to each piece of work, whereas King Vajiravudh wrote his plays single-handedly, and even his adaptations and rewriting of traditional *bot khon* and *bot lakhon* (scripts). It could be said that his "Phra Ratchaniphon" fully deserves its title, "Royal Compositions." Though the king had his plays read to his courtiers for want of external criticism, there were only very rare occasions on which any one of them had courage enough to raise questions or propose alterations in the texts.[10]

Secondly, King Rama II could afford to spend more time on his artistic activities since the country was then enjoying a period of comparative peace and prosperity. The state administration in the Second Reign was in the capable hands of the king's close assistants. During the reign of King Vajiravudh, however, Siam was facing internal political, economic, and social problems as well as embroiled in the international crisis of World War I. The king's deep involvement in dramatic activities and personal pet projects was therefore criticized as luxurious indulgence and as the cause of neglect of administrative responsibilities on the part of the monarch.[11]

Moreover, as the national budget was suffering from economic and financial problems, the king's private expenditure, though paid out of his personal coffer, was, and still is, regarded prejudicially by young historians as extravagance detrimental to the national economy and a cause of national bankruptcy.[12]

King Vajiravudh not only created drama, but also lived it in his daily existence, as if he was acting on a stage in full view of the Thai audience. Whether it was in personal activities, such as saying his prayers, taking meals, reading, writing, playing, or even more so in his public functions, the king was fully conscious of his role and often dramatized it to the extent that he appeared unnatural to his viewers. King Vajiravudh was also in favour of performing the royal ceremonies following the ancient traditions which helped to glorify his presence and semi-divine position. He insisted upon a double form for his coronation, the first to be performed, as tradition demanded, after the death of his father, among the close circle of the royal family and the court, and the second to be performed on a grandiose and spectacular scale for the public and foreign royal dignitaries in the style of Western coronations. The king explained:

> Coronation is a tradition which is regarded by all countries in Europe as a very important and auspicious occasion. Usually it is performed when the funeral of the last king is over. After the mourning period, then the coronation ceremony is performed as a separate joyful occasion, to which the kings and presidents of the allied countries send members of the royal family or senior nobles as representatives to honour the king. . . . therefore the procedures of the coronation ceremony should be revised so as not to contradict the tradition all over the world. . . . there should be two ceremonies. The first is the coronation ceremony to be celebrated in the Royal Palace according to royal tradition, but omitting the royal procession around the city and entertainment. After the royal cremation of King Chulalongkorn, there will be another coronation ceremony as a joyful celebration for the country and to allow all the countries which are our allies to participate.[13]

In this particular ceremony, the king also sat on the *Phra Thaen Manangkhasila-at,* the stone bench of King Ramkhamhaeng in the Dusit Maha Prasat Hall, fully dressed in the royal costume, all of which produced a very spectacular effect for the foreign dignitaries who were present there, representing Great Britain, Russia, Germany, Austria, Denmark, Sweden, United States, France, Italy, Spain, Norway, Holland, and Japan. His serious intention to identify himself with Phra Ruang, the legendary hero king of

Sukhothai and with King Ramkhamhaeng, who is also often identified with Phra Ruang and respected by the Thais as the Father of Siam could not be mistaken here. The king's love of pompous military grandeur in Western style, of Western-sophisticated "salon" society, of an "inner clique," of a cultured elite, and of English manners and social and personal daily activities clearly contrasted with his passion for Thai royal traditions and ceremonies to such an extreme degree in that he insisted on wearing *phanung* (wrap-around pantaloons) for lunch in Thai style and black tie for dinner every day. He often dressed up in traditional royal costumes to preside over old ceremonies which he had revived.

Both King Mongkut and King Vajiravudh had political reasons for reviving traditional royal ceremonies in order to show off to Westerners the rich Thai cultural heritage and the grandeur of the royal court. However, King Vajiravudh was more conscious than his grandfather in his effort to mytho-logize the institution of absolute monarchy and to create a mystical aura of sacredness around his own person, as if he were Vishnu-incarnate. He also initiated the use of the royal appellation "Ram" (i.e., Rama) after his name, intending it to be equivalent to "Rex" in Latin, as well as after the names of his ancestors in the Chakri dynasty. In the initiation ceremony of the *khon* and *lakhon* dancers of the royal court, he acted as a god in pretending to cut off the head of a leading dancer, and then spare his life upon the plea of the *khon* and *lakhon* head teacher.[14] This play-acting followed a Hinduistic religious concept relating possibly to Siva-Nataraj, the Creator and Destroyer, which he had taken from the Sanskrit sources and the *Bharata Natayasastra*. It was for the purpose of sanctifying the ceremony with a touch of religious mysticism.

All these practices reflected his own sense of insecurity, which had de-veloped rather immediately after his succession to the throne, when a group of military officers were caught plotting a *coup d'état* in 1911, only the second year of his reign. This must have shaken him and prompted him to start, in the very same year, the Wild Tigers Corps. They can be seen as a defence mechanism, not so much for the nation, but more directly for his own protection, as they were also his royal guards. In his plays, essays, and speeches, he made very clear the unreadiness of the people to accept the system of democracy, the danger of socialism and communism, the disunity among the elite and power groups, and the irreplaceability of absolute monarchy, in which the king and his people were closely united and which was the best possible system of government for Siam at that particular time. On the other hand, he had made attempts to introduce concepts of liberalism and democratic equality among his "inner clique" and to encourage them to speak in his presence and to write freely in the *Dusit Samit* newspaper published under his "Dusit Thani" (model city-state) project. He also acted with them on stage, sometimes taking the role of a servant, or at one time as Nai Man Pun Yao, a scout of common background in *Phra Ruang* (pls. 28, 29). In one play he even embraced his own fiancée on stage in full view of the court.

Many members of the audience were shocked enough at the daring new idea of the king himself performing *lakhon;* but for him to demonstrate publicly such a romantic act was to them extremely embarassing and below his dignity.

It was this very contradiction in his character and behaviour, being on the one hand very Thai, and on the other hand forwardly *farang* (Western), that often confused his associates. It also created in them doubts about his sincerity. Some of them viewed his life as a *lakhon* performance, in which he was the hero. This role playing may have been psychologically effective for his admirers, but when it was carried to the extreme, outsiders could not help doubting his seriousness of purpose in all the projects he initiated, including the Wild Tigers Corps and his experiment in a democratic system of government in his "Dusit Thani" project, which turned out to be another failure. It appeared as a very expensive investment in perfunctory game playing for the "inner clique" and a private toyland for certain privileged tourists.[15]

Unfortunately, after his death, his personal debts and the near bankrupt condition of the Privy Purse accumulated by the king's various non-official activities and special favours, granted often in terms of wealth and property to his favourite courtiers, caused his brother successor, King Prajadhipok, Rama VII (1925–35), to consider closing down of the Krom Mahorasop and discontinuing court dramatic activities, in order to decrease royal expenditures and help solve the financial crisis. Many court dancers began to find new patrons in other private troupes or palaces. This period has been described as *ban taek saraek khat,* that is, a period of severe disruption of home and family for the members of the royal *khon* and *lakhon* troupes. It was reported that *khon* and *lakhon* properties, masks, and costumes were left unattended. Many were stolen or destroyed during this period.[16]

King Vajiravudh may have failed in his experiments with democratic ideas and modern political and social concepts, largely because of his contradicting inclinations between absolutism and liberalism, monarchy and democracy, tradition and modernity. Nevertheless, he should be given a great deal of credit for having initiated in *khon* and *lakhon* a new political and social function. His essays in the prefaces to all his *bot khon* and *bot lakhon,* and dramatic performances, which expound his ideas and purposes in presenting the plays, were new means to develop the drama as a serious activity in instructing and educating the people. Drama, including dance-drama, was no longer ritual or mere entertainment or an artistic creation as in its traditional role. It became in his reign an educational, social, and political instrument.

DEVELOPMENT OF INSTITUTIONS FOR CLASSICAL DANCE-DRAMA

From the early Ratanakosin period to the reign of King Chulalongkorn, all royal entertainment was under a loosely structured administration consisting of various departments (*krom*), namely, the Krom Khon in charge of Khon Luang, the Krom Hun in charge of puppets, the Krom Piphat in charge of the royal Thai orchestra, the Krom Hok Khamen Ram Khom in charge of acrobatics and the lantern dance, and the Krom Mahorasop in charge of other entertainment such as *mongkhrum, kula ti mai, rabeng, kra-ua thaeng khwai*. Since there was no mention of a "Krom Lakhon," it can be assumed that the Lakhon Luang troupe, whenever it performed, was organized by the royal court dancers for the occasion, whether it be in the style of *lakhon phuchai* (male dence-drama, which was probably performed by the male dancers under the Krom Khon), or in the style of *lakhon phuying,* which was performed by the ladies of the Fai Nai (Inner Court) under the direction and supervision of royal princesses, consorts, and elder dancers who had been in the Lakhon Luang and had trained dancers in the royal court. When new dancers of the Inner Court were good enough to perform for the court, they were presented to the king, who ceremonially initiated them as Lakhon Luang dancers. These dancers would remain in the royal service and perform for royal functions until the end of the reign. When a new king succeeded to the throne and wished to continue the tradition of the Lakhon Luang (King Rama III was the only one of the absolute monarchs in the Chakri dynasty who discontinued the tradition), he would commission the former Lakhon Luang dancers and teachers to form a new Lakhon Luang troupe consisting of former Lakhon Luang dancers and new ones to be trained during the reign. The tradition of Lakhon Fai Nai was thus continued from generation to generation by an independent group, in theory directly subject to the king, but in practice to the head teacher of the Lakhon Luang, who in most cases was either a royal princess, or a royal consort, or even a queen, depending on who was in charge at that moment in the particular reign, or who organized and directed that specific production.

During the Fourth Reign, King Mongkut gave permission to other members of the royal family and nobles to train in and perform *lakhon phuying* and also allowed consorts and Inner Court ladies to leave the royal service and reside outside the Royal Palace. This gave opportunity to some Lakhon Luang dancers and teachers to train and teach in other *lakhon* troupes, some of which became very successful during the Fifth and Sixth Reigns.

During the Fourth Reign, the head of the Krom Mahorasop and Krom Hun Khong Luang was Phra-ong Chao Singhanat Ratchadurong, son of Krom Phra Phithakthewet, son of King Rama II and head of the Kunchon family. He also inherited from his father a *khon* and *lakhon* troupe and continued to train the dancers and their performances with the assistance of the dancers from the Khon Luang and Lakhon Luang. He also succeeded his father as

Commander of the Cavalry. Upon the death of Phra-ong Chao Singhanat, in the Fifth Reign, King Chulalongkorn appointed his son, Chao Phraya Thewetwongwiwat (Mom Ratchawong Lan Kunchon, father of Mom Luang Bupha Kunchon, or "Dok Mai Sot," the female novelist), head of the Krom Mahorasop and Krom Hun, and also put him in charge of three other *krom* for royal entertainment: the Krom Khon, Krom Ram Khom, and Krom Piphat. With these five *krom* under his supervision, Chao Phraya Thewet had almost complete control over the administration and activities of royal entertainment, with the exception of the Inner Court's Lakhon Luang, which in any case, did not exist as a permanent group in this reign, but only performed on special occasions.

Chao Phraya Thewet, with his own *lakhon* troupe which he inherited from his father and with easy access to the royal dancers, performers, musicians, and entertainment properties, was able to produce very successful *lakhon* and train leading dancers at his Ban Mọ Palace. With the ingenious assistance of Prince Naris, he succeeded in development a new form of classical dance-drama, *lakhon dukdamban.* Under Chao Phraya Thewet there were also deputies who assisted him in administering each *krom;* for example, Phra Mahutsawanukit (Luang Mahutsawanukit in the Fifth Reign) was responsible for the Krom Mahorasop.

It is interesting to note also how closely related the military and cultural positions of Chao Phraya Thewet and his father were. It had been a long tradition since Ayudhaya that royal male children and army officers were trained in both martial arts and dance. Even in modern Siam, King Chulalongkorn, when he was still crown prince in the Fourth Reign, and in his own reign, learned the art of sword and baton dance (*ram krabi krabong*) and the victory dances on an elephant (such as *ram phat cha, ram buang suang,* and *ram yoei kha suk*) with weapons swirling in his hands, according to the *Tamnan Kotchasat* (A treatise on elephant lore). He had danced on the neck of an elephant during the worship of the Buddha's Footprint at Phra Phutthabat Temple in 1872. King Vajiravudh was also trained in the art of classical dancing and performed on a few occasions. He even acted as Bharata the Sage, author of the *Nāṭyaśāstra,* in the Initiation and Invocation Ceremony of dancers. He also revived the tradition of having military cadets, officers, and royal pages trained in *khon* and *lakhon* dancing.

The Krom Mahorasop in the Fifth Reign was still loosely structured. Dancers in the Khon Luang did not have to report to work every day. They only turned up for rehearsals and performances. Each leading dancer kept his own *khon* mask at home. Even after the Revolution of 1932, when the Krom Mahorasop was transferred to the Krom Silapakon, in the first seventeen to eighteen years of the new administration, the *khon* and *lakhon* dancers did not come to work every day. They only came for weekly rehearsals on Thursdays (Thursday is Teacher's Day in Thai tradition) and for performances.

However, under the new administration, the *khon* and *lakhon* properties, costumes, and masks were then kept at the department office. It was only after this period that the dancers became civil servants and had to comply with rules and regulations like other government officials. Nevertheless, there is still a relaxed atmosphere and attitude among the Silapakon dancers even today, especially the senior performers and the teachers, since they all regard themselves as artists. They were often be very sensitive about submitting themselves to strict administrative rules and regulations.

In the Sixth Reign, the king reorganized the Krom Mahorasop towards the end of the first year of his reign. Phra Mahutsawanukit continued his service as head of the Krom at the beginning of the reign. Later, in 1911, the king wrote to Chao Phraya Thewet to transfer the Krom Khon and the Royal Pages Orchestra (Phinphat Mahatlek), which had been under the Chao Phraya, to the Krom Mahorasop, and put Luang Sit Nai Wen (later promoted to Phraya Wisukam Sinprasit) in charge of the Krom. The three leading teachers in the Khon Luang, Khun Rabamphasa, Khun Natakanurak, and Khun Phamnaknatchanikon (note the Thai rhyming pattern of the end-syllable with the middle syllable of next word-group linking all three titles, which the king conferred upon these head dancers, viz. Rabampha*sa,* Nata*ka*nu*rak,* Pham*nak*natchanikon), transferred from the Krom Khon to the Krom Mahorasop. They also became teachers of the Kong Thahan Krabi ("Monkey Soldiers," i.e., army of Phra Ram in the *Ramakien*), which was a special battalion attached to the Wild Tigers Corps consisting of officials in the Krom Mahorasop. Since this battalion was the king's favourite, many parents who wished their children to be in the royal service close to the person of the king enlisted them in this battalion. The king therefore set up a special school called Rongrian Thahan Krabi Luang to train these children in the art of *khon* and *lakhon,* as well as in formal education and military training. When the king established the Department of Wild Tigers Royal Scouts and Royal Guards (Krom Sua Pa Phran Luang Raksa Phra-ong) which was developed from the Wild Tigers Corps, he promoted the status of the school to Rongrian Phran Luang (School of Royal Scouts) under royal patronage. There were about one hundred pupils, selected from all walks of life. They were subjected to six years of formal education in ordinary subjects and could pursue their artistic interest by receiving further training in music and classical dance-drama. Under direct royal patronage, these children received free education, meals, lodging, textbooks, clothing, medical treatment, and school equipment. Each boy was given an iron chest, two *phanung* (simple cloth garment wrappings around the lower part of the body similar to the Indian *dhoti*), two shirts, and two uniforms of the Phran Luang (Royal Scouts) cadets. Following the system of an English public school, they were all boarders and resided in four different houses, similar to English public school residence halls. Each house was under the strict supervision of a house father. The school was situated in Suan Misakawan in Dusit Palace where the Rong Khon Luang (Theatre Royal) was also located.

With the setting up of this Rongrian Phran Luang, which was attached on the one hand to the Krom Mahorasop, and on the other to the Wild Tigers Corps, the king's personal political instrument in his movement to propagate nationalism and support of the absolute monarchy, the king was able to implement, instruct and propagate his political schemes and policies through dramatic activities, and to create among these close associates a strong sense of loyalty to the throne, patriotism, and group spirit, which he realized were vital to the unity of the country. In order to have direct, personal control of these activities, the king later appointed his favourite right-hand man, Phraya Prasit Suphakan (later Chao Phraya Ramrakhop), who was also Commander of the Royal Pages and an accomplished dancer in the *phra* (male) role in the Khon Samak Len troupe of the court, Commander of the Krom Mahorasop, and responsible for all departments of royal dance, entertainment, music, and crafts.[17] Unlike in the previous reigns, all these *krom* were no longer under the Krasuang Wang (Ministry of the Royal Palace), but were subject to the Krom Mahatlek (Department of Royal Pages) under the direct command of the king, with Chao Phraya Ramrakhop as his Royal Commissioner for the Affairs of the Royal Pages, a new title invested only in this reign, equivalent perhaps to Lord Chamberlain in the English court tradition.

It is therefore very clear that with the activities of the Khon Samak Len performed by the royal pages and court officials, the setting up of the Rongrian Phran Luang school, and the reorganization of the Krom Mahorasop, the king purposefully centralized all royal entertainment and dramatic activities around his own person in order to use them, not only for his own pleasure and entertainment in the tradition of King Rama II, but more so for his political schemes and ideas, and as a means to strengthen and glorify the institution of the absolute monarchy and to propagate concepts of national unity, patriotism, and great pride in the Thai cultural heritage.

DEVELOPMENT OF CLASSICAL DANCE-DRAMA TEACHING METHODS

It is generally accepted that Thai classical dance and dance-drama was influenced by the *Nāṭyaśāstra* and/or *Bharata Natayasastra* of the Indian classical tradition and that the basic dance movements were introduced by Indian dancers since the Ayudhaya period. The impression to an observer must be that Thai dance movements bear a close resemblance to those of the *Bharata Nāṭyam*. However, there is no historical evidence before the reign of King Rama I of any *tamra fon ram* (text for the training of dancers) written or translated from Indian sources. The first *tamra fon ram,* which describes all the basic dance movements and gestures and which are illustrated with paintings in colour and gold, was written by royal command during the reign of King Rama I. The text was a part of the king's project to reconstruct the Lakhon Luang troupe and set a standard for Thai classical dancing for later generations. Unfortunately, only the beginning part of the text survives today and is kept in the National Library. The last part has been lost.

Since the reconstruction of court dance-drama in the First Reign was closely supervised by authorities of the Ayudhaya royal court, such as Princess Phintumwadi, daughter of King Boromakot, who were knowledgeable in this field, it can be assumed that these dance movements and the training required to perform them imitated rather closely what had been performed by Ayudhaya court dancers. There is another training text with similar types of illustrations consisting of sixty-six (the number of characters in the Thai alphabet) *tha ram* (dance movements), which have been the basic movements in the training of *lakhon ram*. This text is believed to have been written and illustrated in the reign of King Rama II or King Rama III.[18] The names of these basic sixty-six *tha ram* are all in Thai and are related to either the gestures and movements of the gods, or mythological beings, or characters in the *khon* and *lakhon,* or nature. Some examples are *Thep Phanom* (gods in a worshipping gesture), *Phrom Si Na* (Brahma with four faces), *Phra Ram Kong Son* (Phra Ram pulling his bow), *Hanuman Phlan Yak* (Hanuman destroying the ogres), *Chang Prasan Nga* (elephants thrusting each other with their tusks), *Kwang Doeng Dong* (a deer walking in the forest), *Hong Lila* (a swan moving gracefully), and *Nakha Muan Hang* (a serpent coiling its tail). The last movement mentioned here is the god Narai demonstrating to Nonthuk in the *boek rong* dance of "Narai Prap Nonthuk" by pointing his index finger at his knee, and Nonthuk in imitating this breaks his knee by the deadly power of the *niu phet* (diamond finger).

The dance of "Narai Prap Nonthuk" demonstrates how the training and teaching of Thai classical dance have been carried out. There is an interplay between the *khru* (teacher), who demonstrates first each movement and gesture, and the *luk sit* (disciple), who imitates the *khru* as closely as possible. However, in this particular dance, there are only twenty movements, as against the original 108 *karana* (movements) of the *Bharata Natayasastra*. (Incidentally, the Thai term *roi paet tha,* or 108 movements, became an expression meaning "making a lot of fuss," or "being fastidious," i.e., describing a dancer who dances through the complete alphabet of 108 movements and takes a long period of time.)

There is no evidence as to how many of the original 108 movements were taught and performed in the pre-Ratanakosin period, but it is certain that at least these sixty-six of them prescribed in the training texts of the First, Second, and Third Reigns have been carried on to the present. The first complete collection of photographs of these dance movements was taken at the royal command of King Vajiravudh, to be published with the royal standard training text, *Tamra Fon Ram,* which had been edited from the Wachirayan edition and given to guests at the royal cremation of Somdet Phra Chao Nongyathoe Chaofa Chuthathuttharadilok Krom Khun Phetchabun

Intharachai in 1923. In this collection, there were also the aforementioned texts with illustrations of the sixty-six movements taught during the Second or Third Reign. This edition had been obtained from the Palace of the Front. Prince Damrong, the editor of this publication, had also asked Phra Withayaprachong, artist in the Krom Silapakon, and Khun Prasit Chitakam, artist at the National Library, to restore the paintings to their original condition. He included in this publication the *Bot Narai Lọ Nonthuk* (i.e., *Narai Prap Nonthuk;* luring [*lọ*] and defeating [*prap*], the two sequences in the act of Narai destroying Nonthuk) from the *Ramakien* of King Rama I and *Kham Wai Khru* (invocation prayer) of the *nora chatri* of Nakhon Sithammarat, which also contains the basic dance gestures and movements. The gestures and movements of the *nora chatri* are closer to Indian dancing (pl. 17), and therefore are believed to have been directly continued from the traditional *lakhon ram* of Ayudhaya without much alteration or modernization. It was probably a foundation source on which the Lakhon Luang troupe of the Thonburi and early Ratanakosin periods reconstructed their dance techniques and training. However, the refinement and sophistication of the Lakhon Luang under the Bangkok royal court of later periods from the reign of King Rama II to the present are clearly shown when comparing the *nora chatri* (pl. 6), the paintings of the First Reign (pl. 30), and the photographs taken in the Fifth Reign (pl. 20).

The latest photographs of the demonstration of these basic movements may be found in Dhanit Yupho, *The Preliminary Course of Training in Thai Theatrical Art* (Department of Fine Arts, 1990) (pl. 31). From these photographs, we can see that the tradition of *lakhon* has been continued without much alteration to the present day. There have been only a few variations added to certain movements, which has resulted in a slight increase from sixty-six to sixty-eight movements.

The method of training dancers of the royal court was first mentioned in *Phleng Yao Khwam Kao* of the Ayudhaya period,

> They came to be trained in the role of Sisuda[19]
> And tried very hard to dance gracefully.
> They were trained under the old *lamyai* tree,
> At the side of the lawn of Sanphet Prasat [palace].[20]

In *Kraithong* of the First Reign, it is mentioned that the nobles presented their daughters and female relatives to the king to serve at the Inner Court. The group consisted not only Thais but also Chinese, Indians, Laos, Vietnamese, Khmers, and Mons.

> All the *khunnang* [nobles] presented their daughters to the king.
> Those who had only sons presented their nieces.
> If they happened to be childless,

They thought of persuading the sisters of their wives to come.
There were Chinese, *khaek* [Indians or Malays], and Laos, Vietnamese, presented to the court.
They all offered their children to gain favour from the king.
The Khmers, Mons, and people of Chumphon and Chaiya,
People of all languages came under the protection of the king.[21]

It was the tradition of the Inner Court ladies to be trained in various arts. The ones gifted in dancing would become Lakhon Luang dancers and some of them even became royal consorts. King Rama II described the training of these young girl dancers of *lakhon* to celebrate the white elephant in his *phleng yao* at the end of *Kraithong*,

A pavilion was built of pine timber and was crowded with people.
They were rehearsing and correcting [the movements of their dance] in the royal court,
When the new white elephant which had been discovered in that reign was to be presented in the ceremony.
It was decorated with a glorious-looking saddle.
The young *lakhon* dancers were all children.
They befitted the honour, status, and dignity of the king.
There were just people who wished to pledge their loyalty to the king,
And to serve under his feet [i.e., to be in the royal service].[22]

The training of the Lakhon Luang is remembered as being very strict and strenuous, both in the royal court and in private troupes, which were and still are under the direction of Lakhon Luang dancers and teachers. Whipping and beating were common, and long hours of repeated drilling sessions caused many unhappy moments for the dancers of a tender age.[23] In the Ban Mọ Palace of Chao Phraya Thewet, at the sound of the gong announcing the beginning of the dance training session, all dancers in the palace had to be present, or else they would be whipped or punished by some other method. This strict discipline is carried on even today, though the punishment is now lighter, since the new generation of pupils under the modern democratic system would not put up with the traditional beating and have been known to rebel against it. *Khon* and *lakhon* teachers of the Witthayalai Natasin (College of Dance and Music) at present still hold sticks or batons in their hands and use them to tap pupils on the parts of their bodies when they do not move accurately and gracefully.

The first basic drilling dances are *phleng cha* (slow music movements) and *phleng reo* (rapid dance movements). Each dancer has to master these two dances and repeat them daily. Even the leading dancers have to go through these drills to keep fit.

In the *lakhon ram* section of the school, the pupils are divided into two groups: *phra* (male) and *nang* (female) roles. They are selected on the basis of their physical appearances. The *phra* role requires a dancer with a slender, tall, and graceful figure, and an attractive oval face (col. pl. 2), while the *nang* role requires a short, feminine, round figure and an attractive round face (col. pl. 1). In the past, the boys and girls were trained separately, especially the Lakhon Phuying Khong Luang were kept in a restricted area within the Inner Court. Later, starting in the reign of King Chulalongkorn, there began to be mixed casts of male and female dancers in *lakhon* performances. In *khon* the casts had been all male up to the Sixth Reign, after which female dancers sometimes took the female roles. In the post-Revolution period, after 1932, under the Silapakon, male and female dancers are trained and perform together in both *khon* and *lakhon* (pl. 32). (The two dramatic genres have been merged since the Sixth Reign.) Female dancers of the Silapakon have taken the hero (*phra ek*) role as well as the heroine (*nang ek*) role in the *khon*. In some productions, there are two separate casts, one an all female cast (except for the clowns, who are always male), and the other a mixed cast, i.e., male dancers in the *phra* roles and female dancers in the *nang* roles.

In the training of *khon,* the dancers start at a very young age, traditionally at the age of six to eight, at present at the Witthayalai Natasin from the age of thirteen to fifteen (after they have completed elementary education). In private dancing schools they still start out at an earlier age as in the old tradition. They are chosen to be trained in four separate groups of characters: *phra, nang, yak* (ogre), or *ling* (monkey). The *yak* role requires a tall, majestic, strong, and muscular body, while the *ling* requires the opposite, a short, quick, round, and lively figure (pl. 5). These chosen *khon* and *lakhon* roles could be changed within certain limits, and not later than the adolescent years, for example, from *phra* to *nang, phra* to *yak,* or *nang* to *ling.* It is very rare that a *yak* dancer would be able to change to a *ling* role and vice versa, since they have been trained in rather opposite movements, whereas the *phra* and *yak,* and the *nang* and *ling* movements have many similarities. For example, the *phra* and *yak* have angular, open leg positions (the *yak*'s is slightly wider), while that of the *nang* and *ling* have closed leg positions (compare pls. 5, 32).

Since the Witthayalai Natasin was set up to train students in order to become either professional dancers or teachers in primary and secondary schools all over the country, the curriculum and methods of training had to undergo many changes in order best to suit these educational purposes. The dance drills and steps became more simplified and fewer in number.

The present curriculum of the Witthayalai Natasin is divided into five levels:

1) Diploma course for *natasin chan ton:* first level, basic training in *khon* and *lakhon,* six years, starting at the fifth grade.

2) Diploma course for *mathayom suksa ton plai:* last two years of high school, continuing from level 1 for two extra years.
3) Diploma course for *natasin chan klang:* intermediate level, continuing from level 2 for an additional year.
4) Diploma course for *natasin chan sung:* advanced level, continuing from level 3 for two more years.
5) Bachelor of Arts degree in *natasin:* continuing from level 4 for two more years and equivalent to a university degree.

For each of these five curricula, there is a balance between training in the arts and the study of normal subjects as prescribed by the Ministry of Education and the Bureau of State Universities. (See Table 1.)

Starting from the year 1971, the Krom Silapakon set up Witthayalai Natasin in important provincial cities in order to expand education and training in the arts to the provinces. Schools were established at Chiengmai in 1971 offering courses levels 1, 2, 3, and 4, at Lampang, Udonthani, Songkhla, and Angthong in 1977 offering a one-year foundation course to all students in order to promote Thai art and culture, and at Nakhon Sithammarat and Angthong in 1978 for those who have completed grade 6 and level 3. At each of these centres there are also teaching and training in folk dancing, music, and drama at the particular region.[24]

From the first year of school, the pupils spend at least half a day in dance and music training and practice (pl. 33). The best students are selected for character roles in the *Ramakien, Inao,* and other dance-drama, such as *Khun Chang Khun Phaen, Kraithong,* and *Sangthong.* These special pupils receive further training by experts in these roles. It has been the tradition for teachers who were well known in particular roles, such as Inao, Busba, Sida, to teach the techniques and skills of their roles to their favourite pupils. (These dancers and teachers have also adopted the names of their roles and attached them to their own names, for example, Yaem-Inao, Iaem-Busba, Chan-Phra Sang, Kham-Ngo, A-ngun-Rotchana.)

When a new production of *lakhon* or *khon* is rehearsed, these leading dancers would then be trained for the particular episode and learn how to *ti bot* (interpret their roles). The head master, who is also the director of the production, supervises the rehearsals and gives tips on fine points to the leading characters (pl. 34).

Mom Phaeo has contributed significantly to the modernization of the training and directing of *lakhon* and *khon* of the Silapakon (pl. 34). She has the advantage over other teachers in having been exposed to both the old culture of the Thai royal court and to Western culture. She was trained as a *lakhon* dancer in the Sixth Reign in the palace of Prince Atsadang Dechawut, Krom Luang Nakhon Ratchasima, and also became his consort. Later, she became the wife of Mom Sanitwongseni, Thai ambassador to many European

TABLE 1

COLLEGE OF DANCE AND MUSIC ENROLMENT 1992
DEPARTMENT OF FINE ARTS, MINISTRY OF EDUCATION

Student Enrolment

Level	Year	Male	Female	Total	Lakhon	Khon	Khruang sai (string orchestra)	Piphat orchestra	Thai music	Western orchestra	Western music	Western dance
Foundation Level												
	1	60	189	249	134	30	22	21	4	17	3	18
	2	58	148	206	115	30	13	17	5	11	5	10
	3	60	180	240	137	40	11	13	6	15	5	13
Intermediate Level												
	1	47	176	223	137	12	19	25	6	13	5	6
	2	41	156	197	116	17	15	16	4	15	7	7
	3	44	146	190	111	19	15	18	5	13	5	4
Advanced Level												
	1	22	63	85	48	4	8	15	—	4	2	4
	2	21	60	81	51	13	5	6	3	1	—	2
College Level												
	1	33	110	143	85	20	8	9	11	4	3	3
	2	36	95	131	85	18	5	18	5	—	—	—
Total	10	422	1,323	1,745	1,019	203	121	158	49	93	35	67

Faculty

	Experts	Special teachers	Male teachers	Female teachers	Total
General Education	—	—	16	53	69
Performing Arts	4	13	65	74	139

countries. When Dhanit Yupho was director of the Krom Silapakon in the 1950s, he invited her to help develop the Dance Section of the Silapakon. Mom Phaeo, or "Mom Achan" as she is called by her pupils, initiated many new ideas and created many new dances, some of which were inspired by Western ballet and dance (pl. 35), for various productions, all of which were very successful. Among her most notable contributions were the romantic love scenes in *Inao, Phra Aphaimani, Khun Chang Khun Phaen* (col. pl. 3), *Manohra,* her direction and adaptation of *Ngo Pa,* and her numerous dance numbers, such as the Dance of the Nymphs in *Khun Chang Khun Phaen* (pl. 35), which was inspired by *Giselle* and *Les Sylphides.* The Dance of Horses in *Phra Rothasen* was inspired by the Spanish Riding School. Others include Dance of Buffaloes in *Phali Son Nong,* a *khon* production inspired by the Spanish bull-fighting dance, and the Dance of the Mermaids in *Phra Aphaimani.* She also supervised the costume designs for these productions, some of which show definite Western influence, such as the fancy costumes for the water creatures in *Kraithong* designed by Khru Mot, the *kinnari* costume in *Manohra,* and costumes in *Phra Aphaimani.*

Being herself a very accomplished dancer and trained by the best teachers of the Lakhon Luang in the Fourth and Fifth Reigns, namely, Chao Chom Manda Wat (Fourth Reign), Chao Chom Manda Khien and Chao Chom Manda Thapthim (Fifth Reign), Mom Yaem of Somdet Chao Phraya Borom Maha Sisuriyawong, and Mom Ung of Somdet Phra Banthun, Mom Phaeo is able to transmit the most refined and sophisticated art of dancing to her best pupils, some of whom became the best-loved dancers unsurpassed by any others in the 1950s and 1960s. They include Suwanni (Chalanukhro) Chonlamu, Bunnak (Sawettanan) Thanthranon, and in the 1970s Thongchai Phothiwarom and Chindarat Wirayawong.

With this long, continuous line of teaching and training and the transmission of knowledge and techniques from generation to generation, Thai classical dance-drama is able to survive and retain much of its traditional characteristics, despite the modern adaptations and variations. (See Appendix on p. 179 for the list of teachers of the Silapakon who danced in the Sixth and Seventh Reigns.)

APPENDIX

List of Dance Teachers of the Silapakon Who Performed during the Sixth and Seventh Reigns

Teachers of *khon:*
  *Thongroem Mong-khon-nat   Aram Intharanat
  Wong Lomkaeo   Kri Worasarin
  Charoen Wetchakam   Bunchai Chaloeithong

Teachers of *lakhon:*
  *Lamun Yamakhup   Charoenchit Phatharasewi
  *Chaloei Sukhawanit   Chamriang Phutpradap

Teachers of music:
  Thiap Khonglaithong
  Phring Kanchanaphalin

Teachers of singing:
  Sinat Soemsiri
  Usa Sukhan-Thamalai
  Thuam Prasitkun

(*Dancers who performed in the Sixth Reign. The rest performed in the Seventh Reign.)

Chapter V
The Impact of the 1932 Revolution on Drama and Theatre

The Reign of King Prajadhipok, Rama VII, to the Present

BEFORE AND AFTER THE 1932 REVOLUTION

When young King Prajadhipok, Rama VII, quite unexpectedly ascended the throne in 1925 after the sudden death of his brother, who left no male heir, the royal household was facing a serious financial crisis due to the excessive expenditures of the previous reign. The government also had the accumulated debts and national inflation to tend with. The country was entering a new era of moden economy with very little knowledge and experience. Having been educated in the West and taking a keen interest in industrial development, King Prajadhipok expressed serious concern about national economic problems and the urgent need for industrialization through modern technology in order to gradually transform this predominantly agricultural country into an industrial one. He strongly encouraged the new generation to turn to business and commerce instead of the traditional profession in government service and to go into the fields of engineering, sciences, and technology in order to prepare themselves for the new world. His first courageous deed was to cut the budget of the royal household and the king's personal allowance to only 6 million baht from the original 9 million baht allocated by the government.

On 8 February 1925, the first year of his reign, with the consent of the Council of Ministers, the king reduced the staff of various departments in the royal court and the government. Those who were near retirement or who were not vital to the immediate needs and functions of the government were offered early retirement and compensations. One of the most effected departments of the royal court was the Krom Mahorasop (Department of Royal Entertainment). It was considered a luxury that the country could not afford at the time and was therefore temporarily suspended. These drastic changes came as an unexpected shock to the government and court officials and their families, who directly suffered the consequences. The new king was strongly criticized by the old guard and senior military officers.

The leadership of the Revolution of 1932, which consisted of young Western-educated officials and military officers, took this negative reaction within government circles as an opportunity to criticize the monarchy and to personally attack the king. In the Prakat Khana Rat (Proclamation of the People's Party) of 1932, they verbally assaulted the system of absolute monarchy as unjust, corrupt, oppressive, and destructive to the welfare of the country and abusive to human rights and the freedom of the people, who, they insisted, were treated like slaves:

> When this king inherited the throne from his brother, at first, some people had hoped that he would rule the people in peace. However, the situation did not turn out as expected. The king still holds power above the law as before . . . oppresses the people, rules the country without any knowledge and leaves the country to suffer its own fate, as proven by the recent economic decline and depression. . . .
>
> All Thais should know that our country belongs to the people and not to the king. . . . The government forced a great number of people out of work . . . without any pensions.
>
> The people, government officials, and citizens who know well the evil deeds of the government . . . have therefore joined forces to set up the Khana Ratsadon [The People's Party] and have taken hold of the power of the king's government.

Some scholars consider this period as "Ban Taek Saraek Khat" (the era of broken homes, broken baskets holders), signifying the fall of the kingdom, especially with respect to the dancers and dance masters in the Khon Luang and Lakhon Luang troupes. They had to leave the Royal Palace. Some joined private troupes sponsored by other members of the royal family or sought patronage from prominent aristocrats. Others returned to their provincial homes and took up other small jobs or private enterprises with very little or no success due to their lack of knowledge and experience. The dance costumes, masks, and properties of the royal troupe were left unattended or taken home by these retired dancers. There was great damage and loss to the royal possessions of this department.

However, this so-called "dark period" lasted only one year. Meanwhile, the king still maintained the royal Thai classical orchestra. Being himself an accomplished musician and composer, he contributed quite significantly to the development of Thai music. A modern—i.e., Western-style—orchestra was formed for the first time at the royal court. The king's own composition, "Ratri Pradap Dao" (Starlit night), became one of the most popular songs in Thai classical music. Court music flourished during this reign. Many famous court musicians and composers became master-teachers in the Krom Silapakon after the Revolution, notably Luang Praditphairo (later Phra Praditphairo), Luang Snoduriyang (later Phra Snoduriyang), and Montri

Tramote, who still serves as senior advisor to the Music Section of the Krom Silapakon. Many members of the royal family also had private orchestras under their patronage. The best-known were those of Prince Naris and Prince Nakhon Sawan.

The king reduced the status of the Krom Mahatlek (Department of Royal Pages), which had been very powerful during King Vajiravudh's reign, and the Krom Mahorasop (Department of Royal Entertainment) to sectional status under the Krasuang Wang (Ministry of the Royal Palace) and laid off a large number of the staff members. Only a minimum was kept to preserve Thai cultural heritage and to continue the teaching of the arts to the next generation.

In 1926, Phraya Natakanurak, the court dance-master, was called back to head the Krom Piphat (Department of Royal Orchestra) and the Khon Luang troupe and to form again a new troupe of court dancers. The Kong Mahorasop was re-established. On many occasions these new dancers performed for royal guests and foreign visitors. Many of the court dancers during this reign have become leading dancers and teachers in the present-day Krom Silapakon. The long line of court classical dancers was therefore continued without interruption even during those years of political crisis.

Outside the royal court other popular performing arts grew more and more popular. Many new ideas, mostly influenced by Western culture, were introduced into both music and the theatre. The most successful forms were *lakhon rong* (dance-drama with songs, i.e., Thai operetta), *liké* (a folk dance-drama), and film.

Lakhon Rong: A Later Development

Lakhon rong, which began in the reign of King Chulalongkorn (1868–1910), spread all over the country during this reign. There were numerous companies in heavy competition with each other. The most famous were Pramothai, Nakhon Banthoeng, Phathanalai, Chantharophat, Thepbanthoeng, Chaloemkrung, and their off-shoots with common prefixes to indicate their parent troupes: for example, the off-shoots of Pramothai were Pramot Muang, Pramot Nakhon, and Pramot Banthoeng.

The playscripts and songs from popular *lakhon rong* were published and widely sold at 50 *satang* (about 2 US cents) each.[1] Many stories were adaptations of Western and Eastern tales with exciting plots of romantic adventures. The popular songs were mostly sentimental love songs.

The cast of *lakhon rong* were female in major roles with male comedians. The popular actresses who performed the *phra ek* (hero) role became the idols of their patrons, who were mostly women. They sported male attires, hairdos, mannerisms, and behaviour, such as smoking cigars, pipes, or cigarettes, walking smartly like handsome men, and courting ladies in chivalrous manners. Among the most famous were Mae Luan, Mae Chamoi, and later, Mae Srinuan Keowbuasai, who taught Suphan Buranaphim, a famous actress of the 1940s and 1950s. Both Mae Srinuan and Suphan tried to revive *lakhon rong* on television in the 1950s and 1960s without much success. The genre gradually declined and died away. The innovations in the *lakhon rong* during this era were the Western-style band and courting songs, which continued to be the main features in later popular Thai music. The Krom Silapakon revived *lakhon rong* in the 1980s (pl. 11). Recently, in 1992, there is a new movement in commercial theatre to bring back *lakhon rong* with popular film and television stars performed at the Cultural Centre of Thailand. This success shows a new interest among the younger generation.

Liké (Likay)

The origin of *liké,* or popular folk dance-drama, is quite uncertain. While many scholars agree that this dramatic form derived from a Muslim religious chant of the Malays in southern Thailand, others contend that it developed from the Persian Muslim chant of a similar name, *djiké,* as early as the Ayudhaya period, when Persian merchants migrated to Siam. They later served at the royal court and rose to power during the reign of Kings Mongkut and Chulalongkorn. The head of the Bunnag family, Chao Phraya Sisuriyawong, was Regent at the beginning of King Chulalongkorn's reign during the king's adolescent period.

In the *Chotmaihet Phra Ratchakit* (Record of royal activities), for the year 1880 (B.E. 2423), it is recorded that a group of *to khaek* (Muslim religious leaders) came to chant with *rammana* (one-face drums) for the king. A candle was lit behind the *rammana* to project a small shadow puppet. Later in the record of 1888, there is mention of *yiké* (*yikay*) as one type of performing art presented at the Royal Palace to celebrate the anniversary of Prince Phetcharutamathamrong's death. However, there is no clear historical evidence to connect the Muslim chant and this *yiké,* or between *djiké* and *liké.* The common feature is the use of *rammana* as in the *ramtat,* the art of Thai folk singing with exchanges of witty remarks between male and female singers, often with sexual allusions and jokes told in "double entente." These are also important features in *liké.* The dance movements in *liké* are simple, similar to those in the Malay *mayong* dance-drama, with swaying body and hand gestures.

Liké later adopted the stories, music, and dance movements of *lakhon chatri,* but retained its original Malay-like costumes with turbans and embroidered vests worn over short-sleeved shirts and also using *rammana* accompaniment with a Thai *piphat* orchestra. The lower part of the male costume were pantaloons (*pha chong kraben*) wrapped in a fancy manner (pl. 12).

The opening part of the *liké* performance is called "Ok Khaek" (Entrance of an Indian). The term *khaek* can apply to both Indians and Malays, i.e., dark-skinned foreigners. In this dance, the troupe master or comedian wears a white loin cloth (*doti*), a white shirt, a black vest, and a white Indian cap. He holds candle(s) in his hand(s) and introduces the troupe and the story to the audience. In a later period, the narrator gestured with his thumbs in place of the candles. The tune sung in the "Ok Khaek" is closer to the Indian tunes than to the Malay ones. This mixture of singing style is still unexplainable. *Liké* of the later period became completely Thai and closer to *lakhon chatri*. The costumes also became more elaborate, imitating those of aristocrats during the reign of King Chulalongkorn. This style of *liké* with fancy costumes is called *liké song khruang*.

Liké was very popular during the reign of King Prajadhipok in the 1930s and 1940s. There were many famous troupes such as that of Khana Nai Dokdin, and his disciple, Nai Homhuan (Naksiri), who carried it on to the present reign in the 1970s. After World War II *liké* gradually died away due to financial problems and lack of interest among the descendants of the tradition of performing families. It was revived again during Premier Phibunsongkhram's regime in the 1950s during his nationalistic campaign. In 1952 there was a national *liké* competition to recruit artists to propagate government policies on radio. In the late 1950s and early 1960s *liké* was televised and was called *liké thorathat* (television *liké*). The best-known television *liké* troupe was that under the direction of Somsak Phakdi. *Liké* has since been a popular entertainment performed by amateurs or film and television stars. Famous actors and actresses are often invited to perform. This is called *liké dara ngoen lan* (million baht stars *liké*).

At present, *liké* has gained more prestige as many dignitaries in different circles have taken interest in it. It has also been a subject for intellectual discussion, seminars, and research by many scholars and university students. Mom Ratchawong Kukrit Pramoj, a former prime minister and highly respected scholar-writer-dramatist, has been one of the foremost patrons of *liké*. He has not only danced in it at charity shows, but has also produced it at the National Theatre in the 1980s when leading *liké* stars and veteran dancers gave joint performances. His famous short stories *Lai Chiwit* (Many lives) portrays the life of a veteran *liké* star who died in a capsized boat on his way to the national *liké* competition during Premier Phibunsongkhram's regime. The story reflects very well the rise and fall, dreams, and illusions of the *liké* artists.

According to the latest researches,[2] there are at present about 1,000 *liké* troupes and 10,000 *liké* performers. Modern *liké* performances have adopted modern rural-style music and songs called *phleng luk thung* with Western-style bands. The costumes for the female roles are contemporary, with elaborate decoration and Western-style tiaras for the royal characters, while the male costumes remain basically the same with fancy embroidery and head-dresses (pl. 12). Dance movements and gestures are minimal to make the performance faster moving for contemporary audiences. This type of *liké* is called *liké luk thung,* which is quite successful in the provinces. Another custom in *liké* is the patronage of well-to-do fans, mostly women, who shower their admiration by giving garlands of bank notes to their favourite *phra ek liké* (*liké* hero). At present, the troupe masters actually borrow bank notes to make garlands for their leading stars to enhance their popularity, due to the lack of real patrons.

Despite the efforts of well-meaning preservers of the *liké* tradition, this almost two-hundred-year-old performing art exists in only a reduced form and scale, either as comic relief in charity shows and television comedy, or as a national treasure occasionally presented at the National Theatre. However, National Radio still broadcasts *liké* shows quite frequently for the general public. There is also new interest in this folk dance-drama among university teachers and students. Thammasat University is known to perform occasionally political and satirical *liké* as a popular means to criticize the government.

DEVELOPMENT OF THE FILM INDUSTRY

The first imported films introduced into Thailand came from Japan in 1902 in the reign of King Chulalongkorn. They were called *nang yipun* (lit., Japanese leather puppets) referring to leather puppets in traditional shadow puppetry. The term is applied to film since it is also projected on the screen. The Sayam Niramai Company of the Wasuwat family was the first importer of these *nang yipun*. They later produced their own silent films in 1922. The first attempts were records of King Vajiravudh's activities, such as playing golf at Hua Hin, as well as documentaries to promote the Railway Department under the directorship of Prince Kamphaengphet, the king's brother.

The first feature film was produced by the Universal Company from Hollywood in 1923–24 and directed by an American, Henry Macray. It was called *Nang Sao Suwan,* or *Suvarna of Siam.* The story was a typical melodrama with heroic and romantic themes depicting the adventurous lives of a young couple who had to fight through a series of hardships to finally succeed. The exciting final scene shows the heroine taking a train from Hua Hin in the south to arrive in time at Chiengmai in the north to stop the executioner from chopping off the hero's head. One of the major purposes was to show scenic attractions in Siam, that could be offered by the Royal Railway service, as well as Thai customs and culture. However, as Mom Ratchawong Kukrit Pramoj recalled of his seeing the film as a child, the *farang* (white foreigner) director overplayed the traditional element by making the characters *wai* (greet with palms joined together) too frequently until it became ridiculous to Thai viewers.[3]

King Prajadhipok took a special interest in film as a new besiness venture. He commissioned the Wasuwat family to film his coronation in 1925, his return from a royal state visit to the United States in 1931, and the celebration of the 150th anniversary of the Ratanakosin kingdom on 6 April 1932, two months before the Revolution. Even after the Revolution, the king commissioned the company to record his handing the First Constitution over the new democratic government on 10 December 1932 at the Anandha Smakhom Parliament House, including the rehearsals for this great occasion. Also that same year just before the Revolution, the king attended the opening of the first Thai cinema, Sala Chaloemkrung, which still exists today.

Before the Revolution, there were a few silent feature films produced by Thais. The Wasuwat family was again the first Thai producer with the film, *Chok Song Chan* (Double fortune) in 1926–27. In 1930, Mom Ratchawong Anusak Hatsadin produced two other 35 mm silent films, *Ee Nak Phrakhanong,* a story about a female ghost who was attached to her husband, and a romantic war story, *Rop Rawang Rak* (Battle in the middle of love), about World War I.

In 1931, the first "talkie," *Long Thang* (Lost the way), was filmed at the Wasuwat film studio, the first film studio in Thailand using Western techniques. This is considered to be the beginning of the Thai film industry. In 1934 the Sri Krung Film Studio was established in the Bangkapi district of Bangkok. It became a very fashionable centre for young upper-middle-class people. The Sri Krung Studio produced numerous feature films with sound and music and also released phonograph records of popular songs and tunes from box office successes. The fashion of the stars of the silver screen became the model for the young crowd, such attire as short pants and long slacks for women, bathing suits, short and permed hairdos like the Western styles of the 1930s and 1940s. The *phra ek nang* (film heros) and *nang ek nang* (film heroines) were the idols of film audiences. The stories still kept to the same vein as traditional *lakhon:* romantic, melodramatic, and idealistic. The Sri Krung Studio also had a public park with modern entertainment for the movie fans. Young people would come there to socialize and show off the latest fashion.

After the Revolution of 1932, the Sri Krung Film Studio continued to serve the government under the new regime. Their major task was to propagate the nationalistic schemes of Prime Minister Phibunsongkhram. The most popular and influential propagandistic films were *Luat Thahan Thai* (Blood of Thai soldiers) in 1935 and *Ban Rai Na Rao* (Our farm house and rice fields) in 1947 to promote Premier Phibunsongkhram's *patiwat watthanatham* (cultural revolution) for upgrading the status of Thai farmers and encouraging the people to take up agriculture in the depression period during and after World War II. The hero in this film sported an American cowboy outfit to create a new image for Thai farmers. The actor who starred in this film was Air Force Lieutenant (now Air Marshal) Thawi Chullasap, a popular personality in the governments of Field Marshals Phibunsongkhram, Sarit Thanarat, and Thanom Kittikhachon.

Songs and music in film became very popular among the younger generation. It was customary for film stars to sing their favourite theme songs on stage during intermission. This became a tradition in Thai cinemas for many decades until the late 1940s and early 1950s. Even at present, it is still a practice at the gala premiers. There were also dance revues performed during intermission. Phra Chenduriyang and Khun Wichitmatra were the best-known music composers and lyricists. They were also responsible for the composing of the new national anthem, which they secretly created for the Revolution Party. It was said that prior to the Revolution, Phra Chenduriyang had to compose the music in a tram running back and forth until he finally finished it. Among the best-loved songs from these films were "Ban Rai Na Rao" (Our farm house and rice fields) and "Tawan Yo Saeng" (Shining sun), both by Phra Chenduriyang and Khun Wichitmatra, and "Kluai Mai" (Orchids), the theme song from the film, *Pu Som Fao Sap* (Grandfather spirit guarding the treasures) (1933), which is said to be the first *phleng Thai sakon* (Thai modern song). It was composed by a naval officer, Manit Senawinin, who together with Khun Wichitmatra composed many patriotic songs for films, such as "March Trairong" (Tricolour march), the theme song for *Luat Thahan Thai* (Blood of Thai soldiers), and "Tawan Yo Saeng" (Shining sun) for *Luat Chao Na* (Blood of peasants).

The Thai film industry prospered in the early 1940s; however, a lack of business and professional training and modern organization in this family-dominated industry did not allow it to develop to a full international scale and high standards. When World War II broke out, film negatives could not be imported from abroad, resulting in the industry being closed down for two decades. The cinemas were changed into theatres for melodramatic, domestic, romantic, or historical plays. *Lakhon phut* (spoken drama) with songs and music flourished. Film stars, directors, scriptwriters, composers, and technical crews thus returned to the stage theatre business. The theatre of the war period adopted many features from the cinema, particularly the use of a live modern orchestra, dance revues, songs, and comedy shows during intermission.

Film making started again in the 1950s despite inferior technical and artistic quality. It was a step back into the silent film era with sound being dubbed later into the films by voice performers called *khon phak,* which came from the word for the narrator in *khon* performances. The film directors and actors of this period came mostly from the stage. Their peformances and productions still maintained a theatre style quite unsuitable for the film media. It was not until the late 1970s that a new generation of film directors and technicians became well trained in the art. However, the majority of film actors and actresses still lack professional training.

Films in the 1950s and 1960s were mostly melodramas with a Cinderella theme or romantic adventures taken from novels. These repetitious story lines generated a new term *nang nam nao* (films of stagnant, rotten water).

However, the popularity of film heroes and heroines was enough to save the film industry during this struggling period. Some film producers, directors, actors, and actresses even got rich in a relatively short time. Meanwhile, the theatre consequently went into a complete decline.

Modern realistic films containing social themes started to come out in the mid-1970s under the direction of Western-trained professionals, notably Mom Chao Chatrichaloem Yukol, an avant-garde cinematographer. His influence on the younger film directors and producers created a new wave in the film industry. However, with the strong competition from television, as well as financial problems, the Thai film industry at present is again declining. A surplus of film actors and directors who competed to enter into television spilled over into the modern theatre in the late 1980s.

On the whole, the reign of King Prajadhipok, which is often criticized by certain scholars as a "dark age" of Thai drama and theatre, was in fact a period of creativity and modern ideas in the performing arts. Most of its new developments have continued to be influential up to the present day.

DEVELOPMENT OF THE KROM SILAPAKON

In 1932 when the Revolution broke out and the system of absolute monarchy was overthrown, the Kong Mahorasop and Khon Luang underwent another change. The new Krom Silapakon (Department of Fine Arts) was set up in 1933 to take charge of all national cultural activities. It was under the Ministry of Education instead of the former Ministry of the Royal Palace. Cultural heritage in its highest form was to be public property and was no longer attached to the institution of monarchy. In 1934, a school for training in music and classical dance, Rongrian Nataduriyangkhasat, was founded after the French model of l'Ecôle des Beaux-Arts and l'Académie de Danse et Musique through the suggestion of Luang Wichitwathakan, an enthusiastic admirer of French culture, who became Director of the Krom Silapakon and later Minister of Culture. In 1935 the dancers and musicians of the Kong Mahorasop, Piphat Luang, and Khon Luang were transferred to the Krom Silapakon's jurisdiction to teach a new generation of artists, musicians, and dancers in the higher forms of art of the royal court. Royal properties for *khon, lakhon,* and its orchestra were also brought under the administration of the Krom Silapakon for similar educational purposes. The school went through a few changes of name[4] and is now known as Witthayalai Natasin after its promotion to the status of an institution of higher education. The professional training of classical dancers and musicians, which had long been under the authority of the royal court, now came under the responsibility of the government through the Ministry of Education. It is precisely this change in the structure of administration that caused the change in the nature of classical dance-drama, in that educational values and purposes have become the essence of all arts engaged in in some degree of public entertainment.

POLITICS AND THEATRE UNDER THE PHIBUNSONGKHRAM REGIME

When King Prajadhipok abdicated in 1934, the right of succession passed to Prince Anandha Mahidol, who was then studying in Switzerland. Since the king was still a child, during the first period of his reign all the administrative power was in the hands of the leaders of the Revolution of 1932, including Pridi Phanomyong and Marshal Phibunsongkhram (Phibun, in short). The latter, during his two successive regimes (1938–44, 1947–57), many times promoted his nationalist campaigns through the medium of drama under the clever advice of Luang Wichitwathakan, who followed the method of King Vajiravudh in using historical legends and heroic deeds of past kings and national heroes and heroines as materials for *lakhon* productions, such as *Anuphap Phọ Khun Ramkhamhaeng* (The glory of King Ramkhamhaeng).

During the long periods of Premier Phibun's dictatorial rule, drama and the theatre were directly used as political instruments to propagate the government's political, economic, social, and cultural policies. On the one hand, Phibun had to justify his right to rule and to create his own *barami* (merits, glory) as the true leader of the nation in the absence of the king. On the other hand, in the state of political confusion caused by in-fighting between military and revolutionary leaders and by threat from foreign powers, particularly Japan, Premier Phibun had to maintain a strong hold on political power to lead the nation through these crises. His drastic *patiwat watthanatham* (cultural revolution) was imposed on the whole country to accelerate literacy by simplifying the Thai language and eradicating the Sanskrit and Pali elements in it. At the same time, Phibun abolished all noble titles in an attempt to put every citizen on an equal social level. Terms indicating social ranks and status, as well as pronouns signifying different social classes, were replaced by simple, common pronouns as in English, such as *chan* (I), *thoe* (you), and the polite phrase ending *čha* (*ja*) for everyone, instead of variations used in the old regime indicating class differences and royalty (such as *chao kha, phe kha,* and *phaya kha* used when speaking to noble and royal persons).

Another social and cultural change was Phibun's policy of Westernization, with the intention to rapidly modernize the people in their clothing habits and behaviour. In defence of his drastic measures, Phibun tried to explain that his policy would prevent the Japanese from imposing Japanese culture on the Thais and civilize the people through Western culture instead. This explanation, however, was not convincing to most people. Negative reactions were inevitable when the government used police force to control and punish those who failed to follow the orders. Continuous controversies and ambiguities generated by a succession of new orders and rules were major factors which caused rebellious attitudes and negativism among intellectuals and the traditional leaders of society. However, their opinions were suppressed throughout the dictatorial regime. Some members of the royal family refused to change and passively held on to their traditions.

Theatre and radio were the most effective tools of the government. Luang Wichitwathakan (Luang Wichit, in short) was assigned by the premier to create a totally new theatre, completely detached from the old regime. It was a difficult mission for Luang Wichit, who had no proper training. Aware of Premier Phibun's personal lack of understanding and appreciation of classical dance-drama, Luang Wichit modernized *lakhon ram* through the use of modern music, contemporary dialogues, and historical costumes appropriate to the periods in plays such as *lakhon phan thang,* instead of the classical costumes. In short, he made practical use of a combination of aspects from *lakhon dukdamban, lakhon phan thang, lakhon rong,* and *lakhon phut,* all of which were first developed in the Fifth Reign, and brought them up to date, so that they could be presented at the national level. His nationalistic and patriotic plays not only entertained (surprisingly they still do in their recent revivals), but also brought forth very strong and effective political messages. His songs and lyrics were on the lips of most Thai children and adults, since they were played repeatedly on the radio.

The most touching and memorable among his successful patriotic plays are *Luat Suphan* (The blood of Suphan) and *Chaoying Saenwi* (Princess of Saenwi). They still bring tears to the eyes of many audiences whenever they are performed on stage and seen on television today. Being extremely gifted in his ability to produce heart-rending words and possessing a talent for developing intensely dramatic plots, Luang Wichit was more successful than his predecessor, King Vajiravudh, in communicating effectively his social and political ideas to modern audiences. Even at present, his plays and songs are used by the government whenever there is a need to stimulate a sense of national unity and patriotism, such as during the short regime of Premier Thanin Kraiwichien, an extreme rightist who came to power through the support of the military leaders after having defeated the leftist uprising of 6 October 1976.

One mistake among the many that Phibun made, one believed by many royalists to have been the ultimate cause of his downfall, was to imitate, at the height of his power, the life style of past Thai kings and to put himself on a par with the monarchy. When he and Lady La-iat resided at the palace-like villa which once belonged to Chao Phraya Ramrakhop, King Vajiravudh's favourite, they lavishly entertained foreign dignitaries and government guests. There were peformances of classical dance and *lakhon* by the Silapakon troupe very much in the style of the Lakhon Luang troupe at the royal court. The premier also took special personal interest in attractive female dancers, some of whom became his minor wives, in the same way as the royal consorts who were Lakhon Luang dancers. The spirit of pageantry developed again, but this time not for the monarch, but for the military dictator, the pseudo-king. It was not difficult to relate his position as marshal, supreme commander of the three military forces, to that of Somdet Chao Phraya Chakri, founder of the Chakri dynasty. Had he been living two centuries ago, he could easily have become founder of a new dynasty and succeeded to the throne by force. However, the system of democracy, which he had been so much a part of at the beginning, was a preventive measure in itself. Ironically, after his long years in power, his youthful democratic ideals were soon overshadowed by his desire for absolute power. His portrait was shown at the beginning of every entertainment event with the "Maharuk Mahachai" (lit., Great occasion, great victory) anthem, which is used for a royal prince or princess of the highest rank, forcing audiences to stand up to honour him. The portrait of the king was shown at the end along with the "Sansoen Phra Barami" (lit., In praise of the king's merits) anthem.

The accumulated political mistakes, widespread corruption among government leaders and officials, constant abuses of human rights, violence, and injustice, together with conflicts of interests, caused the long regime of Phibun to fall in the *coup d'état* of 1957 led by Sarit Thanarat, his subordinate, who also succeeded as the next military dictator. Phibun went into exile and finally died in Japan. However, the legacy of his rule could still be found in the patriotic plays of the following period.

Chapter VI
Contemporary Thai Theatre

Social and Political Development in the Age of Democracy

After the fall of Field Marshal Phibunsongkhram in the *coup d'état* in 1957, the new government was backed by Marshal Sarit Thanarat, who later became prime minister during the Ninth Reign. It was a shrewd policy of the new military government to revive old royal traditions and ceremonies to promote the prestige of the king, in order to win public approval and to create a sense of national unity. Among the restored royal customs and ceremonies were the Royal Ploughing Ceremony, the Royal Kathin Procession in the Royal Barge, and the Silver Jubilee Celebration (*Ratchadaphisek*) of King Bhumibol, Rama IX, and the celebration of his longest reign, *Ratchamangkalaphisek*. There were also in this middle period of the Ninth Reign more frequent visits of royal guests and heads of states for whom grand parades, balls, music, concerts, and classical dance-drama (both *khon* and *lakhon*) performances were given. The productions were specially created for the occasions with a finale dance celebrating friendship. The king and queen presided over these performances, either for official purposes or for royal charitable causes.

In private, King Bhumibol during the first period of his reign took special interest in promoting traditional dances by inviting leading dancers from many regions to perform at court and photographing and filming their performances. He also started a collection of Thai classical and traditional music on records and tapes. It is well known that his library of films, photographs, and records on these subjects is the best in the country. The king also revived the tradition of initiating the dancers in the *Phithi Khrop* ceremony. King Vajiravudh was the first to play the part of Phra Phrot Rusi (Bharata Rishi, the great teacher of Indian dancing), performing the *Phithi Khrop*, putting the masks and head-dresses of Phra Phrot Rusi and Phra Phirap (the great teacher of *khon* and *lakhon* and a *yak* character in the *Ramakien*) and the *soet* head-dress of *nora chatri* (the earliest form of *lakhon*, and thus the foundation of Thai dance-drama; also Khun Sattha, father of *nora chatri*, is worshipped as a great teacher of *lakhon*) on the heads of the initiated. King Bhumibol also presided over the ceremony at the Chitlada Palace in 1963, in which he initiated Mom Ratchawong Kukrit Pramoj as a dancer and teacher of *khon* and *lakhon,* and again at the Rongrian Natasin (Academy of the Art of Dancing) in 1971. He encouraged senior dancers to perfect their most difficult dances (such as the "sacred dance" of Phra Phirap, which is considered the highest form of Thai classical dance to be performed only by the grand master of the dance) and to teach these dances to their disciples.

In private relaxation periods, however, the king prefers sports such as boat-racing, sailing, badminton, automobiles, and modern jazz sessions. In the 1970s and 1980s the queen greatly supported productions of historical plays to promote patriotism.[1] At present, both of their Majesties spend much of their time visiting different regions, where they reside for a time at one of the regional palaces built for this particular purpose. On these royal visits there are usually tribal or regional dances and *lakhon* performed for them, either in these country palaces or on location during their visits.

At the Chitlada Palace School, which the king founded in order to educate his own royal children as well as other children of all classes, the crown prince, royal princesses, and other pupils were encouraged to learn the art of dancing *khon* and *lakhon* as well as Thai classical music. Crown Prince Vajiralongkorn, as a child, once danced in a school *khon* performance of the *Ramakien.* The study of these traditional art forms is still maintained in the school curriculum at present.

After the student uprising against the military dictatorship on 14 October 1973, Thai classical dance-drama, along with other arts and literature of aristocratic origins, were attacked by leftists as being products of a decadent aristocracy and instruments of the monarchy to glorify its own institution and corrupt the minds of the people. When the military took power again after the so-called "reform," i.e., *coup d'état* on 26 October 1976, the military-backed extreme rightist government of Thanin Kraiwichien (1976–77) made all efforts to counteract the leftist movement by promoting cultural activities, such as organizing in 1977 a grand nation-wide festival of Thai dance and drama, sponsoring productions of historical plays, and publishing books on Thai traditional dance and music.

Among the latest of the patriotic plays in the mixed style of *lakhon ram–lakhon rong* by the National Theatre was *Suk Kao Thap* (The battle of the Nine Armies) performed in 1977. The drama glorified King Rama I, founder of the present Chakri dynasty, when he fought against the Burmese. The music and lyrics in the play were composed by Montri Tramote, head teacher of the Silapakon Music Section, who has been influenced by Prince Naris and is responsible for most of the musical compositions and adaptations of all Silapakon productions since the Revolution of 1932. Achan Montri Tramote was trained in the Piphat Luang and has performed for Thai kings since the reign of King Vajiravudh. He is also an authority on Thai classical music, drama, and dance and has written most of the accounts of these subjects for Krom Silapakon (Department of Fine Arts) since the time when Dhanit Yupho was director.

Another contemporary dramatist who followed in the footsteps of Luang Wichitwathakan in writing and producing historical patriotic *lakhon ram-lakhon rong* is Somphop Chantharaprapha, a former deputy-director of Krom Silapakon and a protégé of Queen Sirikit. Though he calls his plays *lakhon dukdamban* and has established himself as an authority on the genre (he grew up in the Ban Mọ Palace of Chao Phraya Thewet and had close relationships with dancers, singers, and musicians of the Lakhon Dukdamban Theatre), other authorities and the descendants of Chao Phraya Thewet and of Prince Naris have never recognized it as such, nor do they accept his authority on the subject. Somphop uses the same method of dramatizing chronicle tales and historical heroic deeds in a combination of *lakhon ram, lakhon rong,* and *lakhon phan thang.* The dancers themselves both sing and dance. They wear period costumes, instead of the classical traditional garb in *khon* and *lakhon.* The best-known among his plays are *Nang Suang, Sithammasokarat,* and *Somdet Phra Naresuan Maharat.* His latest work is *Samakkhiphet* (1977–78), a dramatic adaptation of *Samakkhiphet Kham Chan* by Chit Burathat, which is a tale on the danger of disunity within the nation. This was written in the Sixth Reign and won a prize for the best work to stimulate nationalism.

Under the new administration of the Krom Silapakon and the Witthayalai Natasin, the public have now more access both as audience and as pupils to the refined and sophisticated art forms which had been more or less restricted to the aristocratic elite. Though it is true that the Khon Luang and Lakhon Luang (with the exception of the *lakhon nang nai,* or *lakhon phuying khong luang*) had been performed for the general public during the old absolute monarchy, and that children of commoners had an opportunity to be trained in the royal dance troupes, the system of public education under the new democratic government allows the training of classical dancers and musicians to spread to a much wider circle in society.

To show off its first fruits under the new regime, the Krom Silapakon sent a troupe of dancers to Japan in 1934. This international activity was to become a show piece of the department and has been carried on until the present day. It serves not only as a means to propagate the cultural achievements of a new government, but also to gain prestige and admiration from foreign audiences on a world-wide scale. The latest cultural mission of this type, considered to be a laudable effort, was the dance tour by the Krom Silapakon in the People's Republic of China in 1976–77 during the government of Prime Minister Mom Ratchawong Kukrit Pramoj, an active patron of *khon* and *lakhon,* who is also an accomplished *khon* dancer, director, and producer. His initiative in training university students in the art of *khon* at Thammasat University since

1973 has been highly praised since the troupe first performed for the king and queen at the bicentennial celebration of the birthday of King Rama II.

It is important to stress here Kukrit's purpose in developing a knowledge of and an appreciation for the art of *khon* and *lakhon* among the new generation of intellectuals, who are the future leaders of Thai society. He follows King Vajiravudh's concept of Khon Samak Len. However, there is a significant difference between Khon Thammasat and Khon Samak Len, in that the latter was exclusive to the "inner clique" of King Vajiravudh, whereas the former is open to all students. In both cases, the new dancers were trained by professionals of the highest calibre, i.e., the teachers of the Khon Luang in the Sixth Reign and those of the Krom Silapakon in the present reign. The Khon Thammasat performed on many occasions in the early 1970s including the Investiture of Crown Prince Vajiralongkorn in 1972. After the student uprising in 1973 it was discontinued due to the political crisis and the political involvement of its producer-director, Mom Ratchawong Kukrit Pramoj. It was revived again in 1978 to celebrate the birthday of King Rama II in February 1978 with the performance of the episodes of *Sida Hai* (Sida's being abducted) and *Thawai Phon* (the monkey army pledge their loyal service to Phra Ram in his pursuit of Sida) from the *Ramakien*. A statement by Kukrit explaining the purpose of the Khon Thammasat is very revealing.

> *Khon* is both an art and a culture of the Thai nation which cannot be found anywhere else. But *khon* is an art which has to live in living human beings. It cannot be written in books, or hung as a painting, or set in place as a statue for worship.
>
> Those who wish to preserve this Thai art and culture, which is called *khon,* therefore have to invest in it by receiving its training, in order to preserve it within themselves.[2]

At present, despite political upheavals, leftist opposition, and a continuous struggle for power among the military officers, Thailand has been able to preserve, maintain and even develop further its classical art of dancing even into modern times. The government institution of the Rongrian Natasin (which is considered the best and the oldest government organization of its kind in Asia giving training in the traditional dance-drama) has taken the place of the royal court in setting a national standard and in producing new dancers and supporting private troupes such as the Khon Thammasat and the Ban Plai Noen Palace troupe of the Prince Naris Foundation, which also performs annually. There are also occasional productions of classical *khon* and *lakhon* in schools and universities all over the country. It is by these activities that Thai cultural heritage is able to survive through all political, social, and economic challenges.

As a natural reaction, the leftist movement, which attempted to destroy Thai traditions and cultural heritage, served only to stimulate more strongly the rightist movement to preserve and glorify Thai culture on a much broader scale, as shown in the grand celebration of the literary and dramatic works of King Rama II at his birthday celebration in 1978. There were not only performances of *khon* (*Ramakien* by the Khon Thammasat troupe), *lakhon nok* (*Khawi* by the Ban Plai Noen Palace troupe [a revival of the dance troupe of Chao Phraya Thewet and of Prince Naris]), but also the rare *nang yai* (*Ramakien*'s "Wirunchambang" episode by the National Theatre troupe), *hun yai* (*Sangthong*'s "Rotchana Choosing Her Husband" episode by the Nai Piak puppet troupe), *he rua* (boat song and procession at Wat Arun, Temple of Dawn), and a demonstration of traditional dishes described in the works of King Rama II. All of these programmes were presided over by H.R.H. Princess Phra Thep Ratanaratchasuda (H.R.H. Princess Mahachakri).[3] The collaborative efforts between government and private organizations on these occasions show a remarkable strength with which the cultural leaders of present Thai society fight against the strong current of modern industrial civilization and the threat of Maoist cultural revolution. It is also through a continuous process of modernization of the other technical aspects of the classical theatre that it is enabled to flow with the current.

INSTITUTIONAL AND CULTURAL DEVELOPMENTS

Contemporary Thai theatre encompasses both classical dance-drama in modernized forms and styles and straight plays in prose or poetic prose on contemporary social and political themes. The former is mainly produced and performed by the National Theatre and the Witthayalai Natasin (College of Dance and Music), which are in the Krom Silapakon under the Ministry of Education. The latter group is within academic circles in universities and among young intellectuals. On television, domestic dramas, some with current social themes, dominate.

Since its gradual development in the mid-1950s, contemporary Thai theatre has been suffering from a lack of financial and moral support from the government and the general public. The classical dance-drama productions continue the conventions handed down from generation to generation with some changes in technical and stylistic aspects in an attempt to attract a popular audience and students who have to study classical drama as a part of Thai literature courses. Since the Ministry of Education prescribes only excerpts from dramatic masterpieces, the National Theatre productions present mostly short scenes from these classical plays in the form of variety shows rather than the complete plays as in the past. Only occasionally are there long episodes from the *Ramakien* re-edited and built around a single character from the beginning of his or her life to the end. This has been the recent trend introduced by the former director of the Dance and Music Department of the National Theatre, Seri Wangnaitham.

Technically, the stage designs and lighting of the National Theatre productions have been significantly improved due to new hi-tech equipment and the modern technical knowledge received from the West. However, a lack of funds and low admission fees prevent the National Theatre from producing high-quality dance-drama. The theatre earns its main income from renting its facilities to governmental, business, and private organizations.

As to university theatres, the productions have been mainly translations and adaptations of Western plays, which are taught in English and Western literature courses. There has been very little attempt to write original plays, except for a few short ones by amateurs, most of which are unsuitable for the productions. The theatres are usually classrooms or auditoriums within the universities attended mostly by students and families and friends of the theatre groups. The circle is therefore very small. The intellectual nature of the plays chosen by this group limits the audience. The general public prefers film and television as in most countries.

One of the major problems in the development of Thai contemporary theatre is the lack of relationship and co-operation or dialogue between the classical dance-drama groups and the new university groups. Probably due to a lack of self-confidence as well as insecurity or pride, each group remains within their own circle instead of sharing ideas and experiences to widen their perspectives. It was not until the early 1970s that the efforts of the Institute of Thai Studies at Thammasat University under the guidance of Mom Ratchawong Kukrit Pramoj and the efforts of the new intellectuals enabled seminars on Thai drama and theatre to be organized. Representatives from all institutions and entertainment circles, including the folk dance-drama and puppet troupes, were invited to attend the meeting, and discussions were carried out on various problems in an effort to encourage closer co-operation among these groups. From then on universities have invited professional artists, dramatists, actors, scriptwriters and technicians to teach or help in their productions. Thammasat University Drama Department was the first and probably the only one to have a classical puppeteer as artist in residence (see pp. 204–6). There are classical dancers teaching traditional dances and dance-drama at the Theatre Arts Department of Chulalongkorn University and the Drama Department of Thammasat University. Thammasat again was first to have its own *khon* troupe under the patronage of Mom Ratchawong Kukrit Pramoj, who continues to be the main supporter of the Thai art and culture programmes of the university. Other universities followed in encouraging dramatic and cultural activities among students. The Bangkok Bank and the Thai Farmers Bank, where top executives are graduates of Chulalongkorn or Thammasat, became sponsors of some of these university activities as a part of their own publicity.

The art and culture scene became brighter from the time of the Bicentennial Celebration of Bangkok in 1982. Then the private sector began to take interest in cultural activities and social development. Theatre productions for charitable purposes, particularly for royal projects, became popular among the upper middle class. Dignitaries and well-known personalities in both government and business performed in many of these productions. Social workers find dance-drama productions or variety shows with songs and dances done in the modern style to be the best medium for fund-raising. Thailand is probably one of most well-known countries where national figures have adopted dance and music as the hobbies. Thailand is probably the only country with singing prime ministers and top government officials.

The period from mid-1985 to the present has been very good for stage theatre and television drama in Thailand. This is due to social, educational, and economic factors.

Firstly, modern theatre, i.e., straight plays on social themes, started during the 1960s in the universities under Western influence initially as a part of the English curriculum or an extra-curricular activity, and later within Drama or Theatre Arts Departments offering undergraduate degrees and elective courses. At present, this media has attracted a large number of advocates in and out of academic life. These are mostly university graduates, members of their families, and friends, who are now more familiar with modern theatre styles and themes and who prefer them to traditional theatre.

Secondly, the circle of modern theatre producers and directors has expanded to the business and commercial sector, which has now taken interest in producing and promoting modern plays for middle-class audiences. They are mostly light comedies and social satires performed in hotel dining rooms and cocktail lounges. Today there are British theatre groups from the West End that comes once or twice a year to perform bedroom farces under the sponsorship of British Airways, the Siam Intercontinental Hotel, and the Landmark Hotel. Thammasat Drama Department was the first to start performing modern, light comedies and musical plays in Thai at the Oriental Hotel as tea and dinner theatre. They are mostly adaptations of Western plays, such as Oscar Wilde's *The Importance of Being Earnest,* Brecht's *The Threepenny Opera,* and *The Siamese Cats* (a Thai version of *Cats, My Fair Lady,* etc.). All of these were very successful. Montien Hotel now has a cocktail lounge theatre, the Monthienthong Theatre, produced, directed, and performed by university graduates and professionals.

As the commercial entertainment companies begin to recognize the profit-earning potentials of modern theatre, they are now more confident about investing their money in promoting productions by young directors. The 1985 production of Brecht's *Galileo* by Group '28 made up of graduates of Chulalongkorn and Thammasat universities was co-sponsored by the German Goethe Cultural Institute and Nite Spot (formerly a very large Thai pop concerts promoter). Nite Spot has very popular radio and television programmes and is able to advertise the play through these media to young radio listeners and television viewers who are regular fans of these programmes. Hence, the play, although a very hard one for a Thai audience to understand, was very well attended by students from schools and universities. Similarly in the 1980s, the Chulalongkorn Theatre Arts Department received support from Nite Spot in promoting their latest stage production, Sophocles' *Oedipus Rex,* which also had a young audience that came probably for the first time to see a Western classic tragedy in the open-air courtyard of the Faculty of Arts. Commercial tactics and approaches in entertainment promotion are main factors contributing to the success of these two modern theatre productions in the 1980s and 1990s. They would not have reached the attention of the outside public, particularly the young age group, if it had not been for commercial promotion. It is therefore an accepted fact that support from the commercial and business sector is necessary for the continuation of high-quality theatre productions. Otherwise, this new genre of drama will definitely decline as other forms have in the past.

Thirdly, newspapers and journals play an even more important role in promoting modern theatre productions in their review, which are usually written by university graduates.

It is interesting to note that modern stage plays from the 1960s onward are mostly translations and adaptations of Western plays by university lecturers and students who have studied modern Western drama either directly in the West or in Thailand. This is similar to the time of King Vajiravudh in the early twentieth century. Original modern Thai plays were written and performed with great success in the 1930s and 1940s. After World War II in the early 1950s, film and television replaced the theatre causing its gradual decline. Theatre scriptwriters changed over to film and television where there is more money. Hence, there is a great lack of original, modern Thai stage plays at present. The writer has produced plays adapted from famous Thai novels such as *Mae Bia* (The cobra; by award-winning novelist Wanit Charungkitauan) in 1989, which was very successful.

With theatre activities being revived again in universities, the choices are being made by new intellectuals who prefer masterpieces in modern Western drama to Thai melodrama and traditional dance-drama, which are thought to be irrelevant to contemporary society. Since successful scriptwriters earn more in the film and television industries, they are reluctant to write for the university and amateur theatres. Modern Thai theatre continues to suffer from this lack of native Thai material. There have been a few new attempts by amateur playwrights. However, due to the lack of stage experience and knowledge in playwriting, their plays were not very successful.

Meanwhile, traditional Thai dance-drama, *khon* (masked dance-drama) and *lakhon* (dance-drama), are still produced and performed by the National Theatre. They are very popular. However, the productions at present tend to be in the form of variety shows rather than complete stories. The scripts now consist of very short lyrics and more comic dialogues to amuse the contemporary audience, which consists mostly of young school students who have to study these classics in school. There is also less dancing. The movements are more simplified and shorter.

As previously discussed in Chapter 3, before modern drama and theatre forms were introduced into Thailand in the late nineteenth century, traditional Thai theatre had been dance-drama in various forms and styles. The oldest forms are *khon* and *lakhon*. During the reign of King Chulalongkorn in the nineteenth century, due to Western influence, there were many changes and new developments in modernizing the traditional forms, in order to make them more suitable to the needs and tastes of the new generation. New types of Thai music and more exotic stories were adapted from foreign sources, both from the East and West. The modernized *khon* and *lakhon* of this period were shorter, i.e., from the traditional three-days and three-nights continuous performance to three to four hours. The productions were divided into acts and scenes, each with a new set painted in a three-dimensional perspective. Longer dialogues in contemporary, conversational prose were added to the scripts, which had traditionally been poetic narratives and lyrics. The lyrics became shorter while the dialogue gained more importance. Towards the end of the nineteenth century, the long prose dialogues eventually developed into prose drama.

One of the latest popular *lakhon phan thang* dance-drama of the Krom Silapakon running continuously for two years (1990–92) was *Phu Chana Sip Thit* (Conqueror of the ten directions) by a famous novelist "Yakhop," adapted for stage by Seri Wangnaitham. The theatre was full at every show, mainly because of the popular male star dancers in it. This modernized version focuses more on the romantic and witty *cheracha* (dialogue) than dancing.

With the introduction of Western concepts and ideas into theatre production, scriptwriting, acting, and directing, the modern Thai theatre emerged in its full form in the works of Crown Prince Vajiravudh at the end of King Chulalongkorn's reign. Though there had been plays written in prose before the works of the crown prince, he is given most of the credit for the development of this new genre. This is mainly because he was able to make it acceptable to the elite society by way of his own informative writings published in journals by himself and circulated among his friends and associates or by experimenting with his courtiers. However, because of the newness of the form and themes, the modern plays did not catch on among the general public until after his reign. In the 1930s and 1940s stage plays were either romantic and melodramatic or home dramas which were popular among the middle-class audience. The stories and themes were less intellectual than the works of King Vajiravudh and hence more widely accepted by the public.

During World War II, foreign films were not allowed into the country. Theatre became the sole public entertainment. This period is often referred to as a "golden age of Thai theatre." There were as many as twenty to thirty theatre troupes in competition with one another in Bangkok and all over the country. Playwrights, directors, producers, and actors enjoyed high income and popularity until foreign films were again allowed into the country in the late 1940s. Theatre went slowly into its decline. Directors, actors, and playwrights switched over to film industry and in the 1950s into television. Modern stage theatre was started again within the university, first at Chulalongkorn Theatre Arts Department and later at Thammasat Faculty of Liberal Arts in the 1960s. At present, in the early 1990s, courses in drama and theatre arts are offered at most universities in Bangkok and in the provinces. Only three universities offer undergraduate degree programmes. They are Chulalongkorn, Thammasat, and Silpakorn. The Witthayalai Natasin (College of Dance and Music) offers an undergraduate degree only in traditional Thai dance, music, and dance-drama, and Western music and classical dance, i.e., classical ballet.

In the 1960s and 1970s there seemed to be no relationship between the university drama groups and the National Theatre and the Witthayalai Natasin. The former are interested only in Western-style modern plays while the latter continue to teach, train and produce traditional-style dance-drama. After a few seminars in which contemporary theatre and its immediate problems were seriously discussed by representatives from the academic and professional circles from both camps, traditionalists and modernists, there is now more cooperation between the two circles. Hence, the 1980s are significant years in the development of contemporary Thai theatre, not only in its expanding activities but also in the interrelationship between various theatre groups. There are now many new commercial theatre groups, such as Dass Entertainment and JSL. They are of popular nature and are targetted for younger audiences.

At present, there seems to be more cooperation and understanding between the classical and modern dramatists. Through successive seminars, conferences, and exchanges of ideas and teachers between universities and the Krom Silapakon and the Witthayalai Natasin, authorities and active artists from all institutions were constantly brought together to share their views and experiences. The newly established Cultural Centre of Thailand[4] plays a very important role in providing a neutral ground for dramatic performances of all types, genres, and styles. Each year the Ministry of Education will allot a budget for the Cultural Centre to sponsor various dance and drama groups, classical, folk, and modern, to give performances for school students and general public. It is also the best theatre for international performing artists.[5]

CHILDREN'S THEATRE

Children have always had a significant part in Thai culture and tradition, though not in the same way as in other countries. While Western children and some other Asian children are protected from the adult world, Thai children are exposed to the facts of life and the realities of the world from a tender age through the indirect means of entertainment, oral and written literature, songs, and music. These realities are often disguised or hidden in symbols or symbolic allusions as in poetry, paintings, sculpture, dance-drama, puppet and shadow plays, games, dances, and songs. This is one reason why Thai children learn from an early age poetic skills in rhyming and symbolizing, verbal witticism, satire, and social criticism. However, all of these are in general expressed with a sense of humour rather than any serious political and social criticism.

As in most countries in the West and Asia, traditional theatre in Thailand was and still is a total theatre for audiences of all ages, young and old. There had been no separation between children's theatre and theatre for adults up to the twentieth century. Though there were puppet theatres and shadow theatres, they have been and still are open theatres for the general public regardless of sex and age. The stories in these plays, performed either by human performers or puppeteers with dolls of various shapes and forms, are mostly tales taken from religious sources, principally *Jataka* tales about the previous thousand lives of Buddha who went through many cycles of lives in different forms, ranging from the lowest forms of animals, human beings of all classes, superhuman beings, or semi-divine beings, gods and goddesses, with typical themes of trial and temptation, wisdom gained through suffering, adventures, romances, separations of loved ones, etc.—all of them usually ending with the happy reunions of loved ones and family, the return of fortune, rewards for the good and punishment for the bad, and confessions of the sinners, followed by forgiveness and atonement.

Many of these Buddhist tales, like old fairy tales in most nations, are unfit for young children. They often describe unpleasant situations, ugly characters, horrifying scenes full of ghosts, goblins, cruelty, and sadistic actions, with the religious purpose of discouraging people from committing sinful acts, and to teach them moral and religious lessons. Most of these tales also have erotic and romantic scenes between the hero and the heroine in their passionate moments, which are often vividly described and demonstrated by performers to the enjoyment of adult audiences, but in most cases harmful to innocent children. However, in one sense, it can be regarded as a method of sex education through literature and drama, which can be naturally and unconsciously absorbed by children and teenagers from an early age. There has always been this curious contradiction between worldly pleasure and religious teaching in traditional Thai drama and literature, a paradox which finds its answer only in Buddhist philosophy. That is to say, the worldly pleasures described in the drama or literature will eventually be shown as the causes of suffering to such an extreme degree that the suffering human beings (the heroes or heroines) wish to search for a way to be released from the seemingly endless cycle of suffering, births, and rebirths. The only way to attain this goal is, according to Buddhist teaching, through the diminishing and extinguishing of the very ultimate causes of suffering, that is, physical and worldly desires. The result is *nirvana*—a total release from the cycle of births and rebirths caused by these human weaknesses.

Ironically, these Buddhist tales are usually told by Buddhist monks in poetic and dramatic recitations. They are one of the main sources of *lakhon* (dance-drama), *khon* (masked dance-drama), *hun* (puppet plays), and *nang* (shadow plays). These monks can sometimes be carried away by the excitement of the adventures and romances. They are in fact dramatic actors-narrators, even though Buddhism forbids monks to indulge in such activities and entertainment. Some of them, self-hypnotized, go into a trance as if possessed by evil spirits or divine beings. Many monks make a profession as prophets and seers or fortune-tellers. King Mongkut, who is known to Westerners as the Siamese king in the musical play, *The King and I,* was the first to forbid such activities by monks when he came to the throne in 1851. He was in fact a very pious king, quite the opposite of the caricature created by American dramatists based on the romantic fantasy of the British governess, Anna, who wrote the story for commercial purposes.[6]

Hun Krabok

Hun krabok (bamboo rods puppets) were created in the reign of King Chulalongkorn as a new form of puppetry. It was slightly influenced by the Chinese Hainan puppets in the form of the puppet itself, but it developed from the traditional Thai *hun lek* (small string puppets with legs and arms manipulated from below), *hun yai* (big puppets with the same style and form), and *lakhon lek* (little puppet dance-drama; the puppets have legs and arms manipulated by rods).

Hun krabok, however, became more popular than these three traditional types and continued to flourish until after World War II. But during the next twenty years, it ceased to be an effective theatre form. It was not until in the late 1970s that a few Thai artists, notably Chakraphan Posayakrit, a famous portrait artist, took a special interest in reviving *hun krabok*. They were at first collectors' items, but gradually Chakraphan began to take lessons from Chusi Skunkaeo, who was then in her late sixties. Chusi is at present probably the best *hun krabok* puppeteer in the country and the only woman classical puppeteer (*dalang*) in Asia. She has been a puppeteer since her early childhood and is the only heir to Piak Skunkaeo, who made *hun krabok* one of the most popular entertainments in Thailand during the 1940s and 1950s. Since Chusi has no one in her family of eleven children who has taken an interest in continuing this traditional art, she is very willing to teach it to other students outside her family. This is in fact a very rare practice and open-minded attitude for the traditional Thai artist. They are usually very jealous of their arts.

Chakraphan also creates many *hun krabok* puppets himself by learning from the old models and restoring them. His puppets are now done in his individual style, far more refined than the traditional ones, having lost the folk qualities of the puppets created by villagers in the old days. In the mid-1970s Chakraphan finally organized a group of young and enthusiastic friends and students under the direction of Chusi to perform *hun krabok* for charitable purposes. His set designs are also more elaborate and refined, unlike the folk style of Chusi's original puppet theatre. This modern improvement by Chakraphan is the main force to attract the sophisticated audiences of the upper-class universities and colleges, and even the Krom Silapakon has begun to take an interest in it. This new style of performance was given at the National Theatre, Suan Pakkat Palace of Princess Chumbhot (col. pl. 4), the Siam Society, and the Bhirasri Art Centre. Chusi was the main puppeteer in all of them. Chakraphan gradually became independent of Chusi and now performs without her assistance. Chusi, or "Pa Chun" (Aunt Chun), becomes only a major performer under Chakraphan's direction. In 1982 he introduced new puppets for the production of a popular Chinese chronicle tale, the *Samkok* (*The Three Kingdoms*), with exquisitely decorated and painted puppets dressed in Chinese traditional costumes of the classic period as in the Peking Chinese Opera.

In 1980 the Thammasat University Drama Department under the author's direction became interested in continuing the art of *hun krabok* for educational and cultural purpose. It started the project by learning the art from Chusi, and finally purchased the whole collection of her puppets. In 1980 the Department also initiated the post of "artist in residence" at Thammasat University, which enabled Chusi to become its first "artist in residence" under the annual sponsorship of a university for the first time in Thai academic history. Each year there are about twenty students and teachers at Thammasat learning the art. They have produced many public performances for children and adults. (See Appendix B on p. 214.)

University and Private Groups of Modern Children's Theatre[7]

Chulalongkorn University, Department of Theatre Arts, Children's Theatre Section The Department started its programmes of producing plays for children in 1972 by adapting Western tales and stories into Thai and eventually writing new plays from Thai folk tales. Students who take courses in children's theatre have to produce or direct short plays as their final projects. These plays are performed by student actors and actresses or amateur volunteers from other faculties and outside the university.

Chulalongkorn puppet theatre started in 1975, again with plays adapted from the West. Their style and types of puppets are also modern under Western influence. They are hand puppets in the style of the "Muppet Show" and "Sesame Street," or modern rod puppets. Thai folk tales have also been adapted for these puppet shows.

The Department presented their works for the first time on television Channel 9 in 1975 under the direction of Onchuma Yuthawong with the sponsorship of commercial enterprises. Their television programmes called "Hun Hansa" (Joyful puppets) were rather popular up to 1981 when Onchuma decided to discontinue the regular shows due to poor administrative and financial problems. The television programmes, however, did stimulate other groups to create quality programmes for children. One other crucial problem which faces most children's theatres internationally, especially the ones depending on students as performers and organizers, is that the students who have graduated from the university rarely continue with the groups or take up this activity as their profession. They are likely to look for other more highly paying jobs which seem more permanent to them.

The groups therefore suffer from the lack of a firm foundation and continuous effort. Financial support from private and governmental sources have not been sufficient for the groups to carry on their creative projects for a long period of time.

Another problem is that most organizations in Thailand are personality-oriented. If the leaders are active, the organizations prosper accordingly. But if the members cease to function actively, the groups die or disintegrate quite naturally. Most activities of this nature are therefore short-lived, especially the non-professional and academic ones. (See Appendix A.)

Thammasat University, Department of Drama, Children's Theatre Section The Department branched off from the Department of English Literature and Language in 1978. It is now an independent department offering courses in Thai, Asian, and Western drama and performing arts. Its main aims are to promote Thai traditional arts and to find ways of modernizing and revitalizing them to suit the taste and pace of life of the new generation, while maintaining traditional aesthetic value and culture. It also makes a serious effort to adapt Western and international modern plays and to apply modern techniques in dramatic and performing arts to traditional Thai arts, in order to preserve our traditional arts as living arts, not as museum collections. In 1980, for the first time in the history of Thai universities, the Department started a programme of supporting "artists in residence" who are famous, professional artists in performing arts under the sponsorship of the university. These artists reside at the university and teach the students traditional performing arts. They also experiment with the Department to modernize their methods of teaching and performing, in order to make them easier and more accessible to those of the general public who are interested in preserving and maintaining the arts. Chusi is the first artist in residence, as mentioned earlier.

The Department has also worked with foreign artists in stage drama, television, and puppetry in collaborative projects as exchange programmes of culture and education. The students and teachers travel to different countries with puppeteers, dancers, and musicians to perform both classical and folk Thai puppet plays, dances, and dance-drama, as well as adaptations of Western plays of international interest. In 1982, the troupe performed its own adaptation of Shakespeare's *A Midsummer Night's Dream* in Thai classical dance-drama for adults and children in England, and also invited small children from the local ballet school to take part as fairies in the play. The children wore traditional Thai dance costumes and learned to do some simple steps in Thai dance to Thai traditional music. It was a great success. The local audiences and parents were extremely proud of their children's participation. They invited the Thammasat troupe to perform there again in 1983. For the puppet show, the Department presented a Thai adaptation of *Cinderella* with traditional *hun krabok* puppets and lyrics set to Thai music. The choreography for the puppets was done by Chusi, and the script was the collaborative work of Chusi, Wandee Limpiwattana, and Chamnian (music teacher, traditional Thai singer). (See Appendix B.)

The Department believes that by way of adapting well-known stories for Thai traditional puppets, it can interest international audiences more effectively than by performing only traditional Thai stories. However, attempts have been made to adapt Thai traditional stories to suit the taste of modern audiences as well. Fortunately, the Department's performing arts in this respect are very flexible and adaptable, and also take great care not to dilute the quality of traditional forms and styles. It is therefore a great challenge to maintain both the traditional aesthetic qualities and the liveliness of modern taste. The dialogues in all of these plays must therefore be very witty, as in all forms of folk arts, in order to attract the attention of young audiences; even adults can be very impatient with lengthy, old-fashioned dialogues and movements. The happy balance and medium, though hard to maintain, is not altogether impossible for the creative and energetic mind.

As to future projects of Thammasat University's children's and adolescent theatre programme, first, there are plans to develop children's theatre in different regions in Thailand, including the hill tribes in the north, to incorporate regional, indigenous visual and performing arts with central Thai arts and modern techniques to create new and effective forms for children's theatre and educational theatre in the regions which would promote regional culture, arts, and traditions and relate to the new generation in the regions.

Secondly, the Department is actively involved in promoting international exchanges with developing and developed countries in the ASEAN countries, other parts of Asia, and the West in performing arts techniques, materials, research sources, performers, directors, producers, libraries, scripts, films, videotapes, visual materials, puppets, actors, teachers, and students. There are plans to promote workshops in which artists from different regions can work together to find ways and means to use traditional art forms relevant to modern needs in educating the public, young and adult, and to pay special attention to young children and adolescents.

Thirdly, efforts will be made to develop adolescent theatre and theatre for young adults. While there is more attention given to young children in creating plays, films, and television programmes, very little attention is directed toward teenagers, young adults, and pre-teens (i.e., ages ranging between 8–13, 13–16, 16–18, 18–20). In a national conference held at Thammasat University in 1982 on this subject, many issues were raised concerning commercial and non-commercial programmes for these particular age groups, which represent crucial turning points in the process of growing up. Young people of these ages are hard to please, because they themselves seem not to know what they want as entertainment and education. While trying to behave like adults, they are generally still childish and immature in many ways. Many of them regard children's theatre as "kid's stuff" and are insulted when forced to participate in it as an audience. One way of finding out what they really want is by organizing workshops for them, in which they could exchange views and ideas, sort out problems and create together new forms of entertainment for their own needs. This type of workshop should be supervised by professionally trained organizers and leaders, who can give them guidance and encourage them to be creative. Traditional arts should tactfully be introduced to them in such a way that they would not reject them. They should be given the opportunity to suggest new techniques or means of making these traditional forms more appealing to them, such as by creating new stories, adapting old folk tales, mixing different forms and media, and using experimental techniques in music and performing arts. They should also be encouraged to travel in their own country to different regions and to live with families in those regions learning to appreciate indigenous cultures and customs. International travel is of course very valuable to them to widen their scope of interest and understanding of the world and people around them. These young people after having been exposed to such an experience become, in most cases, leaders of the new theatre for the young. However, discipline and continuous guidance should also be important elements in their development and training.

Ministry of Education, Department of Educational Radio and Television   The Ministry of Education has started programmes for children on radio since the 1960s, and later in the 1970s they began their television series, monthly at first and later weekly. Their programmes are seen both in Bangkok and in the provinces. The organizers of the programmes are university graduates, some of whom have been trained in the West. The Department was originally headed by Khunying

Amphorn Meesook (Ph.D., Radcliffe). It has been under the direction of Napha Phongphiphat (B.A.Hons. English, Bedford College, University of London; now retired). They have a videotape mobile unit which produces educational programmes and records events or activities of educational value and interest. These videotapes are available for schools, universities, and other institutions.

The types of programmes produced by the Ministry are short plays, games, singing lessons, drawing lessons, story hours, and variety shows. The Department has also received cooperation from the universities, such as Chulalongkorn and Thammasat, in playwriting and dramatic presentations. There is an advisory board of committee members comprised of representatives from educational institutions and professional organizations, including radio and television stations.

Private Troupes   Maya Children's Art and Theatre Group is an independent, loosely structured group of students and graduates started in 1981. Their main purpose is to promote artistic and cultural activities for children and adolescents. They perform various types of plays with actors and puppets, usually in schools, both in Bangkok and in the provinces and in slums and at temples.[8] The group has no permanent theatre. They travel around to different places, mostly congested communities populated by lower income groups. The provinces where they have performed are Kanchanaburi (east), Buriram and Khon Kaen (northeast), and Rajaburi (south). They receive occasional financial support from various organizations, such as the National Housing Department, which sponsored performance in nine communities in Bangkok, and the Thammasat Alumni Association, Class of 1981. At present, due to economic reason as well as the change in their leaders' interest, the group's activities include theatre for adults such as *Sritharata,* a poetic drama adapted from Herman Hess' well-known novel.

Manao Wan (Sweet Lime) Troupe is a volunteers group of Chulalongkorn students started in 1981 with seven members. They perform stage plays, puppet plays, and story-telling for children in Bangkok and up-country at differnt theatres and cultural halls, such as the American Alumni Association Hall and the Bhirasri Art Centre. At present, the group is inactive due to economic reasons.

Thepsiri Suksopha Troupe in Chiengmai province was started by writer-artist Thepsiri Suksopha in 1980. Thepsiri usually writes stories for children. He organized a group of students from Chiengmai University and other colleges in the area to perform puppet plays and tell stories for children. The centre is his own cottage. Due to personal and financial problems, the group has discontinued their activities for the time being. In 1990–91 Thepsiri successfully teamed up with the Chulalongkorn Theatre Arts Department's leading poets and composers to present a "Total Theatre" in poetic recitals and tales for young audiences. The poets included Khunying Chamnangsri L. Rutnin and leading composers, namely, Danu Huntrakun and Bruce Gaston.

Television Programmes

Each of the five commercial television stations in Thailand has its own children's programming, usually shown in the early evening on weekdays and in the morning on weekends. Current programmes are:

1) Channel 3: "Jiu Jaeo Cho Lok" (Jiu and Jaeo discovering the world), an educational programme for children's development.
2) Channel 5: "Phung Noi" (Small bees), produced by the Small Bees Club. Director, "Na Nid" (Auntie Nid, Phatchari), with children singers, dancers, and narrators. This is the longest-running programme.
3) Channel 7: "Nu Tham Dai" (You can do it), a game and quiz show with prizes given by sponsors to promote their products. Director-producer, Atcharaphan Phaibunsuwan. A very popular show with little educational value.
4) Channel 7: "Chao Khun Thong" (The Magpie), teaching Thai language with hand puppets in the style of "Sesame Street," organized by "Khru Aao" (Ms. Kietsuda), a graduate of the Faculty of Education, Chulalongkorn University.
5) Channel 11: "Story-telling Hour" by Ponchan Chanthawimon, Ramkhamhaeng University, with book illustrations and handicrafts teaching.

Most television stations at present have quiz shows for teen-agers and young adults sponsored by such companies as Thai International Airways, Shell Company, Esso Company, Caltex Company, and various banks.

Kantana Film and Television Company of Pradit Kancharuk probably has the longest-running studio for producing moralistic television plays for children and young adults. It has captured many prizes since there are no competitors. At present, it also produces regular television dramas for adults.

The Drama Department of Thammasat University has produced during 1990–91 for the Ministry of Education television programmes for children on "Nature and Environment" under the direction of Wandee Limpiwattana, head of the Children's Theatre and Educational Drama Section. Classical and modern puppetry is often used with actors and narrators in the shows.

Contemporary Issues

It was not until the present century, within the last three decades or so, that Western-educated and influenced Thais began to pay more attention to the children's world in attempting to separate it from that of the adults to prevent the children from the corruption of the world. Cartoon movies from the West and later from Japan were the major sources of influence. In the 1980s national educators and social critics began to take a serious interest in censoring entertainment in mass media: film, television, magazines, newspapers, journals, books, etc. Books for children were published in rather poor imitations of Western models and later of Japanese second-rate publications. The Ministry of Education started programmes for children on radio in the 1950s, which are still continued today. Television programmes for children only started in the late 1970s and are still inferior in quality. Children find entertainment mostly from Western and Japanese films on television, to the point that the Board of Censorship took a serious step to curb violent Japanese and Chinese films. However, the preventive measure is too weak to battle the influx of commercial second-rate films from abroad. These foreign films have succeeded in brainwashing Thai children with values and systems alien to the Thai tradition and heritage. Violent cartoons from Japan and Chinese *kung-fu* films are now major influences in Thai television that corrupt the minds of Thai children. Having realized this danger to the mental health of our national youth, the government put a strict control on the schedule of television programmes and radio broadcasts of all stations. Children's programmes are now presented in suitable late afternoon and early evening hours during the weekdays and most of the daytime during weekends. However, this measure has now been slackened and the adult programmes again occupy the major part of the schedule including the children's hours.

APPENDIX A

Plays Presented by Chulalongkorn University Department of Theatre Arts for Children (1972–present)

1. Stage plays
   Students' projects
   (1) *Hänsel and Gretel*   Dec. 1972, Jan. 1973
   (2) *The Reluctant Dragon*   Jan. 1973
   (3) *The Princess and the Cobweb Witch*   Aug. 1975
   Teachers' projects
   (1) *An Hour for Children* (a variety of small plays)   Feb. 1976
   (2) *Snow White and the Seven Dwarfs*   Jan. 1979
   (3) *Dream of Fantasy*   Aug. 1982

2. Puppet plays for stage and television (Channel 9)
   (1) *The Golden Fish* (an adaptation from an old Thai folk tale)
                                               April & Aug. 1975
   (2) *Bimbo: The Teacher Elephant*   Aug. 1979
   (3) *An Hour for Children* (*Clean Enough, The Little Monkey, The Frogs Choosing Their Master, Thousands of Cats*)
                                               Jan. & Mar. 1980
   (4) *An Hour for Children* (*The Complaining One, The Lonesome One, Boem Goes to School*)   Jan. 1981
   (5) *Monthly Puppet Programme for Children*
                                               1978–81

3. Travelling troupes to the provinces
   "Summer Truck Theatre Project," a combination of stage plays, puppet theatre, and mime performed at schools and orphanages in different provinces throughout Thailand, starting in 1977 and continuing to the present.
   April 1977: *The Pig Who Wants to Fly, The Ugly Frog, The Big-mouth Mouse*
   April 1980: Children's Theatre to the Provinces Project to the North (at Chiengmai and Phayao)
   Oct.–Nov. 1982: Children's Theatre to the Provinces Project to the Northeast (at Udonthani, Mahasarakham, Khon Kaen, Buriram, Surin)

4. *Hun krabok* puppetry

In recent years, Chulalongkorn Theatre Arts Department has taken an interest in *hun krabok* puppetry. Onchuma Yuthawong, head of the Children's Theatre Section, has studied the subject in depth and taken training in the art with Chusi Skunkaeo, artist in residence of Thammasat Drama Department, and Chakraphan Posayakrit, also a disciple of Chusi and a leading artist-puppeteer. Chakraphan's latest *hun krabok* production was *Samkok* (*The Three Kingdoms*), a Chinese classic adapted into Thai, which was jointly performed by Chusi, Chakraphan and his troupe, and Chulalongkorn University students at the Cultural Centre of Thailand. Onchuma has also videotaped the art of *hun krabok* for the National Identity Board, Prime Minister's Office.

5. Educational plays for children

In the 1990s Chulalongkorn Theatre Arts Department presented *Chan Chao Kha* (Dear moon), which reflects the social and economic values of modern children and their parents. The play was performed at the ASEAN Festival in Singapore.

All performances and productions are organized by teachers and students of the Department.

Appendix B

Productions by Thammasat University Drama Department for Children

1. Stage plays
   (1) *The Fat Princess,* 1980
   (2) *Three Little Pigs,* 1980
   (3) *The Little Mermaid,* 1980
   (4) *The Arkansas Bear* (Thai adaptation of Aurand Harris' original American version), 1980

2. Puppet plays: traditional *hun krabok* (bamboo rods) puppets
   (1) *Ramakien: Episode of the Floating Lady (Sida):* 1981 (Thammasat); 1982 (England); 1982 (television, Thailand and England, BBC, ITV, HIV); 1982 (Bangkok Christian College); 1982 (Germany, videotape for Bavarian Television)
   (2) *Phra Aphaimani:* 1981 (staged and videotaped at a temple funeral, Thai Studies Institute, Thammasat); 1982 (Thammasat)
   (3) *Life of a Puppeteer: The Last Performance of Hun Krabok:* 1981 (an autobiographical record of Mrs. Chusi's life and work on videotape, Thai Studies Institute, Thammasat)
   (4) *Sangthong: Prince of the Golden Conch-shell:* 1982 (Suan Pakkat Palace, Bangkok); 1982 (England); 1993 (Thammasat)
   (5) *Khun Chang Khun Phaen:* 1982 (Thammasat)

3. Human puppets (with actors)
   1981: *Phra Aphaimani* (Thammasat)

4. Modern puppets: hand puppets, marionettes, shadow puppets, actors and puppets
   1980: *The Prince Who Never Laughed* (Thammasat), hand puppets
   1981: *Wild Swans* (Thammasat), hand puppets
   Pinocchio (Thammasat), string puppets
   The Urn and the Crow (Thammasat), shadow puppets
   The Wolf and the Lamb (Thammasat), shadow puppets
   1982: *The Adventure of a Young Giant* (Thammasat), hand puppets
   Five Little Ducklings (Chiengmai, Chiengrai for hill-tribe children and teachers), hand puppets
   The Angel and the Frogs from Aesop's tale (Thammasat), hand puppets
   1983–: Numerous students' projects

5. Film for children, 16 mm in colour for the Bangkok Municipality

   A collaborative work of the Thammasat Drama Department and the Department of Mass Communication, Thammasat University, by Wandee Limpiwattana (B.A., Thammasat; M.Ed., Texas; M.A., Wisconsin), Banchong Kosolawat (M.F.A., New York Univ.), and students of the Drama and Mass Communication Departments. This project is for educational theatre film. The stories were adapted from three Aesop's tales of rabbits, 1983: *The Rabbit and the Turtle, The Rabbit and the Coconut Tree,* and *The Witty Rabbit.*

6. Teaching programmes for *hun krabok*

   During 1978–92, the Thammasat Drama Department developed a formal teaching programme for *hun krabok* (originally a folk art, now a new classical form) under the direction of Chusi Skunkaeo, the best-known mistress of puppetry, a National Artist, and now eighty-four years old. The course is organized by Wandee Limpiwattana, who has also brought *hun krabok* performances by her students to different provinces in the country and abroad. Wandee lectures on world puppetry and compares it with Thai classical and folk forms. In 1992, she brought a small group of students to the United States to give a lecture and *hun krabok* demonstration at the Tisch School of Performing Arts, New York University, and other institutions in the area. They also performed for a group of Thai children born in the U.S. and their parents at the Thai Culture Centre in New York. Both the Thai and American audiences, exposed for the first time to this ancient art, expressed a deep interest in its form and technique.

   At present, Wandee is involved in a project to introduce new techniques, more creative and experimental music and scripts, and a more modern interpretation to traditional tales, all to develop a new genre of *hun krabok* for the modern generation.

7. Television programmes

   "Nature and Environment" for Channel 11 and the Ministry of Education. Director-producer: Wandee Limpiwattana.

8. Model theatre for children

   1982 (plays): *Pla Bu Thong, Pinocchio, Little Red Riding Hood, Little Mermaid,* and *Lion and a Rat*

   1983: *Rumpelstiltskin,* a Thai adaptation (at Wat Mahathat Temple School for poor children)

9. Pantomime

   1983: *My Little Cat* (at Wat Mahathat Temple School)

10. Radio and television plays for children and adolescents

    In cooperation with the Ministry of Education, 1980–present. The

Thammasat Drama Department supplies scripts for their regular weekly and monthly programmes on television and radio, and also lectures and seminars to train teachers.

11. Orientations and seminars on children's theatre and educational theatre
    Produced in collaboration with other institutions and the National Council of Education and Culture in 1979 and 1982. Participants were teachers, students, professionals in television and film industry, writers, playwrights, composers, musicians, actors, directors, producers, journalists, and representatives from various mass media.

12. Rural development project theatres
    In 1986, the Department started a theatre for a rural development project in Chiengmai called "Nopphachak" (The Golden Wheel), in which students and teachers spend time in a poor village to perform plays, play games and sports with children and help to develop their social consciousness and artistic talents. The project, which was supported by the Australian government, has expanded to incorporate training of women and youth in income-generating professions for the purpose of preventing child prostitution and abolishing the sex trade.

Collaborative Projects with Western Puppets Troupes and Television

West Germany   Collaboration with Peter Grassinger, Director of Arts and Culture of the Bavarian Television, Munich. Project on the "*Ramayana* in Asian Performing Arts" (1981, continued in 1982 and 1983). Televized in Germany (1982).

Sweden   In 1982, Michael Meschke and the UNIMA troupes collaborated with the Thammasat group in creating new puppets based on both traditional Thai *hun krabok* puppets and Western marionettes to perform the stories from the *Ramayana* for international children.

England   In 1982, an exchage of cultural and educational activities with the Connaught College in Bath. In 1985–86, some puppet troupes in England held a workshop with the Thammasat puppeteers and students to create a new form of peppetry combining traditional Thai and Western techniques and arts for the modern audiences. In 1983, Thammasat Puppets Troupe performed a Thai adaptation of *Cinderella* for English and European children with Thai traditional *hun krabok* puppets using traditional music and songs with new lyrics composed by Chusi Skunkaeo, Wandee Limpiwattana, and Chamnian.

In 1982, Chusi and Thammasat teachers and students performed the *Ramayana* with *hun krabok* puppets for the English audiences in Bath and in London at Covent Garden Market where "Punch and Judy" originated.

In 1979 and 1982, the Thammasat group for children, young adults, and adults produced the author's adaptation in Thai of Shakespeare's *A Midsummer Night's Dream* in Thai classical dance-drama in England.

In 1986 the Thammasat troupe travelled to different cities and towns, including Stratford-upon-Avon, and different countries in Europe.

Japan   In 1984, the Department started an exchange programme in classical dances with Tamagawa University in Tokyo, in which classical dance teachers exchanged training in Thai and *kabuki* dances.

Theatre Construction and Theatre Arts

DEVELOPMENT OF THEATRE CONSTRUCTION

Up to the reign of King Chulalongkorn, Thai dramatic performances were given either in the open air or on temporary stages, with or without roofs, built on the locations of festivals, fairs, funerals, or other ceremonies and social occasions such as the New Year celebration, Buddhist ordination, celebration of a new house, tonsure ceremony, wedding, rice planting and harvesting, and the rain-making ceremony. These temporary platforms were raised in a few days before the performances and were taken down at the end of the functions. Descriptions of these movable or collapsible theatres are given in many literary works (col. pl. 5).

In the chronicles and other historical accounts of the early Bangkok period, there are mentionings of *rong lakhon* (theatres) within the Royal Palace; for example, at the Coronation Ceremony of the Deputy King (*Phithi Upara-chaphisek*) in the Second Reign, it is recorded, ". . . a commission was made to construct a pavilion near the Rong Lakhon [for the deputy king to reside during the ceremony as a temporary residence]."[1]

Again, in the Third Reign, a pavilion was constructed for the deputy king near the Rong Lakhon for the same ceremony.[2] King Rama III is said to practise shooting at the Rong Lakhon which was situated near the gate of Wat Phra Siratana Sasadaram, the Temple of the Emerald Buddha. This indicates that the Rong Lakhon was also used for other non-dramatic functions.

In the Fourth Reign it is recorded in the *Chotmaihet Phra Ratchakit Raiwan* that King Mongkut descended from the royal carriage on the platform in front of the Rong Lakhon and went into the Temple of the Emerald Buddha to attend a royal religious ceremony.[3] In the footnote to that passage, it is explained that the Rong Lakhon was a big hall built in the First Reign and was used not only for *lakhon* performances but also for many royal functions.[4]

In the Fifth Reign, in the *Phithi Uparachaphisek* of Kromamun Bowon Wichaichan,[5] a royal pavilion was set up for him, again in front of the Rong Lakhon, "near the gate of Wat Phra Siratana Sasadaram." But the deputy king did not stay there overnight, as in the tradition.[6] During this same reign the Rong Lakhon was dismantled and the grounds were turned into a grass lawn which is now in front of the Sala Sahathai Smakhom.[7] When King Chulalongkorn returned from his first royal grand tour of Europe, a temporary theatre was built to welcome him with a production of *Inao* by the Lakhon Luang troupe performed by the king's consorts, children, grandchildren, and the elder ladies of the court, under the supervision of the queen[8] (see pl. 36 showing spectacular street decorations to welcome the king on his return).

Introduction of Modern Concepts under Western Influence

Towards the end of the reign of King Chulalongkorn, there were many private theatres built in the palaces of princes and princesses and in the villas of the aristocracy. They gave public performances of dance-drama either in the classical styles of *lakhon nai* and *lakhon nok* or in their modernized variations, such as *lakhon phan thang, lakhon rong,* and *lakhon dukdamban.* Among the best-known private theatres were the Dukdamban Theatre of Chao Phraya Thewetwongwiwat at the Ban Mo Palace, the Prince Theatre of Chao Phraya Mahintharasakdithamrong, and the Pridalai Theatre of Prince Narathip Praphanphong at the Phraeng Nara Palace.

The Dukdamban Theatre of Chao Phraya Thewet, chief of the Krom Mahorasop (Royal Entertainment Department), was built after his trip to Europe in 1891. As mentioned earlier, Chao Phraya Thewet was very much inspired by Western opera and persuaded Prince Naris to produce a modern form of Thai classical dance-drama in the manner of the Western opera or operetta. Chao Phraya Thewet constructed a theatre in the compound of Ban Mo Palace for this particular purpose and opened it up to the public. He called it the "Rong Lakhon Dukdamban" (Dukdamban Theatre). The term *dukdamban* means literally "ancient." It was probably adopted from the ancient Ayudhaya pageant, the *kan len dukdamban* or *chak nak dukdamban,* in which two groups of men pulled a great serpent on each side in a tug-of-war. The pageant represents the churning of the ocean to produce the *nam amarit* (ambrosia of immortality). The *thewada* (devas, gods) and *asun* (asura, demons) stand on opposite sides pulling the serpent.

The name of the theatre was also given to the new type of classical *lakhon ram* performed there. However, *lakhon dukdamban* had no connection with the ancient pageant of *kan len dukdamban,* except for the stories which came from the "ancient" *lakhon* since the time of Ayudhaya and even earlier, such as *Ramakien, Unarut,* and other *Jataka* tales. The style of dancing and the stage techniques were, however, modernized. (See details in Chapter 3.)

The Dukdamban Theatre had a raised proscenium stage, following the Western model. It was beautifully decorated in Thai classical design by Prince Naris (pl. 37). The theatre house had a limited seating capacity. There were special seats for the aristocrats who patronized the theatre and were family friends. King Chulalongkorn, Crown Prince Vajiravudh, and many royal visitors from abroad came to see its *lakhon dukdamban* on several occasions, where a royal box would be prepared for them. The Dukdamban Theatre gave its first public performance on 27 December 1899 for Prince Henry, brother of the King of Prussia.

The theatre under the creative direction of Prince Naris and Chao Phraya Thewet specialized in fantastic and realistic set designs (to be further discussed later in the chapter). Following Western drama, Prince Naris established a new tradition of dividing a play into acts and scenes, each of which had a different set design, developing from a simple one to a very elaborate one in the climax scene. The audiences were attracted to these innovations, waiting patiently for the theatrical surprises. Some came back several times to see a play in order to learn about the stage tricks and techniques used in this theatre.[9]

Since the theatre was small, Prince Naris adapted a new type of *piphat* orchestra, which was later referred to as the *piphat dukdamban*. It was characterized by percussion instruments with cushioned sticks. Noisy instruments, such as the bronze xylophon (*ranat thong*) and the *khong lek* gongs were left out. A set of gongs that were used were struck at long intervals to avoid deafening sound effects which might disturb the audience in such a limited space.[10] These adaptations of musical instruments to suit the physical structure and space of the theatre show a new dimension in the development of modern Thai theatre introduced by creative musicians.

The Prince Theatre of Chao Phraya Mahin was the first public theatre to collect general admission fees. Its name was directly adopted from the Prince's Theatre in London which Chao Phraya Mahin had visited when on an ambassadorial mission with Phraya Montri Suriyawong.[11] "Prince" referred to his princely grandchildren.[12] The theatre specialized in a modernized version of *lakhon nai* and *lakhon nok* which was later known as the *lakhon phan thang*. At the beginning, the theatre gave public performances for one week each month during the moonlit nights, whence derived the term *week,* or *wik* in the Thai pronunciation. (The term refers also to the theatre, i.e., a theatre is called a *wik,* which applied later to *liké* theatre: viz. *wik liké*.) Later, the Prince Theatre extended its performances to two weeks per month, from the eighth day of the rising moon to the seventh day of the waning moon. But the audiences still referred to the performance run as a *wik,* despite the difference in length.[13]

When King Chulalongkorn built the Dusit Palace, he planted many fruit trees, including lychee, that refused to yield any fruit. The king pledged that if the lychee trees bore fruit he would celebrate the occasion with *lakhon* of

Mom Luang Tuan Worawan, consort of Prince Narathip, one of the most famous performers of the time. That year the lychees came in great abundance. The king then ordered the construction of a theatre in a *farang* (Western) style, complete with an authentic stage, at the Dusit Palace to be located between Phra Thinang Amphon and Phra Thinang Phanumat. Prince Narathip composed *Phra Lo,* the middle part, to be performed in this celebration of the *khwan,* or spiritual essence, of the lychees. Mom Luang Tuan arranged the songs, music, and orchestra. Chao Chom Manda Khien, Prince Narathip's mother, was responsible for training the dancers. This was the origin of the Lakhon Luang Narumit before the construction of the "Pridalai" Theatre, a permanent theatre in the Phraeng Nara Palace of Prince Narathip.[14] The king also gave instructions about the decoration and set design for the production; for example, to use panels, high benches, and trees to make the setting more realistic.[15]

The *lakhon* troupe of Prince Narathip had the first permanent theatre in the compound of Wat Saket (Temple) called the "Rong Lakhon Wiman Narumit" (Magic Palace Theatre), hence, the troupe was also called "Lakhon Narumit." Later, when the king granted to it his royal patronage, it was known as "Lakhon Luang Narumit." When the old theatre burnt down,[16] the prince had a new one built in the compound of his own palace at Phraeng Nara and called it the "Pridalai Theatre" (Royal Narumit Theatre). The name "Pridalai" was again attached to the *lakhon* productions there, which were later referred to as "Lakhon Pridalai." Upon the completion of the construction of the new theatre, Prince Narathip wrote modestly to King Chulalongkorn on 2 November 1908, "I have finished building a *kammalo* [impermanent, not of great value or durability] theatre in my compound."[17] As mentioned earlier, King Chulalongkorn, Crown Prince Vajiravudh, and the courtiers frequented the theatre, and on several occasions special performances were given to welcome important state visitors from abroad.

The Pridalai Theatre was open to the public. It had a separate entrance from that of the palace. *Lakhon* was performed on weekends. Admission fees were collected. The theatre was very popular and was almost always full. It was said that each production took in from 2,000 baht on up, which was a very large sum at the time. The most successful performances could make as much as 2,400 baht. They were usually exotic tales or melodramatic, domestic plays in the style of *lakhon rong.*

The Pridalai Theatre was built in the style of a Western theatre with a large seating capacity. It was divided into three seating levels. The stall in the ground floor had six private boxes (six seats to each box) in the orchestra section in front of the stage. This section was reserved for royal or very important guests. Behind the boxes were individual special-class and first-class seats, and ordinary benches at the back. The first balcony had seventeen private boxes of different sizes also for royal and special guests and patrons. The second balcony was for the cheapest seats. The seat prices were 24 baht (orchestra boxes), 3 baht (special class), 2 baht (first class), 1 baht (third class), 6 *salung* (fourth class), and 32 *at* (fifth class). The private boxes in the first balcony ranged from 12 to 60 baht according to the number of seats.[18] The design and the rate of admission fees of the Pridalai Theatre seem to have been the closest imitation of the Western theatre system in Thailand.

King Vajiravudh, when still crown prince, contributed significantly to the development of modern theatre construction in Siam. After his trip to Europe, the United States, and Japan in 1902, the crown prince started a literature and drama club called the "Thawi Panya Smoson," which promoted the artistic, literary, dramatic, and intellectual activities of the elite, many of whom were Western-educated. A small Western-style theatre was built in the compound of the Sranrom Palace to serve these purposes. It was called the "Rong Lakhon Thawi Panya Smoson." As the crown prince wrote in 1904 in one of the *Thawi Panya* magazines, the theatre would hold about a hundred seats for club members. Admission fees were also collected for club activities. The first *lakhon phut* (spoken drama) to be performed at this newly opened theatre was in 1905 to bid farewell to Prince Asadang Dechawut, the librarian of the club. Later, the theatre served on several occasions for the productions of *lakhon phut* under the direction of the crown prince. Its activities continued throughout his reign.

A new concept of a permanent National Theatre was also introduced by King Vajiravudh in the early twentieth century. In the tradition of the Western monarchy patronizing a "Royal Theatre" and constructing theatres in the royal palaces, the English-educated king, when still crown prince, built the first permanent "Royal Theatre" at Misakawan Garden in Dusit Park (opposite the Parusakawan Palace). It was used mostly for performances of royal *khon* and was thus called the "Theatre Royal, Dusit Park." After he became king, the theatre was referred to as the "National Theatre" and was used frequently for royal social functions. One of the very grand occasions was the king's coronation in 1911. The "Theatre Royal" was luxuriously decorated in the style of royal opera houses in European countries (pl. 38).[19]

King Vajiravudh also adopted the practice of European monarchs in changing his residence for each season. As a result, many summer palaces were built in different provinces, each of them with a small theatre or a stage for his dramatic productions. Even on bivouac during his manoeuvres with the Wild Tigers Corps, the dramatist-king did not fail to raise a temporary stage for performances of patriotic plays, which could be considered a very effective political means to create loyalty to the king and a strong sense of national unity, the important values necessary for the modern Thai monarchy to instill in a period of international crises and national anxiety and agitation among the rising upper-middle-class intellectuals and the military, who were anti-royalist and even left-leaning. The best-known of the provincial summer palaces with theatres were the Snam Chan Palace in Nakhon Prathom, Marukhathiwan Palace in Hua Hin, and the Bang Pa-in Palace. The styles of architecture and interior decoration are a mixture of English and French neo-classic and "rococo" with wood-panelling and decorative designs.

The first modern cinema, Sala Chaloemkrung, was built in 1932 during the reign of King Prajadhipok. However, there were minimal cultural and dramatic activities. The national budget had to be drastically curbed to avoid national bankruptcy and to pay off debts accumulated from the previous reign.

After the Revolution of 1932, the first action in reforming the cultural institution of the country was to delegate power from the Royal Household Department to the new government. The Krom Silapakon (Department of Fine Arts) was immediately set up to control all cultural and artistic activities of the nation. On 17 May 1934, the Rongrian Nataduriyangkhasat (Academy of Dance and Music) was founded to train dancers and musicians in place of the private royal households. In July 1935, the Krom Mahorasop (Royal Entertainment Department) and the Krom Chang (Royal Arts and Crafts Department) were transferred from the Ministry of the Royal Palace to the Krom Silapakon. In 1945, towards the end of World War II, there was another reform of the Academy of Dance and Music. Its name was changed to the Rongrian Natasin (Academy of the Art of Dancing), whose purposes were:

1) To be the institution of the arts of dancing and music of "His Majesty's Service" (i.e., of the government).
2) To preserve, promote, and propagate the Thai national art of dancing and music.
3) To raise the status of the artists of music and drama within the country and to achieve international recognition.[20]

The new group of dance and music students at the Academy gave their first two performances in the Royal Palace at the Sivalai Theatre in 1946, when King Anandha Mahidol, Rama VIII, welcomed Lord Louis Mountbattan. When the Allied Forces occupied the country after the fall of the Japanese, they also gave several performances to the soldiers and guests of the government.

In the 1940s the Krom Silapakon remodelled Silapakon Hall, a wooden pavilion near the Siwamokphiman Hall in the Front Palace (later the National Museum), as a temporary theatre for dance-drama productions of the Silapakon and the Academy. The theatre had only one floor with a slight rise at the back and a proscenium stage. Many new theatre techniques and set designs were adopted from the West and Japan (to be discussed later). The seats were divided into three rows with different prices including special, first, second, and third class. The orchestra pit was next to the stage, at a lower level in front of it in the style of a Western theatre imitated by Luang Wichitwathakan who supervised the remodelling of the theatre.

1 *Phra* (male; *centre*) and *nang* (female; *left and right*) roles in *Phra Lo,* a *lakhon phan thang.* Phra Lo, the prince, is in a modernized classical costume, whereas the two princesses (Phra Phuan and Phra Phaeng) are in Northern regional costumes. All three dancers are female. A Silapakon production, 1980s.

2 *Phra* roles: Phra Ram (*left*), hero of the *Ramakien* (male dancer) in classical costume in *khon* mask-dance; Phra Lo (*right*), royal hero of *Phra Lo,* a *lakhon phan thang* dance-drama (female dancer in a male role). A Silapakon production, 1980s.

3 Khru Mot's set design for *Phra Wai Taek Thap,* an episode from *Khun Chang Khun Phaen,* a Silapakon production, late 1970s. The ghost of Nang Wanthong (*left*) is wearing a *krabang na* head-dress; Phra Wai, her son, in an Ayudhaya army general costume.

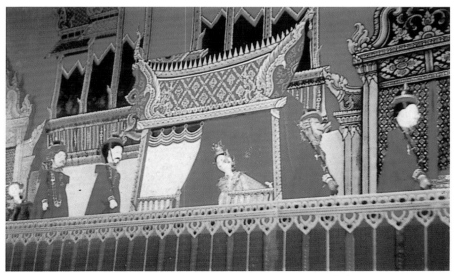

4 Chakraphan Posayakrit's set design for *hun krabok* puppet theatre, 1970s. The procession of the ogress Benyakai in the disguise of Sida (*centre*) in *Nang Loi,* an episode from the *Ramakien.*

5 Temporary theatres for *nang yai* shadow puppetry (*left*) and *khon* (*above centre*) built on a cremation ground, possibly in the 19th century during the reign of King Chulalongkorn (mural painting from the Temple of Emerald Buddha).

6 A Khon Thammasat production, the final scene of *Phiphek Swamiphak,* an episode from the *Ramakien,* to celebrate the Investiture of Crown Prince Vajiralongkorn in 1972. Set and lighting designs by the author.

7 A Chinese opera costume used in
Rachathirat. A Silapakon production, 1980s.

8 Saming Phra Ram, a hero in *Rachathirat*
in a Mon fighting costume with a paper
horse attached to the waist and a lance.
A Silapakon production, 1980s.

9 Inao and Busba in Javanese
costumes. A Silapakon production,
1980s.

36 Street decorations to welcome King Chulalongkorn's return from his first grand tour of Europe, 1897.

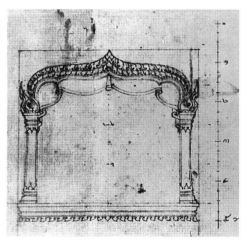

37 Prince Naris' design of the proscenium stage of the Dukdamban Theatre, in the Fifth Reign.

38 The "Theatre Royal" of King Vajiravudh in Misakawan Garden, Dusit Park.

39 Royal *khon* and *lakhon* dancers with musicians, in the Fifth Reign.

40 *Lakhon* scene possibly from *Inao,* in the Fifth Reign.

41 Prince Naris' set design, "The Ocean of Milk," in the Fifth Reign. The god Vishnu (*centre*) reclining on the giant serpent Ananda Nakaraj with the goddess Laksmi (*left*), his wife, and the god Indra (*right*) blowing a conch-shell to awake him.

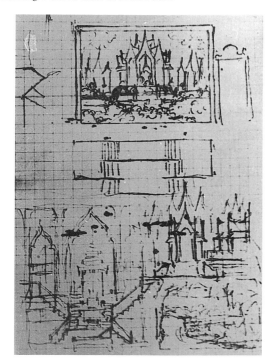

42 Prince Naris' set design sketch for "Daowadung" (God Indra's heaven) in *Sangthong,* a *lakhon dukdamban,* in the Fifth Reign.

43 Khru Mot's set design, a Javanese-style temple in *Inao,* 1960s.

44 Khru Mot's set design for Luang Tangchai's villa in *Khun Chang Khun Phaen,* showing French influence, 1960s.

45 Khru Mot's set design for *Kumphakan Thot Nam* (Kumphakan blocking the river), an episode from the *Ramakien,* 1960s, inspired by Prince Naris. Compare with pl. 25.

46 Thawisak Senanarong's set design for *Phali Son Nong* (Phali teaching his brother), an episode from the *Ramakien,* late 1970s.

47 Chakraphan Posayakrit's set design for Sriwichai Garden in *Sithammasokarat,* 1970.

48 King Chulalongkorn in royal costume for the second coronation ceremony, 1873.

49 Various types of head-dress:
  (a) a *mongkut* crown for *nang*, a royal female character
  (b) a *chada* crown for *phra*, a royal male character
  (c) a *krabang* (tiara) for a lower-ranking or commoner female character
  (d) a *rat klao yot* for a princess in *lakhon nok* and *lakhon dukdamban* dance-drama.

50 Costume and hair style of a court lady from the early Ratanakosin period to the Fifth Reign.

51 Chao Ngo (*right*) without a mask, wearing curly hair and dark make-up. Prince Naris' design, in the Fifth Reign.

During the postwar Phibunsongkhram regime (1948–57), another permanent theatre was built in the Sanam Sua Pa as a part of the Ministry of Culture. It gave many successful performances of patriotic plays mostly created by Luang Whichitwathakan, who was head of the Krom Silapakon and later Minister of Culture. The theatre is still in existence and is used occasionally by the present government.

Towards the end of this Phibunsongkhram regime, the Thammasat University Auditorium was built. Its seating capacity of 2,500 seats makes it the largest theatre in the country. When the Krom Silapakon Theatre burned down and the new National Theatre had not yet been built in its place, the Thammasat University Auditorium was frequently used on special occasions for *khon* and *lakhon* performances to welcome royal state visitors and government guests.

After Marshal Sarit Thanarat took over power from Field Marshal Phibunsongkhram in 1957, a new project was proposed to construct a formal National Theatre in place of the old Silapakon Theatre. A budget of 14 million baht was granted in 1961 for the two-year construction project. The former site in the Ministry of Communication near the Krom Silapakon was given to the Krom. The chief architect was Isra Wiwatthananon, and the chief engineer Dr. Rachot Kanchanawanit. However, fire broke out in the old theatre on 9 November 1960, before the new theatre was completed. This prompted the committee to accelerate the project, which was then transferred to the Municipal Civil Works Department. The construction then proceeded in haste. As a result, it suffered from many architectural short-cuts and changes, not to mention a lot of unnecessary waste, resulting in a total construction cost of 56,484,465 baht, almost five times the original budget.

The architectural design of the National Theatre represents a period of hybrid Thai-Western architecture, with a Thai temple-like roof and a massive concrete flying tower in the back. The theatre was the subject of harsh criticism by the media and the public both for its appearance and the extravagant expense involved.

The dimensions of the National Theatre are 41.5 metres in width, 71.5 metres in length, and 33 metres in height. The stage area is divided into two levels: the proscenium stage (17.5 m, length, x 14.5 m, width, x 32 m, height) and the apron stage (20 m, length, x 10.5 m, width). The theatre seats 1,356 with 893 seats on the ground floor and 463 seats in the balcony.

Due to the inefficiency of the first plan, a new architect, Mom Chao Samaichaloem Kridakon, was commissioned to remodel the theatre which cost another 8,071,974 baht.

In the left wing of the theatre there is a smaller theatre with a capacity of 500 seats and practice rooms for dancers. In the right wing there are two floors of offices and practice rooms for dancers and musicians. The Office of Dance and Music Section of the Krom Silapakon is situated on the first floor of the right wing.[21]

The Cultural Centre of Thailand and Japanese Influence

The Cultural Centre of Thailand was conceived as a grant-in-aid co-operation project between the governments of Japan and Thailand, officially known as "The Social Education and Cultural Centre Project." On 19 July 1983 the Cabinet assigned the Ministry of Education to be in charge of the project. The Japanese government through the Japan International Cooperation Agency allocated 6,385 million yen (638 million baht) for building construction, modern facilities, equipment, and interior decoration. The Thai government made available a plot of land near Rachadaphisek Road. On 1 April 1985, H.R.H. Crown Princess Maha Chakri Sirindhorn laid the foundation stone and graciously bestowed the name "Sun Watthanatham Haeng Prathet Thai" (The Cultural Centre of Thailand) on this latest cultural organization. It now stands as the most modern and best-equipped cultural centre in Thailand. However, during its construction there were negative reactions from many groups of artists, intellectuals, and students against the Japanese influence. A "Sala Thai" (Thai Pavilion) was installed next to the Japanese pavilion to add a touch of Thai architecture to the predominantly Japanese style. The interior of the main auditorium is also decorated in the foyer with two mural paintings in traditional Thai style, and the front curtain is an exquisite tapestry designed by the famous modern Thai artist Chakraphan Posayakrit, depicting a scene from *Traiphum* (The Three Worlds), a Thai cosmology. The tapestry was woven in Japan under the supervision of the artist.

After its inauguration on 11 March 1987, the Centre has fully functioned under the supervision of the Krom Silapakon, Ministry of Education. At present it comes under the Bureau of National Culture of Thailand.

There are three groups of buildings in the compound of the Cultural Centre of Thailand. The main auditorium has 2,000 seats. It is fully equipped with modern electronic equipment, an automated system and sound reflector panels for the concert shell, a computerized modular stage lighting system with pre-programming microprocessor control, simultaneous interpretation equipment for the transmission of four languages to 400 seats and 100 wireless receivers, and projection equipment with wide screens for 16-mm and 35-mm film. Within the main building there are rehearsal rooms, training rooms, a semi-circular rehearsal room for orchestra, seven dressing rooms of various sizes, a greenroom, a modern cafeteria, offices, and ticketing and sales counters. The dimensions of the main proscenium stage including the apron is 19.5 metres in width, 11 metres in height, 23.5 metres deep (main stage, 16 m; apron stage, 7.5 m). There are three motorized elevators: one for the orchestra pit and two for the main stage.

The second building is a small auditorium with 500 seats, seven dressing rooms, and a roll-back stand in two stages for 140 or 240 seats. The hall is also fully equipped with electronically controlled lighting, computerized sound systems and automated stage equipment. There is an adjoining 1,000-seat outdoor amphitheatre in the rear for open-air performances. A Japanese-style pavilion set in a Japanese garden is situated in front of the hall.

Finally, there are the administration buildings: a library, conference halls, exhibition halls, classrooms, language laboratories, a creative education centre for children, meeting and lecture rooms, offices, and a videotape library. Attached to this group are a Thai pavilion and an arts and crafts centre.

Since its inauguration the Centre has conducted many cultural and educational activities including traditional and modern forms and styles of the arts of Thailand and other countries. Despite the negative reaction against Japanese-dominated artistic and technical aspects, the Centre has now gained a highly prestigious position among the Thai public and foreign participants. This is due to the continuous effort of the pioneering administrative staff, the support of the national government through the Krom Silapakon, and later through the National Bureau of Culture. There has been ardent co-operation among many foreign governments in Asia and the West, who have participated in and contributed to royal celebrations and international festivals of folk and classical dance, theatre, and film. The Centre supports both traditional and modern theatre arts to make good use of all the available facilities and modern theatre technology of high international standards. Thai and Western concerts, musicals, dance-dramas, modern and contemporary plays, internationally known troupes of classical and modern ballet and contemporary dance, operas (both Japanese and European) have graced the stages of the main and small auditoriums. The monstrous fortress-like structure, which used to intimidate Thai onlookers and thus stimulated rejection and anti-Japanese feelings, has now become a cultural landmark after only two years of effective operations by the newly trained technical and administrative staff who has dedicated long and often sleepless hours to help transform this foreign phenomenon into a legitimately Thai cultural institution. This in itself is worth recording as a historical milestone in the history of theatre construction in Thailand.

In reviewing the trends of development from the nineteenth century to the present, Thai theatre has successfully synthesized foreign influences both Eastern and Western with its traditions, in order to communicate with the new generations and to relate to economic, political, social, and cultural changes. The transfer of modern technology in theatre building construction and operation has continuously and open-mindedly been accepted by Thai theatre architects, engineers, designers, and artists. However, there is an ingrained nationalistic counter-movement which constantly serves as a balance against foreign influences.

TRADITIONAL AND MODERN STAGE DESIGN

Modernization of the Thai Stage Design

There is very little evidence, albeit historical, literary, or pictorial, of Thai stage design prior to the reign of King Chulalongkorn in the nineteenth century, in which photography introduced by Westerners could capture the pictures of stage designs for the performances of Thai classical dance-drama and its modernized variations. Only in some *lakhon* texts written before this period is there any mention of the constructions of the *rong khon* (*khon* theatre) and *rong lakhon* (*lakhon* theatre) which were, in most cases, temporarily set up for festive occasions. However, there are usually no descriptions of the sets or stage designs for the productions. The only mechanical device often mentioned in *khon* performances on these occasions is the *khon chak rok,* or using pulleys to swing the dancers up and down in the flying or fighting scenes.

Generally, in the past, probably up to the nineteenth century, the stage for *khon* and *lakhon* was an open stage on a raised platform with no painted scenery and furniture, except for a bench or a bamboo bar serving as a bench for *khon rao* (*khon* on a bar or a rod). For *nang yai* shadow plays, a screen with a red border was set up as a backdrop (pl. 14). When *khon* was performed alternately with *nang,* which is called *nang tit tua khon* (*nang* with *khon* characters), the screen was adapted to serve both purposes: it had two entrances with curtains, one on each side of the stage, for the entrance and exit of the *khon* characters. There was a painted scenery on the screen representing the two opposite camps in the *Ramakien*: the palace of Thosakan in Longka on one side, and the pavilion of Phra Ram in the forest on the other side of the screen. Over and above this painted scenery, there were paintings of Nang Mekhala (the goddess of lightning) holding her crystal ball on one side and Ramasun (the god of thunder) with his axe on the other side. There were also pictures of the sun and the moon, one on each side at the top of the screen.[22] In later times, when *khon* was performed without shadow plays, the screen was still present. Hence it is called *khon na cho* (*khon* in front of a screen). Even at present, the screen remains in a reduced size in the form of the painted backcloth in *khon rong* performed in a permanent theatre with a proscenium stage and curtains. It no longer serves any practical purpose. It is maintained only as a sacred vestige from tradition.[23]

In the past, in *lakhon* performance of all types, there was a simple backcloth serving as the only permanent background with two curtained entrances on both sides, through which dancers entered and left the stage. This type of simple, bare stage is still used by travelling troupes in the provinces or on location when they are hired to perform for certain functions, such as a funeral, a wedding, celebration of a new house, entering the monkhood, or a birthday. The furniture is sparse, consisting of only a single long bench, or a few of them, used for all purposes: the throne hall, bedroom chamber, the jungle, and battlefield. The concept is very similar to the stage of the Elizabethan period. In both cases the descriptions of the scenery in the lyrics have to be very vivid and highly detailed to be sung by the chorus and interpreted in descriptive gestures by the dancers (in the Thai *lakhon*) or actors (in the Elizabethan plays). They have to lead the imagination of the audiences and create pictorial images in their minds.

As in Shakespeare's plays, this dramatic technique of scenic painting in the narration, speech, and songs is therefore very necessary due to a lack of actual set design. Interestingly enough, this abstract and suggestive stage design, which reduces all decorations to a bare minimum, made its return to the theatre in the mid-twentieth century, starting in the West and making its way to the East. This is due partly to economic reasons, but principally to the influence of modern art and design. Abstraction and symbolism have always been very important characteristics of Asian theatre. It is an accepted fact that Western abstract modern art was influenced by Asian art, starting with that of the effect of Japanese *ukiyoe* prints on the French Impressionists in the nineteenth century. Ironically, the Asian theatre, including that of the Thai, in the twentieth century began to follow the footsteps of Western theatre, especially in stage design, production, and stage direction, not to mention the mainstream of imports of Western plays and stories.

In some photographs taken during the reign of King Chulalongkorn (1868–1910), we begin to see painted scenery as the background of *lakhon* performances (pl. 20). In this particular picture of a typical *rabam boek rong* (opening dance) of *thewada* and *nang fa* (gods and goddesses), the dancers are in front of a painted backcloth depicting a forest scene with trees, waterfalls, rocks, and open sky. Obtruding from it in low relief is a model of a pavilion. In the far background to the left is another pavilion painted in three dimensions in a rather correct perspective, which shows the influence of Western realistic painting. The set may have also been used for the *lakhon* performance of *Inao* during that time, since the scenery could represent the forest at the foot of Mount Kamangkuning where the twelve kings, queens, princes, and princesses gather together for the *Buang Suang* (sacrifice to the gods). This may also have been the *rabam boek rong* for the *Inao* production of King Chulalongkorn in 1882 to celebrate the Centennial Anniversary of the Capital of Bangkok.[24] This photograph may have been taken on that occasion. Notice that the dancers were dancing on the ground without a raised platform (as in pls. 20, 39). Judging from the costumes, masks, and style of dancing of the apparently female dancers, these two photos are that of traditional *lakhon nai: Ramakien* and *Inao*. The dancers may have been from the Lakhon Luang troupe of the royal court or from another troupe belonging to members of the royal family or aristocracy.

Obviously, plate 39 is not of the actual performance itself, but of the cast and musicians in it who grouped together for the photograph. Plate 20 is *lakhon nai* danced by female performers, and the back screen is painted with a palace scene in three-dimensional perspective. The bench is covered with a Persian (or Arabian) carpet (pl. 7). The *kris* in the belt of the hero indicates that this *lakhon* may have also been *Inao*. In another interior scene (pl. 40), possibly the cave scene in *Inao,* there is a low platform covered with a tiger skin. The author of the book from which these photographs are taken wrote in German, "Abschiedsszene aus 'Inao'" (scene from the performance of *Inao*). The backcloth here is plain, without any painted scenery, probably representing the cave wall in the episode of "Abducting Busba to the Cave."

King Chulalongkorn set a precedent in writing about the detail of stage construction and set design, including the directions for actions, in a separate book for the grand performance of *Inao* in 1882 to celebrate the Centennial Anniversary of the Capital of Bangkok. To the knowledge of this writer, there had never been a book of stage directions and set design prior to this. This practice is still rare in later periods. It shows the king's great concern for historical preservation in order to set an example for the later generations and to keep historical records of all the cultural events during his reign, in which he personally participated.

In the period of the modernization of traditional *lakhon ram* in the forms of *lakhon phan thang, lakhon dukdamban,* and *lakhon rong,* set and costume designs became very important as means to attract the attention of public audiences. Each company competed with its rivals in experimenting with new ideas, some of which were rather adventurous, such as decorating dancers with small electric bulbs which flashed to the rhythm of the music. In one case, it was said that a dancer suffered from electrical shock! Chao Phraya Mahin was famous for these various spectacular stage effects. Some of his dancers had mechanical devices attached to their bodies to create surprises on stage. Flying clouds, roaring thunder, flashing lightning, rain, and water streams were common in these productions.

Prince Naris and Modern Set Design The most artistic and sophisticated set designs, within the limits of technical know-how and good taste, were that of Prince Naris in his *lakhon dukdamban.* It was generally accepted that the productions of the "Rong Lakhon Dukdamban" were the best in town, not only in terms of drama, dance, and songs, but equally important for its exquisite, spectacular, and realistic sets and sound and visual effects. The prince showed mastery of both Thai and Western painting and drawing, the linear, decorative, and abstract designs of traditional Thai art, and Western three-dimensional perspective, scientific studies of architecture, human anatomy, lighting, and shading, all of which added realism and naturalism to his art. Together they created a harmonious unity rather than the awkward hybrid appearing in the works of many Westernized Thai artists of the same period and later. These inferior artists, not being able to grasp the essence of either Thai or Western art, therefore were able to show only superficiality and inaccuracy in their works. In many of their paintings, incorrect perspective and dimensions are rather common features. On the other hand, there is a certain charm in their primitive quality, due to a lack of scientific and technical knowledge.

In the Preface to the *Chumnum Bot Lakhon Lae Bot Khrap Rong* (Collected plays and songs) by Prince Naris, Princess Duangchit Chitraphong, his daughter, wrote,

> The method of performing *lakhon dukdamban,* which he [Prince Naris] invented, was different from that of the traditional *lakhon ram,* in which there were no other decorations than a back screen and a bench for the *lakhon* dancers to sit, the narrations describing the scenes were in lyrics, and the art of dancing helped to create the imagination in the audiences. The *lakhon dukdamban,* on the other hand, was performed on a stage with sets of scenery and mechanical devices to support them. The Prince therefore saw no necessity in having the narrations in the text, since the scenery enabled the audiences to see with their eyes that the scenes were taking place in a forest, a chamber, a palace, or a temple. Moreover, he also showed night time, day time, lightning, and fire by using electricity and mechanical devices in place of the narratives.[25]

Following the structure of Western opera, ballet, and play, Prince Naris divided his *lakhon dukdamban* into acts and scenes and designed a set for each of them individually. His technique was to start off with a simple set design in the First Act and to develop the sets gradually into more detailed and exquisite designs, as the play proceeded to Acts 2, 3, and 4. The most spectacular one was usually the finale in which the climax of the play was to be found, and all the characters were present on stage to do the finale dance and sing the Royal Anthem. In every scene there is usually an architectural design of the location: a part or parts of a palace, a pavilion, a temple, or a throne hall. These were painted in three-dimensional perspective following the Western techniques of realistic stage design with different tones of light and shading, low and high reliefs, and always with elaborate Thai decorative designs. The total effects are rather similar to the baroque theatre designs in France and Italy, which are models for other European countries as well, including England, from where Chao Phraya Thewet, a collaborator of Prince Naris, conceived the idea of *lakhon dukdamban.*

In expediting the change of sets, Prince Naris divided the stage into three sections, the front, middle, and rear, with partitions or painted backcloths in between them. Each section was decorated for each scene with the necessary furniture, painted scenery, and side partitions (also painted with scenery). When the play started, the actions in the First Act would take place in the front section, with the backcloth hiding the middle set. At the end of the First Act, the backcloth or partition between the two sections would be lifted or pushed aside, revealing the second set, which was usually more beautifully decorated than the first one. In the last act, the middle backdrop or partition would be removed to give the whole space of the stage to the grand finale. This Third Act (i.e., the last) was generally the most grandiose, exciting, and spectacular. Because of such a technique, the audiences would not have to wait long for the change of scenery. Music would be played or narratives sung in between the acts to provide the necessary continuation of scenes and actions.

In the temple scene of *Inao* (pl. 25), which is the Second Act in the production, we see the interior of a small, supposedly Javanese, temple chamber, which looks more like a Thai temple.[26] This is where Queen Madewi brings Busba to pray in front of the Divine Image, behind which Inao is hiding with Prasanta. The three-dimensional rendering of the sculpture and architecture is clearly shown here, particularly that of the Divine Image. Prince Naris presents the image in a clever way by showing its side view in order that Inao would be seen behind it in a realistic way and would not have to peer out to let the audience see him hiding as in the traditional stage presentation. The sculpture is drawn with a strong contrast of light and shade to create a *trompe l'oeil* (eye-deceiving illusion of space and depth) effect of a sculpture in the round as in Western Renaissance painting and drawing. Prince Naris may have learned the technique from the Italian artists who came to Siam during the Fifth Reign to design, construct and decorate many palaces and royal halls. The square columns in a three-dimensional perspective, together with the painted window in the rear with round stone bars looking into the dark space behind, create a sense of great depth and mysterious atmosphere appropriate for the interior of the sacred sanctuary and the exciting love scene. This set is preceded by the first scene showing the exterior of the temple and the temple ground, where Inao and his friends are playing games before they are chased by the court ladies who announce the coming of the queen and Princess Busba. The backcloth in this first scene is painted with a picture of the temple building. It is to be lifted when the queen and Busba enter the inner chamber in the second set. In the final act, this second backcloth would again be removed to show the Grand Chamber of the temple where the *Buang Suang* (sacrifice) offered by King Daha and his entourage and the finale dance are performed.

To create realistic effects and stage surprises in the actual production, the prince tied bats on wires and pulled them back and forth a few times across the stage and into the audiences. He never repeated these surprises too often, only enough to attract the attention of the audiences. His motto was "good things are not frequent."[27] The bats were supposed to put out the candles, but this was actually done by Prasanta blowing the candles from behind the statue using a small bamboo stick.

For lighting, he invented stage lamps by using petrol cans with coloured glass plates in front of them to create different colour light effects. Sometimes he used torch lamps in outdoor performances, which gave warm and lively flickering lights.

Sound effects also played a major part in his productions, such as the sounds of birds, cock crows in forest scenes in *Inao,* also lightning, thunder, fire, storm, and wind. Birds and cocks appeared briefly on tree branches or in the holes of tree trunks, then swiftly disappeared.

In other sketches of the set designs for *Khawi* and *Sangthong,* three-dimensional perspectives and architecture are characteristic features. In the forest scene of *Inao,* the painted backcloth representing stone mounts shows an influence from Chinese painting. In the mountain scene of *Sangsinchai* imitation stones made of papier mâché were used together with a painted backcloth depicting the sky and clouds and side partitions painted with pictures of trees to create pictorial depth and space.

In the scene of "Kasian Samut" (Ocean of Milk, or the Milky Way) in the production of *Krung Phan Chom Thawip* (pl. 41), God Narai (Vishnu) is seen reclining on the back of a five-headed great serpent attended by Goddess Laksami and being awakened by the sound of a conch-shell blown by Indra. The great serpent was made of papier mâché. This modern technique of creating big stage properties in papier mâché shows an attempt to present ancient myths in a spectacular fashion, yet with a certain realism. The backcloth is painted with a picture of a dawning sky and rippling sea to add to these realistic effects.

A very modern feature in most of the set design sketches of Prince Naris is a harmonious balance in the composition created, not by traditional symmetrical arrangement, but by asymmetry, such as in the palace scene and the river pavilion in *Khawi:* only parts of the architectural construction of the palace and pavilion of different sizes and appearances are shown on each side in an off-centred composition, paradoxically creating good balance. These techniques of showing only parts of objects, leaving the rest to the audience's imagination and using asymmetrical composition, set a new tradition in Thai stage design which has been followed until the present day.

In another sketch of God Indra's "Daowadung" (heaven) in *Sangthong* (pl. 42), the prince experimented with both traditional and modern asymmetrical compositions. The latter offers richer and grander effects with a majestic staircase leading upward. Prince Naris explained that the secret to the great success of the *lakhon dukdamban* lay in the realism of the set designs and the brevity of presentation, which excited the audiences without boring them with repetition: "To make them wish to see more because it is not enough is better than to give them too much."[28] Alas, such is not the principle of Thai stage designers today!

The creativity of Prince Naris was not limited only to the modernization of the *bot lakhon* (dramatic texts), music, songs, and stage design, but was extended to all areas of the theatre including costume design and make-up (the subjects of which will be later pursued). At the beginning of the reign of King Vajiravudh, Prince Naris was consulted by the king from time to time on performance, *bot lakhon* adaptation, and stage and costume designs. His advice and comments appear in personal correspondence with the king (also to be discussed later).

In the present-day revival production of *lakhon dukdamban* by the children and grandchildren of Prince Naris, the natural landscape of the Ban Plai Noen Palace of the prince at Khlong Toei is used to the fullest advantage in order to recapture the naturalistic atmosphere which he first introduced in his earliest *lakhon* productions, such as *Maniphichai,* performed in a forest to receive a foreign dignitary at Saraburi.

As the audience was limited to close friends of the family, people interested in traditional *lakhon,* and a few foreigners, such a presentation is possible in contemporary time. It gives an atmosphere of a very warm, family-like social gathering rather than public entertainment. The dancers are mostly members of the family, close relations or children of noble and well-to-do families who are interested in Thai classical dance. The dance teachers and musicians are those who themselves, or whose parents, had performed during the heyday of *lakhon dukdamban,* and some are from the Krom Silapakon. According to Princess Duangchit Chitraphong, daughter of Prince Naris, many changes have been made in the present production and performance of *lakhon dukdamban,* since a long period of time has lapsed and the memories of the old days have faded. For economic reasons and for the lack of creative artists today, the remarkable stage techniques and experiments of Prince Naris have not been followed in the modern production. It remains therefore only as a memorial celebration on the prince's birthday to raise funds for the Prince Naris Scholarship for students of Thai archaeology, history, art, music, and dancing.

To conclude, Prince Naris, with these various innovations and creative inventions, introduced to the theatre of the newly evolved "Modern Siam" new methods and techniques of stage design for the modernization of Thai classical dance-drama. He was probably the first Thai artist to succeed in combining Western three-dimensional painting techniques with Thai traditional linear line drawing and decorative design. His work in stage design evolved as totally new creations with a harmonious balance between scientific realism and romantic idealism. They represent a crossroad between tradition and modernity, East and West.

Prince Narathip's Romanticism in Set Design   Another significant contributor to the modernization of set design for the classical Thai theatre during the Fifth Reign was Prince Narathip in his experiment with the *lakhon phan thang* and *lakhon rong,* which gained even greater success and popularity than the *lakhon dukdamban* of Prince Naris and Chao Phraya Thewet. King Chulalongkorn, who was an ardent patron of Prince Narathip's theatre, gave much useful advice to Prince Narathip on the modernization and improvement of stage scenery and set designs, particularly when entertaining foreign visitors. Since the king had observed the first-hand high standards of Western plays, ballet, and opera during his tours of Europe, he was able to convey many new, modern ideas to the prince, as seen in his numerous personal notes and letters, such as:

> Concerning your letter proposing some changes in the decoration of the theatre, I agree with you. . . . It is not necessary to open up the panels. The section of the panels in the lower part should be covered, but the upper part should be left open. . . . Raise the bench behind the panels as high as the covered section. The higher the singing platform, the better the sound. . . . However, about the forest scene, there should be trees. It seems that we have to use big trees that cover up nicely.[29]

The style of Prince Narathip is in contrast to that of Prince Naris. While Prince Naris concentrated on the modernization of stage design for the aesthetic, the classic, and the realistic-naturalistic, Prince Narathip went in for the exotic and the romantic in his approach in all areas: dramatic texts, stories, scenery, costume, and make-up. His plays generally take place in foreign lands or in other regions of Siam that have romantic scenery and local colour, such as Arabia in the *Arabian Nights* (pl. 10), the Lao region in *Phra Lo* (col. pl. 1), and Chiengmai in *Sao Khrua Fa.* The set designs, costumes, and make-up for these plays were therefore challenging and exciting. Moreover, since his plays were inclined towards adventurous romance and melodrama, they appealed more to the average audience, whereas Prince Naris' plays required more sophisticated taste and greater knowledge of Thai literature, drama, music, and art. While Prince Naris maintained the principle of classical balance and restraint, not to give too much and to create the feeling of not having enough, Prince Narathip enjoyed provoking tears and laughters as much as possible. Comic and tragic scenes, in the extreme sense of these words, are the "pièce de résistance" in his plays. Nevertheless, despite their contrast to one another in terms of style, both dramatists complemented each other and greatly contributed to the development of Thai drama at this stage in Thai history. This very contrast created therefore a perfect balance in itself.

Khru Mot and Krom Silapakon Set Design   Theatre and set designs of the Silapakon Theatre from the very beginning, during the thirty-year span between the establishment of the Krom Silapakon in 1933 and 1967, were all under the direction of a single artist, Mot Wongsawat, known as "Khru Mot" (Master

Mot). Khru Mot, who is now a retired National Artist, is still working on the restorations of many temples. Through his long service as chief designer and an art teacher of the Silapakon Theatre, he has gained not only great success and popularity with his spectacular and elaborate designs, but has also trained a great number of disciples, many of whom are now set and stage designers for Thai motion picture and television companies. The fact that Khru Mot remained for such a long period as the sole chief designer of the National Theatre, Krom Silapakon, reveals three significant points concerning the development of Thai theatre.

Firstly, it shows that the National Theatre exclusively use their own official artists to create the sets for all their productions. Hence, being civil servants, and not highly paid, they execute their tasks rather mechanically and are usually taken for granted. Khru Mot himself, however, because of his personal sense of curiosity and love of experimentation, produced many works of high quality, some of them turning out to be very exciting. His elaborately decorative style dominated the classical stage and has established a tradition among contemporary Thai stage designers.

Secondly, due to the first point, the stage designs of the National Theatre tend to lack new challenging works of other artists outside the establishment. There are no opportunities provided for creative artists who are not civil servants and are not attached to the Krom Silapakon. However, in the late 1970s, some changes have been introduced by young artists who designed for the *lakhon* productions by other organizations, which were performed at the National Theatre, such as the *lakhon* of Somphop Chantharaprapha, who attempted to revive the *lakhon dukdamban* by using historical and patriotic stories instead of the traditional ones in the original *lakhon dukdamban* of Prince Naris. The set design for Somphop's plays were by leading contemporary artists and architects such as Chakraphan Posayakrit and Suraphol Wirumrak.

Thirdly, Khru Mot had received a lot of influence from the stage designs of Prince Naris and Prince Narathip. He served therefore as a necessary link between the pre-Revolution and post-Revolution periods. Thai theatrical heritage therefore continues on without any interruption, as in the tradition of dance and music, despite the Revolution.

In a close study of Khru Mot's stage design work for the Silapakon Theatre of the Krom Silapakon (pl. 43), it is quite evident that Prince Naris, whom Khru Mot respects as his master and teacher,[30] had a strong influence on his style in combining Western three-dimensional realism with intricate Thai decorative and elaborate designs. However, while Prince Naris maintained the principle of "classic balance" and "good taste" in not trying to create or to give "too much" and kept his experimentations in reasonable proportion and moderation, Khru Mot at times seemed to be carried away with his fantasy for want of excellence, which he said was the main purpose and principle of his work.[31] Some of his set designs were so elaborate and glittering that they overshadowed the dancers. This caused occasional criticism by Dhanit Yupho, the former director of the Krom Silapakon.[32] However, Khru Mot defended his theory that since classical *khon* and *lakhon* were originally tales of fantasy, the set designs for them should also support the fantastic and romantic, i.e., the non-realistic or even surrealistic, characters of the plays. This concept echoed that of Prince Narathip for whom Khru Mot also has great admiration. The sky, sea, mountains, trees, rocks, streams, ponds, and the underworld, all these natural landscapes in his designs should appear realistic enough in their three-dimensional volumes and surfaces, lights and shades, perspectives, and proportions, yet they should also possess certain mythological qualities in their exquisite beauty, elaborate details, and fairytale like colour schemes. Architectural constructions, such as a royal pavilion, throne hall, royal chamber, or city wall in his productions appeared in great splendour and richness, similar to those of Prince Naris in the *lakhon dukdamban* and of Prince Narathip's "Lakhon Pridalai." However, their "superexcellence" more often than not embarked upon the excessive and the unnecessary. Once Dhanit Yupho politely suggested to Khru Mot that his royal pavilion for Phra Ram in the forest was so glittering with diamond chips that it made the costumes of the dancers look shabby, even though the costumes were all newly made for the production. Khru Mot, being very sensitive to criticism (as most Thai artists were, and still are), replied in anger that Phra Ram's pavilion was created in a miracle by Indra. It should therefore appear in such a heavenly splendour and not as a shabby forest hut.[33] Dhanit, being his superior and a man of a stronger will, managed to make Khru Mot tone down that superlative glitter, of course, to the displeasure and unwillingness of the artist.

Khru Mot was trained as a painter at Phọ Chang Academy (lit., *phọ chang* means to create artisans) and as an architect during the Sixth Reign. The Academy was founded by the Ministry of Education with the purpose of producing a new generation of Thai artists and craftsmen for the future development of Modern Siam. Teachers from England were hired to teach Thai boys in various fields of art. The Academy was first called the "Smoson Chang" (Artists and Artisans Club). Each year it exhibited the works of its students. The exhibitions were presided over by King Vajiravudh. The king saw great value in promoting art education in the country and therefore had the Rongrian Phọ Chang (Academy of Art) established. Khru Mot graduated in one of the first groups to complete their studies. He then entered the civil service at the Ministry of Education in 1918 (one year after his graduation). Khru Mot admitted that he had received direct influence from his British teachers (Mr. Hilley and Mr. Harrap), who were teaching then at the Phọ Chang. Later he learned stage design from Khun Sisuphahat, a chief artist of the Phọ Chang, and worked with him in designing sets for many school plays during the Sixth Reign. Khun Sisuphahat soon saw his great talent and let him design single-handedly, even for the royal premier productions. Apparently the king was pleased with his designs.[34]

After the Revolution of 1932, one of the first tasks of the new democratic government in the area of the arts was to transfer all the departments and sections of the royal court[35] to the government, i.e., to the Krom Silapakon. Luang Wichitwathakan, an advisor to the Revolution Party, was given charge of the Krom as its director. Being deeply inspired by the French theatre, ballet, and opera, Luang Wichit's real ambition was to establish a national public theatre and to expose all the high forms of dance, music, and drama, which had previously been restricted to the royal court and the aristocracy, to the common people, following Western models. However, his personal tastes were inclined towards the West as the centre of civilization. The productions of the Krom Silapakon during this first phase were therefore products of the Westernization of traditional classical dance and drama directly under French influence[36] (pl. 44).

According to his wife, Khunying Praphaphan, who had actively participated in all of his dramatic productions, Luang Wichitwathakan had a personal liking for French revues and operettas, particularly for the spectacle and splendour of their set designs. At the time, Khru Mot was working under Khun Phra Sarotratananimman, a chief architect educated at the University of Liverpool, and Luang Wisansilapakam. Their most representative work is the Assembly Hall of Vajiravudh College, a boys public school founded by King Vajiravudh after the model of Harrow and other English public schools for the children of the Thai aristocracy and upper classes. When Khun Phra Sarot was commissioned to design the sets for the *lakhon* of Luang Wichit, Khru Mot was given the task of designing and creating both the stage sets and costumes for the production. From then on, Khru Mot was attached to the Krom Silapakon and continued to design for it until his retirement in 1967.

In 1934, the same year as the establishment of the Krom Silapakon, Luang Wichit sent a troupe of thirty-six Thai dancers, musicians, and artists to Japan and Taiwan in order to show Thai culture to its neighbours and to expose these performers and artists to the modern theatre of these countries, notably Japan. Khru Mot, who also accompanied them, came back to Thailand with many new ideas, which he had seen in the Japanese theatre. He started experimenting with a revolving stage in the stage design of the episode of "Prasanta To Nok" (Prasanta capturing a bird) from *Inao,* but failed to achieve the proper effect, since Thai *lakhon* dancing and movements were too slow for the revolving stage. In this revolving set, Khru Mot built a complete forest and mountain scenery, which could be seen from all sides like in nature. According to him, "Our *lakhon* is too *cool* [i.e., graceful, slow] and is not *hot* [i.e., exciting, fast, stimulating] enough for such a stage set."[37] He also imitated the Japanese use of *hanamichi* in *kabuki* theatre.[38] In the production of the *Luat Suphan* (The blood of Suphan) by Luang

Wichitwathakan, Khru Mot built a semi-circular bridge walk extending from both sides of the stage and making a semi-circle around the audience for the military processions in the play. The effects were therefore grand and spectacular.

Another stage technique Khru Mot seemed to have received from the Japanese was the use of cloth sheets to produce the effects of water, running streams, flowing rivers, waterfalls, stormy seas, and breaking waves. This technique was very successful in the production of *Kumphakan Thot Nam* (Kumpakana blocking the river) in the *Ramakien* (pl. 45), *Kraithong, Monohra,* and *Phra Aphaimani.* Later he used mirrors which could produce with their reflections an even better water effect.

Khru Mot also used pulleys to swing the dancers up in the air in flying movements (such as in *khon* and the production of *Manohra*). It caused great excitement in the audience, as in *Manohra,* when the *kinnari*[39] princesses descended to and ascended from the Anodat Crystal Pond where they took their baths. Though this device had long been used in the *khon chak rok* since the Ayudhaya and early Bangkok periods, it was from the observations of the French and Japanese theatres that the technique was modernized to produce greater realistic effects.[40]

In 1955 when Luang Ronasithiphichai was the director of the Krom Silapakon, Khru Mot together with Dhanit Yupho (who later succeeded Luang Ronasit) accompanied the director and his wife on a tour of Europe, in order to learn more about the modern theatre techniques and to see the great works of Western theatre. Though the early part of the tour turned out to be a honeymoon trip for the director,[41] Khru Mot and Dhanit managed to slip away and conduct a separate tour to different famous theatres in France, Italy, Germany, and England. Khru Mot admitted that it was in France and England that he got a lot of new ideas and great knowledge of modern theatre designs and techniques, which he later used in his own creations at the Silapakon. From the illustrations of the productions after his return from Europe, in the late 1950s and the 1960s, we can see many new improvements in the colour schemes, composition, lighting decoration, and other stage techniques (col. pl. 3).

Some of Khru Mot's earlier set designs resemble strongly that of French opera-ballet: for example, the haunted forest scene in *Phra Wai Taek Thap* (The defeat of Phra Wai) in *Khun Chang Khun Phaen* (col. pl. 3) came directly from the familiar cemetery scene in *Giselle* or *Les Sylphides.* The dance of the nymphs choreographed and directed by Mom Phaeo was definitely inspired by these two French ballet pieces.[42] The throne hall in *Phra Aphaimani* bears a strong resemblance to that in many of Shakespeare's plays. Khru Mot also greatly admired the set designs in *The King and I,* the musical play version which he saw in London on this trip. Many of his later designs reflected this influence.

The stage designs of Khru Mot as a whole show a steady and continuous trend, since its initiation by Prince Naris to the present, in adapting Western theatre techniques to Thai classical theatre, yet still preserving the Thai character.

Khon and Lakhon Productions from the Late 1960s to the 1980s After the retirement of Khru Mot, a young Thai designer Thawisak Senanarong, who had newly graduated from the Accademia di Belle Arti di Roma in Italy, succeeded him in 1966 as head designer of the Krom Silapakon Theatre, which was later to become the National Theatre. Thawisak had received his bachelor degree in fine arts from Silapakon University. He continued his study in set design in Italy as the recipient of a four-year Unesco fellowship and received a diploma in scenographia.

With such a different educational background, work experience, and artistic training from that of Khru Mot, Thawisak's ideas and concepts about set design and decoration could be termed "new school." The major difference between the work of Khru Mot and Thawisak is that the former maintained the principles and characteristics of the old school of Thai painting in creating an atmosphere of royal grandeur by elaborate, decorative, stylized detail in designs set in three-dimensional perspectives and naturalistic landscape: i.e., a combination of traditional Thai painting and Western realistic presentation. Thawisak, on the contrary, being influenced by modern Western art, prefers the suggestive abstract set design: i.e., using a few symbolic or suggestive architectural and decorative structures to represent the locations of the scenes, such as in his set designs of *Phali Son Nong* (pl. 46). He has also admitted that Italian and French stage designs had influenced his work; for example, as seen in his early designs for *Wiwa Phra Samut* and in the naturalistic landscape with trees and waterfalls in *Ngo Pa,* which is one of his favourite sets. During the 1970s, however, Thawisak gave in to the popular taste for spectacular scenery and stage tricks, such as moving rocks, giants, and fantastic animals on stage for the purpose of attracting and entertaining school-age audiences and to compete with Japanese television adventure films by using the same tricks. This can be seen in his set designs for a number of scenes in *Phali Son Nong* and *Phra Aphaimani.*

After having attended a seminar on Thai classical dance, drama, and music, which was organized by the Institute of Thai Studies at Thammasat University, and where criticism of over-elaborate set designs of the Krom Silapakon was aired, Thawisak and the Krom Silapakon staff seemed to begin applying modern stage techniques and lighting systems to modernize their set designs with more sophistication. The simple, abstract set design and lighting system introduced by this writer in the Khon Thammasat troupe's production of *Phiphek Swamiphak* (The defection of Phiphek) (col. pl. 6), an episode from the *Ramakien,* exerted considerable influence on the design done by Thawisak for the same episode which was produced later in 1976 by the

Krom Silapakon, in that the stage set, as well as the presentation and lighting, were simpler. Nevertheless, it is noticeable that the decorative designs of Thawisak are still more elaborate than those of Khon Thammasat productions.

It could be stated that in modern times, exchanges of ideas and concepts are more acceptable to the new generation of artists than to the more conservative members of the last generation, and that Western ideas exert a greater influence in modern, abstract designs. However, it is ironic that symbolism and abstraction in design and presentation was the original essence of Asian art and a major characteristic of traditional Thai *khon* and *lakhon*. In the past, only a single bench could represent a grand Royal Audience Hall, or a simple log a whole forest. Therefore, the only major contribution from the West in such modern stage design (which has been claimed to be completely and exclusively "Western") is the modern lighting, sound system, and mechanical devices for moving stage properties.

Lakhon **Productions of Somphop Chantharaprapha**   Towards the end of the 1960s, there arose a rightist reaction to counteract the leftist criticism of the monarchy and the Marxist interpretation of Thai history, traditions, and culture. This rightist movement was of course supported by the royal court. Through the encouragement of H.M. Queen Sirikit, Somphop Chantharaprapha, a friend of her aunt, started to write patriotic plays and present them in the style of *lakhon dukdamban* with stories adapted from Thai ancient chronicles and history. From these dance-dramas, Somphop commissioned various young Thai artists to design the sets and costumes.

The major characteristics of these new set designs were the strikingly accurate architectural structures representing the different national settings involved in the stories. They had been researched from historical and archaeological sources. For example, Sukhothai art and architecture was the setting for *Nang Suang* in 1968. The set was designed by Chakraphan Posayakrit, a graduate of the Silapakon University and a leading Thai portraitist, painter, and *hun krabok* (bamboo-rod puppets) restorer and director-producer. (See also his *hun krabok* production of *Nang Loi* in col. pl. 4.) Siwichai (Srivijaya) and Nakhon Sithammarat art and architecture were the settings for *Sithammasokarat* in 1970 (pl. 47); Thai-Chinese scenery for *Chisin* in 1974; and the northeastern Thai-Lao temples and provincial houses for *Phu Wiset* in 1975. In all these productions, it is evident that the use of three-dimensional perspective, architectural structures, and naturalistic landscapes, which had first been introduced by Prince Naris in the Fifth Reign, had been maintained. Only modern lighting systems were added.

Productions of the Khon Thammasat Troupe   Another new concept was introduced by this writer in the set design of the Khon Thammasat production of the episode of *Phiphek Swamiphak* in the *Ramakien* late 1975 to early 1976, under the direction of Mom Ratchawong Kukrit Pramoj, to celebrate the investiture of Crown Prince Vajiralongkorn. This writer, as the set designer, wished to recapture the simplicity and abstraction that had been the essence of traditional *khon* presentations in the past by reducing stage decoration to a bare minimum: therefore, the Pavilion of Phra Ram was presented in a skeleton form, red curtains were used for the Royal Audience Hall of Thosakan in Longka, etc. Also, the platform was moved to the right. Scenery changes were done swiftly through a new technique of using many make-shift platforms on wheels which were rearranged in different patterns for various scenes to provide new settings. The platforms were for the dancers to perform on at different levels in order to create a sense of space without having to have the conventional three-dimensional painted backcloths.

A modern lighting system was a very important feature in this new set design. Different coloured lights were used to create different moods and to represent symbolically the emotional feelings of the main characters in climactic scenes, such as red in the dream scene and the scene of Thosakan's fury; green and blue for the melancholic, lonely wood during Phiphek's exile; and golden-red for the rays of sunset in the last scene when Phiphek takes the oath of allegiance by drinking the consecrated water and Phra Ram manifests himself as the four-armed god Narai (col. pl. 6). Landscape was suggested by abstract forms of trees instead of more realistic trees as presented in Krom Silapakon set designs. This new concept received many encouraging comments in the newspapers; and it was later adopted by Krom Silapakon artists, who took up its stage lighting techniques and also showed a preference for minimizing stage properties. Hence, a trend returning to the simplicity of the past was begun, but with the use of modern theatre techniques.

Development of Set Design for Modern Theatre

Realistic set design for modern theatre started with the *lakhon phut* spoken drama during the reign of King Vajiravudh during the 1910s under the direct influence of English, French, and Italian schools (pl. 26). Two major designers, Khru Mot and Thawisak Senanarong of the National Theatre and the Krom Silapakon (and many other artists who received training from either the Silapakon Academy of Fine Arts or Silapakon University under the Bureau of State Universities), were under the strong influence of the Italian master, Professor Silpa Bhirasri (né Gorrado Feroci), who trained as a sculptor-painter at the Royal Academy of Art of Florence, Italy.

Professor Silpa Bhirasri founded Silapakon College of Fine Arts, and his Thai disciples continue three-dimensional perspective and the *trompe l'oeil* of the Italian school of set design. Professor Bhirasri came to serve the Thai government as a royally commissioned sculptor-painter in 1913. He was given Thai citizenship in 1942. After the Revolution of 1932, he became the director of Silapakon College of Fine Arts, which later developed into a full-fledged university. Most of the well-known modern Thai painters, sculptors, and designers from the 1910s have been either his disciples or students of his disciples and followers of the Italian school in the style of the High Renaissance great masters, principally Leonardo da Vinci and Michelangelo. However, Professor Bhirasri was able to blend Thai aesthetics of the Sukhothai period with Western realism. This curious synthesis has become the essence of Thai modern art and set design.

In the late 1940s during World War II when modern *lakhon phut* theatre was at its height, set designs for historical and romantic melodramas faithfully reflected the Krom Silapakon style until their decline in the 1950s. The style was picked up again in television drama of the same genre. It was not until the 1970s that a more modern style of set design under American influence was introduced within the close circle of university theatres, first with the Theatre Arts Department of Chulalongkorn University and then by the Drama Department of Thammasat University. The new style came naturally along with the productions of modern American plays in translation or adaptation. The most notable were Tennessee Williams' *The Glass Menagerie* (by Chulalongkorn Theatre), *A Streetcar Named Desire,* and Arthur Miller's *Death of a Salesman* (produced by Thammasat Theatre, set design by the writer). The American University Alumni Association has also been responsible for the import of American theatre and theatre arts through its dramatic activities since the 1960s, while the British Council and the Alliance Française have injected Anglo-French styles into various amateur community theatre groups for ex-patriots and Westernized Thai nationals.

Abstract constructivism and Brechtian suggestive styles were introduced in the late 1970s with the Thammasat production of Jean Anouilh's *Antigone* (set design by the writer) and the Chulalongkorn production of Brecht's *The Good Woman of Setchuan*. Brechtian style became more popular in the 1980s, as seen in *The Threepenny Opera* (at Thammasat, designed by the writer), *Mother Courage,* and Strindberg's *A Dream Play* (both at Chulalongkorn, designed by Suraiman Wesayapon), *Galileo, Man of La Mancha,* and *The Visit* (by Group '28, formed by Chulalongkorn and Thammasat graduates). While the university theatre groups search for new ways of expressing themselves and communicating with the new generation, Thai commercial television dramas and films still remain in the traditional, realistic style. The best model of this pictorial realism is the programming on Channel 3.

Kanit Kunawut and Suraiman Wesayapon are now the country's leading Thai contemporary set designers. Both received their training from the United States. Kanit's designs for *Rashomon* and *Kantan* at Chulalongkorn Theatre harmoniously blended Japanese architecture and design with those of the West. Suraiman's unique style features the effective use of lighting on hanging draperies, nets, and textured materials, as in *Mother Courage, Lọ Dilok Rat,* and *Mae Bia* (The cobra).

Multi-media with slide projection are more frequently used for expressionistic and surrealistic effects, as well as for instant changes of scenery as in the historical play *The Empress Dowager* and *The Merchant of Venice* (Thammasat, designed by the writer), *Woman* (Chulalongkorn), and *Camina Burana* (by the combined German-Thai dance troupe, designed by Suraiman).

Thai modern set design has closely followed Western theatre with some Japanese influence in the last decade. It has yet to find its own indigenous creations to meet the requirement of contemporary theatre. However, with the rich natural and cultural resources, more serious research, and new original plays written by Thais, there may be a new generation of Thai design artists who will succeed in finding a true national identity in their creations.

MODERNIZATION OF COSTUME AND MAKE-UP

Research on the costume and make-up of classical *khon* and *lakhon* began during the Sixth Reign, with King Vajiravudh, Prince Damrong, and Prince Naris as its leading contributors. They influenced other scholars, such as Phraya Anuman Rajadhon and Phra Saraprasoet, the two princes' faithful correspondents on the subjects of the humanities and culture, to carry on the task and transmit the knowledge to the next generation of researchers, namely, Prince Dhaninivat and Dhanit Yupho.[43] At present, there are many secondary sources written on the subject by teachers at Silapakon University and other modern scholars. However, as there is little pictorial evidence on the pre-Ratanakosin *khon* and *lakhon* costumes and make-up, scholars have had to depend either on descriptions written in chronicles, literary works, or archaeological findings, or to base their ideas on existing dance costumes and make-up which are believed to have been inherited from ancient forms, such as those of the *nora chatri* of southern Thailand (pl. 6). Pictorial evidence is, however, available in paintings from the Thonburi and early Ratanakosin period, presumably after the models of Ayudhaya (pl. 30).

The earliest evidence is probably in the sculptured reliefs of the Dvaravati period (6th–11th century) found in Nakhon Sawan and Ratchaburi showing the different dance movements of classical Indian dancing: *latita, anchita,* and *chatura.* The first one (pl. 17) shows a bare-chested *kinnari* with wings wearing a head-dress, earrings, and what looks like a thin wrapping from the waist down. The head-dress and earrings are rather silmilar to those of *Kandyan* dancers in Ceylon. Striking similarities in dance movements, musical rhythms, drum beating, and costumes between the *Kandyan* dance and the *nora chatri* of southern Thailand lead one to believe that the latter may have been influenced directly by the *Kandyan* or Ceylonese dance, which may have been introduced by Ceylonese settlers as early as the Sukhothai period and later in the Ayudhaya period, as described in the stone inscriptions.[44] The other two bas-reliefs are also of bare-chested female dancers wearing pointed head-dresses, necklaces, earrings, and long ankle-length *phanung* (skirts) which are pleated in the front, similar to the costume of the *nang* (female role) in Thai classical dance (pl. 3). It is difficult to tell whether the dancers depicted in these reliefs were Indian, Thai, or belonged to some other nationality in the region. However, Lakhon Luang dancers as shown in the paintings from the First Reign wear similar types of costume (pl. 30). Since these paintings were done according to royal command, following the models of the Ayudhaya court dancers, it can be assumed that Ayudhaya dancers wore the same type of costume and danced bare-chested as in *nora chatri.*

According to Prince Damrong, *nora chatri* was brought down from Ayudhaya by Khun Sattha to the south of Siam. However, this theory has been shown by modern authorities to be no longer tenable. Since *nora chatri* appears closer to Indian origins, it is more likely that the influence came from the opposite direction, i.e., from the south and later to Thonburi and Bangkok during the reigns of King Taksin and King Rama I. As has been discussed earlier, King Taksin brought a troupe of southern dancers from Nakhon Sithammarat, who also helped to form his royal Lakhon Luang troupe, and who were highly regarded by the early Ratanakosin dancers. Paintings in the Thonburi period such as in the *Traiphum* show similar costumes of *thewada* (gods), *nang fa* (goddesses), and *yak* (ogre) characters, who also appear in *khon* and *lakhon.*

The dance costumes were without any top garments (probably with the exception of *lakhon nang nai* [dance-drama of the court ladies]) until the Fourth Reign, when King Mongkut ordered his courtiers to wear upper garments at court. Male royal children in the tonsure ceremony before this reign were bare-chested and had ornaments worn on their bodies as in the *nora chatri* dance costumes (pl. 6), while the princesses wore top garments. This topless costume applied only to the costume of the *phra* (male role) which traditionally was the only character wearing a full royal costume with a *soet* head-dress, representing a *thao phraya* (a king or a royal person). He was referred to as the *tua yun khruang* (character wearing a costume), whereas other characters, male and female, wore ordinary costumes, the men with turbans on their heads and the women with shawls covering the upper parts of their bodies. The *yak* characters had lines drawn directly on their faces, and the clown wore a *phran* (hunter) mask in *nora chatri,* which is respected as the mask of a *khru* (teacher). The *phran* represents Phran Suntharik who captured Monohra, the *kinnari* princess in *Suthana Chadok.*

It was probably during the reign of King Boromakot (1732–58) that the costumes of the Lakhon Luang and Lakhon Phuying of the royal court were elaborately developed, and they became the models for the revival that took place during the reign of King Rama I under the supervision of authorities from the court of King Boromakot, such as Princess Phintumwadi. The head-dresses and costumes created during the First Reign were very close to those of the king (pl. 48) and members of the royal family to the degree that the king forbade other troupes to imitate these *khruang ton* (royal costumes), especially the *mongkut* (pl. 49a), a head-dress with different types of top or crest, the *chada* (pl. 49b), a head-dress with a spire-like top, the *kanchiak chon,* a decorative ear piece attached to the head-dress, the *dokmai that,* a flower hanging at the ears, and the *phanung chip chong wai hang hong* (a *phanung*—wrap around skirt with pleated tail like that of a swan). Even the *tua yun khruang* (character representing royalty in a full costume) could no longer wear this type of *phanung* and was allowed only to wear one in the same way as the *yak* character, i.e., without the pleated tail[45] (pls. 5, 32).

In the reign of King Rama II, a new type of head-dress was created for the characters of Panyi and Unakan, who are disguised as forest brigands in *Inao,* to replace the turbans. This is called the *panchuret.* Later the *panchuret* has also been used in other *lakhon phan thang* and *lakhon nok* since the Fifth Reign, such as in *Khun Chang Khun Phaen* and *Kraithong,* for a hero of a common origin, i.e., not a royal person. The tiara (*krabang*) for minor female roles is also believed to have been created in the Second Reign (pl. 49c).

In the reign of King Mongkut, the *khon* and *lakhon* costumes of the royal dance troupe were brought to perfection. The king issued a decree in 1855 restricting the use of these types of costume and accessories to the Lakhon Luang only, as they are similar to those of the king and royal family. These prerogatives were *rat klao yot,* a new type of head-dress created in this reign (pl. 49d), and royal accessories, namely, the *phan thong* (gold pedestal bowl), *hip mak thong* (gold betel-nut case), and enamelled decorative objects, all of which are symbols of royal status.[46] These restrictions became more relaxed in the Fifth Reign, which was a period when many experiments in costume designs were carried out by both the royal court and private troupes. To mention a few significant ones: the light costumes for senior dancers in the production put on to welcome the return of King Chulalongkorn from Europe, the costumes of Prince Narathip's troupe (pl. 10), which had been inspired by the *Arabian Nights,* and the exquisite *lakhon nai* costumes with embroidered slippers (pl. 16). In the *lakhon phan thang* of Prince Narathip and Chao Phraya Mahin, national and historical costumes of the periods were also used, such as in *Phra Lo* (col. pl. 1), *Khun Chang Khun Phaen* (col. pl. 3), *Rachathirat* (col. pls. 7, 8). These new experiments have been adopted by the later producers up to the present day. Costumes as worn in everyday life in a particular period are also used in *lakhon phan thang* (such as those of the court ladies in pl. 50) and *lakhon rong* (pl. 11).

Prince Naris and King Vajiravudh should also be given credit for having introduced natural make-up and realistic costumes in their dance-drama. In his *lakhon dukdamban,* Prince Naris had the *yak* and *ngo* characters (in *Sangthong*) wear their hair in curls (pl. 51) and have their faces done with coloured paints and with lines instead of wearing masks. His dancers also wore Western-style make-up to look more natural than the traditional white mask-like powder make-up (compare pl. 15). The king experimented with human flesh colour make-up in his *lakhon* and *khon*.[47] In his historical plays, the king did research on such historical costumes as appear in *Phra Ruang* (pls. 27, 28, 29). They have influenced other producers of nationalistic historical plays ever since, namely, Luang Wichitwathakan in *Anuphap Phọ Khun Ramkhamhaeng* and Somphop Chantharaprapha in *Nang Suang, Sithammasokarat, Chisin,* and *Phu Wiset,* and Montri Tramote's *Suk Kao Thap.*

During the directorship of Dhanit Yupho, there was an attempt to use archaeological evidence such as sculpture, bas-reliefs, and paintings as a source for dance costumes. Mom Phaeo choreographed a collection of *rabam borankhadi* (archaeological dances), representing different periods of Thai history and costumes. When the Krom Silapakon troupe travelled to Indonesia, Dhanit Yupho was so inspired by the Javanese dance and costumes that he encouraged the production of *Inao* to be costumed in the Javanese style (col. pl. 9), thus creating quite a strange contrast with some characters who still wore the traditional *lakhon* costumes of the Thais.

From Japan and Europe the techniques of modern theatre make-up were adopted and have been used until the present. It has caused some reaction against it among traditionalists who prefer the customary Thai style of make-up, and who disapprove of the blue and green eye make-up which does not suit the dark eyes and dark hair of Thai dancers.

Thus, from the Fifth Reign onward, classical dance-drama costumes and make-up underwent a long process of modernization (or Westernization) in appearing as they do today.

New Creations in Modern Theatre

Contemporary costume and realistic make-up were introduced by King Vajiravudh when he was crown prince in his *lakhon phut* done in both prose and poetry (pl. 26). As mentioned earlier, the crown prince, and later the king, in correspondence with Prince Naris, expressed deep concern about creating more realistic and naturalistic effects in costumes and make-up, following Western trends. The king even conducted serious historical and archaeological study on Thai costumes to make them historically accurate. In some plays, he designed the costumes himself. His influence continued in later periods, especially in the patriotic plays produced from the 1940s to the present day.

During the Second World War, popular plays were mostly melodramas or historical romances, in which both contemporary and period costumes were used in very creative and imaginative ways without much research. The designs were based on the fantasies of the artists or directors of both the theatre and film genres. Due to economic reasons, budgets for costumes have been usually low, producing inferior quality. It was not until the 1970s that university theatres led a new trend in costume design based on historical and archaeological research and proper training in theory and practice. However, low budget for the university productions have been a major obstacle to the development of this field. With increasing support from sponsors in the private sector and the development of hotel theatres, such as the Oriental Hotel (annual performances) and the Monthienthong Theatre (regularly scheduled performances), costume design and construction have greatly improved.

In the film and television industries, it was customary for actors to bring their own wardrobes without any central coordination. Costume and make-up designs suited to the thematic schemes and tones of the productions have only been introduced from the late 1970s starting with Prince Chatrichaloem Yukol, or "Than Mui," in his realistic, social films. This new movement set a precedent for later directors and producers. However, in low-budgeted films and television dramas, the producers can only afford original designs for the main characters leaving the supporting actors to their own whims and personal budgets. During the 1980s television productions have been receiving more support from major dress shops or department stores in return for commercial credits. This practice, though it cuts down on the budget, creates uncoordinated styles and colour schemes unrelated to the themes and total designs of the productions.

Insufficient funds and a lack of qualified costume and make-up designers will continue to be major problems for another decade, until a new generation of producers see the importance of and set a new priorities in this field.

Conclusion

From the study of the development of Thai dance and dance-drama from the Sukhothai period to the present, and from the study of the process of modernization of the dramatic forms, literature, performance techniques, music, stage design, theatre construction, costume, and make-up, the following conclusions can be drawn.

Firstly, in the documented close relationship between dramatic activities and decorum of the Thai royal court, we can observe that the patronization of dance-drama by the royal court, particularly its sponsorship of *lakhon phuying* or *lakhon (nang) nai* (Inner Court ladies dance troupe), was important to the monarchy as an essential attribute to the power and glory of the king. This attribute was greatly emphasized in those times when the monarchs had to prove or justify their position and prestige in the eyes of the general Thai public and/or foreign countries.

As the structure of the court and the style of court life became more complicated towards the end of the Sukhothai period and on into the Ayudhaya period, the Hinduistic concept of *deva-raja* (divine king) was adopted and modified under the influence of the Brahmans, who were advisers to the royal court on the subjects of ceremony and custom. The complexity of the royal court reached a very high degree at the time of the division within the court itself between the Fai Na (the Outer Court for male officials and members of the royal family) and the Fai Nai (the Inner Court, which was restricted to female members attached to the personal life of the king, with the king as the sole adult male at the centre, the only other males being pre-adolescent children). Rules and regulations of the court were drawn up in detail and codified, following the model of the Indian *Manūthammasāt,* in the *Kot Monthienban* (Palatine Laws) from the time of King Boromatrailokanat. This structured decorum further widened the gap between the ruler and the ruled and distinguished the king from even his own siblings and other members of the royal family by setting him above everyone in the realm and equal in position to a divine ruler, or even to Vishnu-incarnate himself.

As the development in refinement and sophistication of the Thai court's art and culture reached its fullest, the classical dance-drama of the Inner Court became a sacred royal prerogative, jealously guarded by the monarch. There was an acceptance of a divinely based absolute monarchy as regards the attributes appertaining to the personal life of the king. Royal ceremonies, customs, language, and personal possessions, and objects were sealed and sanctified with the crest of royalty. They were, and to a certain extent still are, not to be abused, trespassed upon, or even imitated by "mortals" in the kingdom.

The Inner Court's *lakhon nang nai,* being in its origin a dance-drama performed by the consorts and personal female attendants of the king, represented the celestial dancers of a "Deva-Raja" in legendary myths. It was regarded therefore as a *khong tong ham* (prerogative) exclusively reserved for the monarch. The limit of this royal prerogative was extended also to the use of the royal dramatic texts of *lakhon nai,* namely, *Ramakien, Unarut,* and *Inao,* since the first two are stories of Vishnu-incarnate, and the last a story of kings performed exclusively within the royal court and for the closed circle of the royal family.

This exclusive nature of court dance-drama began to change from the reign of King Mongkut, who finally allowed more freedom in dramatic performances, yet still reserved the use of the three texts of *lakhon nai.* King Chulalongkorn gave his royal patronage to all leading *lakhon* companies in and out of the court and even contributed personally to their development. King Vajiravudh started a school to train children of all social backgrounds in the art of classical dance-drama with court dancers as their teachers.

After the Revolution of 1932, which overthrew the old absolute monarchical regime and replaced it with a new system aimed at democratic government, royal classical dance-drama was transferred to the hands of a new middle-class elite and became, as it were, "public domain." The social barriers which had divided the court from the general public were thus destroyed. However, since the teachers at the newly formed Krom Silapakon (Department of Fine Arts) had been dancers in the royal court, the tradition was allowed to continue without interruption, and thus perpetuated not only the sophisticated art of dancing in the court style, but also the sense of superiority shown by which these teachers had distinguished themselves vis-à-vis the other dancers. They maintained the same kinds of responsibility as court dancers in the past in setting the standards for classical dance. Through the national network of education under the new democratic system, this teaching of Thai classical dance could be extended to a wider sphere, though in the process the traditional refinements and sophistication have often been sacrificed for the sake of public enlightenment and entertainment.

Secondly, the absolute rulers of Siam in the past, who wished to establish themselves as great kings, made every effort to patronize, sponsor, and even contribute personally to the dramatic activities within and without the royal court, in order to create an atmosphere of cultural enhancement and wealth symbolic of the peace and prosperity of the reign. This phenomenon can be seen from very early times. King Ramkhamhaeng in the late thirteenth century had written in his first stone inscription the fact of his promotion of freedom within his kingdom through artistic expression in music, dancing, and singing. The mid-nineteenth century royal decrees of King Mongkut, who deliberately revived the classical dance-drama of the royal court in order to counteract the influx of Western culture, and also to glorify his own reign, are further evidence of the great concern of the king that this area of the arts is indispensable to his personal prestige. Hence, each dramatic text that was newly composed, revised, adapted, or modernized for use in royal performances and came to be regarded as a royal standard text and a model for posterity, was stamped with the seal "Phra Ratchaniphon" (royal manuscript, or royal authorship), despite the fact that in many cases it was in reality a collaborative work of the court poets with the king acting only as supervisor, editor, or simply approver of the final draft.

Nevertheless, it should be taken into account that in most of these projects, especially when it concerned a process of modernization of either a dramatic text or stage performance, the initiator was usually the king himself. Moreover, there were several kings who did contribute their personal talents to the works. King Chulalongkorn, in particular, played his role effectively both as a promoter and supporter of creative innovation in dramatic activities within and without the royal court, in addition to being an original and creative modern dramatist in his own right. It was precisely this balance of cultural and social functions and qualities that enabled Thai classical dance-drama during this reign to extend its horizon into many new areas and to open up a new world of modern theatre to the Thais.

Thirdly, at the turn of the age, in the reigns of King Mongkut and King Chulalongkorn, when Old Siam had to respond to the influx of Western civilization in the form of political aggression by the Western powers in the age of colonization, the dramatic activities within the royal court were, for the same political, social, and cultural reasons as above, revived, revitalized, modernized and expanded, in order to cope with the new needs of the up-and-coming leaders and their followers in New Siam. These dramatic activities were an effective means taken by Thai monarchs to gain prestige as great patrons of the arts and garner much-needed respect from their foreign counterparts. New Siam of the nineteenth and twentieth centuries was to be, and still is, a centre of advanced culture and sophisticated civilization in Southeast Asia, as it had been during the time of Ayudhaya.

Fourthly, the initiative, creativity, and ingenuity appropriate to the processes and methods of modernization in Thai classical dance-drama were found more among the artists, dramatists, and musicians in the reign of King

Chulalongkorn. This was the most important turning point in the development of Thai drama and theatre. Thai classical dance-drama had undergone a process of modernization since the early nineteenth century in the reign of King Rama II, who rewrote and adapted the *bot khon* and *bot lakhon* in order to achieve perfection in both aesthetic beauty of the poetry and dancing and the practicality of stage performance. However, it was not until the Fifth Reign, that of King Chulalongkorn, in the late nineteenth and early twentieth centuries that modern dramatic techniques under Western influence were introduced. They were adopted, experimented with, modified and expanded with great enthusiasm and creative vigour resulting in the development of many new forms of dance-drama which were carried on into modern times. The great dramatists of the Fifth Reign asserted their influence so powerfully that all that were to follow have still remained in their shadow until today.

The modern techniques of dramatic text adaptation, music composition for dramatic performance, styles of production, theatrical devices, costume, and make-up, which had been discovered and applied during the Fifth Reign, are still regarded as the standard models for the present generation of theatre artists. On the one hand, this continuity serves as a constant and dominating life force in Thai cultural heritage. On the other hand, it also constitutes an attitude of conservatism, which often delays, and at times obstructs and discourages, new ideas and modern concepts which are always essential to the vitality and creativity of modern theatre. Nevertheless, with traditionalism on one side and liberalism and adaptability on the other side of the scale, a balance can be obtained. However, it seems at present that the harmony between the classical and the modern, the old and the new, is no longer a strong point. This is due to lack of leadership and of self-confidence among the present authorities in the arts.

Since the Revolution of 1932, the cultural struggle, which had been more easily resolved, or at least certainly with much less effort, under the leadership of the absolute monarchs in the past, now seems more complex. It seems to have outgrown the abilities of the new leaders of Thai society.

Under the old regime, the royal court was the one and only standard setter, the nucleus of every aspect of Thai cultural life. The authority of the king and his nobles was therefore readily accepted, respected and adopted as the right way, even when it concerned new schemes of modernization and Westernization, beyond the comprehension of ordinary people. Though questions were raised by members of the elite themselves, some of whom even challenged new ideas introduced by the court, royal prestige provided a shield of defence and security against further abuse. In a modern democratic society, where modern education stimulates more critical thinking among the general public, and where new leaders come from the middle class and may still be struggling among themselves for power and position, it is more difficult for the present generation to accept any single standard of art as absolute.

Being thus insecure in their position and judgement, it is natural for the new leaders of the arts to turn to and search for inspiration and example from an age which they regard as the best possible one, where prosperity and richness in the dance-drama were most apparent: that of King Chulalongkorn, the Father of Modern Siam. The achievements realized in the modernization of the classical dance-drama during that reign have therefore been confirmed as models up to even the most recent times.

Finally, in the analyses of different modernized versions of the *bot khon* and *bot lakhon* and of new forms of dance-drama, it is apparent that there is a steady trend towards realistic presentation and an attempt to balance realism with romanticism; that is, to present the romantic, mythical, and heroic stories of Thai classical dance-drama in a more realistic way for the purpose of communicating better with the modern audiences. This process of modernization involves condensation of the texts, alteration of the lyrics, omission of lengthy narratives and the replacement of narratives with dialogues and actions more realistic and dramatic, action-oriented dance movements, shortened performance time, more detailed stage direction for actor-dancers, a greater variety of musical tunes, realistic-romantic stage set designs, and more effective uses of technical devices, namely, lighting, visual, and sound effects.

The royal court, with its close associates, acted as leader and initiator in most projects relating to modern adaptation and creation in Thai classical dance-drama, as well as in other new genres of entertainment. The court-set new standards were established for the country and for the generations to come.

There is a deep irony which must be noted, however. Thai classical theatre follows the footsteps of Western theatre in the movement towards realism, whereby the original characteristics of idealism, symbolism, and romanticism, which constitute the essence of traditional classical dance-drama in Asia, have often been sacrificed for the sake of modernity. In the reverse direction Western theatre is searching for new inspiration from Asian traditional theatre in order to progress from the realistic plane to a higher plane of symbolism and idealism, and even religious mysticism. These are the levels upon which the impact of ancient Asian dance-drama was experienced.

This irony is even more striking at present when contemporary productions of Thai and Asian classical dance-drama of the 1970s come to be inspired by the Western dramatic techniques turning to idealistic, abstract, mystical, and symbolic presentations, which in truth had been generated from Asian sources themselves. The traditional cliché about East and West never meeting is no longer true at least in the context of the modern theatre; for it is on the very stage itself that the two often meet to counterbalance as well as to complement each other, and thus create, or attempt to create, a harmony between two dramatic polarities. Though perfection is yet an unattainable ideal existing only in the dreams and artistic desires of all dramatists, in the East and West alike, efforts towards perfection, with or without success, have borne fruit and found expression in reality. A universal aspiration to attain perfection is justified. These conflicts, frustrations, and the persistent fire of ambition create in themselves an exciting, provocative, and stimulating drama.

Notes

Chapter I

1. See Dhanit Yupho, *Khon,* and *Silapa lakhon ram, ru khu mu natasin Thai* [The art of Thai dance-drama, or a handbook of Thai dance]; Coedès, "Origine et évolution des diverses formes du théâtre traditionnel en Thailande"; Mahā Vajirāvudh, "Notes on the Siamese Theatre."

2. That is to say, *Prachum phongsawadan* [Collected chronicles] and *Kot Monthienban* [The Palatine Law], etc.

3. For example, De La Loubère, Pallegoix, Crawfurd, etc.

4. See Dhanit Yupho, *Silapa lakhon ram* and *Boran watthu samai Thawarawadi haeng mai* [New discoveries of Dvaravati antique]. See also Coedès, "The Excavation at P'ong Tük and Their Significance for the Ancient History of Siam."

5. See *The Nātyasāstra,* trans. by Monomohan Ghosh; *Bharata Natayasastra,* trans. into Thai by Saeng Monwithu; Prince Damrong, *Tamra fon ram* [The lessons of Thai dance], sec. 1, pp. 8–37.

6. *Catura,* a fast movement—left arm swinging to the right across the breast, right arm lifting upward in an angle, left leg bent, right leg swinging with the toes touching the floor; the left thumb and middle finger pressing together, the index finger pointing out.

7. The *kinnari* figure was found in 1964 at the southern side of a stupa at Wat Khok Mai Khen, Tha Nam Oi village, Phayuhakhiri district, Nakhon Sawan province, on the east bank of the Chao Phraya river, west of the Khok Mai Khen mountain range.

8. *Lalita,* a striding movement—left arm bending upward to the level of the ear like an elephant's trunk, right arm swinging forward and backward, right foot stamping the floor to the rhythm of the music.

9. *Ancita,* similar to the *lalita* movement with the right arm swinging across the body and the left arm lifting to the level of the shoulder.

10. *Krihastaka,* an elephant's trunk position, similar to the *lalita*—right arm swinging across the breast, left arm bending upward, hips swaying to the left with the weight on the left hip, both legs bending with the right one extending a bit in front of the left one.

11. *Vyamsita,* a gesture expressing disappointment—right knee bending forward, left leg extending backward, hands crossing over the chest, then moving downward and upward again.

12. *Kilakahasta,* a gesture expressing love or friendship—wrists crossing over each other, on each hand the thumb and middle finger form a circle.

13. This pose resembles that of the Buddha statue of Trailokaya Vijaya at Jogyakarta

(Majumdar, *Ancient Indian Colonies in the Far East,* vol. 2, pl. 45, figs. 1 & 2; text, p. 303). This dancer figure of the Lopburi period is described by Prince Subhadradis Diskul and A. B. Griswold in *The Sculpture of Thailand* as the "divinity of terrifying aspect." It is in bronze (h. 65/16 inches), 12th century A.D., discovered in the precinct of the Khmer Buddhist temple of Phimai near Khorat, which was associated with Tantric Mahayana Buddhism. The frowning eyebrows, protruding eyes, and two long fangs are marks of the divinity's "terrifying aspect," often seen in Tantric iconography (Bowie, ed., *The Sculpture of Thailand,* fig. 32, p. 69). The striding leg position is the same as that of the Trailokaya-Vijaya of the Mahayana Buddhism in Jogyakarta.

14. Dhanit Yupho, *Silapa lakhon ram,* p. 3.
15. Raikes, "A Brief History of the Mon People," p. 1. See also Hall, *History of Burma;* Halliday, "Immigration of the Mons into Siam" and "The Mons in Siam"; Sut Saengwichien, *Mons: Past and Present;* Smithies, "Village Mons of Bangkok."
16. Dhanit Yupho, *Silapa lakhon ram,* pp. 4–5.
17. Dawson, *A Classical Dictionary of Hindu Mythology and Religion, Geography, History, and Literature,* p. 298.
18. Ibid.; and R. C. Ramachandran, "Temples of Orissa and Bundslkhand" (Bangkok: Chotte Lal Smritigranth, n.d.), pp. 104–5.
19. See further discussion in Mattani Rutnin, "Khwam pen ma khong Phra Phirap" [The origin of Phra Phirap].
20. From an interview with Dhanit Yupho in 1975.
21. Offering to the gods.
22. *Phithi wai khru tamra khrop khon lakhon phrom dua tamnan lae kham klon wai khru lakhon chatri* [Invocation and initiation ceremonies of *khon* and *lakhon* together with history and invocation chants of *lakhon chatri*].
23. See Prince Subhadradis Diskul, *Silapa nai prathet Thai* [Art in Thailand]; Brandon, *Theatre in Southeast Asia;* Bowers, *Theatre in the East;* De Zoete and Spies, *Dance and Drama in Bali.*
24. See Coedès, *Les états hindouisés d'Indochine et d'Indonésie;* MacDonald, *Angkor;* also *Phongsawadan Khamen* [Chronicles of the Khmers] and *Ratchaphongsawadan Krung Khamphucha* [Royal chronicles of Cambodia]; H.R.H. Prince Damrong and H.R.H. Prince Naris, *San Somdet* [Princes' correspondence]; H.R.H. Prince Damrong, *Thieo Nakhon Wat* [Travel to Angkor Wat] and *Nirat Nakhon Wat* [*Nirat* poetry about a visit to Angkor Wat]; H.R.H. Prince Naris, *Pai Chawa* [Travel to Java].
25. This theory, however, contradicts that of H.R.H. Prince Damrong Rajanubhab, an authority of Thai drama and history. In his *Tamnan lakhon Inao* [The origin of *Inao* play], the prince attests that the present *nora chatri* of the south, because of its less refined form when compared with the *lakhon nok* of central Thailand, was probably a degeneration of the Ayudhaya *lakhon nok* and was possibly brought down from Ayudhaya to Nakhon Sithammarat by a so-called "Khun Sattha," supposedly an exiled dancer from Ayudhaya who was said to have taught the dance-drama to the natives of the south. In the *Wai Khru* ceremony text of *nora chatri*, the name of "Khun Sattha" is always mentioned as the founder of the dance-drama. His statue is worshipped by all *nora chatri* performers (*Tamnan lakhon Inao,* p. 6; and Phinyo Chitham, ed., *Nora,* "Bot wai khru" [Songs in worship of the teachers]). However, it is still unclear as to where the dance-drama actually originated.
26. Prince Damrong later wrote to King Vajiravudh on 1 June 1924 that the word *lakhon* probably derived from the Javanese *lagon.* King Chulalongkorn referred to a Javanese dance-drama called *lagon driyo* which was performed for him when he visited Java. See also

Dhanit Yupho, *Khon*, p. 32.

27. See Prince Damrong, *Thieo Muang Phama* [Travel to Burma]; *Phra ratchaphongsawadan chabap phra ratchahatthalekha ratchakan thi 4 . . . ratchakan 5* [Royal autograph edition of royal chronicles in the Fourth and Fifth Reigns]; Dhanit Yupho, *Silapa lakhon ram*, pp. 29–30.

28. See Prakhong Nimmanhemin, *Laksasa wannakam phak nua* [Characteristics of northern Thai literature].

29. Ibid., pp. 24–38.

30. Maung Htin Aung, *Burmese Drama*, p. 44.

31. H.R.H. Prince Damrong, *Tamnan lakhon Inao*, p. 465.

32. Kukrit Pramoj (Mom Ratchawong), *Phunthan thang watthanatham Thai* [The foundation of Thai culture], p. 17.

33. Ibid., p. 16.

34. Lévi, *L'Inde civilisatrice*, p. 136, quoted in Coedès, *Les états hindouisés d'Indochine et d'Indonésie*, pp. 2–3.

35. Coedès, *Les états hindouisés d'Indochine et d'Indonésie*, p. 349.

36. Sørensen, *Archaeological Excavations in Thailand*, vol. 2, p. 147.

37. Ibid.

38. Coedès, *Les états hindouisés d'Indochine et d'Indonésie*, pp. 2–3.

39. Ibid., p. 23.

40. See *Prachum charuk Sayam* [A collection of Siamese inscriptions], part 1; French translation in Coedès, ed. and trans., *Recueil des inscriptions du Siam*. There has recently been a controversial debate on the authenticity of these inscriptions. A new theory introduced by Associate Professor Piriya Krailiksh contends that these inscriptions were written in a much later period, maybe in the Ayudhaya period or even later.

41. *Prachum charuk Sayam*, pp. 51–52; French translation in Coedès, *Recueil*, pp. 37–38.

42. *Prachum charuk Sayam*, pp. 54–55; French translation in Coedès, *Recueil*, pp. 45–46.

43. Ibid.

44. *Kathin*, the offering of robes and necessities to the monks at the end of the *Phansa* (period of retreat during the rainy season).

45. Kukrit Pramoj (Mom Ratchawong), "Kan pokkhrong samai Sukhothai" [The Sukhothai governmental system], pp. 167–68; translation by Mattani Rutnin.

46. Ishii, Akagi, and Endo, *A Glossarial Index of the Sukhothai Inscriptions*, p. 50.

47. Montri Tramote, "Dontri samai Sukhothai" [Sukhothai music], p. 38.

48. A festival in which people float *krathong* (boats made of banana leaves and decorated with flowers) in the river. Originally this may have come from a Hindu festival.

49. *Prachum charuk Sayam*, pp. 129–30.

50. Ibid., pp. 132–33; French translation by Coedès, *Recueil*, pp. 127–28.

51. *Rabam* is, according to Coedès, a word derived from the Khmer word *ram* (to dance) and *rmam* (dancer). In Cambodian it is pronounced *rbam*.

52. Griswold, *Wat Pra Yun Reconsidered*, p. 31.

53. The city of Haripunjaya, now Lamphun, was founded by a Mon princess from Lavo (Lopburi) in the eighth century. In 1369 King Kilana (Gu Na, r. 1355–85), when invited from Martaban, built a monastery near the city for the Mahathera Sumana. The city was the capital of the kingdom of Haripunjaya. When King Meng Rai founded a new capital at Chiengmai in 1296, it remained the cultural capital of the kingdom of Chiengmai for at least seventy-five years more (ibid., pp. 2–3).

54. Mahathera Sumana discovered the Buddha's relic some time between 1340 and 1347 while he was ordained in Udumbarapuppha order in Martaban. He was later invited by King

Dhammaraja to reside at the Mango Grove Monastery, Wat Pa Muang, at Sukhothai (ibid., pp. 10–17).

55. Ibid., p. 13.

56. Quoted in Montri Tramote, "Dontri samai Sukhothai," p. 40; translation in Griswold, *Wat Pra Yun Reconsidered*, p. 13.

57. Montri Tramote, "Dontri samai Sukhothai," p. 40.

58. Lithai, Phaya (King), *Trai Phum Phra Ruang* [The Three Worlds of Phra Ruang], pp. 87, 105, 148–49.

59. Montri Tramote, "Dontri samai Sukhothai," pp. 46–47.

60. *Trai Phum Phra Ruang*, pp. 148–49.

61. Ibid., p. 152.

62. Ibid., p. 199.

63. Ibid., pp. 215–16, 219–20.

64. Ibid., p. 217.

65. Prince Damrong explains in his *Tamnan lakhon Inao* that the Thai *piphat* orchestra derived from the Indian *panja duriyangha*, which consists of an oboe (*pi*), a one-face drum (*attam*), a two-face drum (*vittam*), a leather drum (*attavittam*), a one-face gong (*khong*), and small and large cymbals (*ching* and *chap*).

66. *Prachum charuk Sayam*, p. 72; French translation in Coedès, *Recueil*, p. 70.

67. *Prachum charuk Sayam*, p. 97; *Prachum phongsawadan*, vol. 1, p. 179 (French translation in Coedès, *Recueil*, p. 109).

68. *Prachum charuk Sayam*, p. 113; French translation in Coedès, *Recueil*, p. 109.

69. *Prachum charuk Sayam*, p. 150; French translation in Coedès, *Recueil*, p. 148. The inscription is said to have been written by Phaya Ban Muang for his younger brother, Phaya Ram, ca.1419.

70. *Prachum charuk Sayam*, p. 135.

71. Somdet Phra Mahathera Sri Srattha Rajchulamunisrirattana Lanka Thepa Maha Sami Chao, son of Phrya Kamhaeng, grandson of Khun Pha Muang, was responsible for the building of many Buddhist temples, notably Wat Mahathat, in Sukhothai, which are considered the best examples of Sukhothai art and architecture.

72. *Prachum charuk Sayam*, p. 74; French translation in Coedès, *Recueil*, pp. 74–75.

73. *Khanthap* or *khonthan*, heavenly musicians, servants of the god Indra. In northern Thai mythology, the god of music and dance is called "Sikhan."

74. *Trai Phum Phra Ruang*, p. 224.

75. See Mattani Rutnin, "Phra Phirap."

76. *Trai Phum Phra Ruang*, pp. 223–25.

77. Ibid., pp. 219–20.

78. H.R.H. Prince Damrong, *Tamnan lakhon Inao*, p. 13.

79. *Prachum phongsawadan*, pt. 1, pp. iv–v.

80. Ibid., pt. 2, p. 143.

81. H.R.H. Prince Damrong's preface to *Tamrap Thao Si Chulalak* [Memoirs of Nang Nophamat], pp. 210–12.

82. Ibid., p. 212.

83. Ibid., pp. 213–14.

84. Ibid., p. 212.

85. Ibid. (footnote).

86. The term *mahorasop* is not found in any of the Sukhothai inscriptions, but appears only in the later Ayudhaya and Ratanakosin (Bangkok) chronicles. This is other evidence that the *Tamrap Thao Si Chulalak* was a work of either an Ayudhayan or a Bangkokian.

See Simmonds, *"Mahōrasop* in a Thai Manōrā Manuscript" and *"Mahōrasop* II, the Thai National Library Manuscript."

87. *Tamrap Thao Si Chulalak*, pp. 306, 308–15.
88. Ibid., p. 317.
89. The mention of guns and canons here affirms the theory that the *Tamrap Thao Si Chulalak* was written in the Ayudhaya period when these modern armaments were introduced into Siam by Europeans.
90. Ibid., p. 320.
91. Ibid., pp. 319–20.
92. Ibid., p. 322.
93. Ibid., p. 327.
94. H.H. Prince Dhaninivat, "The Shadow-play as a Possible Origin of the Masked-play," pp. 115–20; and Dhanit Yupho, *Khon.*
95. Dhanit Yupho, *Khon,* pp. 38–40.
96. Ibid., p. 22.
97. Dhanit Yupho, *Silapa lakhon ram*, pp. 8–9.
98. *Tamrap Thao Si Chulalak*, p. 330. *Rabeng*, a dance by male performers who hold bows and arrows for shooting peacocks; *rabam*, a dance such as that of gods and goddesses; *mongkhrum*, a dance by male performers who hold whips in their hands (the whips were later replaced by batons; the performers beat drums while dancing); *hok khamen*, acrobatics; *tai luat*, tight rope walking; *lot buang*, to go under or to go through a loop; *ram phaen*, a dance in which the performers hold peacock feathers as in the "Praleng" dance; *thaeng wisai*, an ancient form of dance; *kai pa cha hong*, a dance imitating birds movements.
99. *Tamrap Thao Si Chulalak*, pp. 332–33.
100. Ibid., p. 335.
101. Ibid., p. 338.
102. Ibid., p. 347.
103. Ibid., p. 349.
104. Ibid., p. 350.
105. Ibid., p. 353.
106. Ibid., pp. 358–60.
107. Ibid., pp. 360–62.
108. *Mahorasop* means a royal entertainment. See Dhanit Yupho, *Khon,* p. 54; Simmonds, *"Mahōrasop* in a Thai Manōrā Manuscript" and *"Mahōrasop* II, the Thai National Library Manuscript."
109. *Rabeng* is one of the five royal forms of entertainment (*rabeng, mongkhrum, kula ti mai, thaeng wisai, kra-oa thaeng khwai*) which were performed in the Ayudhaya and early Ratanakosin periods at royal festivals and celebrations such as the Celebration of the White Elephant and the Royal Tonsure Ceremony, etc.

   The *rabeng* dancers are all males representing kings from all directions marching to Mount Krailat to attend a tonsure ceremony of a royal prince. Each holds a bow and an arrow which he beats together in the march rhythm, while singing verses, starting with "O-la Pho" in each line. The troupe finally confronts God Kala riding a peacock (who should have been Phra Khanta Kuman, since it is God Skanda who rides on a peacock, while Kala rides on a bird). Kala bars their passage. In anger, the kings shoot the peacock and try also to shoot Kala, but Kala knocks them all unconscious. He later brings them back to their senses and they all return to their cities. See Dhanit Yupho, *Silapa lakhon ram*, pp. 254–61; also texts of *mongkhrum* and *kula ti mai*, pp. 261–62.
110. Coedès, *Les états hindouisés d'Indochine et d'Indonésie*, p. 66.

111. Dhanit Yupho states that the *nai rong* (theatre master) was granted a *sakdina* of 200 rai (*Silapa lakhon ram*, p. 14).
112. Prince Damrong, *Tamnan lakhon Inao*, p. 117.
113. Strangely enough, this king has come down in Thai history bearing the posthumous form of royal address (*phra boromakot*) used during the period between a king's death and his cremation when the body is enclosed within a ceremonial urn. This has become tantamount to the established name of this particular king, however, and it is this name that will be used here.
114. Prince Damrong, *Tamnan lakhon Inao*, pp. 120–21.
115. Busakorn Lailert, "The Ban Phlu Luang Dynasty, 1688–1767," chap. 9.
116. Ibid. See also *Latthi thamniem tang tang* [Various customs and manners], vol. 1, part 10, pp. 494–95.
117. Dhanit Yupho, *Silapa lakhon ram*, p. 29.
118. Prince Damrong, *Tamnan lakhon Inao*, p. 122.
119. Ibid., pp. 121–24.
120. Ibid., p. 216.
121. King Chulalongkorn, *Phra ratchawichan chotmaihet khwam song cham Krom Luang Narintharathewi* [His Majesty's critical analysis of the memoirs of Princess Narintharathewi], p. 99.
122. Dhanit Yupho, *Silapa lakhon ram*, p. 25.
123. Ibid., p. 26.
124. Prince Damrong, *Tamnan lakhon Inao*, p. 129.
125. Dhanit Yupho, *Silapa lakhon ram*, p. 28.
126. They are *Karaket, Khawi, Chaiyathat, Phikunthong, Phinsawan, Phinsuriwong, Manohra, Mong Pa, Maniphichai, Sangthong, Sangsinchai, Suwannasin, Suwannahong, Sowat* (Prince Damrong, *Tamnan lakhon Inao*, pp. 129–30).
127. These are *Kraithong, Khobut, Chaiyachet, Phra Rot, Sinsuriwong* (ibid.).
128. Dhanit Yupho, *Silapa lakhon ram*, p. 28.
129. Ibid., pp. 28–29.
130. The council was made up of elder members of the royal family and ministers of state. See Prince Dhaninivat, "The Reconstruction of Rama I of the Chakri Dynasty," pp. 145–68.
131. According to another source, he was presented to Chaofa Thammathibet, the Krom Phra Ratchawang Bowon Maha Senaphithak. See Dhanit Yupho, *Silapa lakhon ram*, p. 32.
132. See Busakorn Lailert, "The Ban Phlu Luang Dynasty, 1688–1767."
133. At the *somphot* of the ashes of the king's father.
134. Somdet Chaofa Krom Phraya Thepsudawadi and Somdet Chaofa Krom Phra Sisudarak, sisters of King Rama I and Somdet Phra Bowonrat Chao Maha Surasinghanat (the second king). See Dhanit Yupho, *Khon*, pp. 36–37.
135. See chiefly Prince Dhaninivat, "The Reconstruction of Rama I of the Chakri Dynasty."
136. *Ruang phra rachanukit,* published under royal commission of King Bhumibol, Rama IX, as a merit to his brother, King Anandha Mahidol, Rama VIII, in 1946.
137. Dhanit Yupho, *Silapa lakhon ram*, p. 33.
138. For example, Khun Morakot (whose name appears in the *wai khru* invocation), Khun Pheng (famous for her role of Phra Ram, teacher in the *lakhon* troupe of Krom Phra Phithakthewet in the Third Reign), Khun Ruang (teacher of the *nang* role in the Lakhon Luang troupe of the Second Reign), Chao Chom Manda Ampha (known for her role of Nang Kanchana in *Inao*, teacher of many troupes in the Third Reign, being a consort of King Rama II and mother of many royal princes and princesses, she did not dance in the Lakhon Luang troupe in the Second Reign; one of her sons, Krom Khun Worachaktharanuphap, became head of

the Pramoj family). See Prince Damrong, *Tamnan lakhon Inao*, pp. 137–39.

139. See chiefly Prince Damrong, *Tamnan lakhon Inao;* Khomkhai Nilprapassorn, "A Study of the Dramatic Poems of the Panji Cycle"; Arada Sumit, "Bot lakhon nai khong luang nai samai ratchakan thi 2" [The *lakhon nai* dance-drama of the royal court in the Second Reign].

140. Pluang Na Nakhon, *Prawat wannakhadi Thai samrap naksuksa* [History of Thai literature for students], p. 285.

141. Neon Snidvongs, "The Development of Siamese Relations with Britain and France in the Reign of King Maha Mongkut, 1851–1868," p. 197. They were Prince Phithakmontri, Prince Chetsadabodin (his son), and the Uparat (his brother).

142. See *Ruang phra rachanukit* of King Chulalongkorn.

143. Prince Damrong, *Tamnan lakhon Inao*, p. 151.

144. See the list of other dancers in Prince Damrong, *Tamnan lakhon Inao*, pp. 152–54.

145. Episode of Sangsinchai falling into a ravine.

146. Episodes of Khun Chang asking Nang Phim for her hand in marriage, and Khun Phaen eloping with Nang Wanthong, and Khun Chang pursuing them.

147. Thepchu Chapthong, *Krung Thep nai adit* [Bangkok in the past], p. 115.

148. See *Ruang phra rachanukit*.

149. *Prachum phongsawadan*, vol. 20, p. 122; emphasis by Mattani Rutnin.

150. *Prachum prakat ratchakan thi 4* [A collection of royal announcements in the Fourth Reign], pp. 161–63.

151. Ibid.

152. Quoted in Dhanit Yupho, *Khon*, p. 48.

153. Prince Damrong, *Tamnan lakhon Inao*, p. 156.

154. Phiphathakosa, Phraya, *Chotmaihet Phraya Phiphathakosa* [The memoirs of Phraya Phiphathakosa].

155. Prince Naris et al., *San Somdet,* letter to Prince Damrong, dated 24 August 1935.

156. *Krom* is a rank given by the king to the royal princes. See Akin Rabibhadana, *The Organization of Thai Society in the Early Bangkok Period, 1782–1873*, p. 54.

157. Prince Damrong, *Tamnan lakhon Inao*, pp. 155–56.

158. Ibid., p. 157.

159. For details, see ibid., pp. 158–61.

160. *Suwannahong* was first produced in 1951, and later in 1959; *Nang Kaeo Na Ma* in 1962. There have been performances of short scenes from the two plays ever since.

161. Prince Damrong notes that he must have inherited them after the death of Krom Phra Ratchawang Bowon, since they were restricted royal properties. See *Tamnan lakhon Inao*, p. 161, n. 1.

162. King Chulalongkorn, *Phra ratchawichan*, pp. 4–7, 147–51.

163. Montri Tramote, "Lakhon chatri," p. 27.

164. Dhanit Yupho, *Khon*, p. 50. Another historical source states that during the long struggle with Vietnam from 1833 to 1845, Phraya Bodin, commander of the Siamese troops, made Battambang his headquarters, and when hostilities ended in 1845, the main army withdrew from Cambodia, leaving only a small covering force in Battambang (Neon Snidvongs, "The Development of Siamese Relations with Britain and France in the Reign of King Maha Mongkut, 1851–1868," p. 94).

165. *Phra ratchaphongsawadan krung Ratanakosin* [Royal chronicles of the city of Ratanakosin (Bangkok)], pp. 29–30.

166. Kukrit Pramoj, *Khrong kraduk nai tu* [Skeletons in the closet], pp. 78–79.

167. Prince Damrong, *Tamnan lakhon Inao*, p. 162, n. 1.

168. See ibid., pp. 164–68 for a list of these teachers.
169. Pluang Na Nakhon, *Prawat wannakhadi Thai samrap naksuksa*, p. 391.
170. Nangklao Chao Yu Hua, Phrabat Somdet Phra (King Rama III), *Phleng yao klon suphap ruang phra ratchaprarop phleng yao konlabot lae konla-akson* [Personal ideas and concepts expressed in *phleng yao klon suphap, phleng yao konlabot,* and *konla-akson* types of poetry].
171. Ibid.
172. Notably the troupes of Prince Lakhananukhun, Prince Phiphitphokphuben, Prince Rakronnaret, Prince Phithakthewet, Prince Phuwanetnarinrit, Chao Phraya Bodindecha, Chao Chom Ampha, and "Chao Krap" (see details in Dhanit Yupho, *Silapa lakhon ram*, pp. 69–74).
173. Ibid., p. 69.

Chapter II

1. See especially Neon Snidvongs, "The Development of Siamese Relations with Britain and France in the Reign of King Maha Mongkut, 1851–1868."
2. Ibid., pp. 108–11.
3. "It has to be recorded that in spite of ardours and faithful labour of the increasing corps of workers and in the face of all encouraging marks of advance in Western civilization, Siam responded very slowly to the spiritual appeal of the Gospel" (D. B. Bradley, *Abstract of the Journal of the Reverend Dan Beach Bradley, M.D., Medical Missionary to Siam in 1835–1873*, edited by George Feltus).
4. William J. Bradley, "Dr. Dan Bradley," a lecture given at The Siam Society, 28 January 1975.
5. Lingat, "Les trois *Bangkok Recorders*"; and Pluang Na Nakhon, *Prawat wannakhadi Thai.*
6. Pluang Na Nakhon, *Prawat wannakhadi Thai.*
7. William Bradley, "Dr. Dan Bradley."
8. See Pluang Na Nakhon, *Prawat wannakhadi Thai;* also *Warasan lae nangsuphim nai prathet Thai sung thi phim rawang phǫ sǫ 2387–2477* [Periodicals and newspapers in Thailand published between 1844 and 1934].
9. See Sittha Phinitphuwadon et al., *Khwam ru thua pai thang wannakam Thai* [Introduction to Thai literature].
10. The chronicles consist of 42 manuscripts and were edited by Prince Damrong in 1914.
11. See Wuthichai Mullasin, *Kan patirup kan suksa nai ratchakan thi 5* [Reform of education in the Fifth Reign].
12. Such an image was not too far from that portrayed by the romantic imagination of Anna Leonowens in her controversial memoirs which was further magnified and fictionalized by Margaret Landon in her *Anna and the King of Siam.*
13. King Chulalongkorn, *Phra ratchaphithi sip song duan* [Royal ceremonies of the twelve months], pp. 1–7 (preface).
14. "In the kingdom [reign] of Phra Bat Somdet Phra Chom Klao Chao Yu Hua [Rama IV], any members of the royal family and *kha ratchakan* [lit., servants in the king's state affairs, i.e., government officials], of high and low status, who wish to perform *lakhon phuchai phuying* [male and female dance-drama] will not at all be rejected [criticized] by the King, for His Majesty realizes that it is good to have many *lakhon* troupes, so that the country will be full of merriment, and it would be an honour to the kingdom" (King Mongkut, "Prakat wa duai lakhon phuying" [Royal decree on the subject of female dance-drama], 1855, quoted in Prince Damrong, *Tamnan lakhon Inao*, pp. 170–71).
    King Chulalongkorn explained in his *Phra ratchaphithi sip song duan*, p. 253, "In truth,

King Chom Klao Chao Yu Hua [Mongkut] liked ancient royal ceremonies very much and had tried out many of them even to the extent of accompanying the gods to the temples in elephant processions [in the *Khachentharatsawasanan* ceremony for the good fortune of the royal elephants] . . . he never missed the *Sa Sanan Yai* ceremony [grand procession of royal elephants, horses, and soldiers in traditional pageantry]. Whenever a new white elephant came into his reign, the King would have the *Sa Sanan* procession."

15. King Chulalongkorn, *Phra ratchaphithi sip song duan*, p. 88.
16. Ibid., p. 96.
17. Ibid., p. 198.
18. Ibid., pp. 198–99.
19. *Phra ratchaphongsawadan krung Ratanakosin, ratchakan thi 4* [Royal chronicles of the Bangkok period, the Fourth Reign], pp. 377–78.
20. *Phra ratchaphongsawadan krung Ratanakosin, ratchakan thi 3* [Royal chronicles of the Bangkok period, the Third Reign], p. 360.
21. Neon Snidvongs, "The Development of Siamese Relations with Britain and France in the Reign of King Maha Mongkut, 1851–1868," pp. xii–xiii.
22. See an account of the illness and death of the princess in Prayut Sitthiphan, *Somdet Phra Chom Klao Chao Krung Sayam* [King Mongkut of Siam].
23. Neon Snidvongs, "The Development of Siamese Relations with Britain and France in the reign of King Maha Mongkut, 1851–1868."
24. King Mongkut, *Chotmaihet ratchakan thi 4* [Historical accounts of King Rama IV], no. 64.
25. Chao Phraya Nikon Bodinthara Mahinthara Maha Kanlayanamit, who wrote the Royal Decree under the command of King Mongkut in 1861, stated,

When the reign [of King Rama III] ended, King Phra Chom Klao [Rama IV] succeeded to the throne and was crowned. At that time, the King wished to follow the meritorious practice of King Phra Nang Klao [Rama III] and not have *lakhon luang* in the Royal Palace as before. However, many members of the royal family and officials of both the Outer Court and Inner Court advised him that in the past reigns from the time of Ayudhaya to that of Thonburi and in the reigns of King Phra Phuttha Yodfa Chulalok [Rama I] and Phra Phuttha Loetia Naphalai [Rama II], there had always been *lakhon khang nai* [dance-drama of the Inner Court] for the Royal Palace. When foreign visitors came to have audiences with the Kings there were performances of *lakhon khang nai* for them as an honour to the Kings' majesty. When there were celebrations to commemorate the capital, or temples, or Buddha images, or *stupa* and *chedi*, and on occasions of royal charity or on having [captured] important elephants, there had been *lakhon khang nai* as a celebration and *somphot tham khwan* [fortune-creating ceremonies]. *Lakhon khang nai* is naturally appropriate to white elephants. In the reign of Phra Nang Klao, there were no white elephants, perhaps because there was no *lakhon khang nai*. They [the court] therefore asked the King's permission to train [dancers] and set up [the royal troupe] according to past tradition. The King graciously granted it saying, "If such idea was reasonable and was agreed upon, let the *thao nang* [princesses], *chao chom* [consorts], and *thao kae* [old ladies of the court with high status and responsibility] of the Inner Court, who had been *lakhon* dancers before, train children of royal officials whose parents and relatives had presented them to the royal court, and let them perform it as their means and abilities would allow them. But let there be no recruiting of children of officials and people whose parents are not willing to present them to the royal court, and let there be no cause of trouble to parents on account of this royal command." At this time, there is not a single girl in the Rong Lakhon Luang Khang Nai [theatre of the dance-drama of the Inner Court] who has been forced into it. Then the King commanded that even though there is training of the Lakhon Luang Khang Nai, let the *lakhon phuying* of princes with *krom*, or of those without *krom* and royal officials, high and low, who have been in practice before or are to be newly trained, be freely allowed to train and perform. As there is no longer suppression, there is no need to hide the activities as in the past. (ibid.)

26. The Royal Decree stated,

> Concerning the *kan len lakhon* [the performing of dance-drama] in the city and country of Siam, in the past, from the time of the old capital of Ayudhaya to the reign of Phra Phuttha Loetla Naphalai [King Rama II], there was a tradition that the *lakhon* with an all-female cast, without any mixing of male dancers, could be performed only in the royal court and the Bowon court [the Palace of the Front of the second king, or deputy king] which are called the Wang Luang [Royal Palace] and Wang Na [Palace of the Front]. These *lakhon nai* troupes belonged to the royal court, or to the "Chaofa" [children of the queens] and "Phra Ong Chao" [children of consorts], all of whom were children of the Fai Nai [Inner Court]. Other than the Royal Palace and the Palace of the Front there was none in the palaces of other members of the royal family, or houses of noblemen, because it was feared that this might create in them an ambition to find beautiful women beyond their *wasana* [fortune they have deserved from merit made in past lives]. It would look as if they were contravening the intentions of the King concerning the Royal Lakhon. In the past, no dancers in the *lakhon phuying* of the King were supposed to be daughters of great noblemen of high rank. Girls were therefore selected who could perform before the public as if they were *chao chom yu ngan* [consorts in attendance on the king] and *phra sanom* [minor wives of lower status than *chao chom*] who were ladies of good families. For this reason, the King had to look for girls, and there were informers who advised the King on recruiting beautiful girls from the populace in different places, both in the city and the provinces. As these recruits from the common and lower officials were not enough, they also conscripted the daughters of higher officials who were *chao chom yu ngan* and disguised them to mix in with the cast and perform. Because of this, people who had beautiful daughters and did not wish to to send them to be virtually imprisoned in the royal court had to force them into having husbands, who would then be their legal owners. Some went into hiding for fear of the informers. Some made their daughters put medicine in their eyes to make them ill, or put medicine on their bodies and wrapped them up to make wounds which later could not be healed and sometimes became cancerous. Some made their daughters pretend to be chronically sick or insane, and so on, as we have all heard from older people for years now. Therefore, the *chao nai tang krom* [princes of *krom* rank appointed to be head of a department] and those who did not have *krom* rank and all the royal officials were afraid of the royal punishment and royal command. They could not train *lakhon phuying*. If they put on performances, they used only male dancers. In general practice, if there were any female dancers, they would perform only the roles of the heroine and the second lady, but in disguise so as to mix them up with the male dancers, and always in secret. Even in the reign of King Phra Phuttha Yotfa Chulalok [Rama I], there was *lakhon phuying* only in the royal court. In the Bowon court, there was only *khon* performed solely by sons of royal officials. There was not a single woman in it. (ibid.)

27. Prince Damrong, *Tamnan lakhon Inao*, p. 169.
28. Dhanit Yupho, *Silapa lakhon ram*, p. 294.
29. See the Royal Command concerning the Invocation Ceremony (Appendix A on p. 89); and "Ram boek rong Narai prap Nonthuk" [Opening dance of God Narai defeating Nonthuk] which was used as a part of the *Phra tamra khrop khon lakhon chabap luang* [*Khon* invocation ceremony, a royal version] and as a royal standard text of the *ram mae bot* (dance of the basic movements and gestures, i.e., in Thai classical dance).
30. "Prakat wa duai lakhon phuying" [The royal decree concerning female dance-drama], in *Nangsu thesaphiban* [Rules and regulations of interior affairs], vol. 8, p. 48 (1 March 1909).
31. Prince Damrong, *Tamnan lakhon Inao*, p. 135.
32. The Royal Decree (1861), in King Mongkut, *Chotmaihet ratchakan thi 4*. In the *Prachum phongsawadan*, it is mentioned that the *Ngiu Wang Na* (Chinese opera of the Palace of the Front) was started in the reign of King Rama II by Krom Phra Ratchawang Bowon Phra Pin Klao, the second king, who had a male Chinese opera troupe which presented themselves to him for his patronage. It is stated, "High-ranking members of the royal family in the past had *ngiu* in their patronage in this way. They did not train the performers themselves" (vol. 11, pp. 132–33).
33. Prince Damrong, *Tamnan lakhon Inao*.
34. These objects were royal exports and merchandise, or royal gifts to foreign rulers and important foreign representatives. In the *Prachum phongsawadan*, it is stated, "rhino horns, elephant tusks, and birds' wings are gifts to foreign customers" (vol. 2, p. 225) and "tin, rhino horns, and elephant tusks are royal merchandise" (p. 239).
35. The Royal Decree (1861), in King Mongkut, *Chotmaihet ratchakan thi 4*.
36. Dhanit Yupho, *Khon*, pp. 53, 55.
37. According to Prince Damrong, the *lakhon khaek* or *lakhon mayong malayu* (Malay *makyong*) may have been brought into Bangkok by the Malays (the *khaek*) from Pattani and Saiburi, but the date is uncertain. The most famous troupe in the reign of King Mongkut was the "Lakhon Ta Sua" troupe. The dancers dressed in Malay costumes and sang in Malay, but spoke in Thai. They performed the *Inao yai* [The greater tale of Inao] of King Rama I. See Prince Damrong, *Tamnan lakhon Inao*, p. 191.
38. Ibid. pp. 189–91.
39. The Royal Decree (1861), in King Mongkut, *Chotmaihet ratchakan thi 4*.
40. Prince Damrong, *Tamnan lakhon Inao*, p. 174.
41. Ibid., pp. 175, 177.
42. In the reign of King Mongkut, a Chinese man called Chin Nim (later Khun Sammatcha-thikon) was the first entertainment tax officer (ibid., p. 175).
43. Ibid., p. 178.
44. Ibid., pp. 179–80.
45. See notes on the subjects of gambling and taxation on gambling (Appendix C on p. 92).
46. Dhanit Yupho, *Khon*, p. 93.
47. Prince Damrong, *Tamnan lakhon Inao*, p. 181.
48. See also Neon Snidvongs, "The Development of Siamese Relations with Britain and France in the Reign of King Maha Mongkut, 1851–1868."
49. Prince Damrong, *Tamnan lakhon Inao*, p. 182.
50. Ibid., pp. 183–84.
51. For example, Chao Chom Manda Wat (later Thao Warachan, grandmother of Prince Dhaninivat), renowned for her role of Inao, became a dance mistress in the Fifth and Sixth Reigns; Chao Chom Manda Khien (mother of Prince Narathip), famous in the role of Inao also, was a dance mistress of the Pridalai Troupe of Prince Narathip in the Fifth Reign.

There were also Chao Chom Manda Sun, Chao Chom Manda Sai, Thao Chun, and many others (ibid., pp. 191–95).

52. "Somnao mai rapsang nai ratchakan thi 4, ruang wai khru lakhon luang mua pi khan cha sok phǫ sǫ 2397" (Prince Damrong, *Tamnan lakhon Inao*, p. 86).

53. King Vajiravudh originated the idea that the mask of the Rishi was that of Bharata Rishi, teacher of the *Bharata Natayasastra* in Indian classical dance (Dhanit Yupho, *Silapa lakhon ram*, p. 296).

54. An ogre in the *Ramakien* who is respected as a great teacher of Thai classical dance-drama (Mattani Rutnin, "Khwam pen ma khong Phra Phirap").

55. *Nora chatri* is respected as the earliest form of Thai dance-drama.

56. Dhanit Yupho, *Silapa lakhon ram*, p. 294.

57. Ibid., pp. 323–34.

58. Prince Damrong, *Tamnan lakhon Inao*, pp. 175–77.

59. Ibid., p. 178.

60. Suthiwong Phongphaibun, *Nang talung*, pp. 2–3.

61. Kukurit Pramoj, "Liké," in *Natasin lae dontri Thai* [Thai classical dance and music], p. 93.

62. See *Prachum phongsawadan*, vol. 12; and *Phra ratchahatthalekha song sang ratchakan nai ratchakan thi 5 lae thi 6* [Royal manuscripts concerning the royal commandments in state affairs during the Fifth and Sixth Reigns], pp. 227–29.

Chapter III

1. Prince Damrong, *Tamnan lakhon Inao*, p. 214.

2. See also King Chulalongkorn, *Phra borom rachowat* [Royal addresses to Crown Prince Wachirunahit], nos. 1 & 2 (1893), published by the Krom Silapakon, Bangkok, 1960.

3. See *Ruang phra rachanukit* of King Chulalongkorn.

4. Ibid.

5. Phra Sawet, captured in Chiengmai, and Phra Maha Raphiphan Khotchaphong, captured in Nakhon Sithammarat in 1870.

6. This dance is a ritualistic dance, depicting thunder (Ramasun), lightning (Mekkhala), and rain (Orachun), which are important in an agricultural society.

7. Prince Damrong, *Tamnan lakhon Inao*, p. 197.

8. All dancers were teachers of *lakhon nai* in the Fourth Reign and had performed this play in the Second Reign in the same roles, namely, Khun Bua (King Samon), Khun Thao Worachanmalai (Phra Sang), Khun Kham (Chao Ngo), Khun Chat (who had performed the role of Lasam in the *Inao* of King Rama II, now performed the role of the elder son-in-law), Khun A-ngun (Sida role in the Second Reign, now Nang Montha), Khun Iam (Busba role in *Inao* in the Second Reign, now Nang Rotchana), and Khun Kham (Bayan role in *Inao* in the Second Reign, now a big sister of Rotchana). As these ladies were rather advanced in age, the production may have been for the purpose of demonstrating the grand style and artistic abilities of these *khru* (teachers) as models for the later generation. A similar type of production in which elderly dancers of the previous reigns performed for the king and his court was to welcome the return of King Chulalongkorn from Europe in 1897 (ibid.).

9. Namely, Nai Tai (comedian, originally belonging to the troupe of Prince Phuminphakdi in the Fourth Reign, now a *khaluang* [courtier] of King Chulalongkorn), playing the role of Orachun (Arjuna, the god of rain), Nai Khamtrae (role of Mekkhala, the goddess of lighting), Nai Ruang (dance teacher in the Second Reign, role of Ramasun, the god of thunder) (ibid.).

10. Ibid., p. 148.

11. Dhanit Yupho, *Khon*, p. 53.
12. Dhanit Yupho, *Silapa lakhon ram*, pp. 77–78.
13. See *Ruang phra rachanukit* of King Chulalongkorn.
14. See chiefly illustrations in Gerini, *Chŭlăkantamaṅgala: The Tonsure Ceremony as Performed in Siam;* and Dohring, *Siam: Land und Volk.*
15. See reproductions in King Chulalongkorn, *Phra racthaphithi sip song duan.*
16. Prince Damrong, *Tamnan lakhon Inao*, p. 199.
17. Ibid.
18. Dhanit Yupho, *Khon*, p. 55.
19. Ibid.
20. Prince Damrong, *Tamnan lakhon Inao*, p. 204.
21. In 1888, Siam lost 87,000 sq.km of territory (twelve provinces in the northeast) to France. The second and the most crucial loss in 1893—143,800 sq.km and 600,000 Thai citizens— deeply affected the king. The third loss in 1903 was the territory on the right bank of the Mekhong River, 62,500 sq.km. The last one, in 1906, was the eastern provinces of Siamrat, Sisophon, and Phratabong, 51,000 sq.km.
22. Prince Damrong, *Tamnan lakhon Inao*, p. 199.
23. Ibid., p. 203.
24. Ibid., pp. 202–3 and 121 (cast list).
25. Ibid., p. 203.
26. Ibid., pp. 204–10.
27. Ibid., p. 205.
28. Ibid., p. 207.
29. Her name Khlai, one of the keepers of caged birds in the royal palace in the Fifth Reign (ibid., p. 151).
30. Ibid., pp. 209–10.
31. Ibid., p. 212. *Chak* (chakra) means a discus associated with the god Vishunu and thus imperial status, "kings"; *wong* (dynasty) is often used as an epithet in the names of the heroes, for example, Suriya*wong*, Thina*wong*, Laksana*wong*, etc. These stories are also called *ruang sam rudu* (stories of three seasons).
32. Prince Damrong's preface to King Chulalongkorn, *Wongthewarat* [Dynasty of the deva-raja].
33. Prince Damrong, *Tamnan lakhon Inao*, pp. 214–16.
34. All later titles of these treachers were granted by King Vajiravudh in his reign.
35. Quoted in Dhanit Yupho, *Khon*, p. 59; emphasis by Mattani Rutnin.
36. King Chulalongkorn, *Samnao phra ratchahatthalekha . . . phra ratchathan Krom Phra Narathip Praphanphong* [Personal correspondence to Prince Narathip], p. 28 (letter dated 15 August 1909).
37. Somphop Chantharaprapha, "Phra Piya Maharat kap kan lakhon" [King Chulalongkorn and drama], lecture given at the American University Alumni Association, Bangkok, n.d.
38. King Chulalongkorn, *Lilit Nithra Chakhrit*, pp. 2, 224. The second known version of the *Arabian Nights* is the *Arap Ratri* by Prince Narathip written in *klon* poetry and published in 1888, ten years after the *Nithra Chakhrit* of King Chulalongkorn. It was also frequently performed in the style of the *lakhon phan thang* in the Fifth Reign and later, for example, by the *lakhon* troupe of Mom Tuan Worawan, consort of Prince Narathip. The publishing house was set up in the palace of Prince Narathip and was hence called the "Rongphim Arap Ratri" (The Arabian Nights Publishing House). See King Chulalongkorn, *Samnao phra ratchahatthalekha . . .* phra ratchathan Krom Phra Narathip Praphanphong, p. 91 (appendix on the Lakhon Pridalai).

39. On this auspicious day, there was a royal ceremony called the *Phithi Samphatcharachin*, a celebration on the 14th–15th days of the waning moon, fourth month, and the first day of the rising moon in the fifth month, in which the *naksat* (the animal of the year) is changed, but the *sok* (the number of the year) is not changed until Songkran Day, which usually falls on 15 April.

40. King Chulalongkorn, *Lilit Nithra Chakhrit*, pp. 222–23.

41. Prince Damrong, *Tamnan lakhon Inao*, p. 198. See also the discussion on the *lakhon phut* on pp. 150–54.

42. King Chulalongkorn, *Lilit Nithra Chakhrit*, p. 226.

43. Krom Mun Phichit Prichakon.

44. They were King Chulalongkorn, Princess Butri, Prince Phichit (Krom Mun Phichit-prichakon), Prince Thewan Uthaiwong (later Somdet Krom Phraya Thewawong Waropakon), Prince Sawat (later Somdet Krom Phra Sawattiwatthanawisit), Phra Sisunthonwohan, and a *nak-ngan* (secretary, clerk, or official). See King Chulalongkorn, *Lilit Nithra Chakhrit*, p. 227.

45. Ibid., p. 224.

46. Part 1, Luang Phisanuseni (later Phra Ratchamanu), teacher of *sepha;* part 2, Phraya Maha Ammat; part 3, Khun Wisutseni; part 4, Khun Phinitchai (later Luang Phiromkosa); part 5, Luang Banhan Atthakhadi (later Phra Phiromracha); part 6, Khun Wisutthakon (later Phraya Isaraphansophon); part 7, Phraya Sisunthonwohan; part 8, Khun Thongsu (later Luang Mongkhonratana); part 9, Luang Seniphithak (later Phraya Ratchawaranukun); part 10, Luang Smoson Phonlakan (later Phraya Smoson Saphakan); part 11, Luang Chakrapani (Prince Damrong's preface to *Sepha ruang Abu Hassan* [*The Arabian Nights* in *sepha* poetry], pp. 1–2).

47. King Chulalongkorn, *Ngo pa*, praface, pp. 1–2.

48. Ibid.

49. *Rua mat*, a barge carved out of a tree trunk.

50. King Chulalongkorn, *Ngo pa*, preface, p. 23; emphasis by Mattani Rutnin.

51. Ibid., p. 4.

52. Ibid.

53. Ibid., p. 2.

54. Wisetchaisi, "Phra Piya Maharat kap Ngo pa" [King Chulalongkorn and *Ngo pa*], p. 38.

55. See the synopsis in Appendix on pp. 155–56.

56. Prince Damrong, *Tamnan lakhon Inao*, p. 212.

57. Pin Malakul (Mom Luang), *Ngan lakhon khong Phrabat Somdet . . . Phra Mongkut Klao Chao Phaendin Sayam* [Dramatic activities of King Vajiravudh], p. 53.

58. Aphon Montrisat and Chaturong Montrisat, *Wicha natasin* [The study of the art of classical dance], p. 106.

59. See King Chulalongkorn, *Samnao phra ratchahatthalekha . . . phra ratchathan Krom Phra Narathip Praphanphong*.

60. Reynolds, "The Case of K.S.R. Kulāp," pp. 63–90.

61. King Chulalongkorn, *Samnao phra ratchahatthalekha . . . phra ratchathan Krom Phra Narathip Praphanphong*, p. 17 (letter dated 15 February 1908).

62. King Chulalongkorn's personal letter to Chao Dararatsami, dated 2 July 1909, collected in Prayut Sitthiphan, *Rak nai ratchasamnak* [Love in the royal court], p. 302.

63. King Chulalongkorn's letter, dated 29 June 1909, in ibid., pp. 311–12.

64. King Chulalongkorn, *Samnao phra ratchahatthalekha . . . phra ratchathan Krom Phra Narathip Praphanphong*, p. 5 (letter dated 23 January 1908).

65. Ibid.

66. Ibid., p. 6 (letter dated 24 January 1908).

67. Prince Naris, *Chumnum bot lakhon lae bot khap rong* [Collected plays and songs], p. 4.

68. Ibid., pp. 4–5.

69. The best example of his architectural design is perhaps the "Marble Temple," or Wat Benchamabophit, in Bangkok, designed and constructed in the Fifth Reign and continued in the Sixth Reign.

70. Pin Malakul (Mom Luang), *Ngan lakhon khong Phrabat Somdet . . . Phra Mongkut Klao Chao Phaendin Sayam,* pp. 26–27, 30–31.

71. Ibid., p. 74.

72. *Ok phasa tang tang* are the variations or improvisations in different languages, i.e., musical languages, or cultures, as earlier discussed in the *lakhon phan thang.*

73. Prince Naris' letter to Phraya Anuman Rajadhon, quoted in Prince Naris, *Chumnum bot lakhon lae bot khap rong,* p. 8.

74. Prince Naris' letter to Phraya Anuman Rajadhon, dated in 29 August 1941, in Prince Naris, *Banthuk ruang khwam ru tang tang* [Notes on various educational subjects], vol. 5, pp. 24–25.

75. Prince Naris then was still H.R.H. Chaofa Kromakhun Narisaranuwattiwong, the king's brother. See Prince Naris, *Chumnum bot lakhon lae bot khap rong,* pp. 373–86.

76. Ibid., p. 331.

77. Ibid.

78. Ibid., p. 332.

79. In the original version of King Rama II, they are Chinese merchants. Prince Naris may have wished to create an exotic Vietnamese lantern dance here.

80. Prince Naris, *Chumnum bot lakhon lae bot khap rong,* p. 195. This note was written later, on 4 September 1933, at the "Ban Somprasong" at Hua Hin.

81. Ibid., p. 207. Personal note written at "Ban Somprasong" at Hua Hin, on 9 September 1933.

82. Ibid., p. 208.

83. Ibid., p. 289.

84. Ibid., p. 28.

85. Ibid., p. 25.

86. Ibid.

87. King Chulalongkorn, *Samnao phra ratchahatthalekha . . . phra ratchathan Krom Phra Narathip Praphanphong,* p. 306 (letter to Chao Dararatsami, dated 24 April 1909).

88. Prince Damrong & Prince Naris, *San Somdet* [Princes' correspondence], vol. 14 (Prince Damrong's letter to Prince Naris, dated 1 December 1938).

89. King Chulalongkorn, *Samnao phra ratchahatthalekha . . . phra ratchathan Krom Phra Narathip Praphanphong,* pp. 306–7 (letter to Chao Dararatsami, dated 24 April 1909); emphasis by Mattani Rutnin.

90. Ibid., pp. 310–11 (letter to Chao Dararatsami, dated 2 July 1909).

91. Ibid., p. 311

92. Dr. Uthit Naksawat, Sinuan Kaeobuasai, and Phraruhat Bunlong, "Discussion on Prince Narathip and the *Lakhon Rong,*" unpublished lecture at the National Library, 1976.

93. Since most performances were given for a week, the theatre was hence called a *week* or *wik* in the Thai pronunciation of English.

94. King Chulalongkorn, *Samnao phra ratchahatthalekha . . . phra ratchathan Krom Phra Narathip Praphanphong,* p. 311 (letter to Chao Dararatsami, dated 29 June 1909).

95. The expression *kam kam bae bae* was coined by Chao Chom Manda Thieng, referring to the inferior dancing of the *Malay Bangsawan* opera-ballet, which was performed in Bangkok after King Chulalongkorn's trip to the Malay Peninsula where it was first presented to the

king in 1891. See Prince Damrong and Prince Naris, *San Somdet*, vol. 14 (Prince Damrong's letter to Prince Naris, dated 1 December 1938).

96. *The Siamese Theatre*, ed. Mattani Rutnin, pp. 263–91.
97. From an interview.
98. King Chulalongkorn, *Samnao phra ratchahatthalekha . . . phra ratchathan Krom Phra Narathip Praphanphong*, p. 43 (letter dated 16 January 1910).
99. Ibid., pp. 37–38 (letter dated 19 December 1909).
100. Ibid., pp. 20–21 (letter dated 25 April 1909).
101. Prince Damrong, *Tamnan lakhon Inao*, p. 168.
102. The full account of her illness and death was recorded in Prayut Sitthiphan, *Somdet Phra Chom Klao Chao Krung Sayam* [King Mongkut of Siam].
103. The *lakhon* troupe of Krom Phra Phiphitphokphuben was known to be the best in terms of dancing quality in the reign of King Rama III. See Prince Damrong, *Tamnam lakhon Inao*, p. 159.
104. King Chulalongkorn, *Samnao phra ratchahatthalekha . . . phra ratchathan Krom Phra Narathip Praphanphong*, p. 89 (Lakhon Pridalai).
105. Ibid., pp. 7–8.
106. Ibid., p. 8.
107. See note 104 above.
108. Prince Damrong, *Tamnan lakhon Inao*, p. 198.
109. Pin Malakul (Mom Luang), *Ngan lakhon khong Phrabat Somdet . . . Phra Mongkut Klao Chao Phaendin Sayam*, p. 269.
110. King Vajiravudh, *Thawi Panya*, 4 May 1904; translation in ibid., p. 54.
111. Ibid., p. 270.
112. Pin Malakul (Mom Luang), *Ngan lakhon khong Phrabat Somdet . . . Phra Mongkut Klao Chao Phaendin Sayam*, pp. 40, 54–57, 88, 90, 91, 94–97.
113. Ibid.
114. Ibid.
115. Ibid.
116. The play *Ngo pa* is written in the traditional form of a *bot lakhon*, without division into acts and scenes. However, for structural purposes, the synopsis that follows is divided into scenes, or *ton*, as it was usually done in actual performance.
117. This scene was later performed for the first time by Khanang under King Chulalongkorn's direction. Khanang also learned to dance the classical movements and steps from Mom Phuan Bunnag, wife of Somdet Chao Phraya Sisuriyawong. One writer recorded the event from memory,

> At first, the teacher was worried that it would be as difficult to train him [Khanang] as to train monkeys in *lakhon ling* [monkeys' dance-drama], but we were mistaken. Though the teacher did not drill him seriously and there was little time for training, when on stage, Khanang was able to dance correctly to the rhythm in every part, albeit the *ram na phat* or *ram chai bot*. Those acquainted with him and fond of him were moved to tears with sympathy in as much as he, being so small and, moreover, a jungle boy, made such an effort to do it so well. (Wisetchaisi, "Phra Piya Maharat kap Ngo pa," p. 38)

Ram na phat is set dances to special tunes for particular actions and emotions, such as *smoe* (going from one place to another); *bat skuni* is the ceremonial procession or walk of a royal person; and *ram chai bot* is an interpretative dance following a narrative or dialogue, i.e., dancing to the lyrics.

Chapter IV

1. Pin Malakul (Mom Luang), *Ngan lakhon khong Phrabat Somdet . . . Phra Mongkut Klao Chao Phaendin Sayam*, p. 54.
2. Ibid., p. 91.
3. They are the *kham phak* and *bot rong* of the following episodes as appear in Valmiki's *Ramayana*: *Sida hai, Phao Longka, Phiphet thuk khap, Chong thanon, Pradoem suk Longka, Sukhrip hak chat, Ongkhot su san*, and *Nakhabat*.
4. They are *bot boek rong* for *khon* performance: *Apisek somrot* (of Phra Ram and Sida, and other brothers of Phra Ram): part 1, *Prap tataka*; part 2, *Aphisek somrot*. The texts were written for the performance of the Khon Samak Len troupe. The story follows Valmiki's *Ramayana*. There are also *bot boek rong* for *lakhon dukdamban*: *Phra Pharot boek rong, Maha Phali, Sudawatan, Rusi siang luk, Phra Norasinghawatan, Phra Khanet Sia Nga, Ramasun ching kaeo*, and *Orachun kap Thosakan*.
5. They are *Nang Loi, Phrommat, Surapanakha ma hung, Phra Ram tam kwang, Phiphek thuk khap, Chong thanon*, and *Sukasaran plom phon*.
6. They are *bot lakhon ram* performed in the style of *khon, Phra Kiatirot, Thammathamma songkhram, Thamma mi chai, Mit mi chai, Phra Nala*; and in the style of *lakhon, Thao saen pom* and *Suphalak wat rup* (*Unarut*).
7. Pin Malakul (Mom Luang), *Ngan lakhon khong Phrabat Somdet . . . Phra Mongkut Klao Chao Phaendin Sayam*, pp. 37–39.
8. Vella, "Siamese Nationalism in the Plays of Rama VI," pp. 181–91.
9. Quoted in Pin Malakul (Mom Luang), *Ngan lakhon khong Phrabat Somdet . . . Phra Mongkut Klao Chao Phaendin Sayam*, p. 145.
10. From personal interviews with Mom Luang Pin Malakul, who was one of the young royal pages chosen to read these plays at the royal dining table.
11. See Atcharaphon Kamutphitsamai, "Kan borihan phaendin nai samai Phrabat Somdet Phra Mongkut Klao Chao Yu Hua" [State administration during the reign of King Vajiravudh].
12. See Phonphen Huntrakun, "Kan chai chai ngoen phaendin nai ratchasamai Phrabat Somdet Phra Mongkut Klao Chao Yu Hua (B.E. 2453–2468)" [National expenditures during the reign of King Vajiravudh, 1910–25].
13. *Chotmaihet Phra Ratchaphithi Borom Rachaphisek Somdet Phra Ramathibodi Sisinthara Maha Wachirawut Phra Mongkut Klao Chao Yu Hua* [Record of the coronation of King Vajiravudh], edited by Prince Naresuanrit, 1923, reprint 1975, pp. 1–2.
14. Dhanit Yupho, *Silapa lakhon ram*, p. 330.
15. See *Dusit Thani muang prachathipatai khong Phrabat Somdet Phra Mongkut Klao Chao Yu Hua* [Dusit Thani, the democratic city of King Vajiravudh]; also Atcharaphon Kamutphitsamai, "Kan borihan phaendin nai samai Phrabat Somdet Phra Mongkut Klao Chao Yu Hua."
16. Dhanit Yupho, *Khon*, pp. 71–72.
17. Those departments include Krom Khon Luang (Royal Khon Department, with Phraya Natakanurak as head), Krom Piphat Luang (Royal Thai Orchestra Department, with Phraya Prasanduriyang as head), Krom Chang (Royal Artisans Department, with Phraya Anusat Chitakon as head), and Kong Khruang Sai Farang Luang (Royal Western String Orchestra, with Phra Praditphairo as head and Phra Chenduriyang as deputy head).
18. Prince Damrong, *Tamra fon ram* [The lessons of Thai dance], p. 1.
19. Sisuda, former wife of Phra Anirut in *Unarut*.
20. Dhanit Yupho, *Silapa lakhon ram*, p. 18.
21. Ibid., p. 41.

22. Ibid., p. 64.
23. A-khom Sayakhom, "Fuk hat lakhon luang nai ratchakan thi 7" [Training of the Lakhon Luang during the Seventh Reign], pp. 131–38.
24. As of 1992 the Witthayalai Natasin has a total of 1,745 students (422 male, 1,323 female), in a four-level curriculum that takes ten years to complete Foundation Level (3 years), Intermediate Level (3 years), Advanced Level (2 years), and College Level (2 years). There are eight fields of study:

> *Lakhon* (dance-drama): 1,019 students (all female)
> *Khon* (masked dance-drama): 203 students (all male)
> *Khruang sai* (classical Thai string orchestra): 121 students (male and female)
> *Piphat* (Thai full orchestra): 158 students (male and female)
> Thai music: 48 students (male and female)
> Western orchestra: 93 students (male and female)
> Western music: 35 students (male and female)
> Western dance: 67 students (male and female)

There are 208 teachers, 139 in performing arts and 69 in general education (see details in Table 1, p. 177).

At the National Theatre itself, there is the Kongkan Sangkhit, a separate Department of Dance and Music with its own experts and performing artists selected from the top graduates of the Witthayalai Natasin. They perform regular shows for the public and special shows for foreign dignitaries, royal visitors, and royal and governmental functionaries. They also travel abroad to promote Thai art, culture, and tourism. There are at present over 100 artists (male and female) in classical dance and music. In larger *khon* and *lakhon* productions, dancers and musicians from both institutions (Kongkan Sangkhit and Witthayalai Natasin) are chosen to perform. During the last decade, these performing artists have had to earn extra income by performing for tourists at restaurants and hotels in order to survive in the present economic hardship. Most of the shows are shortened versions of the classical performances, which is one reason for the decline in artistic quality. However, on the other hand, tourism helps to expand the horizon of Thai dance and music. A leading first-class hotel, The Oriental Hotel, offers regular lectures and training courses in Thai art, culture, and performing arts for their foreign guests and residents. The lectures and courses are organized by the Drama Department of Thammasat University (under the writer's direction), in cooperation with Witthayalai Natasin, Kongkan Sangkhit, and Chulalongkorn University. This programme started in October 1990.

Chapter V

1. There are now over seven hundred stories in the collection kept by the National Library. See *The Siamese Theatre,* ed. Mattani Rutnin, pp. 263–91.
2. Suraphon Wirunrak, *Liké.*
3. "Kukrit kap nang" [Kukrit and film], *Nang* (Thira Kan Phim), 1974, p. 77.
4. From Rongrian Nataduriyangkhasat to Rongrian Silapakon, to Rongrian Sang-khitsin in 1942, and to Rongrian Natasin in 1945.

Chapter VI

1. Many plays, stage dramas, and television programmes based on the heroic deeds of Queen Sisuriyothai of Ayudhaya have been performed in Queen Sirikit's honour to identify the present queen with her Ayudhaya model.
2. Kukrit Pramoj, "Khang sangwian" [At ringside], *Sayam Rat,* 20 February 1978, p. 7.

3. A great variety of traditional and modern performing arts have been continuously presented from 1991 to 1993 to celebrate H.M. Queen Sirikit's sixtieth birthday in 1992. This is apparently the longest celebration for a single royal person.

4. A facility donated by the Japanese government.

5. With the support of ASEAN, many new experimental theatres have presented interesting modernized forms of traditional dance-drama, such as *Singha Kraiphop,* a mixture of *lakhon chatri, lakhon nok,* and modern jazz dance in Brechtian stage design by Patravadi Theatre in 1992–93.

6. According to historical records, Anna was never granted an audience with the king and was a very insignificant English teacher who stayed in Siam for only a short period of time.

7. The writing of this section is based on research findings and a report of Wandee Limpiwattana of Drama Department, Thammasat University, Bangkok, 1985.

8. Their headquarters address is 269 Lad-plao 50, Village no. 11, Wua Thonglang, Bangkapi, Bangkok 10310.

Chapter VII

1. *Prachum phra ratchaphongsawadan* [A collection of royal chronicles], vol. 11, p. 66.

2. Ibid., p. 74.

3. *Ruang phra rachanukit* [Accounts of royal activities], p. 12.

4. *Chotmaihet phra ratchakit raiwan* [Memoirs of the kings' daily activities from B.E. 2411, end of the Fourth Reign, to the beginning of the Fifth Reign], p. 3, n. 1.

5. The last deputy king in the Bangkok period, after whose death King Chulalongkorn abolished the tradition and replaced it by investing his eldest son, Prince Wachirunahit, as crown prince.

6. *Prachum phra ratchaphongsawadan*, vol. 11, p. 107.

7. *Chotmaihet phra ratchakit raiwan*, p. 3, n. 1.

8. Prince Damrong, *Tamnan lakhon Inao,* p. 200.

9. Prince Naris, *Chumnum bot lakhon lae bot khap rong* [Collected plays and songs], pp. 5–7, 10 (Duangchit Chitaphong's preface).

10. Ibid., p. 9.

11. Prince Damrong, *Tamnan lakhon Inao,* p. 206.

12. Ibid.

13. Ibid.

14. King Chulalongkorn, *Samnao phra ratchahatthalekha . . . phra ratchathan Krom Phra Narathip Praphanphong,* p. 92 (appendix on the Lakhon Pridalai).

15. Ibid., p. 47 (letter dated 19 January 1909).

16. Pin Malakul (Mom Luang), *Ngan lakhon khong Phrabat Somdet . . . Phra Mongkut Klao Chao Phaendin Sayam,* p. 53; Dhanit Yupho, *Silapa lakhon ram,* p. 79.

17. Pin Malakul (Mom Luang), *Ngan lakhon khong Phrabat Somdet . . . Phra Mongkut Klao Chao Phaendin Sayam,* p. 53.

18. Ibid.

19. Ibid., pp. 2, 52.

20. Dhanit Yupho, *Silapa lakhon ram,* p. 88.

21. The Witthayalai Natasin (College of Dance and Music) is, however, a separate unit and is situated in the compound of the Wang Na (Palace of the Front) next to the theatre.

22. Dhanit Yupho, *Khon,* p. 39.

23. Thawisak Senanarong, a former director of the Krom Silapakon, in an interview with this writer, once questioned the necessity of maintaining this backcloth screen, since it no longer serves the original purpose. However, having considered its symbolism and ritual

importance, he agreed that it should remain there as an object of worship for *khon* dancers. In its present form, it is only a transparent piece of cloth, almost invisible to the untrained eye.

24. Mentioned in King Chulalongkorn, *Kham cheracha lakhon ruang Inao* [The dialogue of the dance-drama *Inao*].

25. Prince Naris, *Chumnum bot lakhon lae bot khap rong*, p. 5.

26. Prince Naris when drawing this set for the *Inao* had not yet visited Java. He had probably seen pictures of Javanese temples. It was not until after his retirement that he went to Indonesia in 1937–38.

27. Quoted by Princess Duangchit Chitraphong in Prince Naris, *Chumnum bot lakhon lae bot khap rong*, p. 10 (preface).

28. Ibid.

29. King Chulalongkorn, *Samnao phra ratchahatthalekha . . . phra ratchathan Krom Phra Narathip Praphanphong*, p. 43 (letter dated 6 January 1909).

30. From an interview with the writer in 1977.

31. From an interview.

32. Interviews with both Dhanit Yupho and Khru Mot confirm this fact.

33. From the same interviews.

34. From an interview with Khru Mot.

35. Such as the Khon Luang and Lakhon Luang troupes and the Chang Sip Mu (ten groups of artisans who worked in the royal service, i.e., painters, sculptors, woodcarvers, puppet makers, upholsters, etc.).

36. This information was given by Luang Wichit's wife, Khunying Praphaphan Wichituan-thakan, in an interview with the writer in 1976.

37. From an interview in 1977.

38. *Hanamichi*, a forty-five-feet elevated walk running through the audience and connecting the stage with the back of the theatre house in Japanese *kabuki*. It is used as an auxiliary acting area on which important movements of the plays and entrances and exit of important charac-ters are performed in the midst of the spectators. See Bowers, *Theatre in the East*, p. 331.

39. *Kinnari*, a female half-bird, half-woman mythological creature.

40. From an interview with Khru Mot in 1977.

41. This is an example to show how top positions in the government after the Revolution of 1932 were usually given to members of the Revolutionary Party who do not necessarily have the suitable abilities for the posts. It is still in practice today. Trips abroad are often pleasure trips under the label of *du ngan* (observation of work, i.e., in foreign countries for the purpose of learning new methods and techniques of the more developed countries).

42. From an interview with Mom Phaeo in 1976.

43. See Bibliography.

44. See chiefly Sukhothai stone inscription no. 2 (Wat Si-Chum).

45. King Rama I's decree, quoted in Prince Damrong, *Tamnan lakhon Inao*, p. 27.

46. Ibid., p. 171.

47. See King Vajiravudh's note to Phraya Wisutsuriyasak concerning his experiment in using natural make-up for Trichada in *Nang Loi,* quoted in M.L. Pin Malakul, *Ngan lakhon khong Phrabat Somdet . . . Phra Mongkut Klao Chao Phaendin Sayam,* and Prince Naris, "Silapakan taeng na" [The art of make-up] in his *Chumnum bot lakhon lae bot khap rong,* pp. 11–17.

Glossary

Types of Traditional Thai Performing Arts

Words set in SMALL CAPS in the explanation are defined elsewhere in the Glossary.

KHON: Masked dance-drama, traditionally performed by men. Normally the stories performed are taken from different episodes in the *Ramakien* (Thai version of the epic *Ramayana*).

LAKHON: Dance-drama. The various types of LAKHON are:

LAKHON RAM: Dance-drama proper, divided into the following sub-types:

LAKHON NAI or LAKHON NANG NAI: Classical dance-drama, traditionally performed by the ladies of the Inner Court (Fai Nai) exclusively for the king and the inner circle of the royal court. The dance style is very refined and sophisticated. The plays performed in this style are the *Ramakien, Inao,* and *Unarut.* At present, only *Inao* is performed.

LAKHON NOK or LAKHON NOK PHRA RATCHATHAN: Dance-drama performed traditionally by men outside the royal court. Later, there are mixed casts. Characteristics peculiar to LAKHON NOK are a sense of humour, passages of comic relief, and plots based on adventure stories derived mostly from *Jataka* tales, such as *Phra Suthon* (more popularly known as *Manohra*), *Sangthong, Suwannahong, Sangsichai, Kraithong,* and *Maniphichai.*

LAKHON NORA CHATRI: Believed by some authorities to be the earliest form of dance-drama in Siam. There are two theories as to its origin. One theory, expounded by Prince Damrong, states that NORA CHATRI originated in Ayudhaya and was later brought south by Khun Sattha. The other theory purports just the opposite, that the dance-drama was later brought from the south up to central Siam. The plays are chiefly *Manohra* and other *Jataka* tales.

LAKHON CHATRI: Dance-drama developed from NORA CHATRI and LAKHON NOK in central Siam. The stories performed are usually from LAKHON NOK.

LIKÉ: Dance-drama which was developed from LAKHON CHATRI, LAKHON NOK, and *dirke,* the religious chanting of an Islamic sect in southern Siam, the *khaek chao sen* (Malay-Muslims of the Hussein sect). The stories performed are taken from LAKHON CHATRI or from recent or contemporary incidents and situations.

LAKHON DUKDAMBAN: Classical dance-drama operetta created by Prince Naris and Chao Phraya Thewet during the Fifth Reign. The dancers sing and dance without the traditional chorus singing the narrations. The style of dancing and the costumes are similar to those of LAKHON NAI, i.e., refined and sophisticated. The stories are taken both from LAKHON NAI and LAKHON NOK.

LAKHON PHAN THANG: Dance-drama in historical settings with costumes of different nationalities mixed with those of the Thai. The style of dancing is similar to that of LAKHON NOK. The most well-known plays are *Khun Chang Khun Phaen, Phra Aphaimani, Rachathirat,* and *Phra Lọ.*

LAKHON RONG: Dance-drama operetta (originated in the Fifth Reign) in contemporary settings. The actor-dancers sing and speak their parts and perform some dance movements to demonstrate the lyrics. The stories are usually translations from, or adaptations of, foreign tales or contemporary incidents and situations. The costumes are contemporary as well.

LAKHON PHUT: Spoken drama, in which actors speak the dialogue in verse (*lakhon phut kham klon*) or in prose (*lakhon phut roi kaeo*). This is a modern Western import introduced at the end of the Fifth Reign and developed fully by King Vajiravudh.

NANG YAI: Shadow-play in which puppets made of leather are projected on the screen by dancers who perform KHON dance movements while manipulating the puppets.

HUN: Puppets. There are different kinds of HUN:

HUN YAI: Big puppets with arms and legs manipulated by strings from below. They perform classical dance-drama such as the *Ramakien.*

HUN LEK: Smaller puppets similar to HUN YAI, but on a smaller scale.

LAKHON LEK: Small puppets performing stories from LAKHON NOK.

HUN KRABOK: Bamboo rod puppets with arms only, manipulated by bamboo rods. They perform stories from LAKHON NOK and LAKHON PHAN THANG, for example, *Phra Aphaimani* and *Suwannahong,* and later but rarely the *Ramakien.*

HUN CHIN: Chinese puppets.

MONGKHRUM: The ceremonial drum dance.

KULA TI MAI: The ceremonial baton dance.

RABENG: Ceremonial arch and arrow dance of a religious origin.

PHLENG CHOI: Folk singing with male and female singers, exchanging witty words.

NGIU: Chinese opera.

MAHORASOP (Skt., *mahotsava,* "great celebration"): Various types of entertainment at ceremonies and celebrations on important state occasions. Those most often mentioned in the chronicles and literature are: KHON, LAKHON, *nang, rabam,* NGIU, RABENG, MONGKHRUM, KULA TI MAI, *thaeng wisai, kra-ua thaeng khwai, ram prop kai, singto, ram mon, ram dap, tai luat, muai, lot buang, ram phaen, hok khamen, ram khom, krabi krabong, tai luat, phung hok, mai loi, non hok, non dap, khon khrok,* and *yon dap* (Simmonds, "*Mahorasop* II, the Thai National Library Manuscript," pp. 129–30.)

Bibliography I

Primary Sources

Unless otherwise stated, the place of publication is Bangkok.

Anirut kham chan [*Anirut* in *kham chan* poetry]. Krom Silapakon, 1960.

Arun. *Bot lakhon rong ruang Yipun* [*Lakhon rong* script of a Japanese story]. Lakhon Pramothai, 1914.

Bowonbanarak, Luang. *Maha Pharatayut* (Thai translation of the *Maha Bharata* by Takul Rashen Singh). Khlang Witthaya, 1971.

Bun Chiangmai. *Thida Phra Samut* (a *lakhon rong* script), vol. 1. Khana Lakhon Nakhon Banthoen, 1928.

Chindamani, chabap Phra Chao Boromakot [*Chindamani,* King Boromakot's version]. 2 vols. Ruang Watthana, 1971.

Chit Burathat. *Samakkhiphet kham chan* [*Samakkhiphet* in *kham chan* poetry]. Akson Sayam Kan Phim, 1975.

Cho Katchamia ru roi-et ratri [*Cho Katchamia,* or *One Hundred and One Nights*]. 1918.

Chom Klao Chao Yu Hua, Phrabat Somdet Phra (King Mongkut). *Ramakien ton Phra Ram doen dong* [*Ramakien:* Episode of Rama wandering in the forest]. Rongphim Thai, 1919.

Chulachomklao Chao Yu Hua, Phrabat Somdet Phra (King Chulalongkorn). *Abu Hassan* (A tale from *The Arabian Nights*). Silapakon, 1972.

———. *Chulachomklao Chao Yu Hua thi song borihan ratchakan phaendin* [King Chulalong-korn's administrative work]. 4 vols. Office of the Prime Minister Press, 1964–69.

———. *Kham cheracha lakhon ruang Inao* [The dialogue of the dance-drama *Inao*]. Rong-phim Nam Chiang, 1937 (on the occasion of the sixtieth birthday of Chao Chom Manda Sombun).

———. *Lilit Nithra Chakhrit* [*Nithra Chakhrit* in *lilit* poetry]. Rongphim Thai, 1922 (on the occasion of the sixtieth birthday of Somdet Phra Matucha Chao Phra Borom Ratchathewi).

———. *Ngo pa* [The wild Ngo]. Somchet Kan Phim, 1970.

———. *Phra borom rachowat* [Royal addresses to Crown Prince Wachirunahit]. Ruangruang Tham (for Krom Silapakon), 1960.

———. *Phra ratchahatthalekha khrao sadet monthon fai nua* [Personal correspondence: The royal visit to the northern region]. Rongphim Thai, 1922.

———. *Phra ratchahatthalekha ruang sadet praphat laem Malayu mua rǫ sǫ 108, 109, 117,*

120, ruam 4 khrao [Personal correspondence: The four royal visits to Malaysia, R.S. (Ratanakosin, i.e., Bangkok era) 108, 109, 117, 120]. Rongphim Thai, 1925.

Chulachomklao Chao Yu Hua, Phrabat Somdet Phra. *Phra ratchahatthalekha song sang ratchakan nai ratchakan thi 5 lae 6* [Personal correspondence: Royal commands in the Fifth and Sixth Reigns]. Phra Chan, 1964.

――――. *Phra ratchaniphon klai ban* [Royal letters from foreign lands]. 2 vols. Thai Samphan, 1965.

――――. *Phra ratchaphithi sip song duan* [Royal ceremonies of the twelve months]. Phrae Phitthaya, 1971.

――――. *Raya thang thio chawa kwa song duan rǫ sǫ 115* [Journey to Java over two months in R.S. 115]. Sophon Phiphatthanakon, 1925.

――――. *Samnao phra ratchahatthalekha Phrabat Somdet Phra Chulachomklao Chao Yu Hua mi phra ratchathan Krom Phra Narathip Praphanphong* [Personal correspondence to Prince Narathip] (published by Queen Laksamilawan, queen to King Vajiravudh and daughter of Prince Narathip). Sophon Phiphatthanakon, 1931.

――――. *Wongthewarat* [Dynasty of the deva-raja] (published on the occasion of the funeral of Chao Chom Sae). Bamrungnukunkit, 1884.

Chumnum ruang Phra Lǫ [A collection of *Phra Lǫ* stories]. Siwaphon (for Krom Silapakon), 1970.

Kukrit Pramoj, Mom Ratchawong. *Phiphek sawamiphak* [Phiphek's oath of allegiance] (a *khon* script). Thammasat University, 1972.

Lilit Phra Lǫ [*Phra Lǫ* in *lilit* poetry]. Akson Borikan (for Silapakon), 1968.

Mae Bunnak. *Kasat Santoelaf* [King Santoelaf] (a *lakhon rong* script). Lakhon Nakhon Banthoeng, 1922.

Mae Khwan. *Songkhram phǫ kha* [War of the merchants] (a *lakhon rong* script). Lakhon Nakhon Banthoeng, 1924.

Mae Phim. *Luat phayabat* [Blood of vengeance] (a *lakhon rong* script). Lakhon Nakhon Banthoeng, 1928.

Mae Wan. *Rop Yoeraman* [Fighting the Germans] (a *lakhon rong* script). Lakhon Pramothai, 1920.

Mae Wong. *Lang amnat* [Destruction of power] (a *lakhon rong* script). Lakhon Nakhon Banthoeng, 1931.

――――. *Mongkut khwin* [The queen's crown] (a *lakhon rong* script). Lakhon Nakhon Banthoeng, 1924.

――――. *Ratchathida Harem* [Princess of the Harem] (a *lakhon rong* script). Lakhon Nakhon Banthoeng, 1925.

Mahamontri, Phra. *Bot lakhon ruang Raden Landai* [*Raden Landai,* a *lakhon* script]. Thai Samphan, 1961.

Mahasakdipholasep, Somdet Phra Bowonratchao Krom Phra Ratchawang Bowon. *Khun Chang Khun Phaen* (a *lakhon* script). National Library, 1924.

Manohra, bot lakhon [*Manohra,* the *lakhon* script]. Rungruang Tham (for Silapakon), 1955.

Manohra lae Sangthong, bot lakhon khrang krung kao [*Manohra* and *Sangthong:* Ayudhaya *lakhon* scripts]. Silapakon, 1965.

Montri Tramote. *Suk kao thap, lakhon phan thang* [The battle of the Nine Troops, the *lakhon phan thang* script]. Silapakon, 1977.

Nam Khen. *Kon taek* [The failed trick] (a *lakhon rong* script). Lakhon Pramothai (Sophon Phiphatthanakon), 1914.

Namtan Phet. *Khwam phayabat* [The revenge] (a *lakhon rong* script). Thai Khasem, 1969.

Nangklao Chao Yu Hua, Phrabat Somdet Phra (King Rama III). *Phleng yao klon suphap ruang phra ratchaprarop phleng yao konlabot lae konla-akson* [Personal ideas and concepts expressed in *phleng yao klon suphap, phleng yao konlabot,* and *konla-akson* types of poetry]. Thai Publishing House, 1922.

Nangsao Chuchun. *Wira satri* [The heroine]. Lakhon Nakhon Banthoeng, 1929.

Narai sip pang lae phong nai Ramakien [The ten incarnations of Vishnu and genealogy in the *Ramakien*]. Edited by Praphan Sukhonthachat. Siwaphon, 1969.

Narathip Praphanphong, Phra Chao Boromawongthoe Krom Phra. *Phra Lo, lakhon phan thang* [*Phra Lo,* a *lakhon phan thang* script]. Siwaphon (for Krom Silapakon), 1970.

————. *Sao Khrua Fa* [Lady Khrua Fa]. Thai Khasem, 1971.

Narisaranuwattiwong, Somdet Chaofa Krom Phraya (Prince Naris). *Bot lakhon dukdamban chabap phoem toem* [Additional *lakhon dukdamban* scripts]. Maha Makut Ratchawithayalai, 1953.

————. *Chumnum bot lakhon lae bot khap rong* [Collected plays and songs]. Siwaphon, 1971.

————. *Prachum bot concert lae tableaux vivants* [Collected concerts and tableaux vivants scripts]. Siwaphon, 1971.

No Mo Hinghoi. *Rak chat* [Love of the country] (a *lakhon rong* script). Lakhon Pramothai, 1977.

Phaeo Sanitwongseni, Khunying. *Bot lakhon ruang Ngo pa, Khawi, Phra Aphaimani* [*Ngo pa, Khawi,* and *Phra Aphaimani,* a collection of *lakhon* scripts] (adapted and edited by the author). Arun Kan Phim, 1974.

————. *Khawi ton chup tua bot cheracha saek bot lakhon ruang Khawi* [*Khawi:* Episode of the transformation, an additional dialogue for the *Khawi lakhon* script]. N.d.

————. *Khun Chang Khun Phaen ton Phlai Phet Phlai Bua ok suk, bot lakhon* [*Khun Chang Khun Phaen:* Episode of Phlai Phet Phlai Bua going to war, a *lakhon* script]. Edited by the author for the performance at Uttradit, 20–22 February 1969.

Phanida, Sithiwan. *Inao ton Yaran tam nok yung (bot nithet prakop kan sadaeng lakhon nai)* [*Inao:* Episode of Yaran following the peacock, a *lakhon nai* script for demonstration talk on *lakhon nai*]. Edited by the author for the performance on Television Channel 4, 2 May 1971.

Phithayalongkon, Krom Mun. *Sam krung* [The Three Kingdoms]. Thai Samphan, 1968.

Phra Aphaimani, bot lakhon hun krabok [*Phra Aphaimani,* a *hun krabok* puppetry script]. Edited by Niratchada for a television performance by Khana Nai Phiak Prasoetkun. N.d.

Phra Khlang (Hon), Chao Phraya. *Wannakhadi khong Chao Phraya Phra Khlang (Hon) ruam 7 ruang* [Seven literary works of Chao Phraya Phra Khlang (Hon)]. Bannakhan, 1972.

Phra Lak Phra Lam (Ramakien), samnuan kao khong I-san [The *Ramakien* story of Phra Lak Phra Lam, version of the I-san people]. Khemcharithera (for Suksit Sayam), 1975.

Phra Phan Rotchana. *Manila lot-toeri* [Manila lottery] (a *lakhon rong* script). Suphakan Chamrun (for the Lakhon Luang Narumit), 1912.

Phranbun. *Chan chao kha, bot lakhon phleng amata* [*Dear Moon,* an immortal musical play script]. Maen Muang Maen Kan Phim, 1973.

Phutthaloetla Naphalai, Phrabat Somdet Phra (King Rama II). *Bot lakhon nok ruam 6 ruang: Sangthong, Chaiyachet, Kraithong, Maniphichai, Khawi, Sangsinchai* [Six *lakhon nok* scripts: *Sangthong, Chaiyachet, Kraithong, Maniphichai, Khawi,* and *Sangsinchai*]. Khlang Witthaya, 1965.

————. *Bot lakhon ruang Inao* [*Inao,* a *lakhon* script]. 2 vols. Khuru Sapha, 1967.

————. *Bot lakhon ruang Ramakien* [*Ramakien,* a *lakhon* script]. Khuru Sapha, 1967.

————. *Bot lakhon ruang Ramakien lae Bo koet Ramakien* [*Ramakien,* a *lakhon* script, and *The Origin of Ramakien*]. Silapa Bannakhan, 1956.

Phutthayotfa Chulalok, Phrabat Somdet Phra (King Rama I). *Dalang* [*Dalang,* the *lakhon* script]. 2 vols. Phrae Phitthaya (for Silapakon), 1967.

——. *Inao, bot lakhon* (*Inao,* a *lakhon* script). Phrae Phitthaya, 1967.

——. *Ramakien, bot lakhon* [*Ramakien,* a *lakhon* script]. Silapa Bannkhan (for Silapakon), 1967.

——. *Unarut, bot lakhon* [*Unarut,* a *lakhon* script]. Sam Mit, 1971.

Pin Malakul, Mom Luang. *Bot lakhon phut lem mai* [A new spoken drama script]. Khuru Sapha, 1975.

Prachum sila charuk phak 1: Charuk krung Sukhothai [A collection of stone inscriptions, part 1: The Sukhothai period]. Khuru Sapha, 1972.

Prachum sila charuk phak 2: Charuk Dvaravadi, Sriwijaya, Lawo [A collection of stone inscriptions, part 2: Dvaravadi, Sriwijaya, and Lawo]. Edited by George Coedès. Siwaphon, 1961.

Ramakien, bot lakhon chut betaret [*Ramakien,* a collection of miscellaneous *lakhon* scripts]. Chuan Phim, 1976.

Ramakien, chut Phromat, bot khon [*Ramakien:* Episode of Phromat, a *khon* script]. Khon Thammasat (Thammasat University), 1969.

Ramakien, prachum kham phak [A collection of *Ramakien* narratives]. Office of the Prime Minister, 1969. Including adaptations of *khon* and *lakhon* texts by the Silapakon for the performances at the Silapakon Theatre. (See also Silapakon, *Bot khon and bot lakhon.*)

　　Bot khon Ramakien ton Thosakan long suan thung Hanuman thwai waen [*Khon* script of the *Ramakien:* From Thosakan in the garden to Hanuman giving the ring].

　　Ramakien, bot khon [*Ramakien, khon* scripts]. Episodes:

　　"Hanuman a-sa" [Hanuman volunteers]. 1952.

　　"Hanuman hak suan thung Phra Ram rop Thosakan" [From the episode of Hanuman destroying the garden to the episode of Phra Ram fighting Thosakan]. 1973.

　　"Khao suan Phirap" [Entering Phirap's garden]. 1968.

　　"Lak Sida, Sida phuk khọ tai, Chong thanon, Songkram" [Stealing Sida, Sida hanging herself, Building the road, and the War]. 1957.

　　"Lak Sida thung Hanuman sawamiphak" [From stealing Sida to Hanuman's allegiance]. 1974.

　　"Maiyarap sakot thap" [Maiyarap putting the army to sleep]. 1959.

　　"Nakhabat" [Arrows of the serpents]. N.d.

　　"Narai prap Nonthuk" [God Narai defeating the ogre Nonthuk]. 1957.

　　"Phali son nong" [Phali teaching his brother]. 1974.

　　"Phra Ram doen dong [Rama wandering in the forest]. 1958.

　　"Phra Ram khrong Muang" [Phra Ram reigning Ayudhaya]. 1958.

　　"Prap Kakanasun" [Defeating Kakanasun]. 1951.

　　"Sida lui fai" [Sida walking on fire]. 1953.

Sepha ruang Abu Hassan [*The Arabian Nights* in *sepha* poetry]. Sophanphiphattanakon, 1919.

Sepha ruang Khun Chang Khun Phaen [*Khun Chang Khun Phaen* in *sepha* poetry]. Rungruang Tham, 1970.

Silapakon. *Bot khon and bot lakhon.*

　　Inao ton lom hop [*Inao:* The storm]. 1956.

　　Inao ton lom hop chon thung ong Patarakala plaeng Busba pen Unakan [*Inao,* from the storm to the god Patarakala disguising Busba as Unakan], for television production, 1975.

　　Inao ton Prasanta tọ nok [*Inao:* Prasanta catching a bird]. 1950.

Kaeo Na Ma ton thwai luk, bot lakhon nok [*Kaeo Na Ma:* Offering the child, a *lakhon nok* script]. 1962.

Khawi, bot lakhon nok [*Khawi,* a *lakhon nok* script]. 1970.

Khun Chang Khun Phaen ton Phlai Phet Phlai Bua [*Khun Chang Khun Phaen:* The episode of Phlai Phet Phlai Bua]. 1953.

Khun Chang Khun Phaen ton Phra Wai taek thap [*Khun Chang Khun Phaen:* Phra Wai's army defeated]. 1974.

Manohra, bot lakhon [*Manohra,* a *lakhon* script]. 1955.

Phra Aphaimani. Adapted by Seri Wangnaitham. 1975.

Phraya Pha Nong (a *lakhon phan thang* script). 1958.

Rachathirat ton Saming Phra Ram a-sa [*Rachathirat:* Episode of the Saming Phra Ram volunteers]. 1952.

Rai kan chalong 100 pi khong ratchakan thi 2 [A collection of scripts for the centennial celebration of King Rama II]. 1976:
> *Bot mahori Bulan Loi Luan* [*Mahori* script of *Bulan Loi Luan*].
> *Bot lakhon nok Chaiyachet ton Nang Maeo Yoei Sum* [*Lakhon nok* script of *Chaiyachet:* Episode of Nang Maeo Yoei Sum]
> *Bot lakhon nai Inao ton khao fao Thao Daha* [*Lakhon nai* script of *Inao:* Inao in the audience of King Daha].

———. *Bot lakhon nok.*

Rothasen. 1957.

Sangthong ton luak khu lae ha pla [*Sangthong:* Choosing a husband and fishing]. 1954.

Suwannahong (a *lakhon nok* script). 1951.

Suwannahong ton Kumphon thawai ma [*Suwannahong:* Kumphon offering the horse]. 1959.

Somphop Chantharaprapha. *Chisin* (a *lakhon* script). Faculty of Public Relations, Chulalongkorn University, 1974.

———. *Nang Suang* (a *lakhon dukdamban* script). 1968.

———. *Phu wiset* [The superman] (a *lakhon* script). 1975.

———. *Sithammasokarat, lakhon kham klon prakop ram* [*King Sithammasokarat,* a *lakhon* script in *kham klon* poetry with dances]. National Theatre, 1970.

———. *Somdet Phra Naresuan Maharat* [King Naresuan the Great] (a *lakhon* script). Akson Sayam Kan Phim, 1972.

Sri Ayudhya (King Vajiravudh). *Three Little Plays.* The Siam Observer Press, n.d.

Sunthon Phu. *Phra Aphaimani.* Silapakon, 1968.

Suwan, Khun. *Phra Malé Thé Thai, Unarut roi ruang, bot lakhon klon phleng yao ruang Mom Pet Sawan* [*Lakhon* scripts of *Phra Malé Thé Thai, Hundred Stories of Unarut,* and *Mom Pet Sawan* in *lakhon phleng yao* style]. Silapakon, 1968.

Vajiravudh, King. *Chuai amnat* [Coup d'état]. National Library, n.d.

———. *Huachai nak rop* [Heart of a warrior]. Department of Interior, 1974.

———. *Lilit Narai sip pang* [The ten incarnations of the god Narai in *lilit* poetry]. Khlang Witthaya (for Silapakon), 1964.

———. *Madanabadha ru tamnan haeng dok kulap* [*Madanabadha,* or Origin of the rose] (six acts of spoken drama script in *kham chan* poetry). 1924.

———. *Phaya Ratchawangsan kap Samakkhisawek* [*Phaya Ratchawangsan* and *Samakkhisawek*]. Phakdi Pradit, 1925.

———. *Phra Nala* [King Nala]. Mun-nithi Maha Mongkut Ratchawithayalai, 1969.

———. *Phra Non kham luang* [*Phra Non* in *kham luang* poetry]. 2 vols. Rongphim Thai, 1916.

Vajiravudh, King. *Phra Ruang* [King Ruang]. Akson Samphan, 1974.

———. *Phra Ruang ru Khom dam din* [*King Ruang,* or the Khmer spy] (a *lakhon* script). Silapakon, 1952.

———. *Ramakien, chut boek rong* [*Ramakien,* scripts for opening dances]. Including "Orachun kap Thosakan" (Orachun chasing Thosakan), "Sida hai" (Sida abducted), "Phao Longka" (Burning of Longka), "Phiphesana thuk khap" (Defection of Phiphesana), "Nang Loi" (The Floating Lady), "Chong thanon" (Making the road), "Pradoem suk Longka" (Beginning of the Longka War), "Phi thi Kumniphaniya Nakhabat" (Ceremony of Kumniphaniya Nakhabat), "Phromat" (Phromat). Khuru Sapha, 1961.

———. *Ramakien ton rusi sieng luk* [*Ramakien:* The hermit discovering the truth about his children]. National Library, n.d.

———. *Romeo lae Juliet* [Romeo and Juliet]. Khuru Sapha, 1976.

———. *Sakuntala, Madanabadha, Thao Saen Pom, Pramuan suphasit* [A collection of scripts of *Sakuntala, Madanabadha, Thao Saen Pom,* and *Pramuan suphasit*]. Rungruang Rat, 1970.

———. *Sawitri, bot lakhon rong* [*Sawitri, a lakhon rong* script]. National Library, 1924.

———. *Sawitri, khwamriang* [*Sawitri* in prose]. Khuru Sapha, 1983.

———. *Sia sala; Huachai chai num; Huachai nak rop* [The sacrifice; Heart of a young man; Heart of a warrior]. Rung Watthana, 1972.

———. *Tam chai than; Wiwa Phra Samut* [*As You Like It; Neptune's Wedding*]. Charoen Kit, 1971.

———. *Thammathamma songkhram* [War of righteousness]. Rongphim Thai, 1920.

———. *Thao Saen Pom ton chop, bot lakhon thorathat* [*King Saen Pom:* Last episode, a television script], adapted for television by Khunying Phaeo Sanitwongseni, 1972.

———. *Wang ti; Mit thae; Lam di; Wilai luak khu* [The emperor; True friend; Good interpreter; Wilai choosing a husband]. Khuru Sapha, 1969.

Valmiki. *Ramayana khong Phrom Rusi Valmiki* [*Ramayana* of the Bhrama hermit Valmiki], adapted into Thai in *klon don* verse by Suphon Phonlachiwin. Phra Chan, 1971.

Wichitwathakan, Luang. *Anuphap haeng khwam sia sala* [The power of sacrifice] (a *lakhon* script). Rungruang Tham, 1955.

———. *Anuphap Phǫ Khun Ramkhamhaeng* [The glory of King Ramkhamhaeng] (a *lakhon* script). Chaiwat, 1965.

———. *Chaoying Saenwi* [Princess of Saenwi] (a *lakhon* script). Rungruang Tham, 1963.

———. *Chat niyom* [Nationalism]. 1947.

———. *Luat Suphan; Ratchamanu; Phra Chao Krung Thon; Nan Chao* [Blood of Suphan; Ratchamanu; King Thonburi; Nan Chao]. N.d.

———. *Phra Naresuan prakat isaraphap* [King Naresuan declares independence] (a *lakhon* script). N.d.

———. *Suk Thalang* [Battle of Thalang]. Sayam Phanitchakan, 1937.

Withayakon Chiangkun. *Nai Aphaimani* [Mr. Aphaimani]. 1971.

Manuscripts in Thai

Chulalongkorn, King (Rama V). *Inao, bot cheracha klon bot lakhon* [*Inao:* Dialogue in *klon* dramatic poetry]. No. 485, case 113, bundle 201; No. 489, case 115, bundle 201; No. 492, case 115, bundle 201; No. 500; No. 501; No. 502, case 4/1, bundle 202; No. 503; No. 507, case 115, shelf 4/1, bundle 203.

Mongkut, King (Rama IV). *Bet-talet* [Miscellaneous]. No. 10.

———. *Ramakien, klon bot lakhon ruang prap Nonthuk* [*Ramakien:* Defeating Nonthuk, a *lakhon* script]. No. 524, case 114, shelf 4/5, bundle 117.

Phutthaloetla Naphalai, Phrabat Somdet Phra (Rama II). *Inao, klon bot lakhon* [*Inao,* a *lakhon* script]. Book 11. No. 344, case 115, shelf 2/4, bundle 187; No. 358, case 115, shelf 2/4, bundle 188; No. 359, case 115, shelf 2/4, bundle 188.

Book 34. No. 382, case 115, shelf 2/5, bundle 191; No. 428, case 115, bundle 197; No. 451, case 115, bundle 198.

———. *Ramakien.* Book 4, *Ton Nang Loi* [*Ramakien:* The Floating Lady] (a *lakhon* script). No. 293, case 114, shelf 4/1, bundle 93.

Book 12, *Ton Saeng A-thit a-sa rop Phromat; Sida siang busabok kaeo* [Saeng A-thit volunteers fighting in the Phromat Battle and Sida praying to the crystal palanquin]. No. 283, case 114, shelf 4/1, bundle 91.

———. *Ramakien, klon bot lakhon* [*Ramakien,* a *lakhon* script]. From "Ton Intharachit chap Hanuman dai, Hanuman phao Longka" [Intharachit catching Hanuman and Hanuman burning Longka] to "Thosakan khap Phiphek chak krung Longka" [Thosakan exiling Phiphek from Longka]. No. 443, case 114, shelf 4/4, bundle 109.

———. *Sangthong, klon bot lakhon* [*Sangthong,* a *lakhon* script]. Book 1. No. 26, case 114, shelf 5/3, bundle 128; No. 21, case 114, shelf 5/3, bundle 128; No. 22, case 114, shelf 5/3, bundle 129.

Phutthayotfa Chulalok, Phrabat Somdet Phra (Rama I). *Ramakien, klon bot lakhon* [*Ramakien,* a *lakhon* script]. No. 184, case 114, shelf 3/4, bundle 78.

———. *Ramakien.* No. 262, case 114, shelf 4/1, bundle 88.

Rachathirat, klon bot lakhon [*Rachathirat,* a *lakhon* script]. Book 25. No. 26, case 114, shelf 2/5, bundle 59.

Suwannahong, klon bot lakhon [*Suwannahong,* a *lakhon* script]. Book 1. No. 173, case 114, shelf 6/1, bundle 144.

Vajiravudh, King (Rama VI). *Tam chai than, lakhon roengrom khong William Shakespeare* [*As You Like It,* William Shakespeare's comedy], translated at the Phra Thinang Amphon Sathan, 26 May 1921.

Manuscripts in Thai with Illustrations

Phap Inao rabai si lae thong 14 phap [14 illustrations of *Inao* in colour and gold], by Nai Rot, painted in *pi marong* (the year of the great snake). 1880. No. 22, acquired from the National Museum in November 1908.

Samut phap Ramakien rabai si 56 phap [Book of 56 illustrations of *Ramakien* in colour]. No. 16, bought from Mom Luang Daeng Supradit, 1936.

Traiphum 63 phap [The Three Worlds, 63 illustrations]. No. 10. Thonburi.

Bibliography II

Secondary Sources in Thai

Unless otherwise stated, the place of publication is Bangkok.

Achin Panchaphan. *Anuson Phranbun* [In memory of Phranbun]. Krung Sayam Kan Phim, 1976.

A-khom Sayakhom. "Fuk hat lakhon luang nai ratchakan thi 7" [Training of the Lakhon Luang during the Seventh Reign]. In *Silapa lakhon ram,* ed. Dhanit Yupho. Siwaphon, 1973.

Aksonsat Phichan (journal), 2d year, vol. 3 (August 1974). Krung Sayam Kan Phim.

Anuman Rajadhon. *Khwan lae prapheni tham khwan* [*Khwan* and *tham khwan* ceremonies]. Samnak Phim Kao Na, 1963.

Anuson nai ngan rap phra ratchathan phloeng sop Mom Chao Smai [Souvenir book of Prince Smaichaloem Kridakon's cremation]. Phra Chan, 1967.

Anuson Pho Khun Ramkhamhaeng Maharat [In memorium of King Ramkhamhaeng the Great]. Mit Sayam, 1970.

Anuson Suchin Thewaphalin [In remembrance of Suchin Thewaphalin]. Suthiwong Kan Phim, 1970.

Anuson Thet Natakanurak [In remembrance of Thet Natakanurak]. Romgphim Sathan Songkhro Ying Pak Kret, 1968.

Aphichat Kaeosema. "Nang yai Wat Khanon" [Wat Khanon shadow puppets]. *Anakhot* 2 (1972): 31–38.

Aphon Montrisat and Chaturong Montrisat. *Wicha natasin* [The study of the art of classical dance]. Khuru Sapha, 1974.

Arada Sumit. "Bot lakhon nai khong luang nai samai ratchakan thi 2" [The *lakhon nai* dance-drama of the royal court in the Second Reign]. M.A. thesis, Department of Thai, Faculty of Letters, Chulalongkorn University, 1972.

Atcharaphon Kamutphitsamai. "Kan borihan phaendin nai samai Phrabat Somdet Phra Mongkut Klao Chao Yu Hua" [State administration during the reign of King Vajiravudh]. M.A. thesis, Department of History, Faculty of Liberal Arts, Thammasat University, 1975.

Banchong Banchoetsin. *Silapa wannakhadi kap chiwit* [Art, literature, and life]. Thammasat Women's Group; Charoen Wit Kan Phim, 1974.

Bharata Natayasastra. Translated by Saeng Monwithu from the Sanskrit text. 1966.

Bot khwam thi kiao khong kap wannakhadi priap thiap buang ton [Articles on introduction to comparative literature]. Edited by Krasae Malayaphon. Rongrian Satri Neti Suksa, 1973.

Bunlua Thepyasuwan, Mom Luang. *Wikhro rot wannakhadi Thai* [Analysis of Thai Literature: Its flavour, i.e., aesthetic value]. Thai Watthana Phanit, 1974.

Bunlua Thephayasuwan. "Hua liao khong wannakhadi Thai" [The turning point in Thai literature]. In *Wan Waithayakon* [Prince Wan Waithayakon] (literature section), pp. 55–157. Samakhom Sangkhomsat Haeng Prathet Thai, 1971.

———. "Kan lakhon khong Thai" [Thai drama]. Mimeo. 1972.

———. "Kha niyom mai kap wannakhadi Thai" [New values and Thai literature]. *Aksonsat Phichan* (1974): 14–18.

———. "Kho sangket kiao kap khwam pen ma khong kan lakhon Thai lae kan prap-prung" [Remarks on the origin and development of Thai drama]. *Warasan Thammasat,* special issue (1972): 160–99.

———. "Phra Phutthaloetla mai hen dai tham arai" [King Rama II did not achieve anything]. *Chankasem* (January–February 1968): 51–60.

Chai Ruangsin. *Prawatsat Thai samai phọ sọ 2352–2453 dan sangkhom* [The social history of Thailand, 1809–1910]. Kittiwan, 1976.

Chai-anan Nanthaphan. "Phrabat Somdet Phra Pok-klao Chao Yu Hua kap kan pok-khrong rabop rathathammanun" [King Rama VII and the system of constitutional government]. *Warasan Thammasat* (June–October 1973): 144–68.

Chai-anan Samuthawanit. *Kan muang: Kan plian plaeng thang kan muang Thai phọ sọ 1893–2475* [Politics: Changes in Thai politics, 1350–1932]. Faculty of Political Science, Chulalongkorn University, 1976.

Chai-anan Samuthawanit and Khattiya Kanasut. *Ekasan kan muang kan pokkhrong Thai (phọ sọ 1893–2475)* [Source materials on Thai politics and government, 1350–1932]. Faculty of Political Science, Chulalongkorn University, 1976.

Chakraphan Posayakrit. *Ngan sadaeng hun krabok ruang Phra Aphaimani [Hun krabok* performance of *Phra Aphaimani*]. Krung Sayam Kan Phim, 1975.

Chalao Chairatana. *Riangkhwam ruang phra ratchaniphon nai ratchakan thi 6 lae riangkhwam chabap thi dai rap rangwan Phumiphon* [An essay on King Rama VI's literary works and a King Bhumibol's Prize winning essay]. Khuru Sapha, 1961.

Chalao Chaiyaratana. *Phra Ratchaniphon bot lakhon phut nai ratchakan thi 6* [King Rama VI's plays in prose]. Published on the occasion of her cremation, 1967.

Chali Iamkrasin. *Muang Thai samai kon* [Thailand in the past]. Ruangsin, 1976.

"Chamlae Inao: Wannakam sakdina" [Dissecting *Inao:* A literary work of aristocracy]. *Pituphum* (October 1974): 31–38.

Chankasem (journal), vol. 80 (1968). Khuru Sapha.

Chanthima Saowani. "Lakhon Thai yang yu yang yun yong" [Thai drama will prevail]. *Ekalak Thai* 4 (1977): 65–77.

Chanwit Kasetsiri and Suchat Sawatsi. *Prawatisat lae nak prawatisat Thai* [History and Thai historians]. Phikhanet, 1976.

Chiranan Phitpricha. *Lok thi si: Prawatisat na mai khong ying Thai* [The fourth world: A new history of Thai women]. San Sayam, 1975.

Chit Phumisak. *Chom na sakdina Thai* [The image of Thai aristocracy]. Chakranukun Kan Phim, 1974.

———. *Kawi kan muang* [Political poets]. Chiangmai Students' United Front, 1974.

———. *Kawi prachachon* [Poets of the people]. Thammasat Literature Group, 1974.

———. *Khwam pen ma khong kham Sayam Thai Lao lae Khom lae laksana thang sangkhom khong chu chon chat* [Origins of Siamese, Thai, Lao, and Khmer words and social aspects of national names]. Krung Sayam Kan Phim, 1976.

———. *Silapa phua chiwit silapa phua prachachon* [Art for living, art for the people]. 1974.

Chonthira Klatyu. *Chiwit lae ngan Khru Thep* [The life and work of Khru Thep]. Association of Social Sciences of Thailand, 1975.

————. "Kan top patikiriya khong khon run mai Thai mi to wannakhadi Thai" [A response to the new Thai generation's reactions to Thai literature]. *Aksonsat Phichan* (August 1974): 19–42.

Chotmaihet phra ratchakit raiwan [Memoirs of the kings' daily activities from B.E. 2411, end of the Fourth Reign, to the beginning of the Fifth Reign]. Published on the occasion of the cremation of Mom Luang Phra Israsena. Krom Silapakon, 1974.

Chotmaihet Phra Ratchaphithi Borom Rachaphisek Somdet Phra Ramathibodi Sisinthara Maha Wachirawut Phra Mongkut Klao Chao Yu Hua [Record of the coronation of King Vajiravudh]. Edited by Prince Naresuanrit. Sophon Phiphatthanakon, 1923; reprint 1975.

Chotmaihet Phrabat Somdet Phra Chulachomklao Chao Yu Hua sadet praphat laem Malayu khrao rọ sọ 107 lae 108 [An account of King Chulalongkorn's visit to Malaysia, R.S. 107 and 108]. Sophon Phiphatthanakon, 1924.

Chotmaihet ruang rap sadet lae somphot Phrabat Somdet Phra Chulachomklao Chao Yu Hua mua sadet klap chak Yurop khrao raek nai phọ sọ 2440 [An account of the welcoming celebration of King Chulalongkorn's return from his first visit to Europe in 1897]. Sophon Phiphatthanakon, 1923.

Chotmaihet ruang song sadet Phrabat Somdet Phra Chulachomklao Chao Yu Hua sadet Yurop khrang raek mua phọ sọ 2439 [Records of King Chulalongkorn's first tour of Europe in 1896]. Sophon Phiphatthanakon, 1923.

Chomaihet ruang thut American khao ma nai ratchakan thi 3 mua pi phọ sọ 2393 [An account of the visit of the American ambassador during the Third Reign, 1760]. Sophon Phiphatthanakon, 1923.

Chotmaihet sadet phraphat kọ Chawa nai ratchakan thi 5 thang sam khrao [Accounts of the three royal visits to Java in the Fifth Reign]. Sophon Phiphatthanakon, 1920.

Chotmaihet sadet praphat tang prathet nai ratchakan thi 5 sadet muang Singapo lae muang Betawia khrang raek lae sadet phraphat India [Accounts of King Chulalongkorn's first visits to Singapore, Batavia, and visit to India]. 2d ed. Sophon Phiphatthanakon, 1925.

Chua Satawethin. *Prawat nawaniyai Thai* [A history of the Thai novel]. Phasa Thai Udom Suksa, vol. 1. N.d.

Chulalongkorn, King. *Phra borom rachathibai ruang samakkhi lae naeo phra ratchadamri thang kan muang* [The king's clarification of unity and national policy]. With a review by Saneh Chamarik. Chuan Phim, 1968.

————. *Phra Ratcha-karanyanuson lae Ruang Nang Nophamat* [*Phra Ratcha-karanyanuson* royal ceremony and the story of Nang Nophamat]. Khlang Witthaya, 1964.

————. *Phra ratchawichan chotmaihet khwam song cham Krom Luang Narintharathewi* [His Majesty's critical analysis of the memoirs of Princess Narintharathewi]. Published on the occasion of the cremation of Princess Apsonsman Kitiyakon. 1939.

————. *Phra ratchawichan wa dua bot lakhon ruang Inao phra ratchaniphon ratchakan thi 1* [His Majesty's critical analysis of *Inao,* the royal *lakhon* script of the First Reign].

————. *Song wichan ruang phra ratchaphongsawadan kap ruang phra ratchaprapheni kan tang Phra Maha Uparat* [His Majesty's critical analysis of the royal chronicles and the tradition of the Investiture of the Second King]. Phra Chan, 1973.

Damrong Rajanubhab, H.R.H. Prince. "Athibai bot lakhon khrang krung kao" [Commentary on the *lakhon* scripts of the old kingdom, i.e., Ayudhaya]. In *Bot lakhon khrang krung kao ruang Manohra lae Sangthong* [Ayudhaya plays: *Manohra* and *Sangthong*], pp. 1–5. Khlang Witthaya, 1965.

————. *Khwam song cham* [Memoirs]. Rung Watthana, 1971.

————. *Latthi thamnian tang tang* [Customs and traditions]. Khlang Witthaya (for National Library), 1963.

————. *Nirat Nakhon Wat* [*Nirat* poetry about a visit to Angkor Wat]. Phrae Phitthaya, 1971.

————. *Phra ratchaphongsawadan chabap phra ratchahatthalekha* [Royal manuscripts of the royal chronicles]. 2 vols. Odeon Store, 1962.

————. *Prachum bot mahori kap athibai tamnan mahori* [Collection of *mahori* lyrics and explanation about *mahori* tradition]. Sophon Phiphatthanakon, 1948.

————. *Prawat Chao Chom Manda Thapthim ratchakan thi 5 kap suphasit thukkhata son but* [Biography of Consort Thapthim of the Fifth Reign and moral lessons for sons]. Phra Chan, 1938.

————. *Prawatsat Sukhothai* [The history of Sukhothai]. Thamniap Rathaban (distributed by Marshal Phibunsongkhram), 1955.

————. *Rai nam nangsuphim khao sung ok pen raya nai prathet Sayam* [A list of periodicals in Siam]. 1929.

————. *Ruang rao rop Phama khrang krung Si Ayudhaya* [The story of the Burmese War in the Ayudhaya period]. 1920.

————. *Sadet Yurop khrang thi 2* [The second royal visit to Europe]. Bamrungnukunkit, 1971.

————. *Tamnan khruang mahori piphat* [The origin of *mahori* and *piphat* orchestras]. 1972.

————. *Tamnan khruang mahori piphat lae prachum bot phleng Thai doem* [The origin of *mahori* and *piphat* orchestras and a collection of old Thai songs]. Phak 1, 2, 3. Maha Mongkut Ratchawithayalai, 1969.

————. *Tamnan lakhon Inao* [The origin of *Inao* play]. Khlang Witthaya, 1965.

————. *Tamnan Wang Na* [The origin of the Front Palace]. Sophon Phiphatthanakon, 1925.

————. *Tamra fon ram* [The lessons of Thai dance]. Chuan Phim, 1971. First edition published in 1923 on the occasion of the cremation of H.R.H. Prince Chuthathutchadilok.

————. *Thieo Muang Phama* [Travel to Burma]. Phrae Phitthaya, 1971.

————. *Thieo Nakhon Wat* [Travel to Angkor Wat]. Phrae Phitthaya, 1971.

————. "Winichai ruang khruang ton" [A study of the royal regalia and costumes]. *Warasan Silapakon,* 3d year (1949): 73–74.

Damrong Rajanubhab, H.R.H. Prince, and H.R.H. Prince Narisaranuwattiwong. *San Somdet* [Princes' correspondence]. Khlang Witthaya, 1971.

Dhaninivat, H.H. Prince. *Attachiwaprawat* [Autobiography]. 1974. Published on the occasion of his cremation.

————. *Chumnum niphon* [Collected works]. Samakhom Sangkhomsat Haeng Prathet Thai, 1964.

————. *Ruang Phra Ram* [The story of Rama]. Khuru Sapha, 1971.

————. *Ruang phrabat somdet Phra Phutthayotfa Chulalok song funfu watthanatham* [King Rama I's cultural restoration activities]. Phra Chan, 1957.

————. "Wichan ruang nithan Panyi ru Inao" [Critical study of *Tale of Panji* or *Inao*]. In *Chumnum niphon* [Collected works], 158–242. Samakhom Sangkhomsat Haeng Prathet Thai, 1964.

————. *Wichan ruang Panyi ru Inao* [Critical study of *Panji* or *Inao*]. Khuru Sapha, 1972.

Dhanit Yupho. *Athibai tha natasin Thai* [An explanation of Thai classical dance movements]. Krom Silapakon, 1948.

————. *Boran watthu samai Thawarawadi haeng mai* [New discoveries of Dvaravati antique]. Silapakon, 1965.

————. *Fukhat natasin Thai buang ton* [Introduction to the training in Thai classical dance]. Thanakhan Kasikon Thai, n.d.

Dhanit Yupho. "Kamnoet natasin Thai" [The origin of Thai classical dance]. In *Kukrit 60* [Kukrit's sixtieth birthday celebration], 83–115. Samnak Phim Kao Na, 1971.

———. "Kan lalen samai krung Si Ayudhaya" [Entertainment in the Ayudhaya period]. In *Ruam pathakatha ngan anuson Ayudhaya 200 pi* [Ayudhaya bicentennial celebration], 1–61. Khuru Sapha, 1967.

———. "Khletlap nai kan sang lakhon dukdamban" [Secret techniques in producing *lakhon dukdamban*]. *Warasan Silapakon,* 1st year, vol. 1 (1947): 24–31.

———. *Khon.* Siwaphon (for Krom Silapakon), 1968.

———. *Khruang dontri Thai* [Thai musical instruments]. 2d ed. Krom Silapakon, 1967.

———. *Kon phak ton wa dua tamnan lae thrusadi* [*Khon phak:* Origin and theory]. Silapakon, 1953.

———. *Laksana khong tua lakhon nai natakam bang ruang* [Characters in some dramatic dances]. Siwaphon, 1958.

———. *Phithi wai khru lae tamra khrop hua khon lakhon* [Invocation ceremony for and initiation of *khon* and *lakhon* dancers]. Phra Chan, 1959.

———. *Praleng rabeng kap mongkhrum lae thoet-thoeng* [*Praleng, rabeng, mongkhrum,* and *thoet-thoeng:* Traditional, ritualistic, and festive dances]. Phra Chan, 1952.

———. "Prawat lae nayobai khong Krom Silapakon" [History and policies of the Department of Fine Arts]. *Nitayasan Silapakon,* 2d year, vol. 2 (1967): 76–81.

———. *Si lae laksana hua khon* [Colours and characters in *khon*]. Krom Silapakon, 1959.

———. *Silapa lakhon ram, ru khu mu natasin Thai* [The art of Thai dance-drama, or A handbook of Thai dance]. Siwaphon, 1973. Published on the occassion of the sixtieth birthday of Phra-ong Chao Chaloemphonthikhamphon.

———. *Silapin haeng lakhon Thai* [The art of Thai dance-drama]. Phra Chan, 1954.

Duangchit Chitraphong. *Lan pon pa* [Nieces and nephews informing aunts]. Phra Chan, 1968.

———. *Pa pon lan* [Aunts informing nieces and nephews]. Phra Chan, 1968.

Dusadi Malakul, Than Phuying. *Ruang khong khon ha phaendin* [Story of a lady living through five reigns]. Khuru Sapha, 1975.

Dusit Thani muang prachathipatai khong Phrabat Somdet Phra Mongkut Klao Chao Yu Hua [Dusit Thani, the democratic city of King Vajiravudh]. National Library, 1970.

Hua khon [*Khon* masks]. Edited by Praphan Sukhonthachat. Siwaphon, 1971.

Intharayut. *Kho khit chak wannakhadi* [Some thematic ideas from literature]. Charoenwit Kan Phim (for Students' Centre of Thailand), 1975.

Kanchanakhaphan. *Yuk phleng nang lae lakhon nai a-dit* [The age of music and song in film and theatre in the past]. Sihaphan Kan Phim, 1975.

Kasem Sirisamphan and Neon Snidvongs. *Naeo Phra Ratchadamri thang kan muang nai Phrabat Somdet Phra Chulachomklao Chao Yu Hua* [King Chulalongkorn's political ideas]. Siwaphon, 1967.

Kham banyai sammana borankhadi samai Sukhothai [Lectures on archaeology in the Sukhothai period]. Siwaphon (for Krom Silapakon), 1964.

Kham hai kan chao krung kao [Testimonies of the citizens of the old capital, i.e., Ayudhaya]. 2d ed. Sophon Phiphatthanakon, 1925. Translated from the *Chabap Luang* obtained from Burma.

Kham hai kan chao krung kao, Kham hai kan Khun Luang Ha Wat, Phra ratchaphongsawadan krung kao chabap Luang Prasoet Aksonnit [Testimonies of old capital citizens, testimonies of Khun Luang Ha Wat, and royal chronicles, Luang Prasoet Aksonnit's version]. Khlang Witthaya, 1967.

Kho ratchakan nai Krom Mahatlek [Administrative rules of the Department of the Royal Pages].

Wongwiwat, 1957. Published on the occasion of the cremation of Phraya Thewet.

Kiat prawat ying Thai nai a-dit [Honourable biographies of Thai women in the past]. International Women's Year, 1975.

Kingkaeo Atthakon. *Wannakam Ban Nai* [Ban Nai folk literature]. Ministry of Education, 1971.

Korakot Lakphet. "Khon: Ekalak natakam Thai" [*Khon:* National characteristic of Thai dancedrama]. *Ekalak Thai,* 1st year, vol. 4 (1977): 26–32.

Kotmai muang Thai [Thai Law]. Edited by D. B. Bradley. Vol. 2. 1896.

Krung Thai. In *9 ratchakan lae chaofa chai* [Nine kings and crown princes]. Amon Kan Phim, 1973.

Kukrit Pramoj, Mom Ratchawong. "Kan pokkhrong samai Sukhothai" [The Sukhothai governmental system]. In *Pho Khun Ramakhamhaeng Maharat* [King Ramkhamhaeng the Great], 1970.

————. "Kan sup nuang lae kan Thai thot natasin dontri Thai" [The continuation and teaching of Thai classical dance-drama and music]. *Warasan Thammasat,* special issue entitled *Natasin lae dontri Thai* [Thai classical dance and music] (1972): 73–78.

————. *Khrong kraduk nai tu* [Skeletons in the closet]. 1972. Published on the occasion of his sixtieth birthday.

————. "Lakhon nok lakhon nai lae lakhon dukdamban" [*Lakhon nok, lakhon nai,* and *lakhon dukdamban*]. *Warasan Natasin* (Thammasat Students' Club), no. 13 (1971): 30–34.

————. "Natasin lae dontri Thai nai chiwit Thai" [Dance-drama and music in Thai life]. *Warasan Thammasat,* special issue entitled *Natasin lae dontri Thai* (1972): 7–14.

————. *Phunthan thang watthanatham Thai* [The foundation of Thai culture]. Thammasat University, 1971.

————. *Sangkhom samai Ayudhaya* [Ayudhaya society]. Thammasat University, 1967.

————. *Sathaban phra maha kasat* [The Thai institution of monarchy]. Phisanulok: Sinakharintharawirot University, 1975.

————. *Sayam muang yim* [Siam, land of smiles]. Samnak Phim Kao Na, 1972.

————. *Soi Suan Phlu* [Suan Phlu lane]. Samnak Phim Kao Na, 1976.

Kukrit Pramoj, Mom Rachawong; and Phra Sasanasophan. *Phra phuttha sasana kap sangkhom Thai* [Buddhism and Thai society]. Thammasat University, 1971.

Lanthom. "Lakhon kae bon" [Dance-drama as an offering to the gods]. *Chaiyaphruk* 43 (Nov. 1973): 32–33.

Latthi thamniem tang tang [Various customs and manners]. Khlang Witthaya, 1963.

Lithai, Phaya. *Trai Phum Phra Ruang* [The Three Worlds of Phra Ruang]. Khuru Sapha, 1963.

Maharat (journal), special issue entitled *Wannakam phua chiwit* [Literature for living] (May 1973).

Mattani Rutnin. "Kan lakhon samai mai kap kan phatthana natasin lae lakhon Thai [Modern drama and the development of Thai classical dance and drama]. *Warasan Thammasat,* 2d year (1973): 200–213.

————. "Khwam pen ma khong Phra Phirap" [The origin of Phra Phirap]. *Pak Kai* (1975): 45–68. Association of Thai Writers.

————. "Mahakam Ramayana khrang thi 1" [The first Ramayana festival]. *Warasan Thammasat,* 2d year (1971): 96–127.

————. "Phra Phirap." *Sayamrat Sapda Wichan,* 20th year, vols. 24–27 (1973).

————. "Ramayana priapthiap thang wannakhadi" [A comparative study of the *Ramayana* in literature], part 1 & 2. *Warasan Thammasat,* 2d year, vol. 2 (1973): 109–35; 3d year, vol. 1, 103–43.

Mongkut, King (Phrabat Somdet Phra Chom Klao Chao Yu Hua, Rama IV). *Chotmaihet phra ratchakit rai wan b.e. 2411* [Daily accounts of royal activities, 1868]. Siwaphon, 1974.

————. *Chotmaihet ratchakan thi 4* [Historical accounts of King Rama IV]. National Library.

————. *Phra ratchaphongsawadan chabap phra ratchahatthalekha* [Royal chronicles, king's manuscripts]. A-mon Kan Phim (for Silapakon), 1973.

Montri Tramote. "Chatri." In *Saranukrom Thai, chabap Ratchabanditsathan* [Encyclopaedia of Thailand, Ratchabanditsathan's version] 10 (1969/70): 61–95.

————. "Dontri samai Sukhothai" [Sukhothai music]. In *Samana borankhadi samai Sukhothai* (Seminar on archaeology: Sukhothai period). Silapakon, 1965.

————. *Kan lalen khong Thai* [Thai performing arts and games]. Silapakon, 1964.

————. "Khwan taek tang rawang lakhon nok kap lakhon nai" [The differences between *lakhon nok* and *lakhon*]. Silapakon, 1951.

————. "Lakhon chatri." In *Natasin lae dontri Thai* [Thai classical dance and music]. Thammasat University, 1972.

Nangsu banthuk: Samakhom wannakhadi [Notes: Literature Association] (journal). Edited by H.R.H. Prince Damrong Rajanubhab, 1st year, vol. 5, 1932.

Nangsu Court khao ratchakan [Court official news]. Preface by H.R.H. Prince Damrong Rajanubhab. Vols. 1, 2. 1923.

Nangsu ruang Sir James Brooke khao ma kho tham sanya nai ratchakan thi 3 [Account of Sir James Brooke's visit to negotiate contracts in the Third Reign]. Rongphim Thai, 1850. 2d ed. Sophon Phiphatthanakon, 1923.

Nangsu thesaphiban [Rules and regulations of interior affairs] (containing *Prakat wa dua lakhon phuying nai ratchakan thi 4* [Royal decree concerning female dance-drama]). Vol. 8. 1909.

Narathip Praphanphong, Phra Chao Worawongthoe Krom Mun. *Kho khit kiao kap phasa lae wannakhadi* [Ideas on language and literature]. Bophit, 1975.

Narintharathewi, Krom Luang. *Chotmaihet khwam song cham Krom Luang Narintharathewi pho so 2310–2381 lae phra ratchawichan nai Phrabat Somdet Phra Chulachomklao Chao Yu Hua* [The memoirs of Princess Narintharathewi, 1767–1838, and King Chulalongkorn's critical analysis]. Silapakon, 1958.

————. *Narai sip pang* [God Narai's ten incarnations]. Phra Chan, 1976. Adapted and edited from an English version.

————. *Pai Chawa* [Visit to Java]. Phra Chan, 1971.

Narisaranuwattiwong, Somdet Chaofa Krom Phraya (H.R.H. Prince Naris). *Banthuk ruang khwam ru tang tang Somdet Chaofa Krom Phraya Narisaranuwattiwong prathan Phraya Anuman Rajadhon* [Notes on various subjects from Prince Narisaranuwattiwong to Phraya Anuman Rajadhon]. Samakhom Sangkhomsat Haeng Prathet Thai, 1963.

————. *Pai Chawa* [Travel to Java]. N.d.

————. *Lai phra hat song mi to top kap Phra Saraprasoet* [Prince's correspondence with Phra Saraprasoet]. Siwaphon, 1963.

————. "Winichai wa dua samut phap ruang Ramakien" [Analytical study of paintings depicting the *Ramakien*]. *Warasan Silapakon,* 6th year, vol. 7 (1952): 48–56.

Narisaranuwattiwong, Somdet Chaofa Krom Phraya; and Somdet Phra Chao Boromawongthoe Krom Phraya Damrong Rajanubhab. *San Somdet* [Princes' correspondence]. Khuru Sapha, 1961.

Natasin dontri Thai [Thai dance-drama and music]. Thammasat University, 1972.

Natasin lae dontri Thai nangsu prakop kan sadaeng [Thai classical dance and music: Text for the programme]. Thammasat University, 1972.

Natthawut Sutthisongkhram. *Phra borom rachini krung Ratanakosin* [Queens of the Bangkok period]. Phadung Suksa, 1972.

Niphon Suksawat. *Wannakhadi kiao kap khanop prapheni Thai* [Literary works on Thai customs and traditions]. Phisanulok: Sinakharintharawirot University, 1977.

Nitaya Kanchanawan. *Wannakam Ayudhaya* [Ayudhaya literature]. Ramkhamhaeng University, 1972.

Nithatsakan hua khon [Exhibition of *khon* masks]. Silapakon, 1971.

Oraphin Singhaphon. "Lakhon nok nai ratchakan thi 2" [*Lakhon nok* in the Second Reign]. *Chankasem,* 80th year (Jan.–Feb. 1968): 149–76.

Phansi Wichakonkun. "Farang ma Thai nai ratchakan thi 2" [The coming of Westerners to Siam during the Second Reign]. *Chankasem* (Jan.–Feb. 1968): 138–48.

Phichitprichakon, Phra Boromawongthoe Krom Luang. *Prachum Phra Niphon* [Collection of the prince's works]. 1950. Published on the occasion of the cremation of Mom Sun Khakhanang.

Phinyo Chittham. *Nora.* Bamrungnukunkit, 1965.

Phiphathakosa, Phraya. *Chotmaihet Phraya Phiphathakosa* [The memoirs of Phraya Phiphathakosa].

Phithi wai khru tamra khrop khon lakhon phrom dua tamnan lae kham klon wai khru lakhon chatri [Invocation and initiation ceremonies of *khon* and *lakhon* together with history and invocation chants of *lakhon chatri*]. Phra Chan (for Krom Silapakon), 1959.

Phonphen Huntrakun. "Kan chai chai ngoen phaendin nai ratchasamai Phrabat Somdet Phra Mongkut Klao Chao Yu Hua (B.E. 2453–2468)" [National expenditures during the reign of King Vajiravudh, 1910–25]. M.A. thesis, Department of History, Faculty of Arts, Chulalongkorn University, 1974.

Phra ratchahatthalekha song sang ratchakan nai ratchakan thi 5 lae thi 6 [Royal manuscripts concerning the royal commandments in state affairs during the Fifth and Sixth Reigns]. 1964. Published on the occasion of the cremation of Marshal Sarit Thanarat.

Phra ratchaphongsawadan chabap Luang Prasoet [Royal chronicles, Luang Prasoet's version]. Khlang Witthaya, 1967.

Phra ratchaphongsawadan chabap phra ratchahatthalekha ratchakan thi 4, 5 [Royal autograph editions of royal chronicles in the Fourth and Fifth Reigns]. Khlang Witthaya, 1962.

Phra ratchaphongsawadan krung Ratanakosin chabap Ho Samut Haeng Chat [Royal chronicles of the city of Ratanakosin (Bangkok), National Library version]. Khlang Witthaya, 1962. Edition of 1963 under the title *Prachum phongsawadan krung Ratanakosin ratchakan thi 1 khong Chao Phraya Thiphakorawong* [A collection of royal chronicles of the First Reign of Bangkok, Chao Phraya Thiphakorawong's version]. *Ratchakan thi 2; Ratchakan thi 3, 4.*

Phra ratchaphongsawadan krung si Ayudhaya chabap Somdet Krom Phra Poramanuchitchinorot [Ayudhaya royal chronicles, Prince Poramanuchitchinorot's version]. Silapakon, 1942.

Pin Malakul, Mom Luang. *Ngan lakhon khong Phrabat Somdet Phra Ramathibodi Sisin Maha Wachirawut Phra Mongkut Klao Chao Phaendin Sayam* [Dramatic activities of King Vajiravudh]. Thai Watthana Phanit, 1975.

Pluang Na Nakhon. *Prawat wannakhadi Thai samrap naksuksa* [History of Thai literature for students]. Thai Watthana Phanit, 1974.

Prachum charuk Sayam [A collection of Siamese inscriptions]. Translated and edited by Professor George Coedès. Sophon Phiphatthanakon, 1924.

Prachum phongsawadan [Collected chronicles]. Khuru Sapha, 1965.

Prachum phongsawadan chabap Ho Samut Haeng Chat [A collection of chronicles, National Library version]. 14 vols. Samnak Phim Kao Na, 1963–74.

Prachum prakat ratchakan thi 4 [A collection of royal announcements in the Fourth Reign]. Khuru Sapha, 1961.

Prakat kan phra ratchaphithi [Announcements of royal ceremonies]. Rongphim Thai, 1916.

Prakhong Nimmanhemin. *Laksana wannakam phak nua* [Characteristics of northern Thai literature]. Samakhom Sangkhomsat Haeng Prathet Thai, 1974.

Praphan Ruangnarong. "Liké Hulu: Lamtat Thai Muslim" [*Liké Hulu:* Thai Muslim *lamtat*]. *Ekalak Thai,* 1st year, vol. 2 (February 1977): 65–72.

———. "Rong-ngeng." *Ekalak Thai* 4 (April 1977): 116–22.

Prapheni kiao kap chiwit [Traditions and customs relating to daily life]. Silapakon, 1975.

Prathin Phuangsamli. *Athibai tha natasin chut rabam ram fon* [Explanation of dance movements in *rabam ram* and *fon*]. Thai Mit Kan Phim, 1971.

———. *Lak natasin* [Principles of classical dance]. Thai Mit Kan Phim, 1971.

Prathip Muannin. *Wannakam Thai patchuban* [Contemporary Thai literature]. San Sayam, 1976.

Prawat lae bot khap rong phleng Thai bang bot [History and some Thai songs and lyrics], vol. 1. Khuru Sapha, 1973.

Prayun Phisanakha. *9 Phaendin haeng Ratanakosin* [The nine reigns of Bangkok]. Soemwit Bannakhan, 1964.

Prayut Sitthiphan. *Rak nai ratchasamnak* [Love in the royal court]. Khlang Witthaya, 1966.

———. *Somdet Phra Chom Klao Chao Krung Sayam* [King Mongkut of Siam], vol. 1. Samnakphim Sayam, 1973.

Rachaphisek [Coronation: Ceremonies of the Ayudhaya and Ratanakosin periods]. 1936. Published on the occasion of the cremation of Mom Chao Ying Mao Thongthaem.

Rai ngan buang ton kan wichai changwat Phra Nakhon Si Ayudhaya [First report of research on Ayudhaya Province]. Phra Chan, 1971.

Ratchaphongsawadan Krung Kamphucha chabap Ho Samut Haeng Chat [Royal chronicles of Cambodia, National Library version]. Phrae Phitthaya, 1970.

Roekchai Bancha. *Chut kan sadaeng natasin Thai bang chut* [Some performances of Thai classical dance]. Rongphim Montri, 1973.

Ruang phra rachanukit [Accounts of royal activities]. 1946. Published by the royal commission of King Bhumibol as a merit to his brother, King Anandha Mahidol.

Sa-at Buachat. "Kan son natasin lae dontri Thai" [The teaching of Thai classical dance and music]. *Warasan Thammasat,* special issue entitled *Natasin lae dontri Thai* [Thai classical dance and music] (1972): 46–72.

Saeng Monwithu. *Natayasat tamra ram* [Theories and lessons of classical dance]. Siwaphon, 1968.

Saeng Thakoeng. *Silapa kan salak nang yai fi mu chang ek ratchakan thi 2* [The art of carving *nang yai* puppets by master carvers during the reign of King Rama II]. Borisat Kan Chang, 1953.

Samut phap sadaeng khruang taeng kai tam samai prawatisat lae borankhadi [Illustrated book of historical and archaeological costumes]. Siwaphon, 1968.

Sa-nguan Ankhong. *Sing raek nai muang Thai* [First things in Thailand]. 3 vols. Phrae Phitthaya, 1973.

Sa-nguan Chotsukrat. *Prapheni Lanna Thai lae phithikam tang tang* [Various customs and ceremonies of the Lanna (northern Thai) region]. Chiengmai: Rongphim Klang Wiang, 1971.

———. *Prapheni Thai phak nua* [Northern Thai customs]. Sanitphan Kan Phim, 1969.

Sa-nguan Tiyaphaibunsin. "Chon run mai kap natasin dontri Thai" [The new generation and Thai classical dance and music]. *Warasan Thammasat,* special issue entitled *Natasin lae dontri Thai* (1972): 123–59.

Sasanasophon, Phra; and Mom Ratchawong Kukrit Pramoj. *Phra phuttha sasana kap sangkhom Thai* [Buddhism and Thai society]. Thammasat University, 1972.

Satchaphirom, Phraya. *Thewa kamnoet* [Mythology, the origins of gods]. Thammasat University, 1964.

Sathiankoset (Phraya Anuman Rajadhon). *Chiwit chao Thai samai kon* [Thai life in the past]. Samnakphim Bannakhan, 1969.

——. *Khwan lae prapheni kan tham khwan* [*Khwan* and related ceremonies]. Rungruangrat, 1963.

——. *Lao ruang nai Traiphum* [Stories in the Three Worlds]. Rongphim Akson Thai, 1972.

——. *Prapheni kao khong Thai* [Old Thai traditions: Customs related to birth, house building, and death]. Phrae Phitthaya, 1957.

——. *Ruang kieo kap prapheni Thai* [Thai customs: New Year ceremonies and spirit propitiation]. Phrae Kan Chang, 1961.

Satri Thai [Thai women]. Rongphim Withayakon (for Sapha Satri Haeng Chat [National Council for Women]), 1976.

Sawalak Anantasan. "Bot lakhon nok samai Krung Si Ayudhaya" [*Lakhon nok* plays of the Ayudhaya period]. M.A. thesis, Department of Thai, Faculty of Letters, Chulalongkorn University, 1972.

——. *Wannakam ek khong Thai: Khun Chang Khun Phaen* [*Khun Chang Khun Phaen,* a masterpiece of Thai literature]. Rongphim Kan Sasana, 1974.

Sawanit. *Sayam nai adit* [Siam in the past]. Phrae Phitthaya, 1972.

Seni Pramoj. *Pathakatha ruang kotmai samai Krung Si Ayudhaya* [Lectures on Ayudhaya laws]. Siwaphon, 1967.

Silapa Thai: Botkhwam thang silapa [Art: Collection of articles on Thai art]. Thammasat University Press, 1973.

Silapakon. *Kan sadaeng natasin lae dontri Thai* [Performances of Thai classical dance and music]. Khuru Sapha, 1976.

Silapakon, Krom. "Kham athibai ruang rabeng lae kula ti mai" [Explanations of *rabeng* and *kula ti mai* performances]. *Silapakon,* 1st year, vol. 4 (1937): 2–4.

——. "Rup laksana khruang taeng kai khong lakhon ram" [Descriptions of costumes in *lakhon* dance-drama]. *Silapakon,* 1st year, vol. 1 (1937).

——. "Tamra khruang ton khruang song tae boran" [Textbook on ancient royal costumes and regalia]. *Warasan Silapakon,* 7th year, vol. 3 (1953): 65–72.

Sin Sibunruang. *Khao lakhon Thai pai Amerika* [News of Thai drama travelling to America]. Sophon Phiphatthanakon, 1939.

Sittha Phinitphuwadon. *Wannakam Sukhothai* [Sukhothai literature]. Ramkhamhaeng University, 1973.

Sittha Phinitphuwadon, Nitaya Kanchanawan, Sali Siphen, and Prathip Wathikthinnakon. *Khwam ru thua pai thang wannakam Thai* [Introduction to Thai literature]. Krom Kan Pokkhrong, 1972.

Sittha Phinitphuwadon and Prathip Wathikthinnakon. *Roi krong* [Poetry]. Ramkhamhaeng University, 1973.

Snoe Niladet and Manay Arayaphat. "Hua khon phu phalit lae kamawithi nai kan phalit" [*Khon* masks: Their creators and craft]. *Ekalak Thai,* 1st year, vol. 4 (April 1977): 49–64.

Somphop Chantharaprapha. "Lakhon mi chai khong len" [Drama is not a toy]. *Warasan Thammasat,* special issue entitled *Natasin lae dontri Thai* [Thai classical dance and music] (1972): 249–61.

Song Thai [Reflections on Thai]. Edited by Chonthira Klatyu. Suksit Sayam, 1975.

Subhadradis Diskul, Mom Chao. *Silapa nai prathet Thai* [Art in Thailand]. Thammasat University Press, 1963.

Suraphon Wirurak. *Liké.* Hong Phap Suwan, 1979.

Suthiwong Phongphaibun. *Manohra nibat.* Songkhla: Rongphim Ching Ching, 1970.

——. *Nang talung.* Songkhla: Mongkhon Kan Phim, n.d.

Tamra baep thamniem nai ratchasamnak khrang Krung Si Ayudhaya kap phra wichan khong Somdet Krom Phraya Damrong Rajanubhap [Handbook on the traditions of the royal court: Customs and usages in the Ayudhaya period with commentary by Prince Damrong Rajanubhab]. 1950.

Tamrap Thao Si Chulalak [Memoirs of Nang Nophamat]. Preface by Prince Damrong.

Thepchu Chapthong. *Krung Thep nai adit* [Bangkok in the past]. Akson Bandit, 1975.

Thipakon. *Bot wikhro wannakam yuk sakdina khong Chit Phumisak* [Chit Phumisak's criticism of aristocratic literature]. Phikkhanet, 1975.

——. *Silapa phua chiwit silapa phua prachachon* [Art for living, art for the people]. Si Kan Phim, 1974.

Udom Sombat, Luang. *Chotmaihet* [Historical accounts], ed. H.R.H. Prince Damrong Rajanubhab. 1908.

Vajiravudh, King. *Lak ratchakan* [Principles of civil service]. Rungruangtham, 1973.

——. *Yutthaphai lae khwam pen chat doi tae ching* [Military dangers and nationalism in a developing but realistic country].

Walaya Piyarat. "Wannakhadi Thai samai Ayudhaya kap kan muang" [Ayudhaya literature and politics]. *Warasan Thammasat,* 5th year, vol. 3 (Feb.–May 1976): 47–59.

Wan Waithayakon [Collected articles]. 2 vols. Samakhom Sangkhomsat Haeng Prathet Thai, 1971.

Wannakam Thai patchuban [Contemporary Thai literature]. Chiengmai: Chiengmai University, 1973.

Warasan lae nangsuphim nai prathet Thai sung thi phim rawang pho so 2387–2477 [Periodicals and newspapers in Thailand published between 1844 and 1934]. Silapakon, 1970.

Wian Panchasuwan. "Ton trakun nang talung" [The origin of *nang talung* puppetry]. *Fa Muang Thai* 45 (Jan. 1970): 32, 62, 65, 68.

Wichitwathakan, Luang. "Chat niyom di leo yang rai" [How good and bad is nationalism?]. *Warasan Tu Thong,* 1st year, vol. 1: 55–85.

Wisetchaisi. "Phra Piya Maharat kap Ngo pa" [King Chulalongkorn and *Ngo pa*]. *Lalana* 91 (October 1976): 36–39.

Wit Siwasiriyanon. *Wannakhadi lae wannakhadi wichan* [Literature and literary criticism]. Samakon Phasa Lae Nangsu, 1970.

Wiwathanakan khong wannakam Thai [The development of Thai literature]. Thammasat Students' Literature Club, 1970.

Wuthichai Mullasin. *Kan patirup kan suksa nai ratchakan thi 5* [Reform of education in the Fifth Reign]. Association of Social Sciences, 1973.

Yim Banthayakun, ed. *Chomaihet phra ratchakit rai wan pho so 2411* [Record of the king's daily activities]. Silapakon, 1974.

Bibliography III

Secondary Sources in Western Languages

To be consistent with the bibliography of books in Thai, names of Thai authors here are written with first names followed by family names.

Abbreviations:

BSOAS   *Bulletin of the School of Oriental and African Studies*
JSS   *Journal of the Siam Society*

Abrams, Arnold. "Remaking Thai Society: In Wake of Revolution, Students Seek More Power for People." *Asia Magazine* (March 1974).
Akin Rabibhadana, Mom Ratchawong. *The Organization of Thai Society in the Early Bangkok Period, 1782–1873*. Data Paper, no. 74. Ithaca, N.Y.: Cornell University Southeast Asia Program, 1969.
Anuman Rajadhon, Phrya. *Essays on Thai Folklore*. Bangkok: Siwaphon, 1968.
———. *Life and Ritual in Old Siam: Three Studies of Thai Life and Customs*. Translated and edited by William J. Gedney. New Haven: HRAF Press, 1961.
Bailey, Sir Harold. "The Sudhana Poem of Ṛddhiprabhāva." *BSOAS* 29, pt. 3 (1966): 506–32.
Batson, Benjamin. "The Fall of the Phibun Government, 1944." *JSS* 62, no. 2 (1974): 89–120.
Bhattacharya, Asutosh. *The Artistic Performance of the Ramayana: The Ramayana in Chhau, a Traditional Dance-drama of Purelia*. West Bengal: Research Institute of Folk Culture, 1971.
Bidyalankarana, H.H. Prince. "The Pastime of Rhyme-making and Singing in Rural Siam." *JSS* 20, pt. 2 (1926): 101–27. Reprint in *The Siamese Theatre*, 165–85.
———. "Sebhā Recitation and the Story of Khun Chāng Khun Phan." *JSS* 33, pt. 1 (1941): 1–22. Reprint in *The Siamese Theatre*, 187–206.
Blanchard, Wendell. *Thailand: Its People, Its Society, Its Culture*. New Haven: HRAF Press, 1970.
Blankwaardt, W. "Notes upon the Relations between Holland and Siam." *JSS* 20, pt. 2 (1926): 241–58.
Boribalburibhand, Luang. *The History of Buddhism in Thailand*. Translated by Luang Suriyabongs. Bangkok: Chatra Press, 1955.
Bowers, Faubion. *Theatre in the East: A Survey of Asian Dance and Drama*. 5th ed. New York: Grove Press, 1960.
Bowie, Theodore, ed.; Mom Chao Subhadradis Diskul and A. B. Griswold. *The Sculpture of Thailand*. Bangkok: The Asia Society.

Bradley, D. B. *Abstract of the Journal of the Reverend Dan Beach Bradley, M.D., Medical Missionary to Siam in 1835–1873*. Edited by George Feltus. Cleveland: Department of Pilgrim Church, 1936.

Brandon, James R. *Theatre in Southeast Asia*. Cambridge, Mass.: Harvard University Press, 1967.

Bunlua Thephayasuwan, Mom Luang. "A Note on Thai Literary Tradition and Convention When Compared to Western Literature." A paper presented at the English Language Centre, n.d. (unpublished).

Burger, Helga, and Jane Ram. "Chinese Puppets: Drama in Miniature." *The Mandarin* (Hong Kong) 7, no. 1 (March 1976): 18–24.

Burnay, J. "Inventaire des manuscrits juridiques siamois." 2 parts. *JSS* 24, pt. 1 (1930): 29–79; 24, pt. 2 (1931): 93–107.

Busakorn Lailert. "The Ban Phlu Luang Dynasty, 1688–1767: A Study of the Thai Monarchy during the Closing Years of the Ayudhaya Period." Ph.D. diss., School of Oriental and African Studies, University of London, 1972.

Cadet, J. M. *The Ramakien: The Thai Epic*. Illustrated with the bas-reliefs of Wat Phra Jetubon, Bangkok. Tokyo: Kodansha International, 1971.

Charnvit Kasetsiri. "The First Phibun Government and Its Involvement in World War II." *JSS* 62, pt. 2 (1974): 25–88.

――――. *The Rise of Ayudhya: A History of Siam in the Fourteenth and Fifteenth Centuries*. East Asian Historical Monographs. London and Bangkok: Oxford University Press and Duang Kamol Book House, 1976.

Chua Satawedin. "Thai Poets and Their Thoughts." In *The Second Asian Writers Conference, Bangkok, November 1964*, 40–41.

Chula Chakrabongse, H.R.H. Prince. *Lords of Life: The Paternal Monarchy of Bangkok, 1782–1932*. London: Alvin Redman, 1960.

Coedès, George. *Les états hindouisés d'Indochine et d'Indonésie*. Paris: Editions E. de Boccard, 1964.

――――. "The Excavation at P'ong Tük and Their Significance for the Ancient History of Siam." *JSS* 21, pt. 2: 195–209.

――――. "Origine et évolution des diverses formes du théâtre traditionnel en Thailande." *Bulletin de la Société des Etudes Indochinoises*, n.s. 38 (1963): 489–506.

――――. *Recueil des inscriptions du Siam*. Vol. 1, *Inscriptions de Sukhodaya*. Bangkok: Bangkok Times Press, 1924.

Cuisinier, Jeanne. *Danses magiques de Kelantan*. Travaux et mémoires de l'Institut d'Ethnologie, tome 22. Paris, 1936.

――――. "L'infuence de l'Inde sur les danses en Extrême-Orient." *Revue des Arts Asiatiques* 7 (1931–32): 8–14.

Damrong Rajanubhab, H.H. Prince. "The Introduction of Western Culture into Siam." *JSS* 20, pt. 2 (1926): 89–100.

Darling, Frank C. "Student Protest and Political Change in Thailand." *Pacific Affairs* 47, no. 1 (1974): 5–19.

Dawson, John. *A Classical Dictionary of Hindu Mythology and Religion, Geography, History, and Literature*. 9th ed. London: Routledge Kegan Paul, 1957.

De Bary, Wm. Theodore, ed. *Introduction to Oriental Civilizations*. Vol. 1, *Sources of Indian Tradition*. New York: Columbia University Press, 1958.

De Campos, Joaquim. "Early Portuguese Accounts of Thailand." *JSS* 32, pt. 1 (1940): 1–27.

De La Loubère, Simon. *The Kingdom of Siam*. Oxford in Asia Historical Reprints. London: Oxford University Press, 1969.

De Zoete, Beryl, and Walter Spies. *Dance and Drama in Bali.* London, 1938. Reprint. London: Oxford University Press, 1973.

Dhaninivat, H.H. Prince. "Allegories of the Monsoon in Siamese Literature." Occasional Papers No. 1. Bloomington: Asian Studies Research Institute, Indiana University, 1968.

———. "Aspects of King Vajiravudh's Writings." In *The Second Asian Writers Conference, Bangkok, November 1964,* 7–78.

———. "The Chatri." *Journal of the Thailand Research Society* 32, pt. 1 (1940): 43–44.

———. "The City of Thawarawadi Sri Ayudhya." *JSS* 31, pt. 2 (1939). Reprint in *Collected Articles by H.H. Prince Dhani Nivat,* 50–56. Bangkok, 1969.

———. "The Dalan." *JSS* 43, pt. 2 (1956). Reprint in *Collected Articles by H.H. Prince Dhani Nivat,* 169–88; also in *The Siamese Theatre,* 139–56.

———. "The Date and Authorship of the Romance of Phra Lô." *JSS* 41, pt. 2 (1954). Reprint in *Collected Articles of H.H. Prince Dhani Nivat,* 141–44.

———. "Hide Figures of the Ramakien." *JSS* 53, pt. 2 (1965): 61–66. Reprint in *The Siamiese Theatre,* 121–25.

———. "The Inscriptions of Wat Phra Jetubon." *JSS* 26, pt. 2 (1933): 143–70. Reprint in *Collected Articles by H.H. Prince Dhani Nivat,* 5–28.

———. "The Jatri." *Journal of the Thailand Research Society* 32, pt. 1 (1940): 43–44.

———. "King Rama VI's Last Work: *Madanabadha,* or the *Romance of a Rose.*" *JSS* 39, pt. 2 (1952): 181–89.

———. "Note: *Nang talung.*" *JSS* 47, pt. 2 (1959): 181. Reprint in *The Siamese Theatre,* 127.

———. "The Old Siamese Conception of the Monarchy." *JSS* 36, pt. 2 (1947). Reprint in *Collected Articles by H.H. Prince Dhani Nivat,* 91–104.

———. "The Rama Jataka." *JSS* 36, pt. 1 (1946). Reprint in *Collected Articles by H.H. Prince Dhani Nivat,* 73–90.

———. "The Ramakien: A Siamese Version of the Story of Rama." In *Burma Research Society, Fiftieth Anniversary Publications,* no. 1, 33–45. Rangoon, 1961.

———. "The Reconstruction of Rama I of the Chakri Dynasty." *JSS* 43, pt. 1 (1955). Reprint in *Collected Articles by H.H. Prince Dhani Nivat,* 145–68.

———. "The Shadow-play as a Possible Origin of the Masked-play." *JSS* 37, pt. 1 (1948): 26–32. Reprint in *Collected Articles by H.H. Prince Dhani Nivat,* 105–10; also in *The Siamese Theatre,* 115–20.

———. "Siamese Versions of the Panji Romance." *Indian Antiquary* (1947): 95–101.

———. "Traditional Dresses in the Classic Dance of Siam." *JSS* 40, pt. 2 (1952). Reprint in *Collected Articles by H.H. Prince Dhani Nivat,* 129–40; also in *The Siamese Theatre,* 29–39.

———, trans. "The Empire of the South Seas." Translated from the French of G. Coedès. *Journal of the Thailand Research Society* 35, pt. 1 (1944). Reprint in *Collected Articles by H.H. Prince Dhani Nivat,* 57–72.

Dhaninivat, H.H. Prince, and Dhanit Yupho. *The Khon.* Thailand Culture Series, no. 11. Bangkok, 1954. Thai Culture New Series, no. 6. Bangkok: Department of Fine Arts, 1962.

Dhanit Yupho. *Classical Siamese Theatre.* Translated by P. S. Sastri, with an introduction by Phraya Anuman Rajadhon. Bangkok: Hatha Dhip, 1952.

———. *The Custom and Rite of Paying Homage to Teachers of Khon, Lakhon, and Piphat.* Thai Culture New Series, no. 11. Bangkok: Department of Fine Arts, 1968.

———. *Khon.* Bangkok: Department of Fine Arts, 1968.

———. *The Khon and Lakhon: Dance Dramas Presented by the Department of Fine Arts.* Bangkok: Department of Fine Arts, 1963.

———. *Khon Masks.* Thai Culture New Series, no. 7. Bangkok: Department of Fine Arts, 1968.

Dhanit Yupho. *The Preliminary Course of Training in Thai Theatrical Art.* Bangkok: Department of Fine Arts, 1968.

———. *Thai Musical Instruments.* Translated from the Thai by David Morton. 2d ed. Bangkok: Department of Fine Arts, 1971.

Dohring, Von Karl. *Siam: Land und Volk.* Darmstadt: Folkwang-Verlag, 1923.

"English Correspondence of King Mongkut." *JSS* 22, pt. 1 (1928): 1–18.

Feer, M. L. "Les Jâtakas." *Journal Asiatique,* 7 série, tome 5 (1875): 359–434.

Finot, Louis. "Recherches sur la littérature laotienne." *Bulletin de l'Ecole Française d'Extrême-Orient* 17, pt. 5 (1917): 1–218.

The First International Ramayana Festival. Organized by the National Committee for the International Ramayana Festival 1971, Indonesia, August 31–September 17. Djakarta, 1971.

Francisco, Juan R. "Maharadia Lawana."*Asian Studies* 7, no. 2 (1969): 186–249.

Gaur, Albertine. *Les dances sacrées en Inde,* aux edition du seuil. Paris, 1963.

Gerini, G. E. *Chŭḷăkantamaṅgala: The Tonsure Ceremony as Performed in Siam.* 1893. Reprint. Bangkok: The Siam Society, 1976.

Giles, F. H. "An Account of the Ceremonies and Rites Performed When Catching the *Pla Bük,* a Species of Catfish Inhabiting the Water of the River Me Khong, the Northern and Eastern Frontier of Siam." *JSS* 28, pt. 1 (1935): 91–113.

———. "An Account of the Rites and Ceremonies Observed at Elephant Driving Operations in the Seaboard Province of Lang Suan, Southern Siam." *JSS* 25, pt. 2 (1932): 153–214.

———. "A Critical Analysis of van Vliet's *Historical Account.*" *JSS* 30, pt. 2 (1938): 155–240; pt. 3 (1938): 271–380.

Ginsberg, Henry D. "The *Manora* Dance-drama: An Introduction." *JSS* 60, pt. 2 (1972): 169–81. Reprint in *The Siamese Theatre,* 63–73.

———. "The Sudhana-Manohra Tale in Thai: A Comparative Study Based on Two Texts from the National Library, Bangkok, and Wat Machimawat, Songkhla." Ph.D. diss., School of Oriental and African Studies, University of London, 1971.

Green, M. *Tales from the Ramayana.* Told by Margery Green. Madras: Macmillan & Co., 1968.

Griswold, A. B. *Wat Pra Yun Reconsidered.* Monograph, no. 4. Bangkok: The Siam Society, 1975.

Griswold, A. B. and Prasert ṇa Nagara. "The Epigraphy of Mahādharmarājā I of Sukhodaya." *JSS* 61, pt. 2 (July 1973): 91–128.

Groslier, Bernard, and Jacques Arthaud. *Angkor: Art and Civilization.* Rev. ed. London: Thames and Hudson, 1966.

Hall, D. G. E. *History of Burma.* 1950.

———. *A History of Southeast Asia.* 3d ed. London: Macmillan, 1976.

Halliday, Robert. "Immigration of the Mons into Siam." *JSS* 10, pt. 3 (1913): 1–13.

———. "The Mons in Siam." *Journal of the Burma Research Society* 12, pt. 3 (1922): 69–79.

Hutchinson, E. W. "The French Foreign Mission in Siam during the Seventeenth Century." *JSS* 26, pt. 1 (1933): 1–72.

———. "Journey of Mgr. Lambert, Bishop of Beritus, from Tenasserim to Siam in 1662." *JSS* 26, pt. 1 (1933): 215–18.

International Symposium on East Asian Countries' Acceptance of Western Culture, October 3–7, 1966, Tokyo. Edited by S. Iwao and S. Ikuta. *East Asian Cultural Studies* 6, nos. 1–4 (March 1967): 1–249.

Ishii, Y., O. Akagi, and N. Endo. *A Glossarial Index of the Sukhothai Inscriptions.* SEAS Discussion Papers, no. 53. Kyoto: Center for Southeast Asian Studies, Kyoto University, 1972.

Jacobs, Norman. *Modernization without Development: Thailand as an Asian Case Study.* Praeger

Special Studies in International Economics and Development. New York: Praeger Publishers, 1971.

Jaini, Padmanabh S. "The Story of Sudhana and Manoharā: An Analysis of the Texts and the Borobudur Reliefs." *BSOAS* 29, pt. 3 (1966): 533–58.

Jones, Robert B., and Ruchira C. Mendiones. *Introduction to Thai Literature.* Ithaca, N.Y.: Cornell University Southeast Asia Program, 1970.

Kachorn Sukhabanij. "Was Nam Thom the First King of Sukhodaya?" *JSS* 44, pt. 2 (1956): 139–44.

Kamban. *The Ayodhaya Canto of the Ramayana as Told by Kamban.* Translated from the Tamil by C. Rajagopalachan. London: George Allen & Unwin, 1961.

Keyes, Charles F. *The Golden Peninsula: Culture and Adaptation in Mainland Southeast Asia.* New York: Macmillan Publishing, 1977.

———. "The Power of Merit." In *Visakha Puja* (Thai Watthana Phanit Press) (1973): 95–102.

Khmer Classical Dance. Phnom Penh: University of Fine Arts, 1971.

Khomkhai Nilprapassorn. "A Study of the Dramatic Poems of the Panji Cycle." Ph.D. diss., School of Oriental and African Studies, University of London, 1966.

Kukrit Pramoj, Mom Ratchawong. "*Khon* Demonstration." Bangkok: Bangkok Music Group, 1972. Booklet.

Landon, Kenneth Perry. *Siam in Transition: A Brief Study of Cultural Trends in the Five Years since the Revolution of 1932.* New York: Greenwood Press Publishers, 1968.

Landon, Margaret. *Anna and the King of Siam.* London, 1958.

Leonowens, Anna. *The English Governess at the Siamese Court.* London, 1954.

Lévi, Sylvain. *L'Inde civilisatrice: Aperçu historique.* Paris, 1938.

Likhit Diravegin. *Political Attitudes of the Bureaucratic Elite and Modernization in Thailand.* Program of Publication and Research in Political Science, Faculty of Political Science, Thammasat University. Bangkok: Thai Watthana Phanit, 1973.

Lingat, R. "Une lettre de Véret sur la révolution siamoise de 1688." *T'oung Pao,* ser. 2, 31 (1935): 3–5.

———. "Les trois *Bangkok Recorders.*" *JSS* 28, pt. 2 (1935): 203–13.

MacDonald, Malcolm. *Angkor.* London, 1958.

Mahā Vajirāvudh (King Rama VI). "Notes on the Siamese Theatre." *JSS* 55, pt. 1 (1967): 1–30. Reprint in *The Siamese Theatre,* 1–27.

Majumdar, R. C. *Ancient Indian Colonies in the Far East.* Vol. 1, *Champa.* Lahore: Punjab Sanskrit Book Depot, 1927. Vol. 2, *Suvarnadvipa, Part 2: Cultural History.* Calcutta: Modern Publishing Syndicate, 1938.

Manas Chitakasem. "The Nature of Nirat Poetry and the Development of the Genre." Ph.D. diss., School of Oriental and African Studies, University of London, 1974.

Manich Jumsai, Mom Luang. *Thai Ramayana.* Bangkok: Chalermnit, 1967.

Masti Venkatesa Iyengar. *The Poetry of Valmiki.* Bangalore: Bangalore Press, 1940.

Mattani Rutnin. "Modern Thai Literature: The Process of Modernization and the Transformation of Values." *East Asian Cultural Studies* 17, nos. 1–4 (1978): 1–132.

———. "*Nang Talung* and Thai Life." *East Asian Cultural Studies* 15, nos. 1–4 (1976): 45–52.

———. "*Nang Yai:* The Classical Shadow Play and the Wat Kanon Troupe of Rajburi." *East Asian Cultural Studies* 15, nos. 1–4 (1976): 53–59.

Maung Htin Aung. *Burmese Drama.* 4th ed. London: Oxford University Press, 1957.

Mole, Robert L. *Thai Values and Behaviour Patterns.* Tokyo: Charles E. Tuttle, 1973.

Morgan, Bruce. *Thai Buddhism and American Protestantism in Their Social, Cultural, and Historical Setting.* Sinclair Thompson Memorial Lectures, 4th series. Chiengmai: Thailand Theological Seminary, 1966.

Nakhon Phra Ram, Phya. "Who Was Dharmarājā I of Sukhothai?" *JSS* 28, pt. 2 (1935): 214–20.

The Nāṭyaśāstra. Translated by Monomohan Ghosh. Calcutta: The Royal Asiatic Society of Bengal, 1951.

Nayar, S. K. *Kathakali Manjari.* Madras: Government Oriental Manuscripts Library, 1956.

Neon Snidvongs. "The Development of Siamese Relations with Britain and France in the Reign of King Maha Mongkut, 1851–1868." Ph.D. diss., School of Oriental and African Studies, University of London, 1961.

Nicolas, René. "Le *lakhon nora* ou *lakhon chatri* et les origines du théâtre classique siamois." *JSS* 18, pt. 2 (1942): 85–110. Reprint in *The Siamese Theatre,* 41–61.

————. "Le théâtre d'ombres au Siam." *JSS* 21, pt. 1 (1927): 37–51.

Pallegoix, Mgr. *Description du Royaume Thai ou Siam.* 2 vols. Paris, 1854.

The Performing Arts in Asia. Edited by James R. Brandon, with an introduction by James R. Brandon. Paris: Unesco, 1971.

Prachoom Chomchai. *Chulalongkorn the Great.* East Asian Cultural Studies Series, no. 8. Tokyo: Centre for East Asian Cultural Studies, 1965.

Prem Purachatra, H.R.H. Prince. *Magic Lotus.* 1937. 2d ed. Bangkok: Chatra Books, 1946.

Prizzia, Ross, and Narong Sinsawasdi. *Thailand: Student Activism and Political Change.* Bangkok: Duang Kamol, 1974.

Quito, Emerita S. *Oriental Roots of Occidental Philosophy.* First ASAIHL Annual Lecture. Kuala Lumpur: ASAIHL, 1975.

The Raffles Gamelan: A Historical Note. Edited by William Fagg. London: The British Museum, 1970.

Raghavan, V. *The Greater Ramayana.* Varanasi: All-India Kashiraj Trust, 1973.

————. *The Lesser Known Ramayanas.* Reprint. Madras: Asthika Samajam Souvenir, 1970.

————. *The Mahabhavara: Epic Chronicle.* Reprinted from *The Vedanta Kesari.* 1956.

————. *Ramayana and Indian Culture.* Madras: Asthika Samajam Souvenir, 1972.

————. *The Ramayana in Greater India.* Surat: South Gujarat University, 1975.

————. *Ramayana: Triveni.* Madras: Ramayana Publishing House, 1970.

————. *Ramayana Versions.* Madras: University of Madras, n.d.

————. *Some Old Lost Rama Plays.* Annamalai Nagor: Annamalai University, 1961.

————. *The Tattvasanigraharamayana of Ramabrahmananda.* N.d.

————. *Tyagraja's Conception on Rama and Rama Bhareti.* N.d.

Raikes, D. F. "A Brief History of the Mon People"; "The Mon: Their Music and Dance." Bangkok: The Siam Society, n.d. (pamphlet).

Rajagopalachari, C. *Ramayana.* Edited by K. M. Munstri and R. R. Diwakar. Bombay: Bharatiya Vidya Bhavan, 1968.

Rama I, King of Siam. *Ramayana.* 2d ed. Bangkok: Chalermnit Press, 1967.

Reynolds, Craig J. "The Case of K.S.R. Kulāp: A Challenge to Royal Historical Writing in Late Nineteenth Century Thailand." *JSS* 61, pt. 2 (July 1973): 63–90.

Rombongan Kebudayaan Malaysia Ka, Pesta Ramayana Di, Indonesia. Malaysia, 1971.

Sarasin, Fritz. "Prehistorical Researches in Siam." *JSS* 26, pt. 2 (1933): 171–202.

Scott, A. C. *The Theatre in Asia.* New York: Macmillan Publishing, 1972.

Search for Identity: Modern Literature and the Creative Arts in Asia. Papers presented to the 28th International Congress of Orientalists. London: Angus and Robertson, 1974.

The Second Asian Writers Conference, Bangkok, November 1964. Bangkok: Prachandra Printing Press, 1965.

Seidenfaden, Erik. *The Thai Peoples.* Book 1, *The Origins and Habitats of the Thai Peoples with a Sketch of Their Material and Spiritual Culture.* Bangkok: The Siam Society; Prachandra Printing Press, 1967.

————. Review of *Fêtes et céremonies siamoises* by Raymond Plion. *JSS* 30, pt. 2 (1938): 249–51.

The Siamese Theatre: Collection of Reprints from the Journals of the Siam Society. Edited by Mattani Rutnin. Bangkok, 1975.

Simmonds, E. H. S. "Epic Romance Poetry in Thailand." *Samaggi Sara* 32 (Sept. 1961): 2–7; *Sangkhomsat Parithat,* nos. 1–2 (1963): 100–106.

————. "*Mahōrasop* in a Thai Manōrā Manuscript." *BSOAS* 30, pt. 2 (1967): 391–403.

————. "*Mahōrasop* II, the Thai National Library Manuscript." *BSOAS* 34, pt. 1 (1971): 119–31.

————. "New Evidence on Thai Shadow-play Invocations." *BSOAS* 24, pt. 3 (1961): 542–59.

————. "The Shadow Play Treatise on *Nang* for Playing in *Mahorasop.*" Mimeo. N.d.

————. "Thai Literature: A Bibliography of Works in Foreign Languages." *Bulletin of the Association of British Orientalists,* n.s. vol. 3, nos. 1 and 2. London: Association of British Orientalists, 1965.

Sitaramiah, V., ed. *The Valmiki Ramayana.* New Delhi: Shitya Akademi, 1972.

Sivaraksa, S. "Aspects of Contemporary Literature." In *The Second Asian Writers Conference, Bangkok, November 1964,* 69–72.

————. "Prince Naris." *Visakha Puja* (1973): 82–84.

Smithies, Michael. "*Likay:* A Note on the Origin, Form, and Future of Siamese Folk Opera." *JSS* 59, pt. 1 (1971): 33–64. Reprint in *The Siamese Theatre,* 75–101.

————. "Village Mons of Bangkok." *JSS* 60, pt. 1 (1972): 307–32.

Smithies, Michael, and Euayporn Kerdchouay. "*Nang Talung:* The Shadow Theatre of Southern Thailand." *JSS* 60, pt. 1 (1972): 379–90.

Soedarsono. "*Wayang Kulit:* A Javanese Shadow Theatre." *East Asian Cultural Studies* 15, nos. 1–4 (1976): 87–96. A paper presented to an International Seminar on the Shadow Plays of Asia, Tokyo, 18–22 June 1975.

Sørensen, Per. *Archaeological Excavations in Thailand.* 3 vols. Copenhagen: Munksgaard, 1967.

"Stèle du Vǎt Phrǎ Yun, Lǎmphun." *Bulletin de l'Ecole Française d'Extrême-Orient* 25 (1925): 195–200.

Sunardjo Haditjaroko. *Ramayana, Our National Reader.* Djakarta: Djambatan, 1961.

Suriyanbongs, Luang. *Buddhism in Thailand.* Bangkok: Phrae Phitthaya, 1955.

Sut Saengwichien. *Mons: Past and Present.* Bangkok, 1970.

Sweeney, P. L. Amin. *The Ramayana and the Malay Shadow-play.* Kuala Lumpur: National University of Malaysia Press, 1972.

Tej Bunnag. "Hun Krabok." Bangkok: The Siam Society, 1966.

————. "The Provincial Administration of Siam from 1892 to 1915: A Study of the Creation, the Growth, the Achievements, and the Implications for Modern Siam of the Ministry of the Interior under Prince Damrong Rachanubhap." Ph.D. diss., Oxford University, 1968.

Thawat Makaraphong. *History of the Thai Revolution: A Study in Political Behaviour.* Bangkok: Chalermnit, 1972.

Thiphakorawong, Chao Phraya. *The Dynastic Chronicles, Bangkok Era, the Fourth Reign,* B.E. *2394–2411 (A.D.1851–1868).* Translated by Chadin Flood. 5 vols. Tokyo: Centre for East Asian Cultural Studies, 1965–74.

Thompson, Virginia. *Thailand: The New Siam.* New York: Macmillan, 1941.

Tilakasiri, J. "Comic Characters in the Asian Shadow-play." A paper read at an International Conference on the Traditional Drama and Music of Southeast Asia, Kuala Lumpur, 1969.

————. *The Puppet Theatre of Asia.* Colombo: Department of Government Printing, 1968.

————. "The Ramayana Tradition in Ceylon." N.d.

Titima Phitakspraiwan. "The Acceptance of Western Culture in Thailand." In *An International Symposium on East Asian Countries' Acceptance of Western Culture, October 3–7, 1966, Tokyo,* 199–200. *East Asian Cultural Studies* 6, nos. 1–4 (March 1967).

Traditional Drama and Music of Southeast Asia. Edited by Mohd. Taib Osman. Kuala Lumpur: Dewan Bahasa dan Pustaka, 1974.

Transformation and New Development of Traditional Cultures in East Asian Countries in the Course of Modernization: National Language and Modern Literature. Edited by R. Kono. *East Asian Cultural Studies* 15, nos. 1–4 (March 1976): 99–194.

Tulsidas. *The Ramayana.* Rendered into English verse by the Rev. A. G. Atkins. 2 vols. New Delhi: The Hindustan Times, 1954.

Valmiki. *The Ramayana of Valmiki.* Translated by Hari Prasad Shastri. 3 vols. London: Shanti Sadan, 1957.

Van Vliet, J. "Historical Account of Siam in the Seventeenth Century." *JSS* 30, pt. 2 (1938): 95–154.

Vella, Walter F. *The Impact of the West on Government in Thailand.* University of California Publications in Political Science, vol. 4, no. 3. Berkeley, Calif.: University of California, 1955.

———. *Siam under Rama III, 1824–1851.* New York: J.J. Augustin (for the Association of Asian Studies), 1957.

———. "Siamese Nationalism in the Plays of Rama VI." In *Search for Identity: Modern Literature and the Creative Arts in Asia,* 181–91.

Wales, H. G. Quaritch. "The Origins of Sukhodaya Art." *JSS* 44, pt. 2 (1956): 113–24.

Wan Waithayakon, H.R.H. Prince. *Stone Inscriptions of Sukhothai.* Bangkok: Prachandra Printing Press, 1965.

Weys, Ousa, and Walter Robinson, trans. *Phra Law Lilit: A Siamese Poem of Tragic Love.* Bangkok, 1974 (distributed pre-publication).

Wichitwathakan, Luang. "Evolution of Siamese Music." A speech delivered at the Rotary Club, Rong Lakhon Suan Misakawan, Bangkok, 23 September 1937.

Wipha Senanan. *The Genesis of the Novel in Thailand.* Bangkok: Thai Watthana Phanit, 1975.

Wood, W. A. R. "Fernão Mendez Pinto's Account of Events in Siam." *JSS* 20, pt. 1 (1926): 25–39.

Index

Words marked with an asterisk (*) have been included in the Glossary. Colour (*col.pl.*) and black and white (*pl.*) plate numbers are listed in italics.